A Case
of
Sour Grapes

A Cass Elliot Companion Novel

Gae-Lynn Woods

Dead Head Press

Copyright

For Martyn and The Dude, our little savage.

To all the brokenhearted, two words: karma baby.

For the record, Vinnie Mondello, no real life banjos
were harmed during the writing of this book.
(But all bets are off once it's published.)

PROLOGUE

THE KILLER YANKED THE curtains closed and dust motes exploded into a dervish as the body swayed, settling in time to the grisly pendulum's slowing swing. The killer sneezed into the crook of his arm, then took a last walk through the small apartment. Stopping in the hallway, he turned off the air conditioning, thankful for once for the unbearable heat. Given a bit of time and luck, her body would be a seeping abomination when they found her. He almost wished he could be here when they did.

The door snicked quietly closed behind him and he stooped to slip the key beneath the planter of wilting ivy. He took the steps to ground level at a casual pace, checking the street for onlookers. It was mid-afternoon in the middle of Texas' worst drought in a century. No one was out in this heat, and if they were, their one goal was to get inside.

The engine cranked without hesitation and as the tepid air seeping from the vents grew cooler, he closed his eyes and contemplated the future. His conscience had bothered him since he'd decided to travel this road earlier in the year and he'd made a snap judgment last night, deciding to let one of the women live. That act of pardon was a surprise to him, but it gave him peace. It might not be a life worth living once he was done with her, but at least she'd be drawing breath.

Today was the first step on a long path, one he still wasn't sure he was ready to travel. There was so much ambiguity. So much still to research. But given the ease of today's events and how serendipitously the opportunity to kill arose, he thought he could carry on. Regardless, he would move forward one step at a time, watchfully, as he always had.

Slipping the car into gear, he eased down the quiet street and back to work, wondering how fate would present his next victim, knowing full well which woman he'd prefer to kill next.

THURSDAY

THE DREAM

THE DREAM IS ALWAYS the same: a rush of adrenaline as my body throbs to a pounding bass and pulsing lights; the dancing grows wild and sweat builds as bodies crush against me. Then dread creeps in, stealing the light, muting the music, and pressing down, down, down until I can no longer draw breath and just as I explode with need: relief. Sweet air fills my lungs but an image from a horror movie hangs over me, a familiar melting Dorian Gray of a face, eyes distant and dead, breath huffing and foul. A searing pain tears across my chest and a screech rips the fabric of my nightmare.

I woke, swinging at a phantom that didn't exist, drinking in huge gulps of air, heart thrumming against my ribs, scar burning with liquid heat.

With equal measures of relief and rage, I glared at the howling alarm clock, a new addition to my bedroom. I slammed the snooze button and rolled away from the window, glowing with the dawn's early light despite the heavy curtains I'd dragged shut last night. I lay motionless, panting, knowing my memories of dancing that night are real. But I wondered, yet again, which of the rape elements my mind has simply conjured to make sense of that night, and which are true memories buried deep in my subconscious.

Truth versus fiction matters, you see. Because my life is changing direction beginning today, and the hunt for my rapist will gain intensity in the coming months.

The dream always recedes as quickly as it appears and my heart slowed, the sweat slicking my body cooled, and terror released my mind. Cuddled in my down duvet, I pondered yet again whether working for a living was really worth the effort, and drifted back to sleep.

My personality must be quite resilient, because I slipped easily from my rape nightmare into an erotic fantasy. In the middle of a magnificent dream about Daniel Craig in his *Quantum of Solace* days, right when I was easing the button of his shirt through its hole and feeling the warm flesh of his chest beneath my fingertips, just as his lips brushed mine, my cell phone rang with the gutsy opening strains of "Bad to the Bone".

I groaned but answered. "Do you have any idea what you interrupted? Shouldn't you be sleeping until noon? You're off work, you don't have to be up at the crack of dawn."

"It's nine-fifteen, Max. I drove around the square and your car's not there. You're late."

All thoughts of Daniel Craig vanished. "Crap. Thanks. Lunch?"

My best friend laughed the throaty laugh I love and envy in equal measure. "On your first day at the agency? I wouldn't miss it. Call me."

She was the reason I was taking the job, and she was right. Although my Aunts Kay and Babby owned Lost and Found Investigations and I'd been in and out of the office since I was a child, this was technically my first day at work. Running late would only confirm my aunts' belief that I was unsuitable private investigator material. And I had my first assignment: picking up a package from the bank before going to the office. It was time to focus.

I slid the short-barrel pump-action shotgun I keep beside the bed into its case and then ran for the shower. I lathered and rinsed, and lathered again but forwent conditioner, which shows true dedication. My hair begged for a good moisturizing.

It had been some time since I had held a full-time job. Or a job of any kind, really. So it was no wonder my body rebelled when the alarm sounded at six o'clock. But I was determined to get my private investigator's license and while I knew I'd have to pass an exam and get certified to carry a handgun - which sounded pretty awesome - I still wasn't sure about the whole getting up and going to work every day thing.

I yawned at my reflection as I dried my black hair, glad I'd cut it short.

It's worth it, I told myself. *If the only thing you do in this job is find the man who raped you, your best friend, and who knows how many others, and get him off the streets, it's worth getting up early.*

But maybe not until six-fifteen.

THE POINT OF NO RETURN

PARKING AROUND THE SQUARE was a nightmare during business hours, but I managed to slip my Lexus into a spot vacated by the flower shop's delivery van. The hike up the steps to the agency's second floor offices seemed much steeper than I remembered from my interview yesterday. Well, interview might be a little strong. I called Aunt Kay to tell her I wanted to be a private detective, and after she stopped laughing and got the hiccups under control, she invited me to come in for a chat. It took a while to convince her that I was serious, that this wasn't another flight of fancy from her daft niece. She finally relented after I talked non-stop for forty-five minutes. Thank goodness for that. I was going hoarse.

But now that the moment of truth had arrived, standing outside the door with "Lost and Found Investigations - No Job Too Big or Small" written on the frosted glass, nerves fluttered in my stomach. I wasn't sure I was up for this. I knew for sure I wasn't up for being a police detective like my best friend. That girl had balls of brass. Mine were more like copper: warm and pretty, but easily dented.

This is it, I told myself. *The point of no return. Here's to finding my rapist.*

I shifted my lucky Louis Vuitton bag higher on my shoulder and twisted the doorknob before my Blahnik's walked me right back down the stairs. Three pairs of green eyes, each a variation of my own, glanced up at me.

Cousin Cindy smirked. "Maxine Leverman finally arrives. Ten bucks, please. Everybody pay up."

The agency was beautifully designed. Four glassed-in offices opened onto the reception area, one each for Babby and Kay, one for Cindy, and the last for temps or in this case, me. The glass walls were on tracks and remained open unless a meeting demanded privacy. The rest of the walls were a pale blue, and the building's original hardwood floors were covered by Persian rugs and runners. Morning light fell through the skylights and the sense was of an open, airy space. Except for Cindy's office, which had an artfully placed Japanese screen hiding her clutter. The rest of the area housed a conference room, storage closets, a fully equipped kitchen, powder room, and a full-sized bathroom.

Aunt Babby scowled as she dug in her purse. "If you'd waited until ten o'clock, Maxine, I'd have won. Five more minutes. If you're going to be late, do it right girl, and help your aunt win some hard cash."

I pulled off my over-sized shades and placed the bag of donut holes from The Palace on Babby's desk, and the large envelope from the bank on Aunt Kay's desk. "You three had a pool on when I'd get here?"

"Not just the three of us," Cindy said. "Jake the janitor thought you'd make it by ten after eight. Silly man. But Arty was the real skeptic. He didn't think you'd get here until noon."

"Who's Arty?" I asked.

"The gorgeous lawyer who rented the other half of the floor. Cindy's been trying to get her talons into him since he arrived," Kay answered. "He saw you come upstairs yesterday. Cindy filled him in on your less attractive attributes, time-keeping being one of them."

I sipped my extra large coffee from The Golden Gate and watched as Babby peeked in the bag. She seemed to battle with herself for a moment, but finally picked a donut hole and popped it in her mouth. Her eyes rolled. "Grease, flour, and sugar make up for many a shortcoming, sweetie pie, but next time bring me a cinnamon roll."

"Be careful what you wish for, Aunt Babs. With Max's track record, you'll be eating donuts every day." Cindy stood and smoothed the black pencil skirt over her shapely hips and sauntered to the door. "For the record, Arty's into me." She shook her mane of chestnut colored hair and checked her teeth for lipstick in the mirror near the agency's door. "Be back in a flash."

Babby plucked another donut hole from the bag. "I'm off to the post office and bank. Given that it's hot enough to fry chicken, I'll be driving. Show Maxine that financial stuff, Kay. See what she can do with it."

THE SUBTERFUGE BEGINS

IT TOOK KAY ALL of twenty minutes to point out the monstrous mound of pending paperwork and demonstrate how to use the agency's various computer systems. I spent a solid hour trimming the Mount Everest of past due bills down to a cluster of Rocky Mountain foothills before even cracking open the accounting system. I reconciled five months worth of bank statements and realized that with this much cash coming in, it was quite reasonable that three grown women could so completely ignore the paperwork that drives their business.

The whole time I was working I eavesdropped on Kay's phone calls. Ask a question and pause. Ask another question. It sounded like background checks and work proving insurance fraud. I had finished with the foothill containing bills and was printing checks when Kay hung up and stretched.

"Is that what you do all day?" I asked. "Phone work?"

"That's how it goes, honey bunch. I ask a question and get an answer. Then ask another question and get another answer and on it goes." Kay smiled sympathetically. "Not very glam, is it?"

"It's downright boring."

"At times it is. How's the paperwork coming?"

"I'm making progress." I stood and stretched, relishing the pops from my spine. "But I could use a break."

"Where's Cass? You two could go play."

Detective Cass Elliot is my best friend. Has been since, well, maybe not since *before* dirt, but certainly since we were eating dirt. Usually at her house. Mud pies tasted better there, probably thanks to something toxic in the soil.

"Cass and I haven't *played* together in years, Aunt Kay."

She yawned. "You know what I mean. Call her and go to the gun range. If you really want to follow through on this PI dream, I need to know you'll be able to take care of yourself. And Cass needs the time at the range after her shoulder injury. You two grab some lunch after shooting, you're too thin."

I nodded but didn't commit. Kay was right, I was too thin, but a divorce followed by a nasty rape will do that to a girl.

"Change out of the Choo's and Prada before you go, baby. The boys out there will eat you alive if you don't dress a little butch."

"They're Blahnik's, but point taken."

Kay headed for the powder room and I checked the clock. Eleven-thirty. Cass would be done with physical therapy and if I knew her at all, extremely unhappy because Chad, her psychopathic physical therapist, still wouldn't have released her to go back to work. Not that I blamed him. She'd only been shot six short weeks ago. In Cass recovery time, that's eons. In her mind, she should be out saving the world, or Forney County at least, from the criminal element. For the rest of we mere mortals, recovery would've just started. But try telling Cass that and like me, all you'd get is an earful of grief.

I pulled up her number and as I was about to dial, the phone rang. Not my phone, the office phone. I looked towards the powder room. No Kay. I snatched up the handset and in my most professional voice said, "Lost and Found Investigations. Maxine Leverman speaking. How can I help you?"

"This is Blue Ivey out at Cedar Bend Winery. Does your agency find people?"

"Of course. How can we help?"

"I need to find my ex-husband. Not that I *want* to find him, but if I don't find him soon and get him straightened out, I'll have to kill him. We're between white and red harvest and I don't have time to hide a body right now." Her voice carried a silky huskiness that sounded like pure sex, and I wondered what kind of man could walk away from that. Someone called out and Blue covered the phone and shouted something unintelligible. She returned to the conversation with a sigh. "It's lunch prep time and things are crazy. Can you come to the winery? I'll take a break around one. Come hungry."

Another shout sounded before the line went silent. I cradled the receiver and resisted the urge to swing into a happy dance. My first case! Even better? Lunch at one of the best restaurants in East Texas. Not Michelin rated yet, but it certainly would be if Michelin ever made it to Forney County.

And then a cold flush washed over me: how *do* you find someone? Blue Ivey was a smart gal. She'd come to the winery from a neighboring county after starting a posh country club that attracted some of the richest folks in East Texas, and her pedigree trailed a glittering list of such establishments. She also had a reputation as a potter of note, and if I remembered an article I'd read about her not long ago, she had her own kiln out at the winery and had won awards for her art. She was an entrepreneur, an intelligent, feisty businesswoman. If her ex-husband was easily findable, she would've found him. The safest thing to do, the smartest thing, would be to talk to Babby or Kay about the case. But in all likelihood, that would mean turning it over to one of the real detectives.

Like Cindy.

Nobody thought I had it in me to stick to a job, much less a career. I decided to hold off on talking to the aunts until I knew more about this ex-husband that needed finding. I had an ex-husband, didn't I? I knew all about difficult men. Shouldn't be that hard to figure out. And it wouldn't be fair to give them half-baked information.

Decision made, I sat down at my desk and Googled 'how to' articles on finding people and background on Blue Ivey. After a few moments, I was in research heaven.

I was texting Cass to cancel our lunch date when Kay reappeared, tube of lipstick poised over her beestung lips. "Was that the phone?"

"Hmm?"

"Did someone call, darling?"

"It was a sales call."

"That's strange. The business number is on the 'do not call' list." Kay's eyes narrowed. "Maxine, are you sure that was a sales call?"

I picked up my lucky purse and pecked her on the cheek. "If it wasn't, they'll call back."

THE ALMOST EX

CEDAR BEND WINERY WAS one of those rare finds, a true gem set in a beautiful pine forest. It was also a tonic for the deep-fried fare that infused the remainder of Forney County. I waved to the officer in a police car stationed near the winery's entrance and pulled up the gravel drive. The winery was battling a horrific drought, same as counties for miles around, but the vines looked healthy. And, I noted with gratitude, lunch traffic looked light, which meant I would have Blue Ivey's undivided attention.

The roughly elegant interior was peppered with a collection of women of the blue-rinsed variety; pasty middle-aged men in business battle attire; and an assortment of ladies who lunch, passing the time until their offspring finished with swimming and tennis lessons at the country club. A gorgeous man with light brown hair headed my way. I was morphing into Maxine Man-eater mode when I saw the menu he carried and realized he was the host.

Clever, I thought. *Hiring a stud to seat the crusty old ladies. That might explain why more than half of the lunch crowd has double x chromosomes.*

He took me to a table near a window, where I sipped a glass of exceptionally good rosé and nibbled at a plate of cheese and grapes while I waited for Blue, grateful for the opportunity to run through my questions one last time. The sound of shattering pottery came from the kitchen. The diners went silent for only a fraction of a second, and then as if embarrassed they had noticed the commotion, the murmur of conversation resumed.

My phone chimed with a text and I smiled. It was Simon, a new acquaintance from Fort Worth, asking me to dinner Friday night. A bit cheeky, considering it was Thursday afternoon, but I accepted and started planning what time I'd have to leave Arcadia Friday afternoon to meet him by seven.

The hunky host appeared and handed me a copy of *Texas Eats* magazine. A photo of the winery graced the cover, along with an inset photograph of Blue with a man I assumed was Bret Ivey. Blue's smile was wide and natural; she was a beautiful woman with an affinity for the camera. Bret's face was mostly obscured by a wide-brimmed cowboy hat, but the flat planes of his cheeks and his chiseled jaw indicated handsome features.

"Blue apologizes for running late." His lashes were incredibly long over beautiful gray eyes. I caught myself staring as he refilled my glass. "This was published a while back, but there's a story about the winery. We've had a nice bump in traffic from it."

The article recounted the winery's humble origins when Bret planted the first vines almost nine years ago; his pursuit of Blue after she catered an event for a group of clients; Blue's pottery and her culinary career; the winery's exponential growth when they added a full-time kitchen and live jazz; and the awards won by its wines. It was a fabulous love story focused around a unique business. The article also mentioned Bret's passion for music, hinting that he had once played professionally and was working on new tunes when he wasn't busy with the winery.

Bret came off as a serious man of mystery, which surely only heightened interest in the business. In almost every photograph, his face was obscured by the shadows thrown by a hat or the plump grapes ripening on a vine. In only one, the photographer managed to capture Bret and Blue mid-laugh, their faces upturned. The left side of Bret's face was visible, but I wasn't sure I'd recognize the man if I met him face-to-face.

It was quarter after one when Blue emerged from the kitchen and joined me. She was followed by two wait staff bearing plates of sashimi and green salads. Fabulous.

"I'm sorry for the delay. We're between white and red grape harvest, which is wild enough, and one of my staff didn't come in today. I hope you don't mind that I selected lunch for us. The tuna is incredible," she said. She was even more gorgeous in person than in the magazine's photos, even if she looked a little tired. "I have to ask: were there any patrol cars parked out on the county road?"

I nodded.

"That man," she breathed.

"Who?" I asked.

"Sheriff Hoffner's on a mission to shut us down."

"Why?"

"He hates the fact that his dry county has a winery in it. He's had us inspected from top to bottom again and again. Food prep, health and safety, employment law, you name it. But the weird thing?" She leaned forward and puffed an errant strand of silky brown hair from her forehead. I liked the woman already. There was absolutely no pretense about her. "He comes out here regularly."

"And drinks?"

"Two glasses with dinner. If he's with someone else, he'll order a bottle and share it."

"That's a bit hypocritical, isn't it?"

Blue raised her glass to me. "That's Bill Hoffner." She sipped her wine and blushed. "I'm sorry. I'm so wrapped up in our problems I've forgotten my manners." She held out her hand. "Blue Ivey. Which detective are you?"

This question caused me no moral dilemmas. I hadn't misrepresented myself. My potential client had simply assumed I was a private investigator. I handed her a business card bearing only my name and phone number. "Maxine Leverman. It's nice to meet you."

"And you. Great shoes. Blahnik?"

I angled a leg so she could better see my beautiful pumps. "I love them."

"Me, too. But I'm on my feet all day. There'd be no hope for my ankles."

She picked up her wine glass and I goggled at her wedding ring. "Wow."

Blue twisted her hand to give me the full effect. The band was hammered platinum with a huge square cut sapphire surrounded by diamonds. "It's the one thing he gave me that I love. I'm keeping it."

"You should. I've never seen anything like it." I sighed. "At least it's romantic. My husband gave me implants."

Blue looked down at my chest and burst out laughing. "Oh Maxine, I think we'll work together just fine."

The staff served us on blue plates that looked hand-thrown. "These are beautiful. Did you make them?"

A smile curved her lips and brought her features to life. "I did. Pottery is one of my passions, but I don't get to work at it much now. Which is a shame, because one of our new waitresses keeps breaking the plates. You heard the crash?"

I nodded.

"That was Emily. Only three this time. I don't know what we'll do with that girl." She leaned close as the waitress left. "Thank you for coming. I'm at my wits end about Bret. I hope you can find him because he's driving me nuts."

"I'm sure we can help, Mrs. Ivey."

"Call me Blue. I plan to lose his last name as fast as I can get the divorce papers signed."

"I understood you're already divorced."

"Sorry. That's my little fantasy. I'm desperate to get this over with."

"Any particular reason?"

"He keeps spending my money." She sighed and I saw weariness in the gentle bruising under her eyes. "Technically, it's our money, but you'd think he'd turned on the tap and left it running. This can't go on much longer."

I digested this and decided to dig into the details later. "What made you call Lost and Found, Blue?"

She stopped, chopsticks poised mid-air. "I don't have the capacity to deal with another testosterone-fueled ego. I saw your advertisement and loved the concept of an all woman agency."

I ate a bite of tuna and tried not to moan. This wasn't just incredible sushi; this was *otoro*, from the under-belly of the blue fin tuna. It melted in my mouth and it was all I could do not to scarf down the whole plate. I swallowed and said, "I read the article in *Texas Eats* magazine. From that, it sounds like you're living a fairy tale."

"They did the interview and photo shoot last summer. The article came out in the autumn."

"Ah. Tell me what's going on now."

"Bret disappeared a few weeks ago. Which isn't totally unusual. At least not lately. But he always calls to check on the winery."

"You haven't heard from him?"

"No." She stabbed a slab of tuna. "I am so over it. My fondest wish is that he'd disappear and let me run the winery. I'll happily buy him out, as long as he'd just go away."

I wiped my lips. "You said Bret's disappearing act isn't totally unusual. At least lately. What does that mean?"

"We've always spent a fair amount of time apart. With only two of us to run things and promote, we often travel separately. And to be fair, I haven't been here much lately, either. My parents live in Florida and I've been there while my mother recovers from hip surgery. I have a cookbook in the editing phase, so I've traveled to New York. It wasn't a problem when Bret was around, but I didn't realize how bad things had gotten until a few weeks ago." Blue stopped and seemed to compose herself. "He bought a yellow Corvette about a year ago. License plate WINE-O. Who does that?" She didn't wait for an answer. "That's when I noticed. He'd tell me he was going for a drive to clear his head. At the time, the winery was at the tipping point. We were trying to decide whether to shut down or expand. So, when he said he needed some space, I didn't worry. I thought he was enamored with the new car. But it wasn't long before he was staying away until the early hours on the few occasions when we were both home."

"Did you ask him about it?"

"Of course. He had trouble with the Corvette. A flat tire. Out of gas. But he came home smelling not exactly like soap, but certainly not like a man who'd changed a tire. That's when I started to wonder if he was having an affair."

I was quiet for a moment, deciding how hard to push Blue. Then I figured that if I wanted to get anywhere as an investigator, I'd have to ask the hard questions. "Would you have thought him capable of having an affair?"

"Never. Bret's always been so attentive. I never thought I'd have to worry about cheating." She toyed with her wine glass. "I don't mean to discourage you, but it's my experience that marriages don't always turn out like we hope."

"I understand. I'm recently divorced from the implant purchaser. You were married before Bret?"

"He's my fourth husband."

I couldn't help it. I arched a brow.

She laughed, a gorgeous sound. "Believe me, I didn't intend to get married after number three. He was the love of my life. But he died when we were in our late thirties. I thought I was done. I'd had my share of happiness."

Blue had my full attention, even though there was still sashimi on my plate. "But then you met Bret?"

"He took my breath away. He's whip-smart, works like a dog, got a great sense of humor, and," she leaned close, "he's awesome in bed. He wooed me like I've never been wooed. And I don't mind saying I've had my share of amazing wooing."

"How comfortable were you with Bret when you married him?"

"My libido didn't totally override my brain. I've worked hard to get where I am, and husband number three left me very well off. Bret and I signed a pre-nup, but I do have a reputation to think about. I hired one of those all-men agencies. He's been married once, to a woman in California. And he was forty when he married her. No criminal history. The agency pulled credit reports, bank statements, searched his assets, and worked up a financial statement. Other than the winery, he has nothing."

Bank statements? I thought. *Credit reports?* I had no idea private detectives had so much power. "How did his marriage end?"

"Irreconcilable differences, that nebulous catch-all. Maybe I should've thought harder about that. But there's something about Bret. He convinced me he took marriage very seriously, and wanted to find the right woman. Unfortunately, there were serious flaws with the woman he picked. Maybe I'm flawed, too." She sighed then, a deep weariness seeping across her perfect features. "He made me believe I was the right woman for him. But in the end, I wasn't."

"Do you know who he might be involved with?"

"Find the woman with the biggest bottom around." My surprise must've shown because Blue laughed. "Part of his job is to be charming, but every woman he flirts with has a massive backside. Some also have a big chest, but it's the derriere he's interested in."

"Then why...," I started before realizing I was about to be very rude. Blue's a beautiful woman, but her figure is more boyish than lush.

"...did he pick me?" Blue asked, taking my unasked question in stride. "Given the rate at which he's gone through our money, I can only guess it was for my bank account."

"Why are you so sure he's strayed? If the winery was having problems last year, it certainly seems to be doing well now. You've got a beautiful location, the food is superb. Your vines even look good considering the drought. Things can only go up from here."

She toyed with her chopsticks. "Bret has an intense ability to focus. It's always been on me, the business. But over the last year, he's been distracted. Really distracted. I can't imagine what would capture his attention other than a woman."

I considered that. "You think he'd walk away from all this for a fat bottomed girl, to quote the fabulous Freddy Mercury?"

"I do." Blue shrugged. "But at this point, I'm over Bret Ivey. All I want is for him to stop spending so damn much money."

A NOT SO PRIM PENTECOSTAL MASSEUSE

TO TELL THE TRUTH, even after reading the internet articles I was clueless about how to find someone. So I did what every enterprising woman does when faced with a challenge: I had a facial and massage. When at home in Fort Worth, I use a fabulous technician named Jeremy. Handsome and a honey, he's gooey in love with his partner of the moment, Paul. But that won't last. It never does. My relationship with Jeremy has survived at least seven partners. I big-sister him through every break up and remind him of the importance of protected sex when each new love comes along.

Funny, now that I think of it. He does the same for me.

But my options are limited when I'm in Forney County. The best salon I've found is on the Loop around Arcadia, a place called Holy Rollers. It's run by a family of Pentecostal women and let me tell you, despite their own reluctance to doll up, these gals know hair and skin. Janie took one look and ordered me to strip and assume the position on the massage table.

"What's eating you, Maxine?" she asked in a soft voice, covering me with a sheet and placing hot, smooth stones along the back of my left leg and one in each palm.

"I need to find someone, and I'm not sure how to do it."

"Why?" She slicked oil along my right leg and worked the muscles, then gently massaged its length with a hot stone.

"He's just somebody I need to find."

"Nobody's invisible these days. Start with the internet. Use a picture and do a facial recognition thing."

"No photo."

"What do you mean?" Janie finished working my right leg, placed hot stones along its length, and oiled the left leg. I was butter already.

"He hates having his picture taken." I pointed at the magazine in my purse, folded open to the shot of Blue and Bret Ivey laughing. "That's the best his wife has."

"Suspicious."

I rose to twist and look at her, but Janie pushed me back down. "Why?" I asked.

"With all the smart phones around? Given that he runs a winery, there are bound to be pictures of him out there in cyberspace." She hit the ticklish spot on my left thigh with a hot stone and I giggled. "Be still. Google him. See who he's with."

"Pretty smart," I told her. "If that doesn't work, all I know is where he lives and what kind of vehicle he drives. I don't know how to find him when he's not at home."

Janie moved the sheet from my back to my legs and placed hot stones along my spine and on both shoulder blades. The tension in my neck melted away. "Can't you wait until he comes home and then follow him to wherever he goes?"

"He's not coming home, which is part of the problem. And I'd like to be proactive."

"Then you'll have to go wherever he goes."

"I don't know where he goes."

"Well, what kind of things does he like?"

"Leather and Corvettes."

"That's easy," Janie said. She removed the stones from my back and worked the muscles from my lower spine up to my shoulders. "If he stays around here, he'll be at The Golden O over the state line."

I lifted from the massage table and looked over my shoulder. "The biker bar? How in the world do you know about The Golden O?"

Her smile was like the Mona Lisa's, intriguingly unreadable. "I haven't always done hair and nails."

"Janie Chapman. You are full of surprises. You used to strip at The Golden O, didn't you?"

"If you won't be still, turn over." My prim Pentecostal masseuse lifted the sheet and I rolled to my back. "I wore a mask and had my hair pinned up until the final spin combo on the pole. I'd pull a clip out, my hair would swing free, and the dollar bills? Honey, they came a-flying." She laid the sheet over my chest and hips and went to work on my legs. "That's how I paid for beauty school. Don't tell anyone. I couldn't bear for my family to know."

"Given everything you know about my life, your secret is safe with me." I thought for a moment. "I always think of strip clubs as boob focused. He likes big bottoms. Do they have them at The Golden O?"

"Most of the places hire anyone who hasn't been overcome by gravity, so you'll find all shapes and sizes everywhere you go. But try The Bicycle Club. They used to hire women with more Rubenesque figures."

I wiped my hands on the sheet and reached for my phone. "Give me a minute. I need to find an accomplice for tonight's outing."

"Unless you want lots of male attention, choose an attractive woman and pretend you're lesbians." That Mona Lisa smile returned. "It'll ramp the men up, but at least they'll believe you're unavailable."

I stared up at this sweet-faced woman who knew my body almost intimately, and whom I clearly knew not at all. "So how about it?" I asked. "Got any plans tonight?"

HUNTING A MAN TAKES ENERGY

CASS TURNED UP AT eight-thirty, right on time. I opened the door and, as expected, she was dressed in her usual casual outfit of Dockers, button-down shirt, and cowboy boots. Which also happens to be her usual work outfit, although her dark red hair was loose tonight instead of wrapped up in a French twist. She stared at my clothes and burst out laughing. I yanked her inside by her good arm, then reflexively stuck my head outside and checked for strangers. All clear. I closed the door and locked up.

"What *is* that, Maxine?"

I air-kissed her cheek. "What's what?"

She looked me up and down. "Where are we going?"

"That's a surprise. Come on, we've got to fix you up."

———

I TOLD CASS TO take off her shirt and sit at my dressing table, and I swiveled the chair away from the mirror so I could work on her. My gaze fell on the ugly pink pucker left by a crazy cross-dresser's bullet and near it, the thin, pearlized scar spiraling from her collar bone down her chest until it disappeared into her bra. From there, I knew it swooped beneath her breast's curve, looping and swirling up its underside, stopping just short of her areola. I'd only seen her scar once, and only this much of it. But I knew where it traveled because although my scar was newer, it followed the same route. We'd been raped by the same man, a freak who drugged us and wore a Richard Nixon mask. Although we were attacked roughly five years apart, we were almost certain he'd raped other women. Cass had been searching for him for six years, and I had joined Lost and Found for the sole purpose of helping her. I pulled my gaze from her scar and slicked her hair back in a tight ponytail, and then studied her face.

"How was your first day?" she asked.

"Good," I answered, deciding to use foundation. Her skin is flawless, but tonight we needed cover. "I learned a lot."

"Do you still think this is a good idea?"

"Close your eyes." I brushed foundation over her forehead and eyelids. "I do. You wouldn't believe the databases a private eye can dig into."

"That makeup feels really thick, Max."

"It's fine." I finished with her cheeks, nose, and chin. "I don't know how the databases will help, but between the information and contacts you have in the law enforcement community, and those I'll make as a private investigator, we're bound to find other women he's attacked."

"It can only help. So, what did you do today?" Cass asked.

I chose avoidance. "Let me finish your face, then we'll talk."

———

TWENTY MINUTES LATER I spun the chair back around to the mirror. She gasped at her heavily made up face and tightly slicked back hair. "*Maxine*. Take it off." She reached for a cloth but I snatched it away.

"You look fab. Come on, get dressed. We'll be late."

She reluctantly got into the leather pants, white t-shirt, and leather vest I had chosen from my closet. She studied herself in my full-length mirror. "I look like that biker guy from the Village People. It's not even Halloween, Max. Where are we going?"

I turned and stuck my fishnetted leg through the slit in my black leather skirt and struck a pose. "Whiskey Bend."

"The strip clubs? That explains why the bustier is boosting your yays up under your chin." Cass tried to unclip the chain hanging over her shoulder. "I can't go to a strip bar, Maxine, somebody'll recognize me and it'll be in the papers. 'Wounded Woman Cop Lets Hair Down at Topless Bar.' No thank you. Let's take this makeup off and go to the gun range. I'll buy the ammo."

"Tempting," I replied, placing a tight black cap on her head and handing her a pair of mirrored shades. "But we've got work to do."

"I am not taking my clothes off in public, Maxine Wright Leverman."

I laughed. "Your Puritanical values are safe tonight, Cass. We're on a case."

"They gave you a case already?"

"Er, not exactly."

Her pretty violet eyes narrowed. "What do you mean, 'not exactly'?"

I fiddled with fitting a micro camera through my bodice. "The phone rang while everybody was out. It was Blue Ivey from Cedar Bend Winery. She thinks her husband's having an affair and wants proof. I rented a Camry so we'll be less conspicuous." I turned to Cass. "See it?"

"With those boobs? Maxine, nobody would notice a full-sized video camera hanging around your neck, much less one stuck through a buttonhole." She leaned close and squinted at the button hiding the tiny camera. "Where'd you get it?"

"It's a little something I had hanging around."

"Hanging around for what, exactly?"

"Help with my divorce."

"It's excellent for undercover work."

"That's the point."

She straightened. "The point is that you're not licensed. Are you working under either Babby or Kay's direction?"

"Define work," I said.

Cass sighed. "In Max speak, that's a no. Therefore, you're engaging in a criminal act by pretending to be a licensed PI, Maxine. We can't do this. I can't do this. I should arrest you for doing this."

"Please, Cass," I pleaded. "Nobody thinks I can do this job. Aunt Kay's being kind and giving me a shot, but I want her to know I'm serious. The best way for me to prove that is to get the evidence that Ivey is cheating on his wife. You know how important this is to me. To us."

Cass studied me with that intense look that told me she was thinking.

I kept talking. "Okay, so tonight? We're two lesbians out for a good time and I just happen to have a camera in my cleavage. No PI stuff, okay?"

"Lesbians? Guess that makes me the butch and you the femme." She looked in the mirror and adjusted her hat. Finally, she nodded. "No investigating. Do you have a picture of this guy, whoever we're looking for?"

I showed her the photo in *Texas Eats.* "Bret Ivey."

"That's it?"

I nodded.

"Did you Google him?"

I nodded.

"Nothing?"

I shook my head. "He's hiding something."

"Fine. If you happen to see Bret Ivey and get a shot of him fondling a topless waitress, it goes straight to Babby and Kay. First thing tomorrow." She slipped the shades on. "I wish you'd picked dominant and submissive, I'd look good with a whip. What are we eating?"

"Eating?"

"I'm hungry, Max, and you need to put on some weight."

"I do not."

"You're too thin for those fake boobs. Besides, hunting a man takes energy."

THE SEEDIER SIDE OF LIFE

BEING WOMEN OF SOUND mind, we did what any solid sleuths would do before diving into the skank that is Whiskey Bend: we cruised the strip checking for Bret Ivey's Corvette. I've driven this stretch of road just over the state line and into Louisiana numerous times. It's the kind of crammed together place that always makes me slow down and check for drivers who can't stay between the lines. During the day, it's dirty and downright sad. At night, however, it sparkles with twinkling neon signs that distract from the grime and despair.

We drove the half mile stretch of Whiskey Bend at a sedate pace, glancing in the crowded parking lots as we went, searching for a bright yellow Corvette with the license plate WINE-O. We didn't see it, so we agreed to take a closer look at the seedier side of life.

Have you ever been in a bar for bikers? This was my first time, and despite my show of bravado with Cass, I wasn't sure what to expect. Dim lights, sticky floors, inebriated rednecks, scantily clad women with vacant stares. You, too? Well, The Golden O was a surprise. I'd talked it over with Cass, and we decided to work methodically down one side of Whiskey Bend to the last bar, then turn around and work our way along the other side.

Back to The Golden O. It wasn't the kind of place you'd take your mother, but it wasn't as bad as I expected. The parking lot was packed with motorcycles and muscle cars. A flashing neon sign featured the outline of a busty blonde, lips pursed in a sexy 'O'. A bouncer greeted us with a glance up and down, then motioned us inside. I discreetly flipped on my hidden camera. The lights were low, but the floor wasn't sticky. The foyer had a diner-like counter along one wall, fronting a grill where a big man flipped burgers and steaks for five guys perched on chrome stools. The food smelled surprisingly good. Music flowed from deeper inside the establishment and we stepped through a velvet curtain into a wide room with a stage at its center. A busty blonde with mounds of frothy curls who could've been the model for the neon sign stalked along a runway. She was wearing a beautiful black mask and a full-length gown exposing a strip of magnificent cleavage. She peeled off long gloves, one finger at a time, bumping and grinding all the while. The bikers alongside the stage were utterly entranced.

Cass watched the men as they watched the woman. "What gives? I thought the whole reason men came to these places was for the skin."

"It's burlesque," I answered quietly. "It's as much about the tease as the nudity." The stripper unrolled a glove and draped it across one patron's shoulder before whipping it away and slapping him in the face with it. A charged growl went up from the crowd.

"How do you know that?" Cass asked.

"My ex-husband Neil took me to see burlesque shows."

"That didn't bother you?"

"Not until I realized they were men in drag."

Cass cocked an eyebrow.

I focused on the faces around the stage. "It was the beginning of the end for us. If they'd been women, maybe I could've coped."

I felt her gaze and wondered if she would ask more. My best friend and I lost contact while I was married, and other than having been maid of honor in my wedding, she knew very little about my married life. In true Cass style, she knew when to hold her questions. She turned back to the men. "I don't see Bret, do you?"

The dancer tossed her second glove our way and a scrum erupted over the strip of cloth. Amid the chaos, I caught the stripper's glare. I recognized the smoky green eyes behind the mask and blood rushed from my face.

"Oh no," I whispered to Cass. "We're so busted."

"Why?"

"The woman on stage? The dancer?"

Cass glanced up. "What about her?"

"That's Aunt Babby."

HOPELESS

ONCE CASS HAD TAKEN her sweet time confirming I was right, we took our leave from The Golden O, slinking along the walls until we reached the exit. Outside, I bent over and put my hands on my knees, breathing deeply. The bouncer looked curious, and then turned away, probably assuming I'd drunk too much.

Cass was in full detective mode. "*What* is Barbara doing in a club like this?"

"I don't know," I gasped. "But she saw us. She'll know I'm private eyeing without a license."

Her lips puckered. "All she knows is that we were in The Golden O. She has no idea what we were doing." She pulled me upright and headed towards the Camry. "Maybe she's working a case. Who knows?"

"But the cat's out of the bag, Cass," I wailed. "I can't lie to Babby. Aunt Kay and Cindy, no problem. But Babs? She's got some voodoo priestess thing going. It's over. Let's go home."

"It's too late to worry now. We can talk damage control while we cruise the strip again." Cass motioned for the keys. "Buck up, girl. We've got work to do."

EVENTUALLY I CALMED AND we carried on like this for a few hours. Every time we left one bar, we'd cruise the strip, looking for

Bret's yellow Corvette. No dice. In we'd go, me working my charm on bouncers to grease our way into the places, Cass's eagle eyes scanning the crowds. We'd sip at sparkling water and by midnight, we were exhausted and feeling decidedly unclean, but it seemed the night was just getting started. We stopped at a club called The Boom Boom Room. The atmosphere crackled with booze-fueled excitement and I noticed a pattern.

I nudged Cass. "See that guy in the black baseball cap? The one who just sat down at the stage?"

She nodded.

"He was at the burlesque place."

She nodded again.

"You knew that?"

"They're going into shuffle mode, moving from one place to the next, trying to pick somebody up."

I stared at her. "How do you know this?"

"It's the best time of night to arrest drunk drivers. Watch him."

I did. He was a total pervert. Winking at one waitress, patting the well-rounded derriere of another. She gave him the hairy eyeball but instead of backing off, he seemed to take her rebuttal as evidence of desire. It wasn't long until one of the bouncers tossed him out.

I leaned into Cass. "Think he ever scores?"

"It wouldn't surprise me. Look at the chicks at the bar."

Low lights are usually brilliant for erasing years and adding sex appeal, but these gals had been rode so hard and put up so wet that only utter darkness could hide their sleaze. "Nasty."

"The guys are usually drunk enough at this point that anything vaguely resembling a female will do." Cass stiffened and peered into the gloom, then stifled a laugh. "I don't believe it."

"Believe what?"

She lifted her chin at two men with full beards hunkering in a corner. "The Grove twins. Ernie Munk's nephews. I'll be back."

I reached for her. "You'll break our cover, Cass. Let them have their fun. There's no harm in it."

"There's harm in it if they're drunk and try to drive home. I'll be discreet."

I watched her sashay to the bar and speak to the bartender, then return to our table empty-handed.

"What happened?" I asked.

"I ordered chocolate martinis. He'll have to bring them to us."

I gaped. Cass never drank. Ever. "Martinis?"

"A virgin for me. Nobody would believe it about you."

I slapped at her arm. She was right, of course.

A strapping chap in jeans and a tight t-shirt brought two chilled glasses to our table. Cass leaned forward and he bent to listen. "Those two boys in the corner?"

He followed her gaze. "They bothering you?"

"They're underage."

He glanced back to the corner. "They've got to be in their late twenties."

"They're seventeen, tops. That's Matt and Mark Grove. They're nephews of a Forney County police officer." The strapping chap took a step back but Cass stopped him. "I don't want to cause trouble, but it's time for them to go home if they're safe to drive. Agreed?"

He nodded. "And if they can't drive?"

"Take their keys. I'll call their uncle. He'll be discreet."

The bartender turned away and again Cass stopped him. "How much for the martinis?"

"Honey, if those two really are underage, your drinks are on the house."

We watched as the bartender made his way across the room and spoke to the twins. One boy's head drooped and the other punched his brother in the arm.

They followed the bartender from the room and he returned a few minutes later. "One was a little drunk, the other had had one beer. He's driving them home. They won't be back anytime soon. Thanks again for the warning. I'll fire the doorman after closing tonight." He looked us both up and down for the first time. "You two are welcome any time."

I watched him walk to the bar, admiring his posterior assets, and then took a last look around the room. "This is a waste of time. I give up. I have no idea how to find Bret Ivey." A man who might've been handsome before drunkenness overtook him stumbled our way. I tugged on Cass's arm. "The effectiveness of our disguises is waning. Let's go."

In best-friend-pretending-to-be-a-lesbian style, Cass draped her good arm around my shoulders and we headed for the door. "One more pass," she said. "One more cruise up and down Whiskey Bend. I've got a feeling Bret Ivey is nearby."

I glanced over at her. "Really?"

"No, but I'm not letting you quit. Not yet."

A MAN AND HIS CAR

CASS'S PERSISTENCE PAID OFF. We left The Boom Boom Room and turned east to Shreveport, driving at a sedate pace while scanning both sides of the road. Cass pulled into a gas station to turn around, then smacked her forehead. "The back of the bars, Maxine."

"What?"

"We haven't checked behind the clubs." She slipped into the parking lot of the first strip club we came to, and then eased around the side of the building and along the row of parked cars.

I pointed. "The sign says employees only. Why would he park back here?"

"You said he's got a thing for his car, right? It's new and he loves it?"

"That's what Blue said. Why?"

"He'll be careful with it. If he's a regular at one of these places, a big spender, they might send him back here to park."

It was a good theory, and her ability to generate good theories was one of the reasons I wanted Cass along tonight. So we drove up and down Whiskey Bend, dipping into and out of the employee parking lots as we went. Sure enough, we found his Corvette at The Bicycle Club, the place with fat-bottomed girls we'd hit early tonight. He must've arrived after we departed. Cass studied the area for a moment, then pulled alongside the Corvette and hopped out. She touched the hood and returned to the car.

"What was that about?"

"Still warm. He hasn't been here long."

See? The girl is smart. She cruised the remainder of the employee parking lot and then drove around to the front of the building and backed our rented Camry under the overhanging boughs of a thirsty looking oak. She turned the engine off and cracked the windows.

And then she didn't move.

"What are we doing?" I asked.

"Waiting."

"For what?"

"Until he leaves. We'll follow him."

"Like in the movies? A tail?"

"Calm down, Max. Chances are he'll head straight home and you'll be out cruising the bars again tomorrow night."

I chewed on that. "Why don't we go in and see what he's up to?"

"It's almost closing time. There's only one way out of the parking lot. We'll follow and see where he goes."

As much as I itched to get inside, it made sense. I couldn't help it though, I started to twitch.

Cass heaved a sigh. "Where's your camera?"

I pointed to the special button on my bustier.

She laughed. "Not that one. Your big one. Make sure it's set for night shooting and the flash is off."

The girl was good, keeping me occupied doing something practical. I was starting to realize I had a lot to learn about this private detective stuff.

I was adjusting the flash settings when Cass straightened. "We're on."

A chill streaked through my veins. A yellow Corvette eased from beside the building and paused at the highway. I started snapping.

The WINE-O on its license plate was just visible in the glow of neon lights. I looked at Cass. She was peering through the windshield, gaze roving the parking lot.

"Aren't we going to follow?" I asked.

"We'll give him some room."

A wedge of golden light appeared in The Bicycle Club's entrance and two men in cowboy hats stepped into the night. They wobbled, one pointed at the Corvette, and they wove into the parking lot, one hustling like a peg legged pirate. A beep sounded and lights flashed. They climbed into a pickup and an engine roared. I looked back at the road in time to see the Corvette's tires bite gravel and throw it back at the truck.

"Okay," Cass said. "Now we go."

THE CHASE

EAST TEXAS ISN'T AS flat as you might think. Parts of it, in fact, are rather hilly with sharply curving roads. After it peeled out of The Bicycle Club's parking lot, Bret Ivey's Corvette literally headed for the hills, the pickup in hot pursuit. Cass lagged a little behind but was soon up to the same speed. The bright yellow car fairly glowed in the moonlight and she had no problem keeping both vehicles in sight. They wove an easy pattern through the backroads, gradually heading deeper into the Piney Forest. We watched as the Corvette fishtailed around a turn, the pickup gaining as the Corvette lost speed, and Cass dug her cell phone from her back pocket.

I reached for the dashboard as she took the curve without slowing. "Who are you calling?" I asked.

"I want to know who's driving that truck."

She spoke to someone who responded with a name and address. The truck's tail lights disappeared over the hill ahead of us, and Cass floored the engine as she snapped the phone shut. "It's registered to a Jimmy Graves. Reported stolen this afternoon."

"What does that mean?" I asked.

"Either someone's out for a joyride and decided to chase a Corvette, or whoever's chasing Bret Ivey didn't want to use his own car."

We crested the hill and Cass slowed to a stop. A ribbon of dark tarmac stretched away from us, changing to the bony white of concrete as the road became a bridge over the Sabine River, then resuming its silky form about three-quarters of a mile away and climbing into the night sky. The space was empty. In the few seconds the vehicles had been out of our sight, they had disappeared. Cass drove slowly, her eyes on the road, and lowered our windows.

We heard the hissing as our eyes found the skid marks.

Cass stopped near the bridge where parallel ruts slashed the sun-scorched vegetation in the verge. We jumped from the car and worked our way down the incline to the truck, now ticking quietly beside the nearly dry river. It was slow going in my heels, but I was glad I'd forgone the Jimmy Choos that work wonders on my calves and chosen standard pumps for tonight. They'd be destroyed by the rock-hard earth, but it was all in a good cause, like proving my worth. We were about halfway down the hill when the truck's doors popped open. The interior light snapped on and two bodies tumbled from the cab's interior.

"You guys all right?" I called.

They turned to look at us and then stumbled for the trees lining the river. Something shiny arced through the air and I heard a soft splash.

"Hey, wait," I shouted, running as best I could in my tight leather skirt. "Stop. Police. Stop right there."

They easily outpaced me and melted into the trees.

Cass pulled up short beside me. "Good try, Maxine."

We walked back to the truck and she checked its interior before opening her phone, asking for a tow truck and the forensics guy, then squatted to examine the blown rear tire.

I looked us over. "Any chance we could drive back to town and change?"

"I can do better than that," Cass said. "Come on."

THE STORY

BEFORE WE'D LEFT MY apartment complex, Cass had taken a duffel bag from her truck and put it in the Camry's trunk. Now I watched with interest as she whipped the zipper open and then sagged with relief when she pulled normal clothes from inside.

I hugged her. "You are a marvel."

We checked both directions and helped each other strip out of our clubbing attire and into much more comfortable clothes. My feet sighed with relief when I slipped them into a pair of sandals. Cass put our leather into the bag and rearranged a few things.

I peeked over her shoulder. "What else is in there?"

"Standard stuff. Regular handcuffs, tie-wrap cuffs, shotgun and ammunition, pocket knife, emergency medical kit, gloves, and a basic forensic kit."

Spending a night detecting with Cass was an eye opener.

A county-issue pickup pulled to a stop behind us and Cass's hunky boyfriend, Tom Kado, hopped out. The man is a serious honey. Dark hair, gray eyes, great build, and an amazing personality to go with it. He's Forney County's sole forensics guy, and head-over-heels in lust, and maybe even love, with Cass. She's on her way to head-over-heels with him, and I've warned her: if she doesn't get there soon, I'll go into Maxine Man-eater mode and take him for my own.

He pecked Cass on the cheek and I swear the girl blushed to the roots of her auburn hair. Kado studied her for a moment, then looked at me, then back at her. "What have you been up to?"

Her air was total innocence. "Girl stuff."

He lifted an eyebrow as if debating whether to challenge her, and then followed the double tire gashes with his eyes to the pickup, whose cab still glowed from the interior light. "More 'girl stuff?'"

I fumed while Cass gave him the skinny on our evening's activities. She didn't lie to protect me. Or her. Every time I tried to interrupt, she'd hold a hand up and carry on. As if I wasn't there.

When she finished, Kado said, "Makes sense. You were over in Shreveport having dinner and came home down Whiskey Bend, saw the pickup chase the Corvette and did the responsible thing."

"What's that?" I asked.

"Followed at a safe distance," they answered in unison.

"And then called the accident in," Kado said. "You didn't get a plate for the Corvette?"

"Of course we -" I started to answer.

Cass talked over me. "It was too far ahead of us. Not sure what year, but it was a light color. Oh, and they tossed something in the river. Probably a gun. See if the guys can fish it out."

He nodded and started down the incline.

"What just happened?" I asked, sneaking a peek at Kado's broad shoulders and tight backside.

"He's protecting us. You, especially. Technically, he should bust you for not having a license."

I swallowed hard. "Thanks."

"For what? We were out for dinner in Shreveport and came home via Whiskey Bend."

A tow truck and patrol car stopped behind Kado's pickup. Both drivers came to talk to Cass, then joined Kado at the stolen truck.

The tension in my shoulders eased. "What happens now?"

"They'll tow Jimmy Graves' pickup to Arcadia. Tomorrow, Kado will process it to see if he can figure out who stole it. From there, we try to find a link to Bret Ivey."

"How do we do that?"

"Depends on the kind of evidence Kado finds, if any." She opened the Camry. "Let's go. I need sleep if I'm going to keep up with Chad the psychopathic physical therapist tomorrow."

I got into the car and slipped my phone from my pocket and tapped at the screen.

"What are you doing?" Cass asked.

"Texting Simon."

"Who's Simon?"

"A guy from Fort Worth. We're supposed to have dinner tomorrow, but I'm canceling."

"Why?"

"Finding Bret is more important than a date."

Cass looked across the car at me. "That's a first."

"What is?"

"Maxine Leverman finding anything more important than a date."

I couldn't argue with that, so I didn't.

OVER THE RIVER AND THROUGH THE WOODS

THE TWO MEN HOVERED inside the tree line, watching. When no one followed, they inched deeper into the woods, stepping carefully to avoid making loud noises.

They'd crept nearly a quarter mile when the dark-haired man spoke to the blond. "Did you wipe your side of the truck down?"

The blond man blinked. "Um, kind of."

"So, no?"

"Yes, no."

"And the gun? You tossed it because?"

The blond shrugged. "I didn't want them to find us with it."

"You didn't think they might not catch us?"

"Um, no."

"Or because the river is so low they might find it?"

"No."

The dark-haired man sighed and stopped to look around. "You'd better call him."

"Oh, man." It was almost a groan.

"You lost control of the truck."

"I know."

"And you lost BB."

"I know that, too."

"That makes you responsible. You have to call him."

The blond man pulled at his nose. "What do I tell him?"

"What you did, and to come get us."

"Where are we?"

The dark-haired man looked at the river and debated. "Tell him to meet us on the north side of the bridge on Farm-to-Market 699."

"The one we just came from?"

"That one. We'll cross the river and double back. Tell him to give it a couple of hours. They'll take the truck and be gone by then. We'll wait in the woods. If anybody's around, tell him to come back in an hour."

The blond man hesitated. "Maybe we could walk back to the house."

"Maybe not. Dial."

FRIDAY

COMING CLEAN

I WOKE TO THE sound of a small explosion and creative cursing, and added my own disgruntled voicing to the mix as I stumbled to the kitchen. Cass was in one of my bathrobes and Babby was in full office attire, not a hair out of place. Both were glaring at my beautiful espresso machine. Except for the narrow slashes where their bodies shielded the blast path, everything in my kitchen was decorated with a dark mist of wet espresso.

I couldn't help it, I laughed.

Cass stalked past me, swiping grinds from her face. "I'm buying you a Mr. Coffee and some Folgers, first thing."

"She was checking to see if she'd done it right when the thing blew, poor girl." Babby took a sponge from the sink and handed me a damp rag. With a nod at the offending machine, she said, "I'm trainable, sweet pea. After we clean this mess up, you can give me lessons and tell me what you and Cass were doing at The Golden O."

The previous evening came back in a blur, and I scrubbed harder.

"Maxine? You'll have to come clean eventually, no pun intended."

"After coffee, Babby. I can't think without coffee."

"Fair enough. But this isn't going away." She finished with a countertop. "Now, tell me about this apartment."

"What do you mean?"

"How do you pay for this place and your apartment in Fort Worth? I know your trust fund is healthy, but the distributions aren't this generous, are they?"

This was dangerous territory. My father died when I was twelve, but as the practical half of my parent's marriage, he'd made sure my brother and I had a decent financial chance of getting started in the world. The monthly stipend helped, but it wasn't my main source of funds. That came from informal payments my ex-husband Neil made to ensure I kept certain photographs from hitting the internet, and why I'd purchased the button-hole camera and a few other clever gadgets. Since he's a hedge fund manager, the payments are commensurate with his income. Blackmail, some would call it, but I prefer to think of it as a good bargain. I get to live in the style to which he'd made me accustomed, and Neil gets to wear all the frilly knickers he wants.

I couldn't tell Babby any of this, of course, so I lied a little. "Neil helps me with my portfolio."

"I didn't realize the divorce was amicable."

I refused to make eye contact, focusing instead on the coffee grinds stuck in the grout on the floor. "There are some things we agree on."

This seemed to mollify her. It took us the better part of ten minutes to wipe down the kitchen. Babby extracted a compact from her purse and dabbed at her face while I provided instructions on how to successfully produce a delicious cup of coffee. She created three cappuccinos, which was pretty impressive for a first timer. We were sipping and congratulating ourselves when Cass walked into the kitchen toweling her hair dry.

"Hey Babs. Is that rose tattoo on your butt real? And where'd you learn to dance like that?"

Babby blinked. "The tattoo is temporary. But I know a good tattoo artist if you want a real one."

"You're in great shape for your age."

"Careful, sweetie."

"Oh. Right," Cass said. "What I meant to say was that you're in fabulous shape. No cellulite at all. How do you manage that?"

"Trade secret." She pushed a mug across the table. "What were you doing at The Golden O last night?"

Cass sipped. "You first."

"I was working a case. Now, what were you doing there?"

"What kind of case?" Cass asked.

"Your turn." She stared at Cass for a moment, then fixed me with a piercing gaze that held an unnatural power to draw the truth from me. I was struggling to keep my mouth shut and toying with the desire to lie. Instead, I looked to Cass, who shrugged.

"She'll find out sooner or later. Might as well spill."

I chewed my lip and then blurted, "I took a case yesterday. A cheating husband. We were looking for him."

Babby relaxed. "Thank God. I thought you'd found out about my case while you've been filing all the paperwork and wanted to check out an undercover operation." Her expression turned grim again. "You two could've seriously blown my cover."

"How?"

"All that leather and face paint? You stood out like warts on a beautiful bosom."

Cass shot me a glance. "I thought we looked pretty good."

"You did, but nobody dresses like that around here. And did you really think any disguise could hide *you*? You still favor your left arm. And that red hair." Babby reached out and tucked a strand behind Cass's ear. "You're doomed if you ever go undercover. The bartender asked if I'd noticed that 'the hot cop from the papers' had come in, and did I know she was a lesbian." Babby knocked the espresso grounds out of the filter with more force than was needed. "Maxine Wright Leverman, do you have any idea how much trouble you could be in? You were operating as a PI without a license."

I opened my mouth to protest but she talked over me.

"And you, Cass. I would've thought you'd have more sense than to let her get into something like this, much less to go with her."

Cass waited until the machine finished steaming and then put on her detective face. "You're right," she said, which stopped Babby cold. "I tried to talk her out of last night, but not very hard. You know Maxine as well as I do. Once she gets an idea in her head, you can't stop her." She looked pointedly at my aunt, whose expression was thoughtful. "Maxine wants to be an investigator with Lost and Found, but she knows nobody believes she's got any staying power. Am I right?"

"You are."

"Then she did what any determined woman would do: she took matters into her own hands." Cass was in full professional cop mode now, talking with authority to a woman who'd once powdered her bottom. "She told me she'd chanced on an opportunity while she was at the agency yesterday, and decided to show y'all what she was capable of. I believe in Maxine, and I believe in her dream. It's important to me that she become a PI, and I'm willing to help her prove she's capable of becoming a fabulous investigator. You're right, technically, that she was working without a license. But nothing came of it. So if push comes to shove, I'll back Maxine and confirm we were two girls out for a night on the town."

I was near tears.

"It's a compelling argument, but she put herself and the firm in jeopardy." Babby took a carton of yogurt from the fridge and put bowls and spoons on the table.

"If you hadn't been dancing at The Golden O, you wouldn't have known what Max was up to until she decided to tell you."

Babby considered this. "Good point, although Maxine can't keep a secret." She studied Cass over the rim of her coffee mug. "You said it's important to you that Maxine gets her license. Why?"

"Personal reasons that I'm not ready to discuss."

Babby pursed her lips. "There's something you want or need to investigate that has to stay off the county's books, or that you don't want Hoffner to know about." She was sharp, I'll give her that. "Fine. What would make you ready to discuss?"

Cass stole a glance at me. "We might need your help."

"I never could walk away from a mystery." Babby nodded. "Well then, between us, I think Maxine has the potential to make a fine investigator." My eyes lit up. "But," she added, "you absolutely must get licensed and follow the law. Lost and Found can't afford to be associated with any devious behavior. Maxine can work under my supervision until she passes her exam. Frankly, we need all the help we can get right now. We're swamped."

I frowned. "Things seem slow to me. It's all background checks, insurance scams, and misbehaving spouses."

Aunt Babby smiled her seductive smile, looking a little like Marilyn Monroe with coppery hair. "That's what goes on during business hours, boo boo. But one step at a time. Tell me about this case."

"I get to keep it?"

"If it's just a cheating husband, probably. Anything more involved and you'll need help."

Cass nudged me. "It's a good deal, Max. Take it while it's hot."

THE GRUDGE

BABBY LEFT FOR THE office, Cass left for her session with the psychopathic physical therapist, and I was left blissfully alone, basking in the afterglow of success. It's not as good as the afterglow from sex, mind you, but it runs a close second. I considered going back to bed but decided a responsible PI would make notes on what had happened the evening before, while it was still fresh in her mind. I settled at my desk, coffee by my side, and started typing. I had no clue what a detective's file notes should look like, so I rambled. After a quick edit, I thought I had a good start. Then I remembered the photos from my bustier and the big camera. I connected the buttonhole camera to the computer, and let the equipment do its work while I headed for the shower.

Dressed for work, I made a new coffee and sat back to watch.

The film from the button camera was downright entertaining. I'd turned it on when we went into The Golden O and promptly forgotten about it. I caught some great shots of Babby's burlesque act. She was steamy, and the men were seriously into her striptease, evidenced by the currency waving in the air. I wondered if it might be worth going undercover in a strip joint for the tips.

Despite the wealth of footage, I caught no sight of Bret Ivey, so I turned to my big camera. The images I shot in The Bicycle Club's parking lot were grainy but discernible. The first few shots were of the Corvette idling near the road, followed by a smear of neon lights. I must've taken a photo as I swung the camera back to the club's entrance.

The two cowboys were clearly visible as they stopped outside the club's open door. Their cowboy hats threw shadows over their faces, but their clothes were in full view. In the following photos, I'd caught a jawline or a hint of a tattoo creeping from one man's collar, but never enough for an identification. I remembered one man had walked funny and I backed the photos up and viewed them again. Although they weren't a steady flow, one of the cowboys walked with a definite roll to his gait.

My finger went to the delete button, but I stopped myself. They weren't much to go on, but in the end, these photos might be all we had. I saved them to a memory stick and put it and my notes in my lucky purse and headed for the door.

I WAS ON MY way to the office when my client called.

"What happened last night?" Blue's voice was curious, nothing more.

"Good morning. What do you mean?"

"The Corvette is back, but Bret's nowhere around. I figured you'd found him last night and put the fear of God in him."

"Not exactly. I'd love to update you, though. Are you available?" I asked. "I can come to the winery if it's convenient."

"Fridays are a nightmare. Hang on." I heard a keyboard clicking. "Come for dinner. It's flat iron steak night and we've got a great jazz band on. Bring friends, I want to know what they think. You and I can sneak away for a few minutes for that update."

And again, she was gone.

I dialed Cass. Her phone went to voice mail. "Call me. We're going to the winery tonight. See if Kado's available and I'll try to rustle up a date."

I settled back into the Lexus and wondered who to call. Here's the problem: I'd been something of a wild child in high school, sharing the free love thing all over the county. What can I say? I had abandonment issues. I took love anywhere I could find it. But East Texas is a small community. Most of the men I'd bedded back then were either married or newly divorced. And really, I wasn't interested in a replay. I wanted someone new.

This is the challenge with returning to your small home town: it's all a replay, like it or not. Everybody knows everybody else, and memories are long. This is why I live full-time in Fort Worth and only keep an apartment in Arcadia. When it gets a bit too much out here, I can head for blissful anonymity.

I scrolled through the list of available and eligible men in my mind's database. The hottie host from the winery was worth consideration, but I had a hunch he'd be working tonight and a stronger hunch it would be bad to get involved with a client's employee.

And then I realized I could kill two birds with one stone: find a date and get even with Cindy. I decided to stop and see Arty, the lawyer she's chasing. My cousin has an eye for the attractive and well-funded male, even if she can't keep a man. Why am I holding a grudge? She stole Harry Peterson from me back in second grade.

Yes, these things linger.

THE FACE OFF

A RUSTLING SOUNDED FROM behind the Japanese screen, and Cindy emerged wearing a sarong over her yoga outfit. Bright red toenails peeked from the tips of her bejeweled sandals. She dug in a workout bag and strapped on a sports watch. "I can't take the air of expectation permeating this place," she said. She held up her wrist.

"Did anybody charge the batteries? I plan to take a lot of photos today."

"You wore it last, sweetie," Babby said.

"Get better shots this time, punkin," Kay instructed. "All you got last time was his bottom up in the air during Downward Facing Dog."

"It's a nice bottom."

"Be that as it may, butt shots don't prove anything. It's his face we need, preferably while he's seriously contorted."

"Yoga is therapeutic."

"Not some of those harder poses for a man whose back is supposed to be in perpetual spasm. Try to catch him doing the Camel, or maybe the Wheel. Scoot, darling, or you'll miss your class."

Cindy fluffed her hair and sashayed out the door.

"Thank God," Kay said. "I thought she was going to hyperventilate, all that huffing and puffing. It's killing me, too. What's going on?"

Babby checked her lipstick in a small mirror. "Whatever do you mean?"

"Cut the crap, Babs. You walked in late - totally unlike you - wearing the Cheshire Cat's grin. Whose donut did you steal?"

"It's better than donuts. Maxine took a case yesterday, and she's doing a pretty good job of working it."

Kay slapped the desk. "I knew that phone rang while I was in the powder room. She lied to me."

"Can you blame her? Nobody takes her seriously."

"That's her own fault, Babby. It's stunts like this that always got Maxine in trouble." She breathed a sigh. "I wanted to believe in her, but she's still the same little girl that caused so much trouble. She's impulsive. Can't think through consequences or won't take the time to think things through." Kay shook her head. "We both know what she's like. That's the end of her little venture here."

"I know what Maxine used to be like." Babby said. She tapped a fingernail against her coffee cup. "Something has changed. I can't say she's more grounded, but she has a harder edge now."

"Divorce'll do that."

"It will, and that might be it. But she's hiding something. So is Cass."

Kay's eyes narrowed. "Do you think what's-his-name hurt her?"

"Neil," Babby said, waving the comment away. "Of course he hurt her, but she's getting some sort of revenge. I don't think that's what she's hiding, though."

"Did she tell you how she can afford that apartment and still keep her place in Fort Worth?"

"Nope, but it'll come out." She sipped. "About this case…"

"I hope you debriefed her, because she's done here."

"Slow down, Kay. Hear me out."

"It won't work, Barbara. Maxine will never be one to follow the rules. She thinks she knows it all. That'll get her and maybe the agency in trouble. It might get her hurt."

Babby's mouth set in a thin line. "Kay Wooten. I own half of this agency and you will hear me out. Then, if there's an employment decision to make, we'll make it together. Just as our agreement states."

Kay drew a deep breath and stood, straightened her brilliant blue skirt, and stepped to the water cooler. She took her time filling a cup, and then turned to Babby, face composed. "What's the case?"

"A cheating husband."

"Whose?"

"Blue Ivey out at the winery. Do you know her?"

Kay peeled the wrapper from an Atomic Fireball and slipped the candy between her lips. She sucked for a moment. "Only by reputation. I've been to the winery but haven't met her, although I might've met the cheating spouse."

"What's he like?"

"If he's who I think he is, a man's man with the men and a flirt with the skirts. But that's what you'd expect from a guy with the balls to open a restaurant in Forney County that doesn't serve chicken fried steak. And it's pricey. If you want clients, you've got to engage with them, create a personality they remember."

"I need to get out there," Babby said. "I can't remember the last time I had a good glass of wine."

"Last weekend, dear."

"I did say 'good'. That was some swill from across the county line."

Kay sucked her Fireball. "You really think Maxine is serious?"

"I didn't until I saw her out at The Golden O last night."

"Did she make you?"

"Yes, and bolted. Thankfully she didn't give me away."

"How did your gig go?"

"Perfect. The bartender's running hookers from the place. After the show, he asked if I wanted to join his stable."

"Did you get it on film?"

Babby nodded.

"Where'd you put the camera?"

"The wig."

"The big blonde one?"

Babby nodded again.

"I love that thing." Kay sipped her water. "I can't believe Maxine was working a case, without a license, without backup."

"Cass was with her."

Kay slapped a hand over her eyes. "This just gets better."

"They did a good job," Babby said. "Maxine doesn't know how a case like this should be worked, but her approach wasn't bad." She eyed Kay. "They found him."

"They did?"

"They saw his car and followed the truck that was following it until the truck went off the road."

Kay held up a hand. "Start at the beginning. Better yet, let's split an omelet at The Golden Gate. I'm getting weak from all this excitement." She grabbed her handbag. "Don't think that because I've got low blood sugar this is over, Babby. This job, this agency, is the wrong fit for Maxine."

"Let me tell the story, Kay, and then we'll decide." She took her wallet from her purse and locked the door behind them. "I wonder if Stan would protest if I brought a cinnamon swirl into The Gate?"

A SPECIAL KIND OF REVENGE

THE HIKE UP TO the second floor wasn't as hard today. Maybe because my heels were only three inches high, or maybe because I was so excited to be working my first real case I was practically floating. I turned away from Lost and Found's offices and headed for the small law firm down the hall. I hoisted my Louis Vuitton bag onto my shoulder and fluffed my hair before turning the knob. The door eased open on oiled hinges. A man was sitting on the corner of a desk that must belong to the receptionist, swinging one leg, head thrown back in a laugh. They started when I cleared my throat. The receptionist's surprised eyes were the bluest I'd ever seen, and a gorgeous hank of blond hair fell across his forehead. The other man turned, a rush of blood coloring those beautiful high cheekbones.

"I should've knocked," I said.

He stood and smoothed his trousers. "You're Maxine, right? Cindy's cousin? I'm Arty Henderson. Come in."

Yeowza. Based on looks alone, Cindy had picked a winner. Dark hair, a male model's well-defined face, an athlete's lean body - think young Gregory Peck. She was also right about his finances. His hand-tailored suit and shirt, the tastefully decorated office, and the attractive receptionist all indicated he was a honey with money. But she was dead wrong about his sexual preferences. Some things are transparent to the initiated, and thanks to my ex-husband, I'd had more than my share of initiation.

I held out my hand. "She's told me a lot about you. All quite flattering."

He smiled, revealing gorgeous dimples. "And she's told me a lot about you. None of it true, apparently."

"That's Cindy for you. We've always had something of a rivalry when it comes to handsome men." I couldn't let on that I knew he was gay. Lost and Found did a lot of legwork for Arty's firm, and I'd hate to jeopardize that source of income. I smiled at the other man, who was now standing. "Hi."

"I'm Steve, Arthur's receptionist, paralegal, and general gofer."

Arthur and Steve. They made a nice couple.

"I wanted to introduce myself since we'll be sharing the floor," I said.

"You're full time now?" Arty asked.

"Pending my passing the right exams and getting a concealed carry license, yes."

"Congrats. Having another armed woman in the building is a comforting thought. Nobody wants to cross the women from Lost and Found."

I laughed. "Thanks for letting me pop in like this. I hope we'll get to work together soon."

We waved our good-byes and I closed the door behind me before leaning against the wall, a huge smile on my face. I briefly debated saving my cousin the pain of learning that the object of her affection was batting for the other side, but knew I'd be wasting my breath. She'd only think I was chasing Arty. Nope, letting Cindy think she was getting one over on me was a special kind of revenge.

One that might make up for the trauma of losing Harry Peterson all those years ago.

But this left me dateless for tonight and with few options. My heart kept urging me towards something I wasn't sure about: calling Bruce Elliot. Cass has six older brothers. Bruce was the fourth born, eight years older than me and Cass, in his mid-thirties now. A professor at the local college, he's something of a ladies' man and rumor has it that he's bedded all the eligible, and some of the not-so-eligible, women in and around Forney County. We ran into each other at the hospital after Cass was shot and swapped phone numbers and shifts at her bedside until she was ready to go home. There was a *frisson* between us, but Bruce never made a move. Normally, that isn't a problem. If I find a man I want, I go after him.

Therefore, it was disconcerting that neither of us was willing to make the first move.

Maybe I hesitated because Bruce was Cass's brother and had witnessed almost all of the worst moments of my life. Maybe because Bruce had always treated me the same way he'd treated Cass, as his little sister. Maybe because when I was a kid, I'd wished I could trade my one horrible brother for any of the Elliot boys.

My finger hovered over his name in my phone's directory and I decided it was time for that little bit of insecurity to stop.

I tapped a quick text and took three steps towards Lost and Found's door when his reply came back. He wasn't available tonight, but would take a rain check. A smile plastered itself across my face before I realized I was still dateless. I went back through my mind's database of eligible bachelors, finding a psychologist I'd briefly dated who over-analyzed, and a veterinarian who drools too much.

Bottom line: there was no one I wanted to spend my evening with other than Cass and, if he was available, her dishy Kado.

But there was a particular itch that needed scratching, and I sent a text to my trainer, Harvey Osmond, no relation to the white-smiled clan from Utah. We'd slipped into a regular schedule involving cardio and strength training, with the occasional bout between the sheets. Our relationship was purely physical on all fronts, which suited us both. As soon as my text was sent my phone pinged. It was a reply from Harvey with a time later this evening.

Perfect.

THE SOUNDTRACK OF MY YOUTH

WHEN I GOT TO the office, Babby was behind her desk tapping away and didn't even flash me a glance. Although I couldn't see Cindy behind her Japanese screen, I could hear whispers and the occasional giggle. Kay was conspicuously absent and I wondered what she was up to.

I turned my computer on and flipped through the morning's invoices and billing sheets. The ritual of entering data was mindless and soothing, and my thoughts returned to the stolen pickup. I wondered how Kado was doing with the fingerprints.

A final laugh sounded from behind the screen and Cindy emerged, arching her back and stretching a long leg in front of her. "Nice of you to join us, Maxine."

"Who were you slutting around with on the phone?"

"Gathering information from an important source, dearie."

"It was Nicky from First National Bank," Babby said without a break in the tapping. "She uses her phone sex worker voice when she talks to him."

Cindy shrugged. "Whatever it takes, Aunt Babby. Isn't that Lost and Found's motto?"

"Something like that, munchkin. But what a state poor Nicky must be in when you hang up. I'd hate to ask him for a loan right now." She cocked her head, eyes still focused on the screen. "Or maybe now would be the perfect time. I doubt he's capable of reading a credit report."

Cindy turned to me. "Will this be a habit? You wandering in and out whenever you please?"

"I'm not obliged to announce my comings and goings to you. As long as the partners know what I'm doing, that's enough."

Cindy straightened. "Doing? You shouldn't be doing anything but posting invoices. Aunt Babby?" Her voice grew shrill. "Don't tell me she's working a case. She's not qualified to do anything but paperwork, and even that's doubtful."

"Calm down, Cindy. Maxine's doing exactly what I need her to be doing. Right now, that's posting invoices and sending out billing statements, right Maxine?" She picked up the phone and dialed.

I focused on the computer. "Of course it is, Aunt Babby."

Cindy's gaze rested hot on the side of my face. "It's not fair. Maxine gets away with everything."

Ah, sweet memories. That pouty voice was the soundtrack of my youth.

"Get back to work, dumpling. We've got a lot on," Babby said.

"I've got errands to run, anyway." Cindy snagged her handbag and stalked to the door. She pulled it open and a chunky old lady in a flowered dress and Sunday-best straw hat eased inside and sat at Kay's desk. She cracked open a bottle of water and drank deeply. Cindy walked out without a backward glance at the stranger who had invaded Lost and Found.

Babby was deep in a phone conversation about a missing child. I had no choice but to defend Kay's domain. "Excuse me."

The little old lady pulled a dainty handkerchief from a white clutch and dabbed at her hairline.

I stepped over to Kay's desk and bent close. "Is there something I can help you with?"

A pair of eyes so brown they were almost black looked up at me. Her face was a mass of wrinkles that crinkled even deeper, if that was possible, when she giggled. I straightened. The giggle turned into a full belly laugh and I took a step back, glancing at Babby whose full lips were quirked in a half smile.

"What's so funny?" I demanded.

Babby covered the phone and whispered, "Talk to the poor girl."

"It's me, Maxie-moo," a surprisingly strong voice said. "How's my costume?"

It was a voice I knew and a nickname I hated, but I couldn't begin to match it to this shriveled figure. "Aunt Kay?"

She lifted the straw hat and straightened its bow, then peeled a curly white wig from her head, revealing honey-blonde hair matted to her skull. "I'm not doing Elsie again, Babs. Not until it cools down. Wearing this get-up in one hundred degree plus temps is beyond the call of duty. Maybe even suicidal."

Babby fluttered her eyelashes and continued her conversation, jotting notes.

I watched, fascinated, as a set of gnarled fingers tugged at the little old lady's face, pulling a fully formed mask from the forehead and cheekbones to reveal a sweaty Aunt Kay. She turned her desk fan on and breathed deeply from the cool stream.

"Why in the world are you wearing that," I flapped my hand, "outfit? It's Mrs. Doubtfire on a bad hair day, which is saying something."

Kay stood. "Unzip me, sugar pie. I've got to get out of this thing before I explode." I obliged as she explained. "Who are the people nobody notices, Maxine?"

"What do you mean?"

"Those who don't exist because we turn our gaze away. Who are the last people to stick in your memory?"

I helped her peel the floweredy dress off, followed by lumpy pads that rounded out her slender shoulders, hips, and thighs. She stepped out of the puddle of costumery at her feet, wearing only a body suit. "No wonder you were burning up," I said.

"Elsie goes in the closet until it cools down." She padded to the large bathroom at the back of the office, sweat stains dark between her shoulder blades and at the small of her back. "This is an important lesson, Max. Think about it while I'm cleaning up. Who are the invisibles?"

THE INVISIBLES

I RETURNED TO MY desk, half listening to Babby's soothing murmur, and tapped listlessly at the invoice system. *The invisibles*, I wondered. *Those who don't exist because we turn our gaze away.* I made a few notes and then settled into the mindlessness of printing checks.

When Kay returned, it was as if she had never gone out in the heat. She was fresh and perfectly made up, not a hair out of place. The brown contacts were gone and those clear green eyes with the flecks of gold near the pupil and rim of dark blue around the iris were back. "So?" she asked.

Babby was off the phone by then. She stood and stretched. "I'd love to hear this, but I've got to start some cookies."

"Brandon Johnson again?" Kay asked.

Babby nodded.

"Remember the Snickerdoodles. That Sutton kid won't touch a chocolate chip cookie."

"What are you talking about?" I asked Kay.

"Brandon's going through a difficult spell. He's gone missing several times. Always comes home within a few days, and the police don't get too excited when his parents call."

"Aren't they supposed to issue an Amber Alert?"

"Yes, but we must be into double digits by now. We think he's got a hiding place in Deadwood Hollow."

"Aunt Kay! Drug dealers, meth heads, that's where the wacko set up to shoot the Franklins not long ago. It's no place for a kid."

She sipped a fresh cup of coffee. "Of course it isn't. So far, he's come home without a scratch on him. We think they - whoever 'they' is - are protecting him."

"You're kidding."

Kay shrugged. "It's weird, I agree. His parents are so embarrassed, or maybe frustrated, they're calling us instead of the police. We're hitting the juvenile grapevine, plying the kids with cookies. We made good progress with the Sutton kid last time - he's in Babby's Sunday School class. She thinks he knows where Brandon goes."

"What'll happen to him?"

"I think his parents are near the end of their collective ropes. They've tried drugs, psychologists, psychiatrists. The next step is some kind of military boarding school."

"That sounds awful," I said.

"Desperate times, baby cakes." Kay arched a brow. "You weren't far from the military boarding school path when you were a teenager."

Blood rushed to my face. "You might be right. But this kid has both parents. And it seems like they love him."

"Maxine," Kay began. "As much as I dislike your mother -"

And just like that I was close to hyperventilating. Mother was a topic best avoided. At all times. With everyone. "Can we not do this right now?" I interrupted. "Let's talk about invisible people instead. Okay?"

Kay studied me, and I knew she read the terror in my face. "Invisible people. Go."

I drew in a breath laced with the smell of baking cookies and felt calmer. "I'll start with the premise that most people are so absorbed in their own problems, their own day-to-day, they rarely notice anything going on around them."

"I agree. But we don't deal with normal people. We're interested in people who have something to hide."

"Beggars. No one wants to be accosted by someone who's asking for money, whether they're walking down the street or standing at an intersection, cardboard sign in hand." I was talking too fast, but Kay nodded, so I carried on. "The disfigured or infirm. Linger too long, and you're a voyeur. Lift your gaze too abruptly and you're insensitive, a jerk for dismissing someone based on their physical appearance. How am I doing?"

"Good. Keep going."

"The elderly. As long as you appear fit and able, you're part of the ebb and flow of humanity, but as soon as you put on that flowered dress and big straw hat, you become a cliché. A busybody. Someone to avoid or who needs help." I paused for air.

"Anybody else?" Kay pressed.

I shrugged.

"You were right about normal people," Kay said. "We tend not to notice people who are doing normal things, so long as those things are normal within the environment. Few people notice a mother pushing a stroller. A father is a little more unusual, so he might get a second glance, particularly during the week. Someone might remember him. Daddies are supposed to go to work, not stay at home and take care of the kids."

"Why were you in the dress and hat?"

"Creating a normal environment."

I frowned.

"I'm building a character who will become invisible to the person I want to observe. Unfortunately, I picked Elsie. Since I'll suffocate if I dress as her again before winter, I'll have to start over." She traced a pattern on her desk. "Dog walker." She reached for the phone. "If I get to the pound in time, I can make at least one pass today."

I stopped her from dialing. "I'm sorry."

"For what, honey?" she asked.

"Lying to you. Aunt Babby told you about the missing husband, didn't she?"

Kay settled back in her chair. A little steel crept into her gaze. "I understand why you did it, and I admire your initiative, but no more. That was your one lie. We've got too much to lose here. Are we clear?"

The only time I'd heard Kay speak so definitively was when Jerry Crutchfield pushed me down in second grade. She told me he was a bully and bullies only respect people who stand up to them. I'd save myself and people everywhere miles of grief if I'd kick him in the balls as hard as I could next time I saw him. I didn't know what balls were, but Kay advised me to aim between his legs and kick him when no one was around, then make a fast getaway. Her words and my willingness to act did save me much grief, and given that Crutchfield is now a Methodist minister, probably did him a world of good, too.

"Yes, ma'am. It won't happen again."

She reached out and smoothed my hair. "I like this bob cut, but it's time for conditioner, Max. Babby thinks you're serious about becoming a PI."

"I am."

"Why?"

I hesitated. I couldn't tell her the truth: that my goal was to help Cass find the freak who had raped and scarred us. I tried for something that wasn't quite a lie. "I'm a problem solver, Aunt Kay. A good one. Everything you do at Lost and Found revolves around solving mysteries, which are really just problems. I think I can help."

Her eyes softened into the aunt I knew was good for a few cookies, no matter how much red Texas clay I'd smeared into my hair and let dry Medusa-fashion. "Good answer, darling. That'll do for now."

I sent her a questioning look.

"Babby said Cass has an ulterior motive for wanting you to work as a PI, which means you have an ulterior motive." I did my best to imitate Cass and keep my game face on. "I can ride with that as long as you do your work here and do it well."

"I will, Aunt Kay, I promise."

"As with all things, Maxine, time will tell. Babby and I have agreed you're on probation for three months. During that time you'll pursue your license and work on assignments as directed. Once the probation period has passed, we'll evaluate your next steps with the agency," she lifted an eyebrow, "or without."

I couldn't draw a breath. It hadn't dawned on me that I might not get to keep working at Lost and Found as long as I wanted to. Kay was staring me down, so I managed, "Yes, ma'am."

"Babby told me the investigation is getting interesting."

I pulled myself together and filled her in.

"Nice work, honey. We'll loop you in on our status meetings. We have them every couple of days to share information about our cases. When things get busy or we're working on multiple cases, it's easy for something to get dropped. Working together ensures we give our clients the very best." She gave me a pointed look and I blushed, then she went for the coffee pot and asked Babby how long the cookies would be. After filling mugs, she returned to her desk and handed me one. "There are a few things we do behind the scenes that might help. Blue is worried about the amount of money her husband is spending, right?"

I nodded.

"Have you asked for bank and credit card statements?"

I shook my head. "But I'm seeing her tonight. I can ask for them then."

"Text her and tell her you'll run by at lunch to pick them up."

"There's a rush?"

"We need to know what kind of money she's talking about. He can bankrupt them both in short time. And most of us are creatures of habit. His spending patterns might provide a clue about where he is."

"Ah." I pulled out my phone and texted Blue.

"In the meantime, I'll show you how we gather other data. Get a chair. We'll use a case I'm working on as an example."

I waited as Kay clicked on a file and tapped in a password. She paused before hitting 'enter'. "This document," she said, "holds the firm's userIDs and passwords to the databases we use. These are the keys to the kingdom. We only use them for good."

"Wonder Woman stuff, right?" I giggled but she slammed me with a glance. "Got it," I said. "Unlock those doors and let's get to work."

RETAIL WARFARE

BLUE WAS AN ABSOLUTE star and had the documents I needed waiting at lunch time. I stepped inside Cedar Bend Winery to a rush of cool air and the sounds of piped in jazz, and the hunky host met me with a heavy envelope.

He shot me a winning smile. "Blue said you'd come by for this. She also thought you might need a little something to keep you going." He turned and waved to the woman manning the wood-fired oven, who slid a wide paddle bearing an uncooked pizza into the glowing cavity. "She picked a margarita because she wasn't sure what you'd like. We've got salad and desert, too. To go?" I nodded and he motioned to a table. "Iced tea?"

"Yes, please."

I sat and opened the envelope, sliding out a hefty pack of paperwork. Blue had provided personal and business credit card and bank statements going back six months, and I wilted. Paperwork isn't a problem for me, but this was a lot of data. A note from Blue said that any unusual activity on the winery's bank or credit card accounts was Bret's; she always used her personal accounts for personal shopping. I was planning my strategy of attack when the handsome host appeared, winery bag in hand, delicious smells wafting my way.

"I've added a bottle of Blanc du Bois - it's light enough it won't knock you out if you have a glass with your pizza." I opened my lucky Louis Vuitton and he stopped me. "Blue said this is on the house. She wanted to be here when you stopped by, but had to go out, and said she'll see you tonight."

"Tell her I said thanks," I said, giving him my ten-megawatt smile. "What was your name?"

"Will," he said. "And yours?"

"Maxine. Nice to meet you." I stood, flexing a toned leg. "Will I see you this evening?"

Will flashed an equally bright smile. "I certainly hope so."

Well, I thought as I headed into the boiling summer afternoon, *date problem not solved, but I'll have great eye-candy to go with dinner.*

I CHOSE THE RED sofa as my battle station. Its leather is supple, its cushions just the right amount of puffy, and the color deep enough to fuel my fighting bloodlust. I changed into yoga pants and top, opened the bottle of wine, and placed the pizza and salad within reach. Headphones in place with the Barenaked Ladies' *Stunt* album on tap, I assumed the lotus position and scanned Blue's paperwork while I nibbled and sipped.

Marriage to a wealthy man has its advantages. So does divorce when you've got enough dirt to make the monthly stipend generous. Thanks to Neil's decision to see me as a beard to hide his alternative lifestyle, I'd had a fair amount of time on my hands during our marriage. I'd spent it, and a chunk of Neil's income, freely across Dallas-Ft. Worth. As a result, I was on a first name basis with many of the assistants and managers in the establishments on the winery's and Blue's personal credit cards.

With great pride, I speed-dialed the accounting office at one of the poshest department stores in Dallas' Northpark Mall. "Hi Ashley, this is Maxine. Got a minute?"

It took only the tiniest bit of persuading to convince my ex-husband's former secretary to come through for me. I told her my boss had lost her credit card receipts and thought some of her purchases might be tax deductible. Within ten minutes, my inbox held a tidy stack of emails detailing these purchases. After a quick review, I knew Blue was right about Bret Ivey and his love of at least one big bottomed woman.

The receipts were detailed enough to show sizes. I was seeing everything from a woman's trouser size ten to a sixteen. Brassiere sizes ranged from 32C to a 38DD. Curious. The receipts also showed the purchase of some very nice men's boots, jeans, and a leather vest.

On to the other retailers. It took a bit longer and a little pleading, wheedling, and the occasional outright lie, but I got copies of receipts, or at least a description of the goods purchased, from every accounting office I called. After half an hour of phoning and making notes from the comfy sofa, I realized my wine glass was empty and Bret Ivey's shopping activities deserved more respect. I headed for the more practical environs of my office, set up a spreadsheet to capture all the details, and settled in for some real retail warfare. I started with the winery's credit card and bank account.

It didn't take long to figure out the normal shopping activities for the winery versus Bret's personal spending. Although the receipts my digging had uncovered varied in the level of detail they provided, a consistent pattern emerged. With seven exceptions, a charge appeared on the winery's card statement from a breakfast bar in Northpark Mall every Saturday morning for the last six months. Also on every Saturday, charges from a variety of shops located in the same mall appeared, as did lunch and dinner charges from restaurants around town and live venues. On most Saturday nights, Bret charged tickets to the theater, a concert, or a sporting event. From the amount of the purchases, it looked like two people were attending. On Sundays, charges for breakfast and shopping were the norm. During the week, the only charges related to the business. The winery's bank account showed withdrawals of five hundred to two thousand dollars in cash each week. Sometimes from ATMs in and around Forney County. At other times, from ATMs in the Dallas area. There were also good-sized charges for shipping via FedEx or UPS, but those were recent.

I wouldn't have recognized the unusual activity on Blue's bank and credit card statements if I hadn't started with the winery's accounts. Blue's trips to New York to meet with her cookbook editor showed up on the winery's credit card. Her trips to visit her parents in Florida appeared on her personal credit card. She was diligent about keeping her personal spending separate from her business spending. The unusual activity came in the form of gasoline purchases in Dallas on the weekends. Along with occasional charges for a hotel room, usually in one of the more expensive hotels near downtown. I printed the spreadsheet when the numbers started to run together.

I took a half hour for some yoga, then grabbed my spreadsheet. By late afternoon, my balcony is in shade. I slipped on a pair of over-sized sunglasses and studied the people around the pool from behind the French doors. Everyone was dozing under umbrellas except for five kids who were engaged in a furious battle of cannon balls. No strangers were lurking, so I settled into a lounger and got back to work.

Kay's belief in the power of spending patterns was spot on. Bret was, or had been, involved with more than one woman. That's the only logical explanation for the variations in clothing sizes. As I looked closer, the patterns became clearer. Bret never bought different size clothes on the same weekend. He'd been with a size fourteen woman at the same time he was buying clothes for a size ten, but always purchased their clothes on different weekends. The purchases of tens stopped and those of a size sixteen picked up, and still the size fourteen purchases remained, always on weekends when the other sizes weren't purchased. The bra sizes showed a similar pattern, with a 36DD showing up regardless of the other sizes purchased.

And then I connected the hotel room charges, and lack thereof. Bret only used hotels on weekends when he wasn't buying clothes for his size fourteen / 36DD mystery woman.

Which meant the big-bottomed floozy lived in Dallas and he usually stayed with her. The fourteens and 36DDs showed up on more weekends than not on the card statements.

Which meant as long as Bret's dining and shopping patterns remained the same, there was a very good chance I could catch him this weekend at Northpark Mall.

Which meant unless I was totally off my rocker, I had a plan that might actually work.

IN MOTION

HE TOOK A DRAG on his cigarette and was about to press the 'call' button on his phone when his ears perked. He was standing the requisite twenty feet from the building to smoke, but the door hadn't fully closed behind him. She was issuing orders, which was a good sign. Her voice faded as she moved deeper into the structure, and he tapped the 'call' button.

"Come on," he whispered. He wiped his sweaty hands on his white trousers while his orange tennis shoe beat an erratic tempo on the scorched earth. "Answer, you idiot."

On the fourth ring, he did. "Hello?"

"Where were you?"

"In the bathroom."

"Take the phone with you next time. The house is empty."

"How long will she be out?"

"Until ten, at least."

"Are you -"

He snapped the phone shut and slipped it into his pocket, enjoying the rest of his smoke before returning to work.

PARANOIA

THE NIGHT WAS UTTERLY stifling, and I was glad I'd worn linen to dinner. I beat Cass and Kado to the winery and enjoyed following the studly host to our table. In contrast to the relaxing atmosphere I'd experienced at lunch yesterday and today, the winery was heaving with people and energy. Conversations were loud and punctuated with laughter. Servers wove through tightly packed tables carrying trays laden with great smelling food and carrying bottles of wine. A three piece jazz band played on a slightly raised stage in the main room. Several couples danced to "Summer Samba" while the guitar player glanced up and smiled, sending me a nice charge. Small lights twinkled in wine bottles strung in a tight weave from the ceiling, creating a swath of night sky near enough to touch.

I spotted familiar faces, including Forney County's Sheriff, Bill Hoffner, seated a few tables from mine, and it was only as I sat that I got a look at his companion. She was a beautiful blonde, probably in her early fifties and carrying it extremely well. It made me wonder what Hoffner had to offer that would entice a woman like that to have dinner with him. From what Cass had told me and the little I'd experienced of him, the man was a flaming ego on legs. As Blue had predicted, a bottle of wine was chilling in a bucket beside his table.

A muted crash sounded from the kitchen and I winced, wondering if Emily had shattered another stack of Blue's plates. I heard raised voices and then spotted a curvaceous young woman in a ruby blouse bearing the winery's logo headed my way. She hooked a healthy hip into my table as she blew past, fury on her face.

At a set of French doors, she turned and shouted, "This isn't over, you bitch."

The hum of conversation dulled and heads swiveled as she stepped into the darkening evening. But it was barely a moment before the musicians picked up their tune and conversation resumed as if nothing had happened.

The hunky host caught my glance and mouthed, "I'm sorry."

I waved, telling him not to worry, but watched with pleasure as he brought me a glass and a bottle of something pink.

"Everything okay?" I asked.

"Our drama queen. Daphne's a waste of good air, as far as I'm concerned." He poured. "See what you think."

I sipped. "Nice. Fruity."

"Glad to see you again. Are you here alone?"

I thought he was flirting and desperately wanted to slip into Maxine Man-eater mode, but stopped myself. This was business, after all. "I'm meeting some friends, but came a little early. I was hoping to chat with Blue. Is she around?"

"She's in the kitchen. The expediter didn't come in today, and now Daphne's run off."

"Expediter?" I asked.

"The person who keeps the kitchen activities flowing so customers get their food quickly and while it's hot. The expediter's an important role." He glanced at the French doors. A scowl crossed his handsome face and then within a heartbeat, Will smiled at me. "It's going to be a busy night, but I'll let Blue know you're here. Maxine, right?"

I sipped the wine and was idly scanning the room when my heart dropped. Babby and Kay were at a table on the far side of the winery. Kay wiggled her fingers, smiling widely. Babby lifted a wine bottle and motioned me over. I worked my way across the room, wondering why they were here. Didn't they think I was capable of handling Blue Ivey's case? Had they decided to take over? Maybe this was revenge for my lie.

Stop with the paranoia, I told myself, straightening my shoulders. *I am a professional member of the Lost and Found team. I welcome their support and can cope with any sort of involvement or oversight from my aunts. I am a professional member of the -*

Babby poured wine into a fresh glass and my poise shattered. "Don't you trust me?"

Kay held her hand out and Babby slapped a five dollar bill into her palm. "You're costing me money, toots," Babby said.

"How?" I demanded.

"Kay thought you'd be worried that we decided to have dinner here tonight, but I thought you'd cope." She grimaced and slid the glass to me. "Thank goodness it was only five bucks. Sit down."

I sank into a chair. "Well, why are you here?"

"Having dinner, doodle-bug," Kay said. "We want Mrs. Ivey to know she has the full support of the agency." She leaned close. "It makes clients feel special if they think everyone in the business is working for them."

"You're not here because you think I'll screw up?"

Kay patted my hand. "Only for support."

"And to eat. The flat iron steak is scrumptious," Babby said. "As are these dishes. The waitress told me Blue made them. She's a talented woman." She nodded at my untouched glass. "It's good."

She was right. It was a deep red and drier than the pink wine the hunky host had brought. I struggled to decide which I liked better.

Babby glanced over my shoulder and her exquisitely lined eyebrow lifted a notch. "My, my. Bruce Elliot looks downright edible."

I followed her glance and nearly melted at the sight. In a dark blue shirt with French cuffs and fawn-colored trousers, Bruce was quite handsome. He startled when he saw me, but then smiled. My stomach flip-flopped.

"We'll see you in a bit," Babby said.

"Hmm?"

"Maxine." Kay poked me. "We'll drop by your table later. You can introduce us to Mrs. Ivey."

"And the new and improved Bruce," Babby said. "For such a weird looking teenager, he turned out very nice. He's not that much younger than me. If you want him, Maxine, you'd better claim him."

It was my turn to lift an eyebrow.

"Barbara," Kay scolded. "Let the girl have her fun. Run along, Maxine, before your aunt gets her claws out."

WHAT OTHER KIND WOULD HE BE?

I SAT ALONE DRINKING great wine and listening to surprisingly good jazz. East Texas has produced many excellent musicians, but not many of the jazz variety. The trio was guitar, double bass, and drums, and the guitarist crooned a few tunes now and again. Eating alone isn't as hard as most people think and most of the time, I enjoy it. Bruce was within eye-shot and also sitting alone, casting the occasional glance and smile my way. I was chewing my lip and wondering if I should invite him to join me when a sultry brunette entered the winery, scanned the room, and wove through the tables to Bruce. I actually felt my heart drop, and realized he'd probably had this date with the brunette on the books for a while.

Besides, I consoled myself, I had plans with Harvey later. But I still felt hollow inside.

My waitress brought a basket of warm bread and I gave in, buttering a fresh slice of baguette. Cass came through the winery's front door, spotted me, and wove between the tables, bypassing Sheriff Hoffner but stopping to speak to her brother and the stunning brunette.

Cass settled at our table with a sigh.

"You okay?" I asked.

"Fine." She yawned. "I won't make it very long tonight. After last night, I'm tuckered." She opened a menu. "What's good?"

"Everything, I think." I yawned in reply. "Who's Bruce's date? I don't recognize her."

"She's not a date. He's her adviser."

"College adviser?"

"What other kind would he be?"

I looked more closely at the brunette. She was probably in her early twenties. The third finger on her left hand trailed sparkles as she gestured. A smile threatened my lips and I picked up my glass to sip and hide my joy. "Where's Kado?"

"He's working on the stolen pickup."

I topped off my glass and poured pink wine into Cass's glass. She held up a hand.

I stopped and looked at her. "You're not your father."

"I know I'm not. But look what happened the last time I drank."

I reached across the table and took her hand. "That wasn't your fault. You got roofied and raped, like me. And it wasn't my fault, either. You don't have to drink to have a good time, but sometimes it's fun to sip a little wine or have a margarita. Look, there's barely a dribble in the glass. Drink that, we'll have some food, and if you want more you can try another dribble."

She lifted the glass, sniffed, and then took a minuscule sip. "Kind of like Kool-Aid." She sipped again and settled in her chair. "Now, tell me what you found in the financial data."

―――――――――

ONE OF THE MUSICIANS picked up a banjo and started playing "Five Foot Two, Eyes of Blue." His voice was good, but the banjo? Must be an acquired taste. Despite my doubts, my foot tapped in time to the music while I told Cass about my research. She listened with that amazing intensity that makes you believe your stupid ideas are really quite plausible.

When I finished, she sat back and stared at the room's reflection in the darkened French doors. "Go to Dallas tomorrow. I think it'll work."

I beamed. "Want to come with me?"

"I'd love to, but I'm wiped. I don't think I'd be much help. If you make it home tomorrow night -"

I straightened. "I beg your pardon?"

Cass grinned. "There's always a possibility that you'll pick up a man and get distracted, Max. But I meant that if you find Bret Ivey and don't have to stay in Dallas until Sunday, come to the house for supper. Bruce is cooking."

My heart leapt, annoying thing, and I pushed it back into place. "Bruce always cooks."

"Only because he's set up booby traps in the kitchen."

"Maybe because you caught that skillet of scrambled eggs on fire."

"That was years ago." She sipped a bit of wine.

"So, is Bruce inviting company for supper?" Yes, I was fishing. So sue me.

"Only Mitch and Darla. Harry's girls will be there and Kado will come if he finishes working on whatever drama Saturday brings."

The music switched from live to piped in, and I looked up as the guitarist and drummer slowly crossed the winery in our direction, stopping at several tables to chat. They finally made it to our table and asked if they could join us.

"Of course," I answered, offering a hand. "I'm Maxine Leverman and this is Cass Elliot."

They chatted with us for the duration of their brief break, then asked for our numbers. Both were attractive and articulate, and I had no qualms about passing my card to the guitarist, wondering briefly if I should cancel this evening's appointment with Harvey. I watched with interest as Cass handed the drummer a card. They thanked us and headed for the stage.

"I thought you and Kado were an item," I said.

She raised an eyebrow. "There's no risk to whatever relationship Kado and I have, Maxine. My card says I'm a Forney County Detective. He's a musician. There's zero chance he'll call."

CATCHING HIM MYSELF

CASS AND I WERE debating whether the cowboys who chased Bret's Corvette last night were really cowboys when Blue Ivey emerged from the kitchen. She wore a sparkling white chef's tunic over jeans and looked utterly composed, even when she stopped at Sheriff Hoffner's table. He gestured at his steak. Blue nodded, spoke to his companion who shook her head. Blue took Hoffner's plate and disappeared into the kitchen, returning moments later with a fresh dinner. She placed it in front of him and waited while he cut the steak. He nodded and turned to his date, as if dismissing Blue. Hoffner's companion flashed a sardonic smile at Blue, who smiled graciously in reply.

Blue joined us and a waitress placed a platter of cheese, grapes, sliced meats, and dipping sauces on the table. Will, the hunky host, handed Blue a glass of dark red wine and asked if we needed anything else.

"We're fine. Tell Chef I'll be back in a few minutes," Blue said. She yawned and turned to us. "Forgive me for taking so long to get out here. The white grapes are in the tanks and we'll harvest the reds next week. Emily massacred another stack of plates and I had to go dig more out of storage. It's exhausting." Blue sat back in her chair and took a long sip of wine. "I'm sorry if either of you heard the shouting match from earlier."

I waved her off. "Will said one of your cooks didn't show up?"

"My expediter, Annie. She's a star at keeping everything coordinated in the kitchen. This is totally unlike her, but I'm sure there's a reasonable explanation." She held her hand out. "Blue Ivey. Cass Elliot, right? You're even more gorgeous in person than you are in the papers. I love your red hair."

Cass smiled. "Nice to meet you."

"How's the shoulder?"

"Not bad."

"Are you back at work?"

"I know I'm ready to be back, but my physical therapist disagrees."

Blue dipped a slice of baguette into a sauce heavy with chunks of garlic. "You're seeing Chad?"

"How did you know?"

"I hurt my ankle about a year ago. He's a beast, but very good." Blue glanced at me. "The update on Bret. Is it bad enough that we need to involve the police?"

I laughed. "No, not yet, anyway. Cass and I have been friends for ages, and she joined me for some surveillance last night, off the record."

"How'd it go?"

We nibbled and I gave her the short version, telling her we'd found Bret's Corvette, but lost him. "Do you know who would steal a pickup and chase him?" I asked.

"A spurned lover?" Blue answered with a smile. "Maybe not if it was two guys. Seriously, I have no idea who'd be interested in chasing him. If the truck was stolen, it makes sense that they'd run after blowing a tire." She ate a bite of cheese. "If Bret is cheating, could it be an angry spouse or boyfriend?"

"It's possible. The forensic guy is going over the pickup tonight, looking for fingerprints and other evidence. We'll have to see what he turns up."

Blue lifted her glass. "I should thank whoever it was, because at least it sent Bret home. And I might have a chance of catching him myself."

WRECK IT ALL

THE THIRD STEP FROM the top creaked and the blond cringed. The dark-haired man shot him a look, then started opening doors.

The blond hesitated at the music room's threshold. It was packed with instruments and equipment. "I don't know about this."

The dark-haired man carefully took a guitar from its rack and placed it on the floor, and then jumped on it with all his might. It cracked with a discordant twang. He wrenched a piece of wood from the broken top and then peered inside the body cavity. "Why not?"

The blond stepped forward and studied the instruments. "These are old. Lookit. That's a Super 400. I saw one on Antiques Roadshow. And that. That's an old Epiphone Emperor. They must be from the nineteen-thirties or forties." He shook his head. "It's bad luck to destroy stuff like this."

"It'll be bad luck if you don't do what he told us to do."

"I'll tell you what's bad luck."

"What?" the dark-haired man asked.

"His orange shoes."

"His shoes?"

"Yeah. Orange is bad luck."

The dark-haired man dropped another guitar on the floor and smiled when it sang out. "Where do you get this stuff?"

"TV, mostly." The blond pulled at his nose. "And I don't like him."

"You don't have to. You just have to do what he says."

"I don't think he knows what he's doing."

The dark-haired man turned and put his hands on his hips. "Are you going to tell him that?"

"Probably not. What do you think?"

"I'm not paid to think. I'm paid to do what he tells me to do." He landed on the guitar with a grunt and stomped its neck for good measure.

"We could just look inside them," the blond said. "Not break them."

"What did he say?"

"Wreck it all."

The dark-haired man pointed. "Start with the banjos. You always hated those anyway."

The blond shifted from foot to foot. "When will she be back?"

"I don't know. Later. Why?"

"I have to pee."

The dark-haired man sighed. "Make sure you flush. You never flush at home."

WHERE IT ALL BEGAN

I SENSED A PRESENCE and looked up to see Kay and Babby approaching. "Blue," I said. "I'd like you to meet Kay Wooten and Barbara Chandrell. They're my aunts, and also the owners of Lost and Found."

"So glad you could come," Blue said. "Have you eaten?"

"The food is amazing, and it's so refreshing to find good wine that comes from Texas," Babby said. "We don't want to interrupt, just wanted you to know that while Maxine is your main contact, you have the full support of our office."

"See?" Blue said. "This is why I like working with women. They understand the personal touch." She motioned to Will and he brought a bottle of wine and fresh glasses. "Sit, if you have time."

Kay and Babby did and Blue poured. Cass sipped her tiny bit of pink wine without being told, and lifted an eyebrow in my direction. Approval, I assumed.

"How did you get into private detecting?" Blue asked.

I perked up. This was one of my favorite stories.

Kay spoke first. "We lived in boring suburbia where the most exciting thing that ever happened was when a snake came through the septic system and up into a toilet. Not nice. Anyway, family pets started disappearing. At first, it was the ancient German Shepherd down the block. Then it was a pet cat. She was old, too, wasn't she?"

Babby nodded.

"The animals always disappeared in the early part of the week. Babby and I talked about it and thought it was a little strange, but every time we brought it up in bridge club or at a neighborhood party, the conversation would change. We were young -"

"And dumb," Babby added.

"Very dumb," Kay confirmed. "But since we each had dogs, we decided we'd better find out what was going on."

"We called the police," Babby said with a glance at Cass. "But the jerk that Hoffner sent out," she snapped her fingers, "what was his name?"

"Beauford."

"He was an ass. Big gun, big swagger, completely uninterested in our little domestic problems."

"So we decided to investigate. We mounted a surveillance operation on Monday and Tuesday nights."

"Surveillance?" Blue asked.

Kay nodded. "Black clothes, black hats."

"But no grease paint," Babby said. "I'm not sacrificing my skin for a pet."

"Wise choice. It's hard to get off," Cass said.

"What happened?" Blue asked. She was leaning forward, elbows on the table, glass of wine cradled in her hands.

"We worked in shifts. One night I'd be out from dark until two, and Babby would take the two til dawn shift. The next night we'd change. We'd sneak around the neighborhood, looking for lights, checking the houses that still had pets. It took weeks. We lost two more cats and a dog before we figured it out." Kay took a sip of wine and motioned for Babby to continue.

"It was a dark and stormy night," Babby began, then giggled, sounding a little like Marilyn Monroe. "Just kidding. It was July and miserable. Two o'clock in the middle of a blazing hot Tuesday morning. Shift change. Right when Kay showed up at our meeting tree, we saw a flash of light."

"We weren't sure that's what it was," Kay added. "But we checked it out."

"And spotted a shadow scurrying down the sidewalk."

"Dressed in dark clothes and kind of hunched over."

"Like he was protecting something," Babby said.

"What did you do?" Blue asked. Her attention was totally focused on my aunts.

"We followed him," Kay said.

"At a safe distance?" I couldn't help it. I had to ask.

Cass smiled.

Kay looked puzzled, but answered. "Yes, I think it probably was."

"We weren't sure we should even be following this person," Babby said. "Although it was the middle of the night and he was acting suspicious. Anyway, he stopped at a car and raised the trunk lid."

"That's when we heard it," Kay said. "A bark, a yip. Clearly an unhappy dog. So we charged him."

Blue's eyes were huge. "Go on."

Kay's smile was proud. "We hit him hard enough to knock him into the trunk. He banged his head on something and it stunned him."

"Just a little," Babby said.

"Long enough for us to grab the puppy and check her collar. Peaches. She belonged to a new family that probably hadn't been told to keep their pets inside at night."

"Once we realized we had our man," Babby said, "we slammed the lid and I ran for the house to call the police."

Cass and I shared a grin. The good part was coming up.

"Did they arrest him?" Blue asked.

"Nope," Kay said. "They took him to the hospital and arrested us for assault."

Blue gaped. "You're kidding."

"It was Babby's fault. Bill Hoffner wanted to date her back in the day, but she brushed him off. In public. Hoffner never got over it."

"That doesn't bode well for me," Blue said. "He asked me out a decade or two ago, and I said no. He's still sore. Sends his food back every time he eats here and if he's especially pissy, he has a patrol car parked on the county road doing breath-o-lizers. Puts the patrons off." Blue refilled glasses. "Did your husbands bail you out?"

"The cops let us go before our men had to decide to post bail or leave us in jail." Kay frowned. "I'm not sure what Charlie would've chosen."

"Why did they let you go?"

Babby rolled her eyes. "Kay blabbered all the way to the station, talking about how pets had gone missing and we got no help from the police."

Kay grimaced. "Deriding the police while in custody isn't very smart, for future reference."

"The cop who took us in was young, and even though he didn't show it, he was listening." Babby looked at Kay. "Carlos Martinez, right?"

Kay nodded. "He's a detective now."

"When Kay mentioned Beauford, Martinez perked up. After he left us with the fingerprint guy, Martinez went to the petnapper's house and found freshly turned earth in his backyard. He called a detective, took shovels out there that night, and guess what they found?"

Blue grimaced. "Pets?"

"Fresh pets from our neighborhood and older carcasses."

"Who was this guy?" Blue asked.

"The brother of one of our bridge club members. He'd been in and out of mental hospitals over the years and she kept their parent's house in the country so he'd have somewhere to come home to. When he was out, he visited every week, and she noticed the missing pet pattern but kept her mouth shut. Her little old lady friends rallied around to protect him, too, and that's why he went on for so long."

"That's a lot more exciting than what we get up to around here," Blue said, and checked her phone. "If you'll excuse me, I need to check on the kitchen and my expediter. If she doesn't call soon, you might have another mystery to solve."

NO CARDIO TONIGHT

IT WAS AFTER NINE when I saw Blue again. She placed a platter of ribs on a nearby table and chatted with her guests. The woman was a natural at this whole restaurant thing. She glanced at her watch as she passed our table. "I'm sorry I didn't say good night to your aunts. Did they enjoy the evening?"

"Very much. They said to tell you they were sorry they couldn't stay, but Babby's going undercover tonight."

"Undercover. Juicy. How was desert?"

"Marvelous," Cass said. "The best crème brulee I've ever had."

Blue grinned. "The kitchen is under control and I'm heading to the house. Why don't you come with me? Maybe Bret's back. At a minimum, you can see his car and we can chat."

Cass begged off like I knew she would. She'd been sleeping more since the shooting, and I guess her body needed the rest. We separated in the parking lot and I followed Blue behind a workshop. Two golf carts were parked on a concrete slab sheltered by a metal awning. We rode along a curvy dirt path into a dreamy darkness between pine trees so tall and wide they blocked most of the moonlight. The noise from the winery quickly receded, and I asked Blue if her house was far.

"Close to half a mile. But it only takes a few minutes. We've never bothered to have lights installed because the drive is so short."

The scent of pine was overpowering, almost clinical, as we drove. Blue drew a deep breath and I could feel her relax beside me. "I love the winery," she said. "But it's a lot of work. I guess any small business is, but running a restaurant is really taxing."

"It seems like it's doing great," I said. "It was packed all night."

"It's unpredictable. Some weekends are so busy our feet never touch the floor - that's why I can't wear the Blahnik's - and others are so quiet we wonder if everyone's migrated to a different planet."

We broke free of the trees and the dark mass of a house loomed before us. Blue slowed to a stop. "That's strange."

The slight buzz from the wine evaporated and my senses went into overdrive.

"I always leave the outside lights on, and at least the lights in the foyer." She eased the golf cart forward and we bumped onto a flagstone drive. Blue drove through the silvery moonlight and parked at a portico covering the front door. "The power must be out."

"Is the house on a different transformer than the winery?" I asked.

She walked up the steps to the porch. "They're on the same transformer, but we have separate generators for each. If the power is out, the house generator should've kicked on automatically."

I followed slowly, taking in the massive home and scanning the area for the source of my discomfort. Blue pushed open the front door and flipped a switch. A chandelier of antlers illuminated the foyer. "Bret?" Blue called. "Are you here?"

She walked through the downstairs, turning on lights and checking rooms. I followed, taking in the beautiful, rustic decor.

"Nothing's out of place," Blue said. "Maybe he didn't come in the house. Let's grab a glass of wine and then I'll show you the car."

She poured and I followed her through a set of French doors. We wound past a pool big enough to swim laps in. A waterfall gurgled over rocks and splashed into the crystal water. Blue paused and shook her head, staring into the backlit pool. "I don't understand it. All of this," she waved a hand at the house, the pool, the grounds that were swallowed by the moonlight, "was Bret's design. His vision. It was a dream I bought into and believed in. And he walked away from it all. It makes no sense for a man to give up his life's ambition for a big bottom."

"It could be something else, Blue," I said gently. "Let me follow a few more leads before we decide he's cheating, okay?"

She nodded, but it was a slow gesture. "You were there when the waitress stormed out?"

"Yes."

"It came out tonight that she'd been sleeping with him." She shook her head and her eyes cleared as she took a sip of wine. "I should've seen it, but I've been away so much lately. It seems everybody knew but me. Anyway, I fired her. She thought that was unfair and said Bret would have something to say about it." Her laugh was brittle. "Thankfully, Chef and our scheduler had written her up for tardiness and attitude, so it won't be a big deal if she files a complaint. Come on."

We followed a covered flagstone path through a vegetable garden wasted from the drought, and a small orchard that would be lucky to survive the summer. The barn-style garage loomed as we cleared a dying arbor, and I swear, it was as big as the house. Maybe I exaggerate, but only a little. Five bays were covered by heavy wood doors studded with iron work. Blue stepped inside and one by one, the doors rumbled open. A Porsche Cayenne, a Jag of some sort, a Prius, and a Range Rover all sat quietly in their places. A fifth bay was empty except for a pile of sports equipment in one corner.

Blue walked through the open space and straightened a baseball bat and set of golf clubs. "He's gone again."

"But he didn't take anything with him? No clothes, no toiletries, no," I motioned to the sports gear, "toys?"

Blue looked thoughtful. "Let's go check."

Room by room we walked through that big house, with Blue commenting over and over that nothing looked out of place. Until we came to a room on the second floor. She pushed open the door and stopped. I bumped into her and the hair at the nape of my neck stood on end.

"Oh my," Blue said.

It was a music room, packed to the gills with instruments of all varieties. Or what was left of them. Everything was in ruins. Guitars leaned awkwardly on their stands, their tops smashed and torn open. Horns were broken apart and shiny pieces strewn around the room. Drums were slashed.

Blue leaned into the doorframe and I speed-dialed Cass and then sent a discreet text to Harvey. My cardio workout would have to wait.

EVERYBODY HAS TO PEE

CASS ARRIVED BEFORE THE first patrol cars. "What have you touched?" she asked.

"Nothing," Blue said, her voice trembling. "I mean, everything, but not tonight. We opened the door and saw the room and Maxine called you."

Cass surveyed the damage, her violet eyes clouded. "Would your husband do something like this?"

"Bret? Destroy his own instruments? Never. He loved this stuff." She motioned with her chin to a tangle of wires and smashed metal boxes in a corner. "That's new studio equipment. He wanted to start recording again."

"Again?" I asked.

Blue pressed her fingertips to her eyelids. "He was in a band when he was teenager. A punk group, I think. Or maybe folk. Music was a safe topic lately. Anyway, he bought this stuff and played old tapes. They sounded horrible to me, but he seemed so happy. He'd been practicing and when I asked him about it, he said he was trying to find that original sound." She half choked a laugh. "You'd think he was some aging rock star who'd been out of the game and wanted back in. I thought it was part of the whole mid-life crisis thing."

Cass turned us away from the room and led us back down to the first floor. "Walk me through what happened tonight."

Blue took us to the kitchen and put a kettle on to boil, then pulled mugs and tea bags from a cupboard while she explained our earlier traipse through the house and out to the garage. The familiar activities seemed to sooth her.

"There were no signs of forced entry?" Cass asked.

Blue shrugged and looked to me.

"Do you always leave the front door unlocked?" I asked.

"Yes."

I faintly heard Cass draw a slow breath and wondered if she was counting to ten. "This place is remote, but you get a lot of traffic at the winery. Why would you leave your doors unlocked?"

The kettle whistled and Blue poured boiling water into our mugs. "I wasn't comfortable with it at first, but Bret was insistent. We keep some stock for the restaurant here and we're always back and forth. The staff constantly come and go. We've never had any trouble. Sometimes I remember to lock up at night, but it hadn't crossed my mind that I'd need to during the day. Besides, we keep a set of house keys at the winery in case we forget and leave the doors locked."

Cass opened her mouth and I felt a scolding coming, but a knocking sounded and she left to go check the front door.

Blue's eyes were red-rimmed when she looked at me. "Who would do something like this? Come into our home and damage nothing except Bret's instruments? Is it some sort of revenge? Could Bret be hurt?"

I didn't have an answer, so for once, I kept my mouth shut and just squeezed Blue's hand.

———————

IT TOOK KADO AND that handsome young officer called Scott Truman the better part of two hours to examine the house, the grounds, and Bret's music room. Blue was right; everything but the music room appeared untouched.

Kado followed Truman and Cass into the kitchen. They all looked as bushed as I felt.

"I've got loads of fingerprints from the music equipment. Can you get a list of all the people who've been in that room for me?" Kado asked.

Blue nodded. "It's mostly the winery staff who use it. But some people came from the music shop to set up the recording equipment."

"Don't freak out when you see the fingerprint dust in the bathroom," Truman said. "We took prints in there, too."

At Blue's quizzical look, Truman explained, "Whoever did this spent a lot of time in the music room." He shrugged. "Everybody has to pee."

Truman's expression was so sincere that I couldn't help it: I giggled. Blue joined me, and then Cass, and pretty soon the girls were howling while the guys looked on in amused confusion.

"I need sleep," Blue said, sniffling back a chuckle. "And I'm sure y'all do, too. But one question before you go. Why do you think he spent a lot of time in the music room? It looked like someone walked in and started bashing."

"Most of the destruction is methodical," Kado said. His gray eyes were bloodshot but he was as sexy as ever. I wondered how serious he and Cass were, then chided myself for the thought. "The instruments are destroyed and although the damage looks random, there's a precision in how they were taken apart. The banjos got hit especially hard. It feels like he was looking for something."

I was stumped. "What would that be?"

"Drugs?" Kado answered.

"No," Blue said absolutely. All the humor was gone from her face. "Not Bret."

"Then money."

"Who hides money in a banjo? Or a guitar?" Blue asked.

"Maybe it's neither of those things. Maybe they stole something. Did you notice if anything was missing?" Cass asked.

"I don't know what he had. In all that mess, I'm not sure I would notice."

"Were the instruments insured?"

Blue nodded.

"Find the inventory and see if you can determine if anything is missing." Cass looked at Kado. "If the fingerprints don't pan out, searching for a stolen instrument might be our only lead."

I SEE RIGHT THROUGH YOU

BLUE KNELT AMONG THE ravaged remains of her husband's instruments and stifled a sob. It was a rare occasion when she gave in to self pity, but it wasn't supposed to be this way. Bret wasn't supposed to leave, to abandon her, their marriage, the winery. He wasn't supposed to walk out and leave Blue to deal with the business and now the whole mess from the break-in. What had happened to the man she married? Her lip quivered and tears hung on her lashes. What had happened to her? How in the world had she missed the fact that he was shagging the help? Probably on the warming counter, God help us. And given the size of the girls he bedded, she'd better check the supports under the counter.

At that very practical thought, she threw her head back and laughed. The tension in her chest eased and she wiped her nose, then swapped Adele for Alanis Morissette in the CD player, cranking the volume up. "We Could've Had It All" and more songs of lost love, even sung by a voice as fabulous as Adele's, weren't what she needed right now. Morissette's "Right Through You" and "You Oughta Know" were the kick-ass tonic that would get her through this awful night.

The inventory list she'd scavenged from Bret's desk was a huge help. The horns and amplifiers were quick to identify because there weren't many pieces to put back together. But the stringed instruments were a nightmare. Blue had no idea whether this neck fit on that guitar or the other banjo, or even if that guitar body was supposed to have a neck. Bret was notorious for buying fixer-upper instruments and never getting around to the fixing part. She'd had some luck checking serial numbers on the instruments that had them and was down to a collection of instruments with no serial numbers, a stack of parts that didn't seem to belong together, and an alarming number of instruments that weren't checked off the inventory. The night was passing from young to old at an amazing pace.

The CD stopped and she stretched, watching her blurred reflection in the beautiful floor to ceiling windows creating the walls of this room. Suddenly she wondered if she should leave the inventory until daylight. She was a perfect target, perfectly visible to anyone watching. Never, until the last few days, would Blue have entertained the thought that she wasn't safe in her own home. Now she found herself jumping at the smallest sound and seeing shadows flit around the room.

"Get a grip, girl," she said to the quiet room. Then she stepped into the hall and headed for her bathroom. "There's nobody here and no point scaring yourself to death. Let's get some sleep and see if we can figure this out in the morning."

———————

IT WAS JUST AS she was floating in that blissful but often elusive space between wakefulness and sleep that Blue heard the creak. Her sleep had been light, her dreams restless and filled with images of a sun-washed car accompanied by the deep rumble of a growl from a big cat's chest. White teeth flashed against tanned skin in a broad smile that disappeared into a startled 'o' at the intruding sound. Blue's eyes snapped open and her breath caught in her chest. That creak belonged to the third step from the top of the staircase. The only way to avoid it was to miss that step entirely, which meant whoever was coming up the stairs wasn't familiar with the house, or didn't care if they made noise. Blue ran her fingers gently along the bedside table and found her cell phone. She slipped it under the covers and had pushed 9-1- when she heard a whispered, "Blue?"

She froze. That voice. "Bret? Bret, is that you?"

"It's Will, Blue. Are you okay?"

Blue sank back into the mattress. "Will?"

"Yes. I saw the police cars earlier and decided to come check on you. I grabbed the spare house keys from the winery. Are you all right?"

She switched on the lamp, grateful she'd worn pajamas to bed. "Come in."

The handsome young man she'd hired only a couple of months ago poked his head around the door. "I'm sorry to bother you, but it looked like the cops were here a long time. Is everything okay?"

Blue blinked, torn between gratitude that someone had noticed something unusual was happening here, and irritated because she'd never get to sleep now. "Yes. I mean, no. Everything's not okay. But it is okay."

Will cocked his head to one side.

"What time is it?" she asked, pushing up to a sitting position.

"Almost two. We've closed up and everybody's gone home. Chef put kitchen assignments up for tomorrow and left a shopping list. We ran out of specials tonight. And Toni got a call from her mom - they've taken her dad to the hospital. It looks like a heart attack and they're Care Flighting him to Dallas. She won't be in tomorrow."

Blue's mind flew into planning mode and she pushed the covers back. "Meet me in the kitchen. Do you know where the kettle is?"

WHAT PAPA GETS

"NOTHING? HOW COULD YOU find nothing?" The small man paced the narrow room and glared at the two men sitting mute before him. "Nothing?"

The men shook their heads.

He slapped a cigarette from its pack and lit up. The blond opened his mouth to speak, but the dark-haired man bumped his shoulder. Instead, the blond pulled on his nose.

"You broke it all?" the small man asked.

They nodded.

"Then it's at the Dallas house. Go there tonight."

"But that place is armed to the rafters," the dark-haired man protested. "And the neighborhood. There's all kinds of cops. All the time."

A set of brilliant white teeth gleamed in the light from the bare bulb. "That's why you get the big bucks."

"What do we do?"

"Same thing. Search the music room and all his files. Wreck everything."

"We didn't -" the blond started, but the dark-haired man pinched his thigh. "Ouch."

"What was that?" the small man asked.

"Nothing," the dark-haired man answered, glaring at the blond.

"Some of that stuff is valuable," the blond man offered. "What if we stole it instead?"

"Destroy it," the small man said. "That's what Papa wants, so that's what Papa gets."

THE TRUTH AT LAST

BLUE JOINED HIM, DRESSED in jeans, a long-sleeved t-shirt, and sandals. He slid a steaming mug to her as she slipped onto a barstool.

"Is chamomile okay?" Will asked. "I'll never sleep if I have caffeine this late."

"It's perfect. What's happening with Toni? How is she?"

"She was freaking out when she left. Chef had someone drive her home, she was shaking that bad."

Blue reached for a pad of paper and a pen and made notes, talking as she wrote. "We'll send flowers and a snack basket to the Dallas hospital. I'll call Clover Leaf Ranch first thing and see if they can get some more steaks to us early tomorrow. That's usually not a problem, but they had a big order going to New York this week." She tapped the pen against the pad, and then ran both hands through her hair. "We're two wait staff and one expediter down. College is out for the summer, but do you know anybody who has extensive restaurant experience who's dying to work a night of madness for low pay and bad tips on short notice? The food is good, if that's any incentive."

Will grinned. "I do."

Blue perked up. "Really?"

"Some friends are taking summer classes. I'll call in the morning. You want two more staff?"

"Three, if you can get them. It'll help with the learning curve."

"I'll see what I can do." Will blew across the top of his mug and sipped, then drew a breath. "Can I, uh, ask something?"

Blue felt her insides grow still. "Sure."

"Is Bret coming back?" He glanced up at her and hurried on. "We haven't seen him for a while now, and with the infidelity -"

What a word that is, Blue thought. *Totally bereft of emotion. How perfectly inadequate a word to describe what he's done.*

"- everyone's wondering if you'll stay married. And if you guys divorce, what'll happen with the winery."

Blue opened her mouth to speak and tears stung her eyes. She pressed a dishcloth to her face and felt Will tense across the expanse of granite covering her kitchen island. After a moment, his fingers touched hers and she clutched at his hand, feeling waves of fear and desperation threatening to pull her under. She drew deep breaths and searched for that place of serenity she'd cultivated long ago. Life had never been easy for Blue Ivey, but she'd decided early on that no one could give her the life she wanted: she'd have to find it, build it, and do whatever it took to protect it. Regardless of the choices Bret made, the winery was hers and she would push it to success. And at that thought, she felt the fight return.

She dried her eyes and nearly laughed at Will's look of concern. "It's okay," she told him. "I guess we need to get some of this stuff out in the open. Do you think that would help?"

"I do." Will grimaced. "There are some things you need to know, too."

Butterflies stirred in her stomach, but Blue sipped her tea. "Like what?"

Will had the grace to squirm.

"Like what?"

"Like who he's been sleeping with." Will bit his lip and watched her.

"Have there been more than Daphne?"

Will nodded and Blue heaved a great sigh.

"How do you know all this, Will? You've only been with us for a few months."

"People talk. There's tension in the winery, you've noticed, right?"

It was Blue's turn to nod. "I thought it was because I was traveling so much. Demanding so much from the staff."

"They're okay with that. You've got some loyal people working for you. They'd walk on hot coals if they thought it would help you."

"They're not loyal to Bret?"

He shrugged. "With Daphne and Annie gone, I think the balance has swung in your favor."

Blue's blood ran cold. "What do you mean, with Daphne and Annie gone?"

"I really hate men who do this, Blue, especially to women as nice as you." Will hesitated. "Annie was his latest conquest."

"Good Lord. I had no idea. Is that what Daphne was upset about? Why she was acting so strange? Bret dumped Daphne for Annie?"

He nodded.

Blue's eyelids slid closed. "These girls are what? Late teens? Early twenties? What is he thinking? Has anybody heard from Annie?"

"Several people have called and texted, but she hasn't made contact. She's a great expediter, and the staff really like her."

Blue straightened her shoulders. "Who else?"

"Daphne and Annie are the two I'm sure about. There were only a couple of others, from what I've heard."

"*Only*," Blue snorted. "When was the last time you saw Bret?"

"A few weeks ago. No, maybe a couple of weeks ago. But he's called the winery since then." He hesitated. "And you?"

"I haven't seen him in almost a month, or talked to him in almost two weeks."

"So, what happened here tonight, with the cops, it wasn't about Bret?"

"What do you mean?"

"Someone saw the Corvette pull in earlier. He's got a temper, and we wondered if the two of you had had a fight."

"No, nothing like that. Someone trashed Bret's music room."

Will's eyes went wide. "His instruments?"

"All of them."

"Man. He's got some expensive stuff."

"He does?"

"Yeah. Some of those instruments were old. He had banjos from the 1920s and a few pre-war Gibson guitars. Who would do that? Why would somebody destroy his gear?"

"No idea. But that reminds me: the forensic guy wants fingerprints from the staff to eliminate everyone." Blue pushed her mug away. "Okay. Staff meeting at ten o'clock tomorrow morning for whoever can make it. I'll send a text first thing. We'll get all this crap out in the open and do the fingerprint thing. Sound good?"

"I'll see you then. Glad everything is okay. You know, relatively speaking." He put their mugs in the sink. "You're good people. In some ways, you remind me of my mom."

Her smile was warm. "Thanks, Will. That's very kind of you. It'll all work out. It always does."

Saturday

I'M WORKING WITH A WOMAN

"HURRY."

"SHUT UP AND let me work," the dark-haired man said. He snipped the wires and then wiped sweat from his face. "That's it. Check out front again."

The blond peered up and down the street, pulling at his nose. Occasional cones of golden light filtered through the tree branches. Cars passed on the main thoroughfare at the end of the block, but all was quiet on this street. "It's clear," he whispered.

"Then get this door open."

The blond patted his pockets. "Uh oh."

"What?"

"My picks."

The dark-haired man sighed. "Where are they?"

"In the truck. I think."

"We have one job to do tonight. One job. In a hot part of town. And you leave your tools in the truck?"

"I was in a hurry when we parked. I had to pee."

"I swear, I'm working with a woman."

"I think it's my prostate."

"You're gonna have bigger problems than your prostate if you don't get us in this house. Right now."

The blond looked at the dark-haired man, worry on his face. "What now?"

"I have to pee again."

TO BOND OR NOT TO BOND

WITH DEEP FOREBODING, I pulled into Cindy's driveway at five-thirty Saturday morning. A deep rose tint was creeping into the eastern sky, but it would be an hour before the sun would make an appearance.

Cindy slammed her front door and hopped into my Lexus, pulling a smirk at my beautiful car. "Black is classier."

"Red is cooler in Texas," I retorted, and backed out of her drive. "Had you rather take your stylish Buick?"

She slipped a massive white tote bag over the console and into the backseat.

"This is a day trip, Cindy. No need to pack a bag."

"Oh ye of little faith. The contents of that bag have saved many an investigation." When I asked what she meant, Cindy ignored my question and looked me over. "Not bad."

"It's better than not bad. You said to wear a light colored sun dress and sandals. That's what I did." I pointedly looked her up and down. "Although if I'd known we were dressing alike, I would've rebelled."

She again ignored my comment and twisted around to dig in the bag, then sat with a smaller purse in her lap. She switched my radio from the nineties station I love to talk radio. I switched it back.

"It's good manners to let your guest pick the station," she said.

"You're not a guest. And it's good manners to ask before changing the station." I motioned to a travel mug in the console. "It's Kopi Luwak. You take your coffee black, right?"

"Yes." She took a cautious sip. "That's good. Where's it from?"

"The guts of an Asian cat-like thing called a palm civet."

She thought about that. "This is cat poop coffee?"

"Well, no. But kind of. See, the civets eat berries that have coffee seeds in them, then poop out the undigested seeds. The enzymes in the cat's guts change the flavor of the beans."

"I'll bet," Cindy muttered.

"Somebody cleans the poop off before turning the beans into coffee."

She placed the mug back in the console. "I could've done without the details."

"You asked. It's the most expensive coffee in the world."

"Of course it is. Because you can afford the best, as opposed to we poor schmucks who have to work for a living."

I refused to engage with Cindy on the subject of money. "I'll drink it. It's better than you deserve."

She popped a Kindle from her purse and turned it on. I glanced over but couldn't catch the title.

"What are you reading?"

"A series by a Hawaiian gal called Toby Neal."

"What genre?"

"Crime fiction. I'm at a good part. Shut up and drive."

Dallas is roughly three hours from Arcadia. We passed most of it in silence and, thankfully, without stopping. Cindy has a notoriously small bladder. The roads were almost entirely clear this early on a Saturday morning, as everyone with any sense was still tucked up in bed. We hopscotched our way across East Texas with three eighteen-wheelers, two guys in a silver Camry, and a woman in a white Kia who took turns tailing us for a while, then would speed up and pass us, only to slow down again. Seriously annoying, but I consoled myself by finishing my coffee and Cindy's. I needed it after my two late nights.

She came up for air as we neared the Terrell exit from I-20 to Highway 80. "What are we doing today?"

I glanced at her, wide-eyed, and almost rear-ended a lumbering eighteen-wheeler that changed lanes without signaling. "Babby didn't tell you?"

"No. And I tried to get it out of her. All she said is you're working a small case and she thought it would be good for us to spend some time together. To bond. And," my cousin said with a pointed look, "it would be good for you to have a licensed PI with you."

So there we were, at something of a stalemate. I didn't want Cindy here, but I needed her credentials. She didn't want to be here, but she was dying to know why I was working a case. Inwardly, I sighed. Babby was right. Cindy and I needed to bond, to the extent that bonding was possible between a warm-blooded mammal and a reptile like my cousin. I really have to pass that PI exam. In the meantime, if we were going to work together, we'd have to find a modicum of trust in our relationship. So I filled her in, leaving out the inflammatory bits, like how I got the case and worked it without Kay or Babby knowing. When I got to the part about the credit card and bank statements, Cindy pulled a notebook from her bag and jotted notes.

She was silent after I finished, studying the one decent photograph of Bret Ivey from *Texas Eats*. "Your plan is to try and find Bret when he shows up at this bakery in Northpark Mall?"

"He's there every Saturday morning, regular as Uncle Phil on prunes."

Cindy actually laughed at that. "It's a better plan than cruising Whiskey Bend, hoping to see his car."

"It worked," I said. "We found him."

"And lost him. What happens if we see him today?"

I'd thought long and hard about this. I could approach him, tell him who I was, that Blue had hired me to find him because she was sick of his hemorrhaging money, and beg him to return her calls. Or, I could do what Blue hired me to do, which was find him. "We follow him. Find out where he's staying and let Blue know. From there, she can tell us what she wants us to do."

Cindy chewed on that. "Plan B?"

"For what?"

"If this is the one Saturday he doesn't show up."

"We'll be at Northpark. We shop."

Traffic grew heavier once we hit Mesquite but the ride to the upscale mall was uneventful. We argued over where to park, and although I hated to leave my Lexus in the boiling Texas sun, I agreed that given the trail of receipts he left through his past visits to the mall, Bret would most likely leave through Nordstrom's. I snugged the car next to a tiny tree, hoping for a bit of shade, and we both groaned as we got out of the car and stretched.

Cindy pulled the large tote from the back seat. She extracted two white baseball caps with the Dallas Stars hockey team logo on the front and handed me one.

"No, thanks."

"Your first lesson in tracking: disguises are invaluable."

"A sun dress and a baseball cap?"

"Watch and learn, grasshopper."

I grudgingly put it on and Cindy tucked my hair behind my ears, then pulled her chestnut hair into a ponytail and stuffed it through the opening in back of the cap. "That's better. I hope this bakery does some sort of protein. I'm starving."

"Their Eggs Benedict are wonderful."

"As long as their coffee isn't made with cat poop, I'm in. Speaking of, let's find a bathroom."

A KIND OF REVENGE

BLUE GAVE IN TO a yawn as she rounded a curve and broke free from the pines separating her house from the winery, driving the golf cart by rote when her eyes squeezed shut. She gave a gasp and nearly drove off the little road when she opened them again. "Oh no," she moaned.

She left the little road to drive along the row of vines nearest the workshop. They and several other rows were wilting, and Blue checked to ensure the irrigation lines were in place. Then the chemical scent of weed killer hit her. Fury flushed through her system and her hands shook on the steering wheel. Face grim, she parked the golf cart under cover and stalked to the winery.

She unlocked the front door and reached for the phone, then hesitated, letting her anger abate. It seemed every decision these days was driven by an action taken by idiots, whether it was her husband, one of her staff, or some random act of hatred. For once, she would let her head clear and then decide whether to call the police.

She went behind the bar to make a cappuccino, and then took it out onto the winery's wide front porch and sat in a rocking chair. The porch faced west and was bearable despite the onslaught from the morning sun that was steadily baking her vines. Blue sipped and rocked, and rocked and sipped, reaching for that place of inner calm. She sighed deeply when she felt her muscles releasing their tension.

Her mind wandered over the past few days, thinking about the work going on at the winery and the contract laborers. Was it possible one of them had grabbed the wrong container and sprayed the vines with weed killer? But that made no sense. Given that harvest was under way, there was no reason for anyone to spray.

She went inside to make another cappuccino, then sipped and rocked, coming back to the snap conclusion she'd reached when she saw the damage: it was Daphne.

Given the degree of distress the vines were showing, they must've come into contact with weed killer last night. Everything was stressed this summer. The intense heat, the lack of rain. Every plant in East Texas was more vulnerable to damage than normal. Contact with weed killer in any concentration would wilt the vines faster than normal.

Tires sounded on the gravel drive and Will's car stopped at the far side of the parking lot. His smile was wide as he opened the door. "What are you doing here so early?" he called.

"I could ask you the same thing."

"Thought I'd help Chef get ready for the staff meeting."

She forced a smile. "You're planning a takeover of the kitchen?"

He eased into the rocking chair beside her. "No way. Kitchen people are crazy. And they have knives. What brings you out so early?"

"I couldn't sleep."

"Were you worried about whoever broke in?"

"Maybe. A little. You're probably too young for this to happen, but sometimes your mind switches on and won't shut off."

Will looked out across the parking lot, a wistful look on his face. "I know something about that." He glanced at her cup. "Can I get you another?"

"I've already had two."

"You'll need the caffeine before the morning's over."

"Go on, then."

Will returned quickly with two cappuccinos and sat next to her again. "This is my favorite time of day."

"Is it?" Blue asked. "Why?"

"Everything is fresh and new. Yesterday's problems might still linger, but there's hope to get through them today."

Blue studied him. Will was a handsome young man and from everything she'd seen, solid emotionally. His features were even and strong, and his eyes a unique gray with long, beautiful lashes tipped with gold as if he'd spent considerable time in the sun. His optimism made her think of Bret in the early days of their relationship. "I like that. And I'm glad somebody has hope, because we're going to have to replant three rows of Cynthiana."

"Which ones?"

"Those nearest the workshop."

"No way. I was out there yesterday and they looked fine, given the conditions. The drought finally got them?"

"It wasn't Mother Nature. There's a human culprit."

"What do you mean?"

"They were sprayed with weed killer. Undiluted glyphosate, I think."

Will started. "Who would do that?"

"Who left mad last night?"

"Daphne?"

"Who else?"

Will was quiet. "Did you call the police?"

Blue looked out at the vines. "She's lashing out. And I was thinking about replacing all the Cynthiana vines anyway. They've never produced well out here."

"You have to call the police, Blue."

"Why?"

His words were slow in coming. "Daphne's volatile. I mean, her ups are way up but when she's mad or down, she's a wild one. When Bret dumped her," he glanced at Blue who returned his gaze without blinking, "she promised she'd get even. Not just with him, but with you."

"You don't think she had anything to do with the music room, do you?"

"It's a big coincidence if she sprayed the vines but didn't bash the instruments."

"Maybe," Blue said. "Maybe you're right."

"Maybe I am. The police can check for fingerprints on the jugs of poison. If it's not her, no big deal. If it is, she needs to be dealt with. Harshly, in my opinion." He hesitated. "Please call, Blue. You're important to me and to everyone at the winery. None of us want you to get hurt."

She watched him as he spoke, taking the measure of his words. She sensed nothing untoward in them, only a genuine concern.

Chef's little Mercedes rolled into the parking lot and he backed under a shade tree. Will took Blue's empty mug. "If I can give the boss instructions, your first job is to call the police. Your second is to call about tonight's flat iron steaks."

WHEN A MAN WANTS INTO YOUR PANTS, OR YOUR WALLET

NORTHPARK WAS QUIET, PEOPLED with early mall walkers and staff coming in before the shops opened at ten. Three tables were occupied when we got to the little bakery. Two women and one guy in a dark suit who looked vaguely like Bret Ivey, if a little on the young side. I detoured to pass his table and saw 'Steve' on his name tag.

We took turns in the ladies room to make sure we didn't miss our target, and then placed orders for Eggs Benedict and coffee. I traded air-kisses with two of the staff I hadn't seen in several months and spent a few minutes gossiping about changes in the mall. I finally got around to telling them I was looking for a friend's lover, a guy who had dumped her and refused to pay child support. Yes, I lied, but it was for a good cause. Both of these gals had deadbeat husbands who didn't pay child support. They were sympathetic and knew exactly who I was talking about, and promised to let me know, subtly, when he arrived.

Our Eggs Benedict arrived before Bret did, and Cindy gasped when she took her first bite. It seemed there *was* something we could agree on. We'd finished breakfast and were lingering over our second cups of coffee when Cindy shifted ever so slightly in her chair. I glanced up to see her gaze flick to the counter. Just then, one of my waitress friends walked up and asked if we wanted another orange juice when she refilled our coffee. It took a moment but I remembered that this was our prearranged signal. I handed over my mug and turned to look at the counter.

There stood a man and a woman, their backs to me. The woman had big hair and was curvy, her hips a definite size fourteen. From behind, the man had a nice shape. He wore a baseball cap, black t-shirt, jeans, and black boots, everything just tight enough to highlight his assets. I waited impatiently for him to turn around.

Cindy tapped my shin with her toe. "Close your mouth."

I frowned. "Stop bossing me around."

"Maxine," she said quietly. "His bimbo is doing a periscope. Lord. Look at those boobs. They're bigger than yours, and hers look real. Not now, Max. She'll tag you if you keep gawping. Look at me, and pretend we're having a conversation."

"Oh. Right. About what?"

"You're supposed to be the clever one. Make something up. How about your favorite topic, shopping?"

I couldn't help it. I looked at the counter again. Cindy kicked me. "Ouch." I rubbed my shin and glared at her. "What?"

"Stop. Looking. At. Bret." Cindy waited until my gaze met hers. "They're sitting by the window, right in my line of sight. Say 'cheese'." She held up her camera and snapped a photo. And then another. And another. "I'll let you know if they decide to leave."

"But I want to see," I protested. "Are you sure it's them?"

"Maxine," she growled, passing me the phone.

I squinted. "I'm not sure."

"I'm almost sure. Tell me about the shops in this mall, and then go to the bathroom. Try not to drool as you walk past."

"What kind of shops?" I asked, still pouting.

"Which one is your favorite?"

"That depends. Nordstrom's has a brilliant personal shopping service and spa. I love the soaps at L'Occitane and the cosmetics counters at Neiman's." Yes, I am that easy to distract. "There's a sweet little shop that sells cards and notepaper, and I love the bath fizzies at Lush. What are you in the market for?"

"Lingerie."

"What do you need lingerie for?"

Cindy glared. "I'm making conversation, Maxine." She lifted her chin. "They've got their food. Go to the bathroom and don't make a spectacle of yourself."

I stood with as much dignity as I could muster, straightened my sun dress, and sauntered past the table by the window. There Bret Ivey sat with a wide-bottomed million-dollar bimbo, big as life. He was one of those men who wavered on the edge of handsome, but his personality and high-wattage smile tipped him over the edge. He and the bimbo held hands across the table, ogling one another over their breakfasts. He gave her one of those "you're the only one for me" shit-eating grins I knew all too well. It was the kind of smile a man gave you when he wanted into your pants. Or your wallet.

They were still in that lovey-dovey pose when I returned to our table. It had been cleared and the dishes replaced with to-go cups.

"They didn't have cat poop coffee, so I got Sumatra," Cindy said. She stood and slung her bag over her shoulder. "Let's go. And make happy with me, like we're friends."

"Go where?" I whispered. "They're still here."

"They'll notice if we linger too long. We can shop nearby and keep an eye on them. Come on." And with that, she picked up her coffee and headed for the lingerie store.

COMING OUT

BLUE RESISTED THE URGE to pour a glass of wine and opted instead for coffee and orange juice. She selected a warm croissant and fruit from a tray, and waited while the staff served themselves. She studied the faces in the room. Only Daphne, Toni, and Annie the expediter were missing.

Normally an uproarious lot, the staff was subdued. The usual cliques sat apart from one another and conversation was muted. Will sat near the back and gave her a small smile.

After everyone was seated, Blue cleared her throat and stood. "Thank you for coming in this morning, especially those of you who aren't working today. It seemed best to have this conversation with everyone at once. But first, Toni texted this morning to say that her father is stable, but they're still calling his condition critical. She's not sure when she'll be back, but she promised to keep in touch." She took a sip of coffee. "Has anyone heard from Annie?"

No one replied.

"No one's seen her?" Blue asked.

One of the wait staff spoke. "I drove by Annie's house on my way here this morning. I didn't see her car, but it might've been in the garage."

"Does anybody know what's going on with her?"

Blue heard the shifting of bodies in chairs, but no one replied. She decided to change tack.

"I understand questions have come up about the future of the winery, given the fact that Bret hasn't been here for a while. I'll get it out in the open: I know he was cheating with Daphne." Blue felt color bloom in her cheeks and heard her voice crack. Everyone exchanged glances. Blue slowly counted to ten and lowered her voice. "If you worked last night, you'll also know that I fired her. Not for sleeping with Bret, but for problems related to her performance. I also understand he's had affairs with other women who've worked at the winery, Annie included."

Blue studied the room and saw several faces turn red, those of both men and women. She wondered if Bret had been sleeping with these girls, or perhaps with these guys.

Chef spoke up. "The girls he's been with are gone, Blue. He started up with Annie in the last couple of weeks, but he's already dumped her. Daphne found out about it and blew a gasket. Bret hasn't been around much so she took it out on Annie."

"How?" Blue asked.

"Snide remarks, bumping Annie while she was handling dishes. I think Daphne dumped extra salt on a dish that was ready to go out, but Annie dealt with it."

"Why didn't anyone tell me about all this?" When no one replied, she nodded. "I know I haven't been around much, but surely you know you can tell me anything. Some of you have been with the winery since it opened. Didn't you think I deserved to know what was going on?"

Again Chef spoke. "Nobody was sure what to say, Blue. Bret hasn't exactly threatened anybody, but you know what his temper is like. If we said something to you and Bret found out, he would've fired us. And as weird as things have been around here, it's still a great place to work."

Several of the staff nodded.

Blue felt the iron band that had been wrapped around her chest for the last several weeks loosen. Only a little, but it helped. They wanted to be here, and that was all that mattered. "It may not have been great lately, but in the future I'll make sure it doesn't suck as bad as it has."

A few chuckles sounded and the band loosened further.

"Here's where things stand between me and Bret: I've begun divorce proceedings and as soon as I can find him, we'll finalize things. Some of you know I've hired a private detective to help me track Bret down. He's not returning my calls. Has anyone seen him or heard from him?"

Heads shook in the negative and Blue felt her old self return.

"My detective's name is Maxine. Give her whatever help she needs. Answer whatever questions she asks. The sooner we find him the sooner this is over and we can get back to whatever passes for normal in this madhouse."

One of the wait staff stood and got another cup of coffee. She asked, "How's your mom doing?"

Blue's heart expanded. "Better, but she's still shaky. Truthfully, her recovery is going slower than the doctors had hoped."

"So you still need to travel?"

Blue hesitated, then nodded. "This is really crappy timing. I'm the only kid available to help my parents, and I know some of you understand that. I've thought about bringing them here to make it easier for me, but that would probably drive me crazy in the end. I know some of you understand that, too."

The staff relaxed a bit, and several others refilled their plates and glasses. A tall young man with glasses, new to the kitchen, asked, "Is the cookbook still on track?"

Blue smiled then. It was the first genuine smile to cross her lips that morning and it felt wonderful. "It is. Again, it's bad timing given everything that's going on with Bret, but the editor and publisher are so excited that I hate to slow the process down."

"It'll be great publicity for the wines and the winery, Blue," Chef said. He looked around the room. "You'll probably have to make a few more trips to New York to finalize everything, but we can hold the fort while you're there and in Florida. Don't worry about us."

A pair of hands clapped, then another joined in, and soon the room was awash in applause and Blue felt tears sting her eyes. "Thank you," she said when the applause slowed. "I can't tell you what your support means. Will's bringing in a few people who might be interested in working as wait staff. Any other questions?"

The winery's front door opened and Kado poked his head inside. "Is now okay?"

Blue motioned him in. "Everyone, this is Forney County's forensic person, Tom Kado." She glanced at the young man with him. "And this is Officer Truman. Everybody's here and they're all okay with having their fingerprints taken for elimination purposes. I'll go first."

Will spread butcher paper over a small table and Kado and Truman took white cards and black ink pads from a case. The staff stood and stretched while Blue was fingerprinted. Some wandered into the kitchen to finish lunch preparations after they were printed, and a few came by and hugged Blue, telling her how glad they were it was Blue and not Bret who would run the winery.

Chef cleared his throat. "Do you think you could find it in your heart to forgive Annie?"

Blue looked at him, a question in her eyes.

He squirmed. "She told me how guilty she felt and I told her the last thing she needed to do was sleep with the boss." He bit his lip. "She said she didn't have a choice, she was falling in love with him."

Blue's eyelids slid closed. "What a guy."

"She was devastated when he dumped her. I don't think she has much experience with this kind of stuff."

"And you want her back?"

"She's the best expediter I've ever worked with."

Blue nodded slowly. "I guess we've all been screwed by Bret, one way or another. I'll go check on Annie and see if I can get her back in the kitchen."

EMPTY HANDED

"NOTHING? AGAIN NOTHING? DID you trash the place?"

The small man breathed heavily into the phone. His accent grew thicker when he was irritated and the blond could barely understand him. He tried to hand the phone to the dark-haired man who was driving, but he refused. The blond pulled at his nose and spoke. "Um, we trashed the music room like you said. Smashed everything up."

"The rest of the place?"

"We searched it."

"And you're sure it's not there?"

"Yeah. We're sure." The phone went silent. "Are you there?"

"There's at least one more woman, but I don't know how to find her."

"Another chick from the winery?"

"No. Frannie. He talks to her on the phone."

"We can follow him," the blond said, and the dark-haired man shot him a look.

"Where is he now?" the small man asked.

"Um, we don't know."

"Then how will you follow him?"

"He has to go back to the Dallas house."

"Why?"

"He and the woman left their luggage there when they came home."

"You're watching the house?"

The blond nodded and then realized the short man couldn't see through the phone. "Yeah."

"Fine. Follow him. But keep in touch."

The line went dead and the blond looked at the dark-haired man. "He said to follow BB."

"You offered to follow BB."

"I did?"

"You did."

"That's a good idea, huh?" the blond asked with a smile.

"If we could keep up with him, yeah, it might be a good idea."

"What do you mean?"

"We're in a beat up truck, you loser. He's in a Corvette. How are we going to follow him?"

The blond pulled at his nose. "Yeah, right. Um, could you find a gas station?"

"Don't tell me."

"I've gotta pee again."

ON THE TRAIL

CINDY WAS THE MOST frustrating woman I'd ever shopped with, until I realized she was digging through the sale bin of panties for the third time only so she could watch Bret and the bimbo. They stepped out of the bakery and headed straight for the wall display of nighties, holding hands and oblivious to everything around them. I watched from the corner of my eye, changing position as they moved around the shop. The bimbo was a big-haired blonde, heavily made up, with a bottom wide enough to comfortably seat two, a tiny waist, and a hefty shelf of boobs, no doubt a 38DD.

Cindy drifted deeper into the shop and I followed, stopping to finger an orange silk pajama set. She selected a bra and met me at the PJ display. "I'll take the lead. You follow."

"What are you talking about?"

She rolled her eyes. "When I see them headed for the cash register, I'll get in line in front. You hold off until there are a couple of customers between you."

"You want me to buy something? Here?"

"You can afford it."

"That's not the point. I wear La Perla."

"Your panty preference is not the point," Cindy said. "We can return the stuff if you don't want it. The point is to get something in our hands so we look like we're here for a purpose. And we can stop and look at what we've purchased if they head into a shop we don't want to go into."

"Like what shop?"

"I don't know, Maxine. A fancy jewelry shop? Somewhere with not many people or displays. Where we might be noticed."

I checked the size on the pajama set and put it over my arm.

Cindy tsked. "Not your color."

I held it up and looked in a mirror. Score one for the cousin. I picked out a pale blue set and then looked for Bret and the bimbo again. My heart jumped. "They're gone."

"They're in the third dressing room on the left."

"What?"

"Bret was looking eager. We might hear banging in a minute. Keep shopping until they come out."

I'd read that tailing people was a boring job, but tailing Bret and Bimbo was anything but boring. We followed at a very safe distance, and often didn't even go into the shops they did. Sometimes we followed them into a store; other times, we split up and took positions on opposite sides of their shop so we'd have an easy way to tail them if they left. Let me tell you, cell phones are a necessity in these situations. For calling your partner, for one thing, but also for gazing at the screen, pretending to be absorbed. That kind of behavior renders you invisible. You can watch discreetly and your target will ignore you.

Bimbo clocked us as they were coming out of Mont Blanc and I thought we were blown. Cindy backed us off and over a three hour period, Bimbo only glared at us once more. Bret never noticed us, or if he did, gave no indication. The happy couple made their way through the mall to Nordstrom's. They ordered coffee at Ebar and sat at a little table where they took out their phones. Cindy pulled me into a mall restroom and popped her tote bag open. She thrust a pair of dark leggings and matching top at me, and dug out a pair of sandals.

"Change," she ordered.

"Why?"

She pulled the baseball cap off my head and put it in her bag. "Bimbo's seen us. We need to look different for the next phase of this operation." She took her ball cap off and fluffed her hair, then pulled a pair of skinny jeans on under her sun dress, peeled off the dress and replaced it with a black t-shirt. She put on a pair of ballet slippers and slid sunshades onto her head. Then she turned the tote inside out to reveal a black interior, and stuffed everything back inside. "We've been in light colored dresses with hats on. Now we're in dark pants, hatless. People they haven't seen before."

She took my lingerie bag and put it in a shopping bag from Williams Sonoma she took from her tote. Again, score one for the cuz. She looked totally different.

"That's pretty good," I told her.

"Yes, it is. We've been happy and smiling, it's time for dark and brooding. Let's get coffee and see what they're up to."

ROCK PAPER SCISSORS

WHEN KADO AND TRUMAN finished taking fingerprints, Kado found Blue in the kitchen. "Would you show me the damaged vines?"

The sun was climbing in the clear sky, the heat near searing. Sweat popped out on Blue's forehead as they stepped off the porch and she pointed when they rounded the workshop's side. The vines looked even worse than they had earlier this morning.

"You're sure it's not the drought?" Kado asked.

"I'm sure I smelled weed killer this morning. Can you take a sample from the leaves and see if there's a chemical on them? I can show you the stuff we use. It's in the workshop."

Blue unlocked the padlock on the door and flipped a switch once they were inside. Fluorescent lights stuttered to life, revealing a high-ceilinged building that was already sweltering in the morning sun. Equipment, tools, and supplies were neatly organized.

"Is the workshop always locked?" Truman asked.

"No," Blue answered. "All our keys hang inside the winery's kitchen door. Whoever needs to get in the shop first each day unlocks it. Someone is always assigned lock up duties at night and returns the keys to their hooks." She lifted her chin at a row of metal shelves. "The first set contains weed killers. The second holds fertilizers."

Truman studied the plastic containers. "Some of this stuff is powerful. We use Sahara on the farm under our electric fences."

"That's where we use it, too. We use the brushy weed killer out in the woods to keep the elm and Chinese tallow down. It works, but you have to keep spraying it."

"That stuff is hard to kill. Do you use any of these chemicals around your vines, or see anything out of place?"

Blue reached out to turn a container but Kado stopped her. "Fingerprints."

She pointed at a jug on the top shelf. "That's undiluted glyphosate. And that," she pointed at a container on a middle shelf, "is brushy wood killer. Both should be on the bottom shelf. We keep the most potent stuff on the lower shelves in case there's a leak. None of the weaker chemicals gets contaminated."

"Is it possible someone put it in the wrong place?" Kado asked.

"Of course. But it's unlikely. The guys who work the vines and the wider property have been with us for several years. They all know the system."

"That stuff would kill your vines?"

"Definitely. It's absorbed by the leaves and travels through the plant's system to its roots."

"How do you apply it?"

"Usually with a backpack sprayer." Blue pointed to several hanging on a wall. "For bigger jobs, we use a big sprayer we carry in a utility vehicle." She pointed to a bucket resting on its side near the shelves. "Technically, you could mix it up in a bucket and throw the stuff around."

"You think a member of your staff did this?"

Blue hesitated. "I fired one of our wait staff last night, and she was very angry."

"Why did you fire her?"

"For tardiness and attitude, but you might as well know that she'd had an affair with my husband. I understand he broke up with her."

"So she had reason to be mad at both of you."

Blue nodded.

"Revenge is a great motive."

"It could be an accident," Blue clarified. "But after the break-in, I'm worried enough that I'd like to know for sure if it wasn't." She checked her watch. "I need to run. Are you okay on your own?"

Kado looked at Truman. "It's hot in here. It's hot out there. Rock, paper, scissors. Winner calls vines or jugs."

MONEY LIKE THIS

BY THE TIME BRET and Bimbo finished their coffee, I'd picked out a new Furla handbag and Cindy was cooing over a pair of Cole Haan driving moccasins that were way out of her price range. Bret and his woman strolled through the department store and just like Cindy said, never noticed us.

I hooked up with her in the shoe department. "Do we follow at a safe distance?"

"What?" she asked, giving the moccasins a longing look as she returned them to the display.

"Never mind. I hope they're in the Corvette. It'll be easier to spot in traffic. Let's go."

Bret must've missed out on his morning nooky in Victoria's Secret because he had his arm around Bimbo's back and was reaching for a breast as they hurried across the blistering parking lot to that bright yellow Corvette.

"Lordy," Cindy muttered as we ducked into the Lexus and surrendered our shaded space to a Mercedes. "They need to get a room."

"I have a feeling they're headed straight to bed. Do not pass go, do not collect two hundred dollars. Although Bimbo might be a hooker, it looks like she's giving it to Bret at no charge."

We spotted them pulling onto Park Lane and followed as they turned south on Central Expressway. Traffic was heavy enough that I stayed close, allowing only one or two cars to come between us. They exited on Lemmon Avenue and nipped down to Turtle Creek

Boulevard, then turned onto Hall Street and pulled into a circular drive in front of a sweet little cottage.

"Holy cow," I said. "This is where the money's going."

"What do you mean?"

I cruised past and stopped farther down the street. "This is Turtle Creek." I swiveled to watch Bret walk around the Corvette and open Bimbo's door. "Or maybe it's Uptown."

Cindy snapped photos with her phone. "So?"

"This is a pricey part of Dallas. That little cottage goes for a million, easy."

"Get out."

"Probably a tad more."

"For that?"

"It's small," I agreed, watching Bret stroke Bimbo's bottom as she unlocked the front door. "But property around here is worth a fortune." I slipped the Lexus into gear. "Get the house number."

"Why don't we park here?" Cindy asked. She dug in her purse and jotted a note.

"Money like this doesn't miss a beat."

"I guess you'd know all about that."

"Let it go, Cindy. Let's find somewhere to eat. We can decide what to do from there."

AFTER CIRCLING BACK TO Lemmon and waiting for a parking spot to open, we settled into a Starbucks. The place was overrun with afternoon shoppers, but Cindy snagged a table and fired up a small laptop. By the time I delivered paninis and iced coffee, she had the property owner's name: Nicole Ivy. She spelled it for me. "He spells his with an 'e', doesn't he?" she asked.

I nodded, swallowed. "Coincidence?"

"I think not."

Cindy finished her sandwich, wiped her fingers on a napkin, and went to work. Within ten minutes we had Nicole's life story, including her marriage certificate to a Bretton Baxter Ivy from 2002, but no divorce decree. A warning bell went off in my brain. Nicole's social media pages showed the big bottomed bimbo we'd followed through Northpark, and the occasional photograph with a man that could be Blue's Bret. In the few shots that included him, he rarely looked directly into the camera, and usually had a hat tipped to shade his eyes or his head turned, hiding most of his face.

"It's got to be him," I said. "But why would he spell his name differently?"

"And be married to two women at the same time?" She went back to work on the computer. "Give me another ten minutes and an espresso. And you need a muffin. You're too thin."

I cocked an eyebrow at my assertive cousin, but did as she bid. I returned with coffees for us both but sans muffin, and scooted my chair closer. The stuff these databases house is amazing. Instead of searching for more information about Nicole Ivy, Cindy was focusing on the man we knew as Bret Ivey. The deeper she dug, the less we found about him.

"Interesting," she muttered.

"What?"

"He's legit. But barely."

"What does that mean?"

"It means he has a semblance of a life out there. Stuff that's verifiable, but doesn't reveal too much."

"For example?"

Cindy twisted the laptop so I could see better. The open website showed a photograph of grapes on a vine. A gorgeous view of mountains slideshowed onto the screen, followed by a shot of a rustic front porch. A man sat alone at a table, toasting the photographer, his face mostly obscured by shadows.

"That's not Cedar Bend Winery," I said.

"Nope. It's out in California. A place called Stony Pike Winery. Owned by Bret Ivey and his lovely wife Imelda Sanchez Ivey, until they divorced in 2006."

"But you said he married Nicole in 2002, right?"

"Right."

"So he's a polygamist as Ivy and Ivey, at a minimum."

"But why?" Cindy asked. "Why would a man choose to be married to two women at the same time?"

"Isn't that every guy's fantasy?"

"Imagine the cost of maintaining two households. Kids, cars, whatever."

"The Imelda marriage is legally over?"

She switched to an online database. "Looks like it."

I pointed at the computer. "Can you find out how much Nicole Ivy is worth?"

"Why?"

"Maybe his wives maintain him."

"Sugar mommas?"

"That's what Blue is," I said. "Why not Nicole?"

"Naughty boy," Cindy whispered, and started typing.

I CHECKED MY WATCH. We'd been gone from the fat bottomed Nicole's home for almost an hour. "Any luck?"

Cindy stretched and checked her espresso cup, which was empty. "I can't say for certain, but her name is on five properties in the Dallas area alone. The overpriced cottage and four commercial locations."

"Mortgages?"

"Doubtful. She's a principal in the law firm of Ivy, McLellan and Brown."

I raised an eyebrow.

"I know," Cindy said. "But I checked their website." She motioned to the screen. "There she is, big bottom and all."

The same blonde from the mall stood with two silver haired men on steps leading to a chic office building. A sign bearing the firm's name graced the wall next to the door.

"There's a brain in that head?" I asked.

"She's got something that led to her name getting top billing, but it might not be a brain."

"What kind of law do they practice?"

Cindy clicked the 'About' link. "Entertainment."

"He's got a nose for money. I wonder how he hooked up with her?"

"No idea. What are you going to tell Blue?"

I chewed my lower lip. "The truth. That's what she hired me for."

"Good girl," Cindy said.

"I'm not your dog."

"Calm down, Maxine. I meant that I agree with your choice. Depending on how she feels about her marriage, the news will either be good or bad for her. But that's not our call. She hired *us*," she emphasized the word, "to find him, and that's what we've done. Do you want to call her now?"

"Should we take another look at the house, see if he's still there? I'll call her on our way back to Arcadia."

Cindy closed the computer. "It can't hurt. At his age, the love fest is bound to be over."

WRECKING MY LIFE

BLUE STOPPED IN FRONT of the garage apartment but hesitated before opening her car door. The piece of her heart she'd given to Bret was already healing, and she was resigned to the end of her marriage. But she was conflicted about approaching one of Bret's lovers, and about having her back at the winery. Until last night, Blue had had no idea Annie was involved with Bret. The girl was young but composed, and Chef was right: Annie was a natural expediter. Good with people, good with order details, a good sense of timing. It was hard to find someone with the right set of skills to keep the kitchen flowing together. From that perspective, Blue couldn't ask for a better employee.

But she had slept with Bret. Annie might be naive when it came to relationships, but she was a grown woman, surely able to tell the difference between right and wrong when it came to a sexual relationship with her boss. How would she react once she was back in the kitchen? How would Blue and the rest of the staff react?

Blue shook herself and opened the car door. This wasn't about Annie. In truth, she was a very young and inexperienced woman who had been manipulated by a man who'd manipulated an older and much more experienced Blue. And although she didn't totally feel it, Blue told herself Annie deserved compassion, not anger. Blue's whole life had been about moving forward and shaking off failures. This marriage would be no different. She straightened her shoulders and headed for the stairs.

THE SIRENS WAILED FROM a great distance, and Blue barely registered the pounding of feet up the stairs and the bump of a body as it eased past her. A light brown form sat beside her. Blue heard urgent sounds that must've been words, but couldn't bring her mind to tune in to their meaning. She had no point of reference for what was happening, so Blue responded in the way every well-bred Southern female is trained from birth to respond to a stressful situation: with a polite smile.

Then she fainted.

DETECTIVE MITCH STONE SAT next to Blue on the tailgate of his truck and told her to take another sip of Dr. Pepper. He was parked on the street under the arching branches of a cedar elm that was dropping its leaves due to the drought. A slight breeze stirred the air but his face was slick with sweat and he dried his forehead with a handkerchief. The area around Annie's garage apartment was alive with activity, and the scent of decomposition rode the breeze. He waited quietly until Blue seemed to notice the motion around her. She looked at him, almost in confusion, and he smiled when her eyes cleared. "Better?"

"I never drink this stuff," she said, touching the cold can to her forehead.

"There's nothing like sugar for dealing with shock."

"I'm not in shock."

"You fainted because you got overheated?"

Blue hesitated. "Maybe I am a little shocked."

"You're Blue Ivey?"

She nodded. "How did you know?"

"I lost a bet with my wife and had to take her to your winery not long ago."

Blue blinked. "Had to?"

"Wrong words. I *got* to take her to your winery."

"I'm sorry, did we meet there? So many people come through the place…"

"No, we didn't. I called in your license plate and got the registration details."

Blue's gaze locked on her Prius, parked in front of the garage doors. A shudder ran through her and Dr. Pepper sloshed onto her hand. She instinctively licked it away and realized she still had Annie's key in her hand. Blue held it out. "Annie keeps this under the ivy."

Mitch put the key on the tailgate between them. "I'm Mitch Stone, with the sheriff's department. Can you tell me what happened?"

Blue forced her attention back to him. His kindly blue eyes were mesmerizing and Blue found it easy to talk. "One of my employees lives here. She hasn't been at work for a couple of days, hasn't called in, and no one's been able to contact her."

"One day, two, three?"

"Today's Saturday?"

Mitch nodded.

Blue thought. "Tuesday. I'm pretty sure she was at work Tuesday."

Mitch jotted a note. "I'd imagine running a winery keeps you pretty busy."

Blue nodded.

"Do you check on all your staff personally?"

"No. Well, sometimes. Today, it seemed appropriate that I come check on her."

"Why today, especially?"

A pickup truck pulled up behind Mitch's, and flame-colored hair flashed through the windshield. Cass stepped from the cab and joined them. "Hey Mitch, Blue."

"I thought you were helping Bruce cook," he said.

"Nobody helps my brother cook," Cass answered. "He's an animal in this new kitchen. Thinks he's Gordon Ramsay."

Blue perked up. "That's good and bad."

"The food is good," Cass said. "The attitude has to go. Where're we at?"

"You're not on duty," Mitch said.

"I'm not on duty," she agreed. "I heard the call on the scanner, recognized Blue's name, and decided I'd be more use helping my partner than being abused in my own kitchen." She looked at Blue. "You reported a death?"

Blue tried to swallow and found that her tongue had stuck to the roof of her mouth. She took another sip and nodded. "My expediter, Annie." Her gaze flew to the apartment over the garage. "She's in there."

"Blue was telling me why she came to check on Annie instead of sending someone else," Mitch said.

Cass leaned against her truck's hood.

Blue looked down at her hands and then focused on Cass. "Annie was having an affair with my husband." She looked at Mitch. "She was one of several girls he's slept with at the winery. Apparently he broke up with her in the last few days."

Mitch shifted. "This Annie worked for you and was sleeping with your husband?"

A small car slowed to a stop a few houses away. Blue watched as a thin man hung a camera around his neck. He nodded at the little trio, then stepped onto the lawn.

"Not too close, Wally," Cass called. "They're still working."

He nodded again and raised the camera to take a photo of the garage.

"Annie?" Mitch said, drawing Blue's attention back.

"She worked for both of us. And yes, according to my staff, she was his latest conquest."

"How did you feel about that?"

"I only found out about it last night. Mostly, I feel sorry for her. Bret's quite manipulative and she's pretty young."

"It's unusual that anyone who's been cheated on wouldn't feel angry."

"Oh, I'm angry all right," Blue said, color returning to her cheeks. "I'm furious. At Bret. For all he's put me through. For how bizarre his behavior has become. For spending all our cash. And especially for cheating on me. But I'm angriest that he's put the winery at risk by doing all this. I've spent nearly five years helping him build it, and now he seems determined to destroy it all."

Mitch cocked an eyebrow at Cass, who motioned for him to be quiet. A heavy van rumbled to a stop behind Cass's truck and the county's lanky Medical Examiner, John Grey, and his skinny assistant Porky Rivers stepped out.

Blue drew herself together as she looked from the van to the garage. "I hope she didn't do this because of him," she whispered. "He's doing his best to wreck my life, but I'd hate to think he could push someone to suicide."

THE BREAK-IN

TWO HIGHLAND PARK POLICE cars were parked in front of Nicole Ivy's residence, blocking the yellow Corvette in the driveway. A sedan so ugly it had to be city issued was parked at the curb. Nose-in behind it was a crime scene van. A gaggle of folks were gawking at the house as I cruised slowly past. Cindy turned to watch as I made a left at the next corner. I pulled to the side of the road and parked. "What is that about?" I asked.

"It can't be good. Does he have a temper?"

"Blue didn't mention it if he does. Let's chat with the neighbors."

I pulled to a stop half a block away. The police cars and gawkers were still in place. No uniformed presence was visible. We walked up to the small crowd and Cindy whispered, "Watch and learn, Maxine. Keep your mouth shut."

I started to protest but Cindy was already in motion. She gently bumped one of the elderly women.

"I'm so sorry," Cindy said. "I didn't hurt you, did I?"

"No, honey. We shouldn't be blocking the sidewalk like this." She was a doll-like thing, barely five feet tall. Her beautiful white hair and wrinkles made her look close to one hundred.

"What's happening?" Cindy asked.

"A break-in, dear."

Cindy took a step back. "We're looking at houses in this neighborhood. I thought Oak Lawn would be safe."

"It's usually very safe around here," a young man in jogging shorts and a sweat streaked t-shirt said. "Whoever broke in knew what they were doing. The alarm wasn't triggered."

"Maybe he didn't set it," Cindy said. "If the neighborhood is so safe, the owner might not've thought he needed it."

"Not he, she," he said. "Nicole's ex-husband was a brute. She always sets the alarm, even when she's home."

Score one for Cindy. She'd just confirmed her online findings.

"If the alarm didn't go off, how was the break-in discovered?"

An elderly man wearing a Texas Rangers ball cap mopped his forehead and said, "Nicole and her husband, this is her second husband, came back from breakfast and found his music room ransacked."

The hairs on the back of my neck stood up and I fought to keep my eyebrows from shooting to my hairline.

"It happened this morning? In broad daylight?" Cindy wrapped her arms around herself. "That doesn't sound good."

"Could've been last night," the old lady said. "Nicole flew back from Los Angeles this morning and Baxter was away on business last night." She unzipped her purse. "I look after Ted while she's gone."

"Ted?" Cindy asked.

"Their toy poodle." She glanced at a ball of fluff poking from her purse and I realized it was a dog. "Nicole and Baxter got back about an hour ago and I was bringing Ted home when the police rushed the place." She leaned close and I caught a whiff of lavender. "Lights flashing, sirens wailing. We haven't had that much excitement since old Mr. Simpson dropped dead during his morning constitutional. Do you remember, Jack?"

The old man nodded sagely. "Aneurysm. Took him right out. We should all be so lucky."

"Did anyone see anything? A getaway car?" Cindy asked.

"Marjorie spotted a pickup truck when she was out for her jog this morning," Jack said. "Did you get a plate?"

The old lady shook her head and dabbed at her face with a hankie.

Jogging? At one hundred? Man, I had a lot to look forward to.

"They've had workmen in and out lately. It never crossed my mind that it shouldn't be there." She patted Cindy on the arm and smiled at me. "Don't let this put you off, dear. This is a safe place for everyone, even your type."

I frowned, struggling to find her meaning. Cindy put her arm around my shoulders and pulled me close. "Thank you. It's hard to know what kind of people live in a place until you move in."

And then it dawned on me: Marjorie thought we were lesbians. Score another one for the cuz for handling it so well.

"Is the husband a famous musician?" Cindy asked.

The old man looked thoughtful. "He certainly makes enough racket to be a professional musician. I've never heard such tortured sounds coming from a banjo. But I think he's some sort of traveling salesman. He's gone enough."

"And the wife?"

"Now *she's* famous. A lawyer. Works with all those artsy-fartsy types in Hollywood. She travels a lot, too."

"How long have they been married?"

"No idea. They've only lived here a few years."

Four men in police uniforms and a woman in a suit came through the front door and turned to speak to Nicole, who was standing at the threshold. I subtly shifted behind Cindy.

"What's wrong?" she whispered.

"I used to date one of those cops."

"Date or screw?"

"Whatever. We know each other. It would be bad if he saw me."

We watched as they piled into cars and drove away, leaving only the crime scene van at the curb. I relaxed.

The group murmured goodbyes and drifted away.

Bret rushed out of the house and hurried to the Corvette. He nearly clipped old Marjorie as he backed out of the drive and sped down Hall Street, pausing at the stop sign and rounding the corner with a squeal of tires.

I grabbed Cindy's arm. "Let's follow him."

"We'll never catch him now," she whispered. "Let's go home. You can report to Blue and see if she wants us to follow Bret any longer."

A CREATIVE THINKER

"YOU CALL," THE BLOND said, holding the phone across the pickup's cab. "You didn't even try to follow BB."

"Really?" The dark-haired man rubbed his eyes. "In this traffic?"

"I could've followed him."

"You could?"

"Yeah. Get out in traffic and go."

The dark-haired man twisted the key and the old truck coughed and sputtered to life. "Really?"

"You should've stole a better one."

The dark-haired man squeezed the steering wheel. "Did you see the women? One with black hair and one with red?"

"The hot ones?"

"Yeah. They look familiar."

"They do?"

"They're from Arcadia, but I don't know who they are."

"More of BB's girlfriends?"

"I don't think so, but I don't like it." The dark-haired man fiddled with the air conditioning. "You call him. This was your idea."

"I always call him."

"They're always your stupid ideas."

The blond pulled at his nose. "They're not stupid. I'm a creative thinker."

"Ah, that's it. For all these years, I thought it was stupidity."

"There's no need to be nasty."

The dark-haired man slipped the truck into gear. "Call him. Tell him we're coming back and see if he can figure out where that other woman lives."

"Can we stop first?"

"You have to pee again?"

"I'm hungry, too. It's as easy to get bawled out on a full stomach as it is on an empty one."

The dark-haired man gazed at the blond. "That's the first intelligent thing you've said in ages. Let's eat."

THE SCENT OF DEATH

MITCH WATCHED TWO UNIFORMED officers help Grey and Porky work the gurney down the steps from Annie's garage apartment and around Blue's Prius. Mitch had told her they'd need to keep it at the scene a little longer, and had one of the uniformed officers drive her home. Once the gurney reached the van, the medical examiner wiped the sweat from his forehead and motioned to Mitch to join him. Cass followed.

"See anything unusual?" Cass asked.

"I thought you were on medical leave," Grey said.

"I am."

Grey raised a bushy brow at Mitch, who shrugged. "She's bored."

"I would be, too. Given the state of her body, it's hard to say. The air conditioning was off, and the heat buildup in the apartment accelerated decomposition. We'll know more after we autopsy her. Kado was muttering to himself. He may have something."

"Thanks. I'll check in later."

The thin man with the camera approached, his movements sleek, sinuous. This was Wally Pugh, reporter for the local radio station,

KOIL, and the Forney Cater, the county's newspaper. He'd supported the police department, if not the sheriff, during recent trouble with a cult and a cross-dressing murderer.

"Hey, Wally," Cass said.

"Sounds like suicide."

"Might be," Mitch said.

Wally looked a question at him.

"Better safe than sorry when you're reporting, right? Call the ME's office later and confirm."

"Was that Blue Ivey earlier?" Wally asked.

Mitch nodded.

"She know the girl?"

"Annie worked for her. You can probably find somebody out there to give you a quote about her."

Wally nodded and put the lens cap on his camera. "How's the shoulder?" he asked Cass.

"Good," Cass said.

"You back at work?"

"Not yet."

"But you're investigating an unattended death with Mitch?"

"Nope. I was out for a drive and stopped by."

Something like a smile moved Wally's lips. "I'll keep you out of the article."

"Thanks."

They watched him leave, then Mitch and Cass headed for the garage. He stopped and eyed the steps.

"Leg bothering you?" Cass asked.

"It's been months now."

"You sure?"

Mitch grunted. "Yup."

"Want me to go first?"

"Might be faster."

"I'll see you at the top."

————

MITCH PAUSED IN THE open doorway, took a deep breath, and scowled. "Why do dead people have to stink?"

"Missing the crutches?" Cass asked.

"I haven't needed crutches in weeks. It's the decomp. Got any Vick's?"

Cass pulled a small container from her pocket and tossed it to him.

"The sheriff would have a fit if he knew you were out here," Mitch said.

"I won't tell if you won't. And Wally said he wouldn't. Let's see what Kado's found."

Even though Grey had taken Annie's body away, the scent of death still stained the air. Kado and Truman were dusting for prints and bagging evidence. The only thing out of place was a stepladder lying on its side in the living room.

"Find anything useful?" Mitch asked.

"She wasn't much of a housekeeper, which is good for us. There are loads of prints in most of the places you'd expect to find them," Kado said. "There's a partially empty wine bottle in the kitchen along with one wine glass. That is the rope," he motioned to a neatly wrapped blue pile, "she cut her noose from. Her computer is open to a video demonstration of how to tie a noose, and there's a note in the printer tray lamenting the loss of an unnamed love and her decision to get involved with him."

Mitch opened his mouth but Kado silenced him with a raised finger.

"However, there are no fingerprints on the door knobs and you couldn't learn to tie this knot," he lifted the noose they'd removed from Annie's neck, "by watching that video."

"Murder?" Mitch asked.

"If so, it's clumsy. But it's a real possibility."

SOMEBODY NEEDS TO DO SOMETHING ABOUT THAT MAN

WE MADE EXCELLENT TIME on the return trip to Arcadia, even though Cindy demanded a potty break in Lindale. The woman's bladder is the size of a shot glass. I called Blue on the way and told her we had news, asking if I could come by the winery. She told me to come to her house instead. Her voice sounded shaky but when I asked if she was okay, she said she had to go.

I dropped Cindy at her house and after the tiniest internal debate, thanked her for helping me.

She shrugged. "It's my job."

"I know, but I appreciate that you gave up your Saturday to help me."

"I wasn't helping you, Maxine, not directly. I was making sure the agency doesn't get a black-eye thanks to one of your patented boneheaded moves."

Ouch.

I licked that wound all the way to Cedar Bend Winery. The parking lot was nearly empty, which seemed strange given that it was five o'clock on a Saturday evening. I found a host of cars outside Blue's house and had to leave the Lexus parked down her long driveway. I trudged through the steaming afternoon and mounted the porch steps to find the front door open a crack. I called a greeting as I pushed it closed behind me and felt the blissful wash of conditioned air hit me.

A head poked around a corner and I recognized one of the winery's waitresses. She sniffed. "Maxine?"

I nodded.

"Blue's in here."

I followed the girl into the kitchen and found Blue stirring a pot of sauce on her massive stove. Her eyes were bloodshot and the tip of her nose red, but it still took a moment for me to realize that she, and almost everyone else in the room, had been crying.

"Thanks for coming," Blue said. "Everyone, this is the private investigator I told you about, Maxine. Please give her whatever help you can."

"Won't the police be asking questions?" a tall man asked.

The police? What had I missed?

"Of course. But Maxine may need information as well." She put a lid on the pot. "Tonight and the next few days will be hard, but we've got to get back to work. I'll speak to Annie's parents about the timing of the funeral. Chef, would you take everyone back to the winery? Finish your prep work and I'll see you there shortly."

A slow parade of sagging bodies left Blue's kitchen and it was all I could do to wait until the door closed behind the last of them. "What happened?" I asked as gently as I could.

"Annie is dead."

It took a moment but I remembered Blue mentioning that her expediter hadn't come in to work last night. I sank onto a barstool. "What happened?"

"She committed suicide," Blue said. Her eyes filled and she worried at a bandage on her thumb. "I found her hanging from a rafter in her apartment."

"I'm so sorry. Was she depressed?"

"Maybe. It seems she was sleeping with Bret and he dumped her earlier this week."

"Do you think -"

"I hope not. Not over Bret. He isn't worth it." She drew a deep breath and looked at me. "Speaking of my personal devil, what did you find out?"

"It's not good news."

Blue pushed back from the island and stood at the stove. She took the lid off the pot and stirred. "Go ahead."

"Bret is married to another woman." When Blue remained silent and kept stirring, I continued. "Her name is Nicole. She lives in Oak Lawn, is an attorney."

"That explains a lot. How long?"

"Pardon?"

"How long have they been married?"

"Since 2002."

Her laugh was harsh. "That means *I'm* the other woman. Here I was feeling slighted because he was sleeping with the staff."

"I'm sorry, Blue."

"Me, too." She stirred. "Do you have a physical address for the original Mrs. Ivey?"

I slipped a piece of paper onto the island. "And the name and address of the law firm. We can probably get a home phone number for her. It may not matter, but she spells her name without an 'e' in the Ivey."

Blue stopped stirring, a frown on her face. "Why would she do that?"

"I don't know. The man she married in 2002 is Bretton Baxter Ivy."

"But he's Baxter Bretton Ivey, with an 'e'. Why would he change his name? Are you sure it's the same man?"

I showed her a photo on my cell phone.

"That's him. Is that Nicole?"

I nodded.

"Big rump. I told you."

A small smile crept onto my lips. "You did."

She tasted the sauce, put the lid on the pot, and turned the stove off. "So he was cheating on me, but with his own wife, right?"

I chewed on my lower lip. "And probably with others."

"What do you mean?"

I explained my theory about the variety of clothing sizes Bret purchased, speculating he was with other women on the weekends Nicole was traveling.

"He was cheating on Nicole and me? I mean, he was cheating on Nicole with me, but he was also cheating on both of us with other women? In addition to the girls here at the winery?"

I nodded. "It looks that way."

"Good Lord. Is he still there?" Blue slipped her apron over her head. "At Nicole's?"

"He wasn't when we left the neighborhood." I remembered the spooky feeling when we were talking to the neighbors. "Something strange happened, though. The music room in Nicole's house was ransacked."

Blue started. "By the same people?"

"I have no idea. The crime scene people were still there when we left."

She rubbed her eyes and then shook her head. "Two break-ins, a suicide, and who knows how many affairs. He's left a trail of destruction in his wake, and everybody suffers but Bret. Somebody needs to do something about that man."

THE ELLIOT FAMILY

I ASKED BLUE IF there was anything else I could do for her, and she said she'd need to talk to her lawyer about her legal status. If Bretton Baxter Ivy and Baxter Bretton Ivey were the same man, she might not be married at all. If so, untangling their affairs might be easier. Blue told me to send her a bill for our time and that she'd be in touch if she needed anything else.

I'd expected to be shattered after leaving so early for Dallas, but I was oddly exhilarated after all we'd discovered. Instead of heading home, I called Cass and asked if dinner was still on.

"At the Elliot house?" she said. "Of course it is."

I should explain a bit about Cass and her family. She's the youngest of seven kids, and the only girl. Her oldest brother, Jack, has been in prison for rape and murder since Cass was four. I know with absolute certainty he didn't do it, and once I get a grip on this PI stuff, I'll prove it.

There's more tragedy. Her mother died when Cass was five. Abe, her father, is a drunk. Well, sometimes. Sometimes he goes on a sobriety kick. It never lasts.

Two of Cass's older brothers live in the family home with her and Abe. Harry is the second oldest and going through a nasty divorce. Bruce never really left home, which isn't such a bad thing. He's putting his construction talent to use remodeling the house. It needs serious work, believe me, and he's the right man for the job.

Regardless of how ramshackle it is, for my entire life the Elliot house felt more like home to me than my own. I always felt loved there. Accepted. Maybe it was because I was one of many and disappeared in all the chaos. In my own home? When she wasn't ignoring me, I was on my mother's 'most wanted' list. Being an Elliot seemed like heaven to me. Still does.

I pulled into the short drive and admired the front porch. Bruce and Cass had worked to bring the thing back to level and make the repairs it needed to be functional again. It took them a couple of weeks when she was suspended for shooting a baddie back in the spring. Forney County's sheriff took six weeks to bring her back to work, which was a dereliction of duty on his part and should've resulted in impeachment or whatever they do to stupid sheriffs. After all, the bad guy needed killing. She should've gotten a medal instead of suspension.

My cell phone rang and I looked at the screen. Kay was calling. "Hey," I answered.

"Hi, sweetie. I heard things went very well today. Have you talked to Blue?"

I was a little miffed that Cindy had taken it upon herself to report to the higher-ups on my case, but I stifled my irritation. "I just left her."

"How did she take it?"

"She was upset, but found it funny when she realized that she was the other woman."

"Good job, baby love."

I filled Kay in on Annie's death, her relationship with Bret, and told her Blue had found the body.

"How terrible for Blue. And for Annie. Blue will do well to get rid of this husband. Let me know if she asks for anything else. Otherwise, enjoy what's left of your weekend."

I basked in the glow of my aunt's praise, imagining myself as a partner in the agency. My fantasy ended as the heat in the car grew oppressive. I opened the door and heard the laughter of little girls floating on the sweltering evening air, and knew at least two of Harry's daughters were here. I also smelled the aroma of beef cooking on an open flame and my stomach growled.

Harry's daughters met me as I was coming around the side of the house and squealed. I swung the youngest, Phoebe, around and around until we were both laughing and in peril of landing on our butts. Macy, the middle girl, was too mature at eight for twirling so we exchanged air kisses. Phoebe grabbed my hand and skipped me into the back yard. Handsome Harry ordered the girls into the house, kissed my cheek, and apologized for leaving, saying his almost-ex-wife Carly was in a tizzy and wanted the girls home that night.

Those beautiful smells and a fair amount of smoke were coming from an unmanned grill, and I joined Abe Elliot and Goober at a picnic table where they were engaged in a heavy-duty game of checkers. Goober. If you're from a small town, you'll have your own version of Goober. The poor guy was abandoned as a toddler on Arcadia's town square, adopted by an elderly widow, and now lives in the trailer house she left him when she died a few years ago. He must be in his forties or fifties and makes ends meet by doing odd jobs. I've never had a problem with him, but there's a slowness to him that makes you wonder if he was dropped on his head when he was a baby.

Abe hung an arm around my waist and squeezed. I discreetly sniffed and smelled soft aftershave, detecting no alcohol or extreme breath freshener. A positive sign. Abe released me and watched in disbelief as one of Goober's kings jumped five of his checkers in a series of forward and backward moves.

"That's not legal, Goober," Abe said.

"It is," I said. "I was regularly thrashed by my best friend's dad -" I raised a brow at Abe, "- who had no qualms about wiping out as many checkers in one go as humanly possible."

"Those were little girl rules. We're playing man checkers."

"It's all the same, Abe. You're still a sore loser."

"Might be true. But I think we need a replay on Goober's last move."

"Hey Maxine," Goober said with a shy smile.

"Hey Goob. Don't give up without a fight."

"I won't. I know the checkers rules."

"You here for dinner?" I asked him.

Goober fingered the hook on his overalls. "Abe said I could stay tonight."

I glanced at Cass's dad. Abe is a good-looking man considering that he's in his sixties. His hair has gone a beautiful white and his eyes are the color of honeyed oak. He's also one of the kindest individuals on the planet. When he's sober. After a drink, all bets are off.

Abe glanced at the other man. "Goober's been staying with us since he found that burning zombie."

Goober shuddered. "It gave me nightmares."

"It did," Abe agreed.

"It would me, too." I glanced at the house. "Is Cass around?"

"She's in the house. Go check out the kitchen and let me finish thrashing Goober," Abe said. "We'll console him with red meat."

WE SHOULD'VE DONE THAT THE FIRST TIME

"THIS WAS SMART," THE blond said. "Waiting to call until he's at work. He can't yell."

"Just dial," the dark-haired man said.

The blond did, and left a cryptic message. They were parked in a rest area north of Arcadia. The return call came quickly.

The blond answered and pressed the phone to his ear. "We lost him."

"What's he saying?" the dark-haired man asked.

The blond covered the microphone. "He's cussing us in Mexican. Hold on." He made soothing noises into the phone. Finally he disconnected. "He said we have to go back to the house behind the winery."

"What for?"

"To search it, like we did the Dallas house this morning."

The dark-haired man covered his eyes. "Ah man, I knew we should've done that the first time."

"He didn't tell us to the first time."

"I'm getting tired of this. He's a little piss-ant tyrant."

"What else can we do?"

The dark-haired man checked his watch. "Let's give it an hour or two and go back to the winery. You hungry?"

"Nah, I'd rather wait 'til after and go to the boats in Shreveport."

"You got money to gamble with?"

The blond nodded. "I won last time, remember?"

"No, I don't."

"That's because you lost."

"Well I'm hungry now. You don't want to eat? I know you need to pee. Let's go."

USING FOLK AND PUNK IN THE SAME SENTENCE

I HADN'T BEEN OUT to the Elliot house since Bruce and Cass had finished remodeling the kitchen. The screen door still had that comforting squeak, but the kitchen itself was in a new dimension. "Wow."

Bruce turned from the stove and smiled. I melted and hated myself for it. "Wow? That's it?"

"Very wow." I touched the cabinets. "Cherry?"

"Nice, eh?"

"You did all this?"

Cass stepped into the kitchen, her red hair damp. "He did the fun part," Cass clarified. "I did all the hot work, ripping the old kitchen out. Bruce got to build the new stuff."

"Only because you got shot in the shoulder and wimped out," Bruce said.

A dog barked and I knew Darla and Mitch Stone had arrived. "Can I do anything?"

Bruce motioned me to the stove. "It's hollandaise. Keep it off the double boiler and add the butter cubes a couple at a time and keep stirring. Put it back on the double boiler if it's too cool for the butter to melt."

Cass raised an eyebrow as I walked past. "Nobody but Bruce has touched that stove since he installed it."

The words came out of my mouth before I could stop them. "There's something sexy about a man who cooks."

Bruce grinned on his way out the door and Cass followed, carrying plates and cutlery.

"I hope you're setting up a fan," I called through the screen door.

"Bruce brought one from the college," Cass said as she came back inside, wiping her forehead. "And a tent thing for shade."

Bruce followed her in, took over stirring duties, and I escaped to help Cass take food and iced tea outside. A foil-covered platter waited on the picnic table, now devoid of checkers. Abe and Mitch were adjusting a white tent that covered the patio and part of the yard. A gale-sized breeze hit me as Cass turned on an industrial-sized fan.

"Who won?" I asked.

"Goober," Abe said, and I swear he was pouting.

A lanky greyhound slurped water from a bowl and when he was done, presented himself for an ear rub. "Hello Zeus," I cooed. "Sit with me. I'll sneak you plenty of scraps."

"Maxine," Mitch scolded as he folded himself into the picnic table. He'd suffered severe injuries in the spring when he and Cass were trying to stop a cult. And although he was moving pretty well, if you knew what had happened, you could still see the stiffness in his right leg. "He farts when he eats people food."

"Ignore him, Maxine. He farts no matter what he eats," Mitch's pretty wife Darla said as she hugged me. "And yes, I mean Zeus and Mitch."

Mitch groused as his wife slid onto the bench and scooted him over, but the love they felt for each other was palpable. I tried not to, but I envied them.

It felt so natural to crowd around the picnic table with these people. We settled in to an amazing dinner of ribeyes cooked to perfection and drenched in a velvety hollandaise, corn on the cob, mashed potatoes, green beans, and a massive salad. I think I'm falling in love with Bruce Elliot based on the quality of his cooking alone.

"How'd it go today?" Cass asked between bites.

"We found him."

"Awesome." She high-fived me. "What's the poop?"

I summarized our day, ending with details about Baxter Bretton Ivey's multiple names and marriages.

"I've never understood why a man would want more than one wife," Mitch mused.

"Hey," Darla protested. "You got a pretty good deal here."

"I do. Why risk ruining a perfectly good marriage by adding a second wife?"

"I think it's for the money," I said. "Nicole Ivy is a hotshot lawyer who works with Hollywood types. Blue is independently wealthy, even though she doesn't flaunt it."

"What's Blue going to do?" Cass asked.

"Talk to her lawyer about whether she's legally married. Technically, her husband was married to Nicole before he married her. Blue's marriage might be void." I sipped tea from a glass weeping condensation, then glanced at Goober and lowered my voice. "She told me about her expediter. Did you go to the scene?"

"It was unpleasant. How was Blue?"

"Holding it together. What happened?"

Mitch and Cass exchanged a glance. "Blue said no one had heard from Annie in several days, so she went to go check on her."

"Blue thought she might've committed suicide because Bret broke up with her."

An engine growled from the driveway and then shut off. Kado emerged from around the corner of the house and slid in next to Cass. She tried to hide it, but I caught her smile. It was nice and made me want one of my own. I sneaked a look at Bruce, who was filling a plate for Kado.

"So?" Mitch asked.

"It's homicide," Kado said.

"Who?" I asked.

Kado glanced at Mitch. "Give us the cliff notes," Mitch said. "Wally Pugh was nosing around. It'll be in the papers tomorrow."

"Annie. Grey found evidence on her body. The irregular evidence I told you about earlier points in that direction, too."

It took me a moment to catch on. "You mean someone killed her and made it look like suicide?"

Kado nodded.

I looked at Cass. "Could it be Bret Ivey?"

Mitch frowned. "Why would you think Bret Ivey did this?"

"He dumped her. Maybe she wouldn't let go."

"Maybe," Cass said. "But let's see where the evidence takes us." Sometimes her logical nature drives me nuts. She nudged Kado. "Tell Max about the fingerprints from the truck."

Kado swallowed a bite of steak. "I got hits on two people. Sugar Murphy and William Garcia."

"Sugar?" I asked.

"That's what the system says. Both from California. They've done time for breaking and entering and William Garcia's prints show up on a guitar damaged during a robbery in Arcadia a couple of weeks ago."

"Where?"

"The VanZandt's."

"What are California boys doing in East -" I started to ask, but Mitch interrupted me.

"Man, I don't believe it."

"Believe what?"

"Poison Ivy and the Dismembered Bunnies." He looked around the table as if expecting recognition. "Really? Nobody?" Mitch put his fork down. There was still food on his plate. This was major. "Poison Ivy and the Dismembered Bunnies was the hottest folk punk band in the early eighties."

"How can you use 'folk' and 'punk' in the same sentence without your head exploding?" I asked.

Mitch frowned.

"Oh yeah," Bruce said. "You and Jack were really into them. He had one of their albums, didn't he?"

"Their first and only album, which is a shame. They were young, late teens or early twenties, and had years of musical life left. They played loads of venues in the late seventies. Most of them crappy, but I think they hit CBGB in New York and that gave them a big boost."

He was speaking a language only he and Bruce understood.

"The band broke up, right? The drummer spontaneously combusted?" Bruce asked.

"That was Spinal Tap. With the Bunnies, it was murder. They were almost done with a week's recording session when Sonny Arellano up and went to Mexico."

"Whoa. Arellano as in the Arellano-Felix drug cartel?" Kado asked.

Mitch nodded. "Something happened while he was there. A shooting? An attack on the family business? Sonny never resurfaced and as far as I know, is assumed dead."

"The band broke up when Sonny died?"

Mitch nodded. "The studio burned, and the unmastered recordings from their last session went missing. It kind of gave them cult status."

Nobody was eating now, which is huge when you think about the Elliot family and how vital food is to their functioning. Even Zeus was interested in the conversation. Or maybe in the lack of scraps.

"The guys who left fingerprints in the truck, Murphy and Garcia, how do they fit in?" Cass asked.

"They were band members. BB Ivy, Big Billy Garcia, Sugar Murphy, and Sonny Arellano."

"BB Ivy was Poison Ivy?"

"Yup."

"You think BB Ivy is Bretton Baxter Ivy?" Cass asked.

Mitch nodded. "Gotta be."

Kado speared a bite of steak. "It makes sense when you consider we found their fingerprints in Blue Ivey's music room, too."

I was stumped. "Back the truck up. If we assume the Murphy and Garcia who are leaving fingerprints all over Forney County are the same guys who played in a band with Bret Ivy back in the day, what are the chances they're the same people who broke into Nicole Ivy's house in Dallas and ransacked the music room there?"

"Pretty good," Cass said.

"But why?" Darla asked. Her pretty face was troubled. "If Bret Ivey has been out of the music business for decades, why would his former band mates steal a truck and chase him? Why destroy his instruments? What are they after?"

A SACK OF ROCKS

THEY WERE PICKING THEIR way through the pine forest surrounding BB's house when they heard shouting. The men stopped in their tracks, and then the blond crept forward.

"Sugar," the dark-haired man whispered. "Let's get out of here."

"Come here, Billy. I think it's BB."

Big Billy followed and they stood inside the tree line near the garden. A man stood absolutely still as a woman screamed and jabbed him in the chest.

"What was that?" Sugar asked.

"Something about Annie. Be quiet."

She continued to rant and it seemed he was trying to soothe her.

"You see that?" Sugar asked.

"What?"

"He's BB's twin. From back in the Bunnies days."

Billy took a step closer. It was eleven o'clock and although the garden was dark, a bright moon shone in the sky. The man was young and strong. Tall, with a healthy head of hair. He was a white kid, but tanned. Had kind of a surfer look going on. Billy looked closer. Sugar was right, from this distance, the kid looked a lot like

BB back when they were playing together. But a lot of kids wore the surfer look.

"Nah," Billy said. "Any kid with bushy hair and a tan looks like BB to you."

He started to ease back into the forest but stopped when the woman picked up a bat and pulled back to swing at the man. He caught the bat mid-arc and laughed, a clear, happy sound, before smacking her in the head with it.

She dropped like a sack of rocks.

"Oh man," Sugar whispered. "That was brutal."

"Let's get out of here."

"What about the house?"

The man was standing over the fallen woman, and at last he bent to pick her up, slinging her easily over his shoulder. He disappeared around the house.

Billy shuddered. "After that? I'm not going near the place. Ever."

"Then you call and tell him."

"No problem. Let's go. I need a drink."

SUNDAY

BEAUTIFUL FLOWERS

CHEWIE RODRIGUEZ BACKED HIS zero-turn mower off its trailer and let it idle, listening to the engine. It was early Sunday morning but the VanZandts were out of town, and the house's location on ten secluded acres ensured no neighbors would be bothered by the noise. Although it was unusual for him, Chewie was in a hurry. His new niece's baptism was today and Uncle Chewie wouldn't miss that for the world.

Once the engine was suitably warm, Chewie tied his hat's straps under his chin and adjusted the blade height. He mowed in a contented bubble of engine hum and dust motes, focusing on aligning each pass of the mower with the last to maximize the reach of the blades and minimize the amount of gas and oil he used. Chewie Rodriguez ran a landscaping business that was growing in reputation, but he still guarded every penny of every expense as if it were his last.

He rounded the house to start on the backyard, drawing to a stop as he saw the car parked in the driveway, still shrouded in early morning shadows. It belonged to the VanZandt's daughter, Daphne, a striking young woman who rarely stopped to speak. Daphne always parked in the three car garage attached to the house, but he'd understood she would leave Saturday night to meet her parents wherever they were traveling. That was one reason he'd felt confident in showing up so early on a Sunday.

Chewie turned around. He'd come back after the christening, when it was more likely Daphne wasn't sleeping. And then he saw the shoe and a flush of goosebumps shivered across his arms. He eased the mower forward, wishing he could ignore what was surely a bad omen.

A black tennis shoe lay forlornly in the rose bed near the driveway, and almost hidden behind the shoe, a bottle. They were incongruous in this landscape. Mrs. VanZandt was fastidious with her home's appearance, and Chewie couldn't imagine any sort of trash had been here when she left for vacation.

Chewie looked over his shoulder at the little car sitting alone in the drive, and then at the stone steps to the front door. He considered picking up the shoe and bottle, leaving them on the front mat, hoping someone would reunite the shoe with its lonely partner. But something made him turn the mower around and creep back to Daphne's car.

The shade was so deep on the west side of the house that it wasn't until he was nearly on top of it that he saw the sparkle. A sprinkling of diamonds lay scattered at the car's front end, and rubies littered the ground at its rear. Instead of pinstripes, the car sported a jagged decoration along its flank, and its tires were flat.

He turned off the mower. The quiet was immense. A sixth sense prickled the short hairs along Chewie's neck, and he moved to the car as if in a trance. The jagged decoration morphed into letters and then into words and his eyes could hardly believe the hatred in them. "NOW it's over, bitch." The urge to flee hit Chewie hard, but his feet stepped forward against his will.

She was buried deep in the sheltering arms of the morning's shadows, her body leaning back in the driver's seat, her face tilted to look in the rearview mirror.

Against all logic, Chewie tapped on the window. Receiving no reply, he knocked harder, and then walked around to the driver's side of the car, avoiding the diamonds and rubies. The same message was scrawled in the paint on this side, and through the window Daphne's skin was the perfect alabaster of a calla lily. A wooden handle protruded from her long neck and a crimson stain the color of a Scarlett O'Hara rose spread downward, disappearing into the neck of her blouse.

Chewie debated. If he called the police, he might miss his niece's christening. But if he didn't call, the police would see part of a mown lawn and discover he'd been here. So Chewie did the right thing: he crossed himself, uttered a prayer for Daphne's soul, and pulled out his cell phone to dial 911.

A SENSE OF LOSS

SUNDAY IS MY 'DO not disturb' day, when I sleep in, often until early afternoon. This Sunday found me wide awake by seven o'clock. Yes, alone. And surprisingly, I wasn't disturbed by that fact. Instead, my head was swimming with thoughts of folk punk music, lost recordings, and irate band members. As strange as that was, I offered up a prayer of gratitude: it must've saved me from the rape nightmare.

I hopped in the shower and, after running the usual safety checks, put on my big shades and a floppy hat and rode my bicycle to The Golden Gate Café.

The Golden Gate is something of an institution in Forney County, although it hasn't always been that way. Stan and Sally Overheart moved from San Francisco to Arcadia about a decade ago, and opened the little eaterie. Located just off Arcadia's square, it's homey but not clichéd. They serve all the normal country fare, but also offer a selection of healthy options.

At first, the locals shunned The Golden Gate because Stan is tattooed and has a ponytail. Sally is thin as a whip and her frizzy hair gives her something of a wild look. Never mind that the tattoos are fading, the hair is gray-streaked, and they must be in their fifties or sixties, folks assumed that because Stan and Sally came from San Francisco they must be hippies. And hippies mean only two things in the Bible Belt: devil music and drugs.

Over time, the locals thawed and people came to appreciate The Golden Gate for being a safe place for kids to hang out and offering wholesome music and food. We have another coffee shop located on the square called, ironically, The Coffee Shop, but The Golden Gate is my favorite, both for the food and for Stan and Sally.

I stepped through the door at eight-fifteen, slipped my hat and shades off, and wiped the sweat from my face. I doubt if the temperature had even dropped into the eighties overnight, and the humidity was already unbearable. The café was busy this time of morning, with people grabbing breakfast before heading to Sunday School or early church services and I waved at several faces I recognized.

My bare legs made a horrible skidding sound as I slid into a red-vinyl covered booth. Sally buzzed my table and left a glass of ice water and a mug of steaming coffee. "Stan'll be around in a minute, Max. There's a Forney Cater in the rack if you're interested. You can steal the funnies from the Pettigrew brothers. I think they're done with them."

I unstuck my sweaty legs and scooted out of the booth to grab a copy of the paper, sans funnies. The front page bore a smiling photograph of the woman who must be Annie from Cedar Bend Winery. The byline was Wally Pugh and the story was bare bones, offering her short history, a few details about how she was found on Saturday, and statements from Blue and others at the winery about what a sweet girl Annie was and how shocked they were.

Although Cass was right and evidence had to be pursued, I wondered if Bret Ivey really could be a suspect. And then it struck me like a bolt of lightning - for all intents and purposes I was done with Blue and Bret Ivey. I'd done what Blue asked me to do, which was find Bret. The stolen truck, the break-in at Blue's house, the break-in at Nicole's house, the mystery over the missing recordings and the band members - none of it was my business. When Aunt Kay told me that I'd done a good job last night, she meant it in the sense that I'd delivered my assignment.

I tried to resist it, but I felt a sense of loss as I sat there alone in The Golden Gate Café that Sunday morning. I almost felt sorry for myself. There I'd gone and done my job. The chase, the rush to find Bret, all of that was exciting. But the rest of the investigative business? I wasn't sure I wanted to pull on yoga pants and take pictures of insurance malingerers with their boom-booms in the air. How boring.

Stan Overheart slid into the booth opposite me and flipped his pony tail over his shoulder. A faded tiger tattoo rippled on his hairy forearm as he readied his order pad. "Hey Maxine. How's tricks?"

"Slow, Stan. Slow. Anything new?"

"Only you. I've never known you to come in so early. What's up?"

I hesitated, only because now it was none of my business. "Nothing."

"It's something. What can I do for you? We're headed into that lull when Sunday School starts. Now's the time."

I struggled to keep my mouth shut. I really did. But maybe my insane degree of nosiness will turn into an asset when I'm a private detective. "Do you remember a group called Poison Ivy and the Dismembered Bunnies?"

Stan's face lit up. "One of the great musical mysteries of our time. Why do you ask?"

I chewed my lower lip. Most of what I was about to reveal was public knowledge, except for the names of the suspects. They would come out soon enough. And I couldn't help myself, I had to figure this out.

I leaned forward. "Can you keep a secret?"

A REAL LIVE CARRIE UNDERWOOD

KADO WIPED THE SWEAT dripping from his chin, then stepped into a slice of shade left by the hungry sun. The black powder smearing the car's exterior revealed no prints, and he could do nothing more until the Medical Examiner arrived. Mitch and Cass were talking to the landscape guy, and Kado winced as she reached up to touch her left shoulder. Cass insisted she was ready to go back to work, but Kado suspected she was in more pain than she revealed, and that single touch told him he was right.

A rumbling sounded from the drive and John Grey backed the medical examiner's van into a spot next to Kado's truck.

"That's a real live Carrie Underwood," Porky Rivers said as he and Grey approached.

"What is?" Kado asked.

The painfully thin black man circled the car. "That song she sings about the chick who's been cheated on. This is what she does to his car."

"The cheated on chick?"

"Yup. Knocks his headlights out with a baseball bat, scratches his paint, slashes his tires, and writes her name in his seats." He peeked through the passenger window. "They missed that one."

"You think somebody did this based on a song?"

"Looks like it," Porky stated. "But those words, the 'NOW it's over, bitch.' That's not part of the song. She just uses her key to mess up his paint."

Kado looked at Grey, who shrugged. "I don't listen to pop music," he said.

Porky scoffed. "It's country, man. We've got to get you out more."

"I'll stick with show tunes, thanks. Is it locked?"

The door opened easily when Kado pulled the handle. The medical examiner was six feet eight inches tall and had to bend almost in half to look in the driver's door. "What is that?"

Kado leaned in next to him. "Some sort of tool."

"Can you get prints?"

"If there are any, yes. The door and handle were wiped down."

Grey eased himself upright and looked over the car at Porky. "Grab the bag. I need to get her temperature."

"I haven't seen any signs of a struggle outside the car. Is it possible she was killed in her seat?" Kado asked. "I'd expect some spatter from that wound."

"Given the amount of blood that's drained down her chest, it looks like he hit her carotid artery or jugular vein. If he'd pulled the tool out, I'd expect spatter. But if he didn't move it, it's possible it's stopping the blood from running out too quickly." He examined her hands where they rested in her lap. "No sign of defensive wounds. Do you want to get photos?"

Kado nodded and took shots from the open driver's and passenger doors, then motioned for Grey to take her temperature. As the medical examiner lifted her blouse and made a small incision, her body moved.

"Grey," Kado said. "There's blood on the headrest."

The ME gently turned Daphne's head. Blood matted her hair.

"Fracture?" Kado asked.

"I'll check during the autopsy. But I'd guess he hit her with something outside the car, then put her in here."

"He did it carefully," Kado said. "There's no smear across the headrest, and she's not a small woman. Whoever did this was strong enough to position her without making a mess."

A mower started and they watched Chewie Rodriquez drive to his trailer. Mitch and Cass walked up the drive.

"Anything?" Mitch asked.

Grey pulled the thermometer from her body and his lips moved as he calculated. "Given her body temperature and the heat, she died late last night or early this morning."

"Is she wearing shoes?" Cass asked.

Kado looked at the foot well. "There's a black tennis shoe on her right foot."

"Its mate is in the roses." She gestured along the drive. "Along with an empty bottle from Cedar Bend Winery."

"I'll print it."

Cass and Mitch circled the car, taking in the damage.

"This looks like 'Before He Cheats', that country song," Cass said.

Porky nodded. "See, I told you."

"And that was about revenge, right?"

Porky nodded again. "She was mad at her boyfriend for cheating and she busted up his car."

Cass looked at Mitch and Kado. "We'd better talk to Blue Ivey."

"You think this is one of Bret's girls?" Mitch asked.

"She's got a big bottom," Cass answered. "Just the kind Blue says her husband likes."

POISON IVY AND THE DISMEMBERED BUNNIES

STAN DELIVERED MY VEGETARIAN omelet and two mugs of fresh coffee, then opened the jukebox and fiddled with it. I'm usually not picky about eating meat, but given the amount of ribeye I consumed Saturday night at the Elliot's, I decided to give my digestive system a break. Sally brought a stack of pancakes and a jug of syrup to the table, and I told her they weren't mine.

"You're too skinny, Maxine. Eat them." And with that proclamation, Sally walked off and Stan slid into the booth.

"Sally has spoken," he said.

"That must be a million calories."

"Only half a million. Listen," he said.

A great caterwauling came from the jukebox. I noticed the Pettigrew brothers exchanging a look as they left the café, and I couldn't help it, I grimaced. "That's them?"

"Poison Ivy and the Dismembered Bunnies, a song called 'Stick to the Trees, Boys'."

"Angry," I said, and took a bite of an exceptionally good omelet.

"It was punk. Everybody was angry."

I listened, surprised the lyrics were so political. "He's bashing Reagan and Thatcher?"

Stan nodded, tapping a thumb to the music. "Lots of music is politically charged, but these first two songs are very explicit. This one focuses on the economic state of the U.S. back in the eighties. The next one is about the Mexican drug cartels."

"Their singer was part of a drug family, wasn't he?"

"Yeah, and that's what broke them up in the end."

"Who was who in this band?"

"BB Ivy and Santiago 'Sonny' Arellano collaborated on lyrics and music. BB played banjo, a little guitar, and mandolin or violin. Sonny played guitar, keyboard, accordion, and washboard. Both sang. Sugar Murphy played bass and Big Billy Garcia played drums and other percussion instruments."

"Is Sugar his real name?"

"Single mom. Flower child."

"Poor kid."

"No doubt."

"Only four guys?"

Stan nodded.

"What's the big mystery?" I asked.

"All the recordings for their second album went missing."

I shrugged. "Mitch mentioned that. So what?"

"They were on the verge, right on the tipping point, of breaking out. Their first album, *Hand to the Throat*, was picking up airtime when they went back into the studio. The band's manager was making a big deal about how explosive the second album would be. A real hot potato, even angrier. Rumor had it they were calling it *Fist Full of Nuts* and BB wanted the band to be photographed naked, grabbing their uncovered nether regions."

"Radical," I said, raising an eyebrow.

"At the time, it was."

"You said Sonny Arellano's being part of a drug family was what caused the band to break up. Mitch said he got killed in Mexico. Is that what you meant?"

"He did disappear while they were recording that second album, and popular theory has it that he resurfaced in Mexico. Some think his family was pissed off about the second song on the first album, 'Tequila Baby, Not Bullets'. It's possible that was true. The song - here it comes - is an outright indictment of the drug violence. Sonny was related to one of the big honchos. He might've been grabbed one night, or he might've honored a summons. I also heard Sonny and BB were at each other's throats. They were kind of a Simon and Garfunkel team: brilliant, but huge rivals for musical credit."

The song had a rough Latin feel and the lyrics damned the violence originating with the Mexican cartels. "He was killed in a gun fight?" I asked.

Stan sipped his coffee. "Never confirmed. He could be alive and living in Mexico for all anyone knows. Or buried in a mass grave with others who objected to the cartels."

"All the recordings from the second album, the unmastered tapes, right?" I asked. Stan nodded. "What happened to them?"

"That's the mystery. The band waited for Sonny but ran out of recording time. They were righteously pissed. Sonny had a beautiful National Triolian guitar, and BB busted it up in a fit when the studio kicked them out. And that was that. The remaining band members rocketed apart. Big Billy and Sugar tried to start another band, but nothing came of it."

"Then why does the second album matter?"

"*Hand to the Throat* was selling well. A solid second album would've pushed them over the top and they would've been into some big money."

"They had a following?"

Stan shrugged. "They were more of an underground band when Sonny disappeared, but that was set to explode. All the anger in *Fist Full of Nuts* was directed at the cartels. Sonny had written a couple of songs for his mother, accusing an uncle of having her murdered to keep her quiet."

"Is it possible somebody got wind of what this second album was about and decided to shut Sonny down?"

"That was one of the theories, but most people think he went to Mexico willingly and for whatever reason, didn't make it back."

"It had to be an important reason for him to leave a recording session."

Stan nodded. "It did."

"If those unmastered tapes still exist, do you think they'd be worth anything?"

"Thirty-plus years later? Who knows? But it's possible."

Sally swept by the table and topped off our coffee. "The Bunnies are scaring the customers."

Stan fiddled with the juke box again and Willie Nelson crooned gospel through the speakers. He winked when he slipped back into the booth. "She's right. Poison Ivy and the Dismembered Bunnies are a bit rough for this town. You think this Bret Ivey is BB Ivy?"

"Mitch does. And it seems too big a coincidence for him not to be."

"What are you thinking?"

"That if he is BB Ivy, he might have the tapes. That would explain why Sugar and Big Billy were chasing him and have trashed his stuff."

"Did you get a picture of the guys who were chasing Bret?"

I nodded. "I got some video as they were leaving a strip club. But it didn't come out very well."

"The Big Billy Garcia I'm talking about has a limp."

My eyebrows shot up. "One of the guys was limping."

"They all had tattoos, if that's any help. Hang on a minute." He disappeared into the back of the café and returned with an album sleeve encased in clear plastic. I reached for it and he pulled back. "I need a solemn promise, Maxine."

I held up my first two fingers. "I promise to do my best. To do my duty to God -"

"That's the Cub Scout Promise, Maxine. Wrong gender. I'm serious. There aren't many of these around. It's worth some money."

"I promise I'll take good care of whatever you've got there."

Stan placed the album cover on the table. A quartet of pimply-faced shirtless teenagers stood defiantly on what might've been the bow of ship, steel cuffs around their necks, dirty bunny ears on their heads, heavy chains stretched tight by Ronald Regan and Margaret Thatcher look-a-likes. Although they each wore an expression of teenage angst, they were unique. One was toned and with his heavy thatch of blond hair could've passed for a surfer dude once the smirk was off his face. Another kid was darker skinned with masses of black hair and a sexy, pouty lower lip. A tall blond kid stood at the back of the group and while he was still skinny, he was broader through the shoulders than the others. The fourth member of the group was shorter and a ghostly white with black hair slicked straight back. A bunny head tattoo was visible on each of the boys, one on the neck, another on the arm, one on the chest, and the fourth peeking from the surfer dude's cut-offs.

Stan pointed to the surfer dude. "That's BB."

Then to kid with the sexy lower lip. "Sonny."

Then to the tall blond at the back. "That's Sugar Murphy, and that one," he touched the ghostly white kid, "is Big Billy Garcia."

"He's not very big," I said.

"Nicknames are like that," Stan said.

I looked closer and felt an itch of familiarity. It was hard to tell if the surfer dude glaring from this forty year old photograph was the Bret Ivey who lived in Forney County and liked big bottoms. I pulled out my phone and found a photo of Bret and Bimbo. I enlarged his face. "What do you think?"

Stan looked back and forth between the two. "Hard to say, but there is some resemblance. If you promise to return this in the same condition, I'll lend it to you for research purposes."

"Is the album in there?"

"Nope. Do you want it?"

I nodded. "It's not really my style, but maybe I'll learn something about BB and the boys."

He opened the juke box again and carefully removed an album, then slipped it into the sleeve and handed it to me. "Mitch could be right about Bret Ivey being BB Ivy." Stan collected his order pad and stuck it in his apron. "But why would Sugar and Big Billy start looking for the tapes after all this time, if BB even has them?"

I thought about the article in *Texas Eats*. "You know Stan, I think it's taken them this long to figure out where to look."

ALL VERY NEAT

KADO PICKED UP THE phone and dialed. Mitch answered on the first ring. "Have you been to see Blue Ivey yet?" Kado asked.

"We're on our way now."

"Cass is with you?"

"She is."

"Stop by the courthouse. I've got news."

———

"SO?" MITCH ASKED AS he pushed opened the forensics room door. Cass followed him in and although he relished the sight of her, Kado wanted to get this briefing done. Mitch was right, if Hoffner saw her in the courthouse and knew she was working a case, he'd blow a gasket.

"Cut and dried," Kado answered. "Hoffner's ready to arrest Blue Ivey."

"What's he got against her?" Mitch asked.

"She didn't go out with him years ago," Cass supplied. "Hurt his ego. And she won with the county over Hoffner's protests when she wanted to open the winery."

Mitch sat at the wide forensics table and studied the reports Kado handed him, scanning each before passing it to Cass. She looked them over and laid them out in neat rows. Truman backed into the room balancing two carry out containers of coffee from The Golden Gate Café and passed them around. John Grey ducked through the doorway, dropped two files on the table, snagged a cup of coffee, and folded his lanky body into a chair.

Mitch absently took a cup, and then looked up at Kado. "This is all very neat."

"Isn't it?"

"Do you believe it?" Cass asked.

"You're not here," Mitch told her. He looked at Kado and then at Truman. "Do you believe it?"

Kado shrugged. "Fingerprints are fingerprints and the places where we found those," he nodded at the rows of paper, "implicate Blue Ivey. Tell them what you think, Scott."

Truman spun a chair around and sat next to Cass. "I think there's about a twenty-five percent chance she killed them."

Mitch raised an eyebrow.

"The DA could make a case that Blue murdered the two girls, based on her fingerprints alone. At Annie's garage apartment, Blue's prints are on the wine bottle. Blue's and Annie's are on the wine glass. Both contain traces of tetrahydrozoline."

"Annie was drugged using eye drops?" Mitch asked.

Grey shifted in his chair. "We won't know for sure until her tox screen comes back."

Mitch chewed his lip. "Were Blue's prints anywhere else in the house?"

"In the kitchen on one of the burner knobs, on the fridge door, and there were a few in the living room," Truman said.

"On the computer, the mouse, or the printer?"

"Nope. Annie's are on both, but they're smudged in some places."

"You said there were no prints on the door knobs?"

"Correct."

"Like someone wiped them off," Mitch stated. Cass was squirming and Mitch relented. "You can be here for a few minutes. Go ahead."

"So you think," she began, "Blue went to Annie's with a roofied bottle of wine, convinced Annie to drink it or pretended to drink with her, and when Annie passed out, Blue strangled her in cold blood, wrote and printed a suicide note, looked up a video on how to tie a noose, and managed to hang a girl who outweighed Blue by at least forty pounds? She wore gloves for some of these activities and didn't for others, and wiped her fingerprints off some surfaces but not others?"

"I said there was about a twenty-five percent chance," Truman clarified. "The stepladder had Annie's prints on it, and again, some of them were smudged."

"Twenty-five percent because..." Cass asked.

"Blue had motive: jealously or revenge."

"Means and opportunity?"

"You'll have to see if you can find eye drops out at the winery or in Blue's house and check her schedule around the time of Annie's death."

"Which was?"

"Wednesday, probably in the afternoon," Grey answered.

"The other seventy-five percent?" Mitch asked.

"This is where it gets interesting," Kado said. "We found a wine glass in the dishwasher with Bret Ivey's and Annie's prints on it."

"With tetrahydrozoline residue?"

"Yes."

"Were his prints anywhere else in the house?"

"Everywhere," Kado said. "Her bedroom, the bathroom, the living room, the desk where the computer sat. We also found guitar parts in a box in her bedroom."

"No guitar?"

"No, but the instrument they came from had been broken. The headstock still had the tuners on it, but it had been broken from the guitar's neck. A piece of the body still had the pickup on it. Another piece had the volume and tone control knobs on it."

Mitch frowned. "Bret went to his house and got pieces of one of the broken instruments and brought them to Annie's apartment?"

"Or pieces from several instruments. But given that she died on Wednesday and the instruments didn't get smashed until Friday night, it's more likely the guitar was at Annie's when it was smashed."

"That's a reasonable bet," Truman said. "The door frame had been recently repaired, and Annie's landlord said someone broke in a week or so ago. They took her DVD player and television, but she didn't file a police report."

"Why not?" Cass asked.

Truman shrugged. "The landlord said she didn't have renter's insurance so a report wouldn't have mattered. When I pushed him, he said he didn't want a report filed either. It might make it difficult to rent the apartment in the future."

"But you don't think the break in is related to her murder?"

"Maybe, maybe not. There's no evidence anyone has broken in since." Truman sipped his coffee. "I think Annie knew her killer and opened the door to him."

PHYSICAL EXERTION

IT WAS AS I finished breakfast at The Golden Gate that I realized how deeply entrenched I was in the mystery surrounding the missing Poison Ivy and the Dismembered Bunnies tapes. The cover for their first album was quite good, once you got past the shock of seeing two world leaders holding four boys as slaves. The composition was solid, their expressions perfect for the situation. It must've generated some controversy at the time.

I stood and stretched, realizing that although I'd been honing my detecting skills over the last few days, I'd neglected my physical fitness. And then I remembered the date I'd had to cancel Friday night with Harvey. I sent him a text and took a sip of coffee. By the time I put my cup back on the table, I had a reply.

With a smile, I picked up the album, waved to Stan and Sally, and prepared for a late morning bout of pleasurable physical exertion.

HALF AN HOUR LATER, I hovered over Harvey, watching with satisfaction as his eyelids slipped shut, closing the window on those gorgeous chocolate eyes. He groaned and I smiled.

"That's it," he whispered. "The sweet spot."

Sweat glistened on his handsome brow and I hunched a shoulder to wipe away a drop from the tip of my nose. I couldn't change position. Not now. I took a moment to look down, relishing the sight of his sculpted torso beneath me. His biceps bulged and he squirmed, finding a better spot.

"Easy now," I said. "No hurry. Nice and slow. That's the way."

He looked up and followed a bead of sweat as it ran from the hollow of my neck down between my breasts. "Oh, Lord. You're killing me."

His muscles contracted and he grunted, then thrust the barbells up and placed them gently in the rack over his shoulders. He lay panting while I stood behind him.

"Nice work," I said. "That was three hundred."

"Told you."

"Seeing is believing, big guy."

Harvey stood and grabbed me by the waist, lifting me over the rack and setting me next to the bench. He waved a hand at the weights. "Your turn."

WHAT ARE THE ODDS?

"DO YOU THINK IT'S more likely Bret killed Annie than Blue did?" Cass asked.

"We think the odds are about even, which takes care of fifty percent of Truman's estimate," Kado said. He looked at the young officer. "Tell them the rest."

"The scene at Annie's has been manipulated, and it's possible someone is trying to make it look like either Bret or Blue killed Annie. Like Cass said, it doesn't make sense that someone would be careful about fingerprints with one thing and not with another. So, I think there's a fifty percent chance someone is trying to set up either Bret or Blue, or provide enough confusion that we'll never identify her killer."

Mitch and Cass digested this, and then Cass asked, "What about Daphne?"

"Everything we have points to Blue."

"What's everything?"

"The wine bottle has Blue's thumb print on it. In blood," Truman said.

Cass raised an eyebrow. "Daphne's?"

"Type doesn't match," Kado said. "It's probably Blue's. Maybe she hurt herself during the attack."

"What else?"

Truman held up a plastic baggie that held a bloody sharpened brass tube protruding from a wooden handle. "This is a round hole cutter, used in pottery making."

"So?"

"Blue Ivey has a reputation as a potter. All the crockery at the winery is stuff she's made. She even has a kiln out there."

"Where?"

"In the workshop next to the winery," Truman said. "I saw it yesterday when we were processing the bottles of weed killer."

Cass cocked her head to one side. "I think I've missed something."

"Me, too," Mitch said. "Why were you processing weed killer?"

Kado looked sheepish. "I should've told you, but we got busy with Annie's apartment and then with Daphne's car this morning. Somebody poisoned some vines out at Cedar Bend Winery on Friday night. They were wilting pretty badly Saturday morning. We swabbed them and the chemical matches the weed killer they use on woody brush. They have several jugs of it in the shop, and a bucket tested positive for the stuff."

"Somebody did it on purpose?" Mitch asked.

"Daphne did it, and given that Blue fired her Friday night, she probably did it on purpose. Her prints were on the bucket and the jug."

"So Blue has two reasons to get even with Daphne: for sleeping with her husband and for killing her vines."

"She had means," Cass added. "If that pottery thing is something she used. Were Blue's fingerprints on it?"

"No," Truman said. "It was wiped clean."

"And again, we'll have to wait and see on opportunity," Mitch said.

"We have another connection between the girls," Kado said. "Truman found pieces of a guitar in the trash at Daphne's house. They were in a big curb-side can the family keeps in the garage."

"The VanZandt's alarm system went off a couple of weeks ago," Truman said. "Their alarm company responded. Someone had broken a window. They stole some small electronics and tried to break into a gun safe. Mr. VanZandt included the smashed guitar on the inventory report he gave to the officer who responded, but he said no one in the family played the guitar and it might've belonged to one of the kid's friends."

"Or maybe to Bret Ivey," Cass said.

"That crossed my mind," Truman said. "But I don't know why he'd leave instruments at his girlfriend's houses. These weren't cheap guitars. One had a Martin headstock and the other was a Gibson with a script logo. That means it was made before 1948, which would make it very valuable."

"I wonder if Bret could've done this?" Mitch asked. "He'd dumped Daphne, right?"

Cass nodded.

"Maybe she wouldn't leave him alone and he decided to get rid of her permanently and make it look like Blue killed her."

"We need to find the man and ask him," Cass said. "Or talk to Blue. Or both."

Mitch looked at Grey. "Did anything come up on autopsy for either girl?"

The medical examiner opened the folders and pushed them across the table. "There are two sets of marks around Annie's neck. The horizontal marks," he demonstrated by placing his hands around his throat, "were left when she was strangled."

"Did the strangling or the hanging kill her?" Cass asked.

"The strangling. Whoever did this crushed her wind pipe."

Cass bent over the photos. "I see finger marks and rope marks along that path. They used both?"

"I think so. He could've crushed her wind pipe with the rope, but it makes sense when you look at the damage that he did it with his hands. The bruising on her neck here," he pointed, "is dark, as if he pushed his thumbs into her throat."

"Or her thumbs," Mitch said. "If the killer is a woman."

Cass lifted an eyebrow.

"She'd have to have strong hands," Grey said. "But yes, a woman could strangle another unconscious woman."

"And then get her into a noose. Did you see any scrapes on the rafter she hung from?" Cass asked Kado.

He looked at Truman. "Pull up the crime scene photos. I don't remember any."

They studied the photos on Kado's computer screen. Cass pointed. "There are no marks on the rafter."

"What are you thinking?" Kado asked.

"He didn't toss the rope over the rafter, hook the noose around her neck, and pull her body upright. Whoever did this was strong enough to throw a rope over the rafter, position the noose at the height he wanted it, and get Annie's head up into the noose without her weight dragging the rope on the rafter."

"You don't think Blue could do that?"

"It would take some upper body strength. Probably more than she has. I think Bret's a more likely candidate for Annie's murder."

Mitch held up Daphne's autopsy file. "A baseball bat? Are you sure?"

"Almost one hundred percent," Grey said. "The shape of the depression would match a bat, and we found blue paint flakes in her scalp. There were no splinters, so the bat is probably metal."

Kado nodded. "That makes sense. Some bits of head- and tail-light glass we swept up have small amounts of blood on them. A lot of blue paint scraped off on the jagged edges."

"Someone whacked her in the head and then went to work on the car," Mitch said.

"Looks that way. We found no blood on the driveway or in the grass."

"There wouldn't have been much," Grey said. He found an autopsy photo. "The split in her skin is small."

Cass turned to Truman. "If there's a fifty percent chance Bret or Blue Ivey killed one or both of these girls, what's the other fifty percent chance?"

"Unknown," Kado said. "There's no evidence anyone else was at either crime scene when these girls died."

"Except the fact that there's no evidence anyone else was there."

"Correct."

Mitch looked at Cass. "You want to be not on duty for a little longer and take a ride out to the winery? We need to find a bat."

KNOCK YOURSELVES OUT

SUNDAY'S LUNCH SERVICE WAS in full swing when Mitch and Cass arrived at the winery. They found Blue in the barrel room, climbing down a ladder attached to a massive dimpled stainless steel tank. She held a damp rag in one hand and a small bucket in the other, and stopped on the third rung from the bottom to remove a face mask and breathe deeply, then joined them.

"Is everything okay?" she asked, unstrapping a tank from her back and turning a knob. Sweat plastered her hair to her head and she turned her reddened face into the breeze created by massive fans blowing across the room to wide open doors.

"What is that?" Mitch asked.

"Breathing equipment. The grapes are fermenting and the amount of carbon dioxide in the atmosphere around the tanks can kill you." She lifted the mask over her head. "It looks extreme, but everybody who works around the tanks, especially this time of year, wears one. That's why we keep the fans going, too. What can I do for you?"

"Daphne's dead," Mitch said.

Blue took a step back. "What happened?"

"She was murdered," Cass said. "Is there somewhere we can talk?"

———

"YOU THINK I KILLED her, don't you?" Blue asked in a low voice.

They were seated at one end of the winery's wide porch. She reached for a glass of tea that was already sweating in the extreme heat. Ice rattled when she lifted it from the table.

Mitch hesitated, then said, "We have evidence that suggests you were at the scene where we found Daphne's body, and both you and Bret were at Annie's."

The glass stopped mid-air. "Annie committed suicide."

Mitch shook his head, his eyes never leaving Blue's.

"She didn't?"

Mitch shook his head again.

"Are you sure?"

He nodded.

Blue placed the glass back in its sweat ring. "Those poor girls." She drew a deep breath. "I didn't kill them, but I doubt you'll take my word for it. I can't imagine Bret killing anyone, either. He's an ass and I can't wait until he's out of my life, but he's not a murderer. What do you need?"

"We'd like to search your home and the winery."

"For what?"

"Evidence."

"I could ask for a warrant, right?"

Mitch nodded.

Her fingers danced in the condensation dripping down the glass, and at last she spoke. "I didn't do it. I doubt Bret did it." She gestured to the wider property. "Knock yourselves out."

SUBMERGED

THEY RETURNED TO THE barrel room in less than an hour. Blue had a mop and bucket and was scrubbing the floor around a tank when they appeared at the wide open doors, faces grim. She wiped sweat from her forehead. "Well?"

Cass held out five plastic bags, each containing a bottle of eye drops. "Are these yours?"

"If they came from the house, probably."

"When was the last time you used them?"

She shrugged. "Over the last few weeks, during harvest. Why?"

Cass didn't answer, but instead held up a soft leather roll. "And these?"

"They're my pottery tools."

Cass rolled the tools out. "Is anything missing?"

Blue frowned. "One of my hole cutters."

"When was the last time you used them?"

"Ages ago. Months. Maybe a year." She looked up at Cass, and then at Mitch, her eyes clouded. "One of my tools was used to hurt these girls?"

Mitch opened a paper bag and pulled out a softball bat. "Is this yours?"

Blue gasped at the ruddy smear on the bat's barrel. "Is that blood?"

"Is this your bat?" he asked again.

Blue closed her eyes and drew several deep breaths, seeming to compose herself. When she looked at him again, her eyes were clear. "Where did you find it?"

"In the garage bay where the Corvette is parked."

She blinked. "Where the Corvette is parked?"

"The end bay farthest from the house. A yellow Corvette, license plate WINE-O is parked there. Is that your vehicle?"

"It's Bret's, but he's not here."

Mitch glanced at Cass and then back at Blue. "Does he drive another vehicle?"

"Occasionally the Range Rover. Were all the cars there?"

"All the bays were full, if that's what you're asking. Where can we find him?"

"If he's here at the winery or somewhere on the property, I'm not aware of it. He wasn't in the house this morning when I left."

"Are you sure?"

She hesitated. "I didn't check all the rooms. But the alarm was still set when I went to leave. The security log should show whether it was disabled in the night and reset."

Mitch motioned to the bat.

Blue nodded. "If you found it in the garage, then yes, it belongs to Bret. Or, more accurately, to the winery. We have a pile of sports equipment used by the staff or for special events."

"Where would your husband be on the property?" Mitch asked.

"We have a hundred acres. About twenty of it is vines, but most of it is uncleared woodland. He could be anywhere." She pulled her phone out. "If he's here and has heard about Annie and Daphne, maybe he'll answer."

She tapped a contact and lifted the phone to her ear. After a moment, a distorted double ring sounded. Blue looked around the barrel room. "Do you hear that?"

Mitch and Cass moved away from the doors, heads cocked.

The ringing stopped and she looked down at her phone. "Voice mail."

"Try again," Mitch said.

The distorted ringing sounded again. Cass stopped in the middle of the wide barrel room and turned in a slow circle. "Turn off the fans."

Blue did, and tried calling again. Mitch and Cass honed in on the massive silver tank where Blue had been working.

"It's coming from in there," Cass said. She started for the ladder welded to the side of the tank.

"No," Blue called. "Don't go up there."

Cass turned, a frown on her face. "Why not?"

"The carbon dioxide. That's a tank of Vermentino grapes. The cap is raised to let the gasses out so the tank doesn't explode. You need the right safety equipment. I can go up."

"No, ma'am. If Bret's phone is in there, the tank could be a crime scene." Cass looked at Mitch. "What do we do?"

He shrugged. "Call the fire department."

AN OBSCURE BUNNY BAND

"WHAT'S UP WITH YOU, Maxine?" Harvey asked in that gravelly voice. His gym was now open for business and gaining traction from the late Sunday morning crowd. Energizing music with a steady beat thrummed through the speakers, and a barrage of running shoes pounded the treadmills in a steady cadence. Although my personal session with him was over, Harvey still hovered.

I was rowing my little heart out when he spoke, and looked up with a start. "What do you mean?"

"You're not your usual snarky self. You're preoccupied, which is out of character. You need to talk more than you need to work out. What's up?"

I followed him to the juice bar and accepted a glass of freshly squeezed orange juice, then opened up. Maintaining client confidentiality as best I could, I told him.

"You're hung up over an obscure Bunny band that might or might not've recorded a second album back in the eighties?" he said, summarizing my plight.

"Essentially, yes."

Harvey smiled at a trio of girls who were headed for a Pilates class. "Why do you care if the tapes are missing?"

"It bothers me that these guys have turned up all of sudden. Why now? What's changed?"

"You think they're messing with this other guy, the one who played the banjo?"

"I do."

"Then go find out, Miss Private Eye. And don't come back until you have the answer. This mystery is interfering with my libido."

THE UNLUCKY HARVEST HAT

THE BARREL ROOM WAS a hive of activity as a fire crew helped two burly men into breathing apparatus that looked like scuba gear. After signaling that air was flowing, they hurried across the room.

Blue's mop was still in its bucket, and it leaned against the tank. Kado had already dusted the ladder's handrail for prints, and the two men climbed up the steps to the catwalk running above the tanks.

Blue put her hands on her hips. "Be careful," she called. "Those grapes make some of our most expensive wine." After a moment, she added, "And don't you dare take off those masks."

One man held his thumb up in acknowledgment, then helped his partner raise the cap higher. They eased a net on a long pole into the tank and lowered it until the pole was nearly submerged. Together, they swept through the fermenting grapes. After a few moments, they stopped and looked at each other, then down at the crowd watching from below. One reached in the tank and withdrew an object. He let it drip and then held up a sodden mass.

Blue gasped.

"What is that?" Mitch asked.

"Bret's hat," she whispered. "His lucky harvest hat."

––––––––––––

"I'LL KILL HIM IF he's not in there," Blue fumed, watching a hose pulse as fermenting grapes pumped through it. "Do you know much this will cost us? Arturo's moving the wine to a new tank. He's an amazing vintner, but even he can't save it. That means no Vermentino unless we buy the grapes in, and there's not a chance this late in the season. Every grape is sold. We'll have to wait another year."

She paced behind the yellow crime scene tape separating the barrel room from the rest of the winery and the firefighters edged out of her way. Mitch and Cass watched her stalk back and forth, a caged cat with nowhere to go. At last she turned and disappeared into the dining room, returning shortly with a trio of waitstaff bearing trays of wood-fired pizzas. Blue cleared paperwork from a desk in a corner, and they placed the food and cutlery on it. She motioned the firefighters over. "Eat. The girls will bring tea and water."

Kado climbed down from the catwalk and took his face mask off. Mitch and Cass stepped away from Blue to join him.

"Any prints on the cap?" Mitch asked.

"Not a one."

Cass watched the wine maker adjusting a pump and the hoses. "Do you think he's in there?"

Mitch shrugged. "I'd hate to see Blue get hold of him if he's not." He motioned to the mop and bucket. "She was mopping around that tank earlier, Kado."

The forensics man squatted. "I'll take a sample and we'll see what it is. Fermenting grapes, I'd imagine."

"From that tank?"

"Maybe. You think she's washing away evidence?"

"She wiped down the tank and mopped the floor. Seems like it to me."

"Hold up," Cass said. "All we've got right now is a hat that might belong to Bret Ivey, and his phone ringing in that tank. Which makes me wonder, how could a phone survive in that much liquid?"

"Cases are great nowadays," Mitch said. "I got Darla a waterproof one after she dropped her last phone in the tub."

"She was taking a bath and talking on the phone?" Kado asked. "Women do that?"

"Heck no. My wife is a sophisticated multi-tasker. She was giving Zeus a bath and talking on the phone. That's when she dropped it."

"If the phone survived," Cass said, "we can see who he was talking to and texting."

"It looks open and shut to me, Cass," Mitch said. "Blue found out he was cheating, killed the competition, and then killed him."

"I don't think it's that straight-forward," Cass answered. "If she was running around killing these girls, why would she hire Maxine to find Bret?"

"So she could kill him, too."

"That wouldn't be very smart, would it? She would've been better off to keep her mouth closed and let the bodies turn up where they turned up. We'd struggle to figure out who killed the girls."

"Except that we have evidence. Kado, do you have enough gear here to test the softball bat for blood and fingerprints?"

"It's too convenient, Mitch," Cass persisted.

"Cass, most people are dumb when it comes to killing. They get in a fit and smack somebody in the head and think nobody will know they did it, or they're too dumb to clean up after themselves."

They watched as Kado tested the bat's barrel for blood. "Positive," he said, and dusted its length for fingerprints. "It's clean."

He turned to the eye drop bottles next, and lifted several sets of fingerprints. He laid the cards out side by side and then stacked them into piles. He scanned three images into his laptop and compared them to saved files. "Blue's prints are on all of them, and one bottle has another set I can't match out here."

Cass looked back at the tank. "If he's in there, do we arrest her?"

Mitch nodded. "I think we have to."

Arturo turned off the pump but left the hoses in place and turned on the fans again before joining Blue at the crime scene tape. Kado, Mitch, and Cass walked over.

"I can't believe Bret would do something like this," Arturo said. He was a strong man with a serious demeanor. "Work around a tank while the wine is fermenting. He knows the dangers."

"I haven't understood anything Bret is doing for a while now, have you?" Blue asked.

The wine maker grimaced. "No. It's all totally out of character."

"Maybe the carbon dioxide got to him and he dropped his phone and hat," Blue said. "But I don't understand why he didn't tell someone, or try to fish them out himself." She looked at Kado. "Who should help you?"

Kado shook his head. "I can manage."

"Not alone. Even though it's been drained, I want someone outside to pull you back if you're overwhelmed." She motioned to her wine maker. "Arturo knows the most about working around these tanks. Are you happy that he helps you?"

"How about Arturo and one of the firefighters?" Mitch said. "That would give you Arturo's knowledge and somebody independent on the outside."

Kado nodded.

"You'll need wellies and a shovel," Arturo said.

"A shovel? What for?"

"The wine is gone," Arturo said. "But the dead yeast remains."

THE BODY IN THE TANK

CASS ONLY REALIZED SHE was holding her breath when her body forced her to breathe again. Her relationship with Kado was still young, but her heart had already cracked open to let him in. Blue stopped pacing and watched as Kado disappeared into the dark hole, then started walking again. Cass fought the urge to join her. Mitch and the firefighters stared at the dark hatch as if they could will Kado to come back out.

Cass turned her back to the tank and touched her left shoulder, the place where a bullet had passed through her flesh only weeks ago. The gesture was reflexive rather than driven by pain, and she'd almost broken herself of the habit. But when she was stressed, her body seemed to need to touch that weak spot, almost as a reminder that she'd pulled through bad situations before.

Through the roar of the fans, she heard a commotion and turned to see Arturo struggle to grasp a form covered in a white-ish paste. Head and shoulders emerged first from the hatch. Before Cass could stop her, Blue slipped under the crime scene tape.

"Oh my God. Is that Bret?" A fireman caught her around the waist and shoulders, and Blue strained against him. "Is it him?"

Arturo grunted with the body's weight and Mitch and another fireman grabbed the shoulders. The rest of the body slithered through the opening like a slippery infant sliding from the womb, and Kado crawled from the hatch behind it. His face was streaked with sweat and he held up a dripping rectangle. "The phone," he croaked.

Blue squirmed harder and broke free, then fell to her knees next to the motionless body. She wiped gently at the pasty face, clearing sludge from eyes, nose, and mouth. "Bret?" she whispered. "Bret?"

Arturo touched her shoulder. "Blue."

She shook him off and scraped the yeast from his ears. "Bret? Can you hear me?" When he didn't respond, she put her head to his chest and murmured his name.

Cass exchanged a look with the fireman and mouthed, "Check."

He lifted a bushy brow but pulled a stethoscope from a bag and knelt beside Blue. "I need to check for a pulse, ma'am." When she tightened her grip, he added, "I won't hurt him, I promise."

Blue straightened and stroked Bret's forehead. One side of her face was matted with yeast and tears traced a path through the white sludge on her cheek. The fireman struggled with the slippery top few buttons of the shirt and slipped the stethoscope inside. He listened for several moments, watching the chest and moving the stethoscope around, and then looked up at Cass and gave a slight shake of his head.

"I'm sorry," he said to Blue, and eased away from the grieving woman who only moments ago had promised to kill her husband.

A RICH WIFE

I TOOK HARVEY'S ADVICE and cycled home and showered in record time. I carefully unsleeved Poison Ivy and the Dismembered Bunnies' first album and put it on my turntable, then plugged my headphones in. No point irritating the neighbors with music like this, was there?

I plopped down on the red leather sofa with my laptop, a glass of sparkling spring water, the shotgun within reach, and folk punk on low volume. My cursor found its way to the Google search bar, and I wondered what to type. Compulsion might be my middle name, but like Harvey said, who cares about a thirty-year-old musical mystery?

I did. I was no longer employed by Blue Ivey and didn't understand why I couldn't let go of the puzzle surrounding Bret's band. I needed to know where the missing tapes were, and what happened to Sonny Arellano.

Undaunted by my doubts, I typed in the band's name and clicked links. Stan's story matched the online version of the band's history, with the exception of a minor detail. An update on the Arellano crime family noted recent sightings of a man believed to be Sonny Arellano who was acting in a leadership capacity in the drug cartel. My high school Spanish was rusty, but I worked my way through a news briefing on a Mexican website where the government said it believed this rumor was untrue, that the family was led by one of the four sisters. One mystery solved. Maybe.

I sat back and sipped my water, choosing to believe the reports were true. It seemed more than coincidental that Sonny was spotted in Mexico in the months leading up to the break-in at Bret's houses. If Sonny Arellano was alive and heading a drug cartel, why would he be interested in finding tapes from an old recording session, if the things even existed?

I printed the articles and decided to look deeper into my main man, Bret Ivey. If he'd misspelled his name on one marriage certificate, who was to say he hadn't done so on others? While incredibly useful, Cindy's dive into the databases on Saturday morning had been perfunctory. It was time for some serious searching.

Since I didn't have the keys to the kingdom, i.e., the usernames and passwords for the industrial strength databases, I started with public marriage and divorce records in the California wine country where Stony Pike Winery, now owned by Bret Ivey's ex-wife Imelda Sanchez, was located. I found a marriage certificate from 2001. A divorce certificate from 2006. No other records for Bretton Baxter Ivey. Recent articles from local newspapers and magazines were flattering about Stony Pike and the woman who owned it. They referenced her tough upbringing as one of eight children born to immigrant parents. She had a knack for numbers and made a bold move into day-trading that morphed her initial baby-sitting money investment of one thousand dollars into a seven-figure fortune in the 1990s. She 'retired' and moved into wine-making as a joint venture with her new husband in 2001.

Aha. A rich wife.

To make sure I had the full picture, I searched Bretton Baxter Ivey, and then swapped the first and middle names. I did it again with Ivy. I tried last names only. Big fat goose egg on all fronts.

A map of California showed the counties neighboring the one where Bret and Imelda married and divorced, so I expanded my search geographically in widening circles. I hit pay dirt on the third county to the south: Bretton Baxter Ivy climbed on the marriage treadmill with a Mary Sterling way back in 1983. They divorced in 1987. I searched local newspapers but online archives were sketchy before the mid-90s.

Probably not a rich wife.

I expanded again.

Bret moved farther south and in 1991 married a Susan Spikes. They divorced in 1997. The local society magazine was helpful. Susan was the only child of the man who owned the local bank. She and Bret Ivy met while he worked for her father. According to the tidbits of gossip in the local paper, Susan dumped Bret for the rich son of another banker. The merger of the two banks swiftly followed. Local gossip hinted Bret was quite the eligible bachelor given the windfall he received in the divorce.

Another rich wife.

I opened a note pad. Bret and his marital activities were confusing.

I worked my way to the California counties bordering Mexico, and decided my abilities didn't extend to prying open the official records of another country. Yet. So I went north again, back to the counties radiating up and out from Imelda and her winery. And hit the lottery once again.

Baxter Bretton Ivye married a Karen Smythson in 1999. They divorced in 2004. For the record, Karen was the daughter of a local artist of some note. Karen ran his gallery in a little seaside town up near the border with Oregon.

Yet another rich wife.

My note pad was a mess, so I organized his marriages into timelines and all was revealed. Well, as much as I could gather so far. Bret started his polygamous habits in 2001, when he married Imelda

Sanchez Ivey in California. At that time, he was already married to Karen Smythson Ivye. He married Nicole Ivy in 2002 for a total of three wives at one time. He didn't unburden himself until 2003 when he divorced Karen, and then again in 2006 when he and Imelda divorced.

Three names, Ivy, Ivey, and Ivye, and I finally understood why they changed.

I drained my glass of now room-temperature water, stood, and stretched. I considered calling it quits. After all, this was my time. The dirt I was digging on Bret Ivey wouldn't matter one whit to Blue. But that wasn't the point.

I was angry. Angry at the way he'd lied to and presumably manipulated these women, much as he had Blue. Men like that weren't worth the price of the leather on their soles. They needed to be hunted down and dealt with.

I didn't stop to consider what I'd do with the information. I settled back on the couch, changed my search references to Texas, and went at it again.

THOSE THINGS'LL GIVE YOU CANCER

BIG BILLY GRUNTED AND rolled onto his side, squinting at the light flowing through the filthy windows. A buzzing sounded and he swatted the air around his head before realizing it was the cell phone. He raised up on one arm and swayed, letting the nausea pass, then snatched the phone from the floor. He poked Sugar. "Wake up and answer this."

Sugar peered through gummy eyes. "Wha?"

"Answer it."

"My head, man." He squinted at the screen. "It's a message."

"Listen to it."

"You listen to it."

Billy lay back and put his arm over his eyes. "Nope. Those things'll give you cancer."

"They've done studies -"

"They lie so you'll buy more phones."

"You don't care if I get cancer?" Sugar asked.

"No."

"Don't say that. Of course you care."

"No, I don't. Listen to it."

Sugar did, and slowly sat up, his mouth hanging open.

"What is it?"

He carefully closed the phone. "There's two messages. One bawling us out for getting drunk last night. The other one says BB's dead."

Billy sat up, one hand to his head. "He's what?"

"BB's dead."

"Who killed him?"

"He doesn't know." Sugar pulled at his nose. "You know what this means?"

"What?"

"We're done."

"What do you mean?" Billy asked.

"If BB's dead, it doesn't matter anymore."

Billy eased to his feet, opened a bottle of water, and took a long drink. "Even if BB's dead, it's still out there."

"But it doesn't matter anymore. 'Cause BB's dead."

Billy sat at the grungy kitchen table. "Let's face it, man. He'll never let it go. If it's out there, somebody could still use it against him. No." He breathed a long sigh. "We're not done. Not yet."

SOMETIMES IT AIN'T WHAT IT IS, IT'S WHAT IT AIN'T

CASS PULLED MITCH TO one side. "I don't like this."

"You don't think she did it?"

"I don't think it adds up."

"We've convicted people on less, Cass."

She looked back at the woman on the floor, cradling her dead husband's head. "There's too much inconsistency in the evidence from the three scenes."

"Evidence is rarely clear cut."

"I know, but…"

"But you still don't like it."

"Right. And once you make an arrest, the DA walks down this path with this woman, and we could miss the real killer."

Mitch winced and shifted his stance. "Who else had motive to kill those two girls and Bret? It's not a coincidence that two of Bret's girlfriends ended up dead, and he dies right after they do."

"We don't know his death wasn't natural."

"You think an experienced wine-maker like Bret Ivey would work around these tanks without safety gear?"

"Maybe he was drunk, or showing off, and fell in."

"Cass, that's stretching it."

"We've seen stranger."

"If I wait for Grey to tell us whether Bret was murdered? Would you feel better about arresting Blue then?"

"I don't know. So much doesn't make sense. Why wipe down the bat but leave a wine bottle with your prints on it at a crime scene? Why wipe down parts of Annie's apartment but leave your fingerprints on the wine bottle and glass that had tetrahydrozoline in them?"

"I agree that not everything ties up neatly, but when you take all three deaths -"

"If Bret was murdered," Cass said.

"If Bret was murdered," Mitch echoed. "Then when you take all three deaths, Blue is the only suspect who makes sense." Mitch studied her, his blue eyes thoughtful. "If I don't arrest her, how do I explain that?"

"Call her a person of interest but keep looking for suspects."

"Based on what? What evidence points to another suspect?"

"Inconsistency and absence of evidence," Cass said. "That's all we have."

"Sometimes it ain't what it is, it's what it ain't," he murmured, and then blew out a breath of air. "I hate to do it, but I'll call Hoffner and see what he thinks."

"He'll want her arrested. That's three murders cleared in short order, and that's all Hoffner cares about."

———————————

MITCH STEPPED OUTSIDE AND stood in the shade from the winery's front porch, away from the noise of the fire truck and fans. Hoffner answered on the second ring. Mitch explained the situation and asked the sheriff's opinion.

"Murder evidence rarely comes tied up with a bow, Mitch."

"True," Mitch agreed. "But Blue Ivey's got a lot of good will around here. I wanted to know what you think before I arrested her."

"Good will for pizza, Mitch. There's nothing to making a pizza."

Mitch blinked. "There's more on the menu than pizza. And the wines have won some awards. There's even an article in -"

"I've seen it," Hoffner growled. "A bunch of fluff."

The medical examiner's van rumbled into the driveway and Mitch motioned them to the back of the winery. "Grey just got here."

The sheriff grunted. "Wait and see what he says. If Ivey was murdered, arrest his wife. She's arrogant enough to have done this and think she can get away with it."

"Do you think she's the type to sue for false arrest?"

"With her ego, probably, but we'll deal with that if it happens."

"And the press?" Mitch asked. "You know they'll turn up once word gets around that we've arrested her."

"You just bring her in quietly. I'll handle the press."

That's what I was afraid of, thought Mitch.

OPTIMISTIC THINKING

WHEN MITCH RETURNED TO the barrel room, Grey and Porky were hovering over Bret Ivey's body and talking in hushed tones. Blue and Cass were gone, and Mitch waited with Kado at the crime scene tape.

"Can you do anything with that phone?" Mitch asked.

"If it was ringing in the tank, we should be able to extract whatever data's on it," Kado said. "Depends how long it takes to crack the password."

"If there is one."

"That's the kind of optimistic thinking we need."

Grey motioned them over. "I don't know for certain that he was dead when he went into the tank, but chances are that he was." He and Porky turned Bret's body, and he pointed to the back of the man's head, still covered in yeast. "There's an indentation, similar to the one we found in Daphne's skull."

"Baseball bat?" Mitch said.

"I'll know for sure later, but from what I can feel right now, he was hit once."

Mitch looked at Kado. "You'll test that bat for more than one source of blood?"

The forensics man nodded.

Mitch turned back to Grey. "So this is definitely murder."

"Given the trauma to his skull, I can't see him staggering up the ladder and falling in without some sort of help. If he was alive when he went in, he might've been mobile. More likely, he was hit in the head and either died instantly or was rendered unconscious."

"And then put in the tank," Mitch said. "Which would need someone who was strong enough to lift him, carry him from wherever the attack took place, and up those steps."

"And smart enough to know they needed safety gear," Kado added. "That probably explains why Blue was cleaning the tank and floor. When Bret went in, wine splashed out."

Mitch straightened and sighed. "If he was stunned, Grey, he could've walked here under his own steam?"

Grey shrugged. "Maybe, with help getting here and up those steps. You don't have any idea where he was attacked?"

"No. His Corvette is in the garage, but there's no sign of a struggle. Kado, it might be worth checking for blood spatter there, but I suspect he was hit either in here or near the winery building. I can't see someone carrying him very far."

"I'll see if Truman can join me and we'll check out both." He looked at the ladder wrapped around the tank. "You think Blue couldn't have done this if Bret was unconscious?"

Mitch shook his head. "He's what? Six feet or more and weighs one-eighty or one-ninety? She's too small to lift him."

"But if he was only stunned…"

Mitch looked towards the dining room. "Then I'd better go get her."

IN CHARGE OF SOFT THINGS

BLUE WAS AT HER desk writing on a pad of paper. Several staff stood around taking notes and looking stunned. The yeast caked in her hair was drying and she absently tried to rake her fingers through it, then gave up. Cass was watching from a corner of the room and joined Mitch as he entered.

"I heard Grey's van. What did he say?" she asked in a low voice.

"Bret was hit on the head, possibly with a baseball bat."

She nodded. "You're going to arrest her?"

"I have to." Cass was silent for several moments and Mitch eyeballed her. "What?"

"I don't think she did it, Mitch."

"We need evidence someone else did."

"I know."

"So?"

"Since Sheriff Hoffner would freak out if he saw me at the station, I'll do a little nosing around on my own."

"You really don't think she committed these murders?" Mitch asked.

"I can't reconcile her behavior to that of a murderer."

"Maybe she's a sociopath."

"If so, she's a very good one who can fake empathy. It's possible, but it doesn't feel right. I need more."

"I still have to arrest her."

"Hoffner?"

171

Mitch nodded.

"You won't stop me from investigating outside your investigation?"

"Nope, and I'll keep you posted on what Kado and Grey learn. You've got a good gut. We need to follow it."

Cass headed for the wide doors of the barrel room.

"Where're you going?" Mitch asked.

"To get started," she said, and was gone.

———————

BLUE RAISED ONE FINGER in a 'just a minute' gesture when Mitch approached. "I hope I'll be back tomorrow, but you've got staffing assignments for the next week," she said to the small group of employees who looked on with disbelieving faces. "The daily menu is ready and food orders are in. Arturo, you may have to start harvest without me, but you've got everything you need, right?"

"Right, boss. But -"

She cut him off. "Empty the Vermentino. We'll never sell it now that we've had a body in it." Her voice hitched on the word 'body' but she regained her composure. "The publishers are sending the same photographer who covered white grape harvest to take photographs next week. Please give her what she needs." Two employees were crying, and she stood to hug them. "I didn't kill him. Or Daphne. Or Annie. None of them. I trust our detectives to find out what really happened, so give them all the help you can."

A crash sounded from the kitchen. Blue closed her eyes. "Chef, keep Emily away from the dishes."

"But she's a waitress," he protested.

"Put her in charge of soft things. Maybe the laundry." She turned to Mitch and held her hands out. "How's the food in prison?"

"Unless you're planning to make a run for it, I don't think we'll need handcuffs. And you're going to the county jail, not to prison. The food stinks, but maybe you can give the kitchen convicts some tips." He eyed her. "Why don't you take a shower first? You're all crusty and the showers at the jailhouse are clean, but the towels are rough."

"You trust me to go home and do that?"

His eyes twinkled. "I'll put officers at your front and back doors, just to be safe."

She touched her stiffened hair. "I hope it's not too noisy in prison. I could use some rest."

COUNTING THE WIVES

I WAS ADMIRING MY timeline of Bret Ivey Ivy Ivye's marriages when a thudding sounded at my door. I picked up the shotgun and peeked out a window. Cass stood on the mat carrying an easel and several plastic bags. I unlocked the deadbolts and let her in.

"Three flights is a long way up," she complained.

"What's all that?" I asked as I stuck my head outside to check for strangers before throwing the deadbolts again.

She put everything on my dining room table and turned to face me. "You really want to be a detective?"

I nodded.

"We found Bret Ivey in a tank of wine."

"Doing what?"

"Not breathing."

It sunk in. "He's dead?"

She nodded.

I buried my head in my hands and groaned.

"That's an extreme reaction for a man you've never met." Cass headed for the kitchen. "Glasses?"

I dragged behind her, moping, and pointed at a cabinet. "I just did all this work figuring out who Bret was married to and when. All that time. A total loss."

She filled a glass with ice and water and sat at the island. "How many wives has he had?"

"I've found four in California and three in Texas."

Cass choked. "Seriously?"

"I may have missed some. I need to finish Texas and there are forty-eight states I haven't checked yet."

Her face took on a ferocious look that would terrify most people, but just told me she was thinking. "Show me."

———————

CASS FINISHED WRITING ON a giant sticky note and stuck it on the wall in my study.

"That won't hurt my paint, right?"

"Nope." She stepped back and studied the notes she'd copied from my pad, which filled several of the giant stickies. She stuck those up, too. "What a guy."

"Yeah, but so what?"

"What do you mean, so what?"

"What does it matter how many wives he's had? He's dead now. If they're smart, they all took out life insurance policies on him."

Her smile was sneaky. "If we're lucky, they all took out life insurance policies on him."

"What are you talking about?"

"We need a suspect."

"For what?"

"Bret's murder, of course."

My lips formed themselves into a perfect little 'o'. "He was murdered?"

"I didn't mention that?"

"No, you didn't."

"Did I mention Mitch arrested Blue for all three murders?"

I gaped. "Three?"

"Guess not. Daphne was killed last night." She turned to the kitchen. "I haven't eaten since breakfast. What have you got?"

I was still reeling from the news that three people were dead and Blue was in jail. It took a moment for me to respond. "Salad, yogurt, some hummus."

Cass stepped back from the fridge. "Real food, Max. Do you have a grill?"

I nodded.

"Heat it up. I'll be back."

BOOKED

"SUZANNE BLUE IVEY," SHE said. "No, a double 'n' in Suzanne. Blue like the color. Does it always smell like this?"

"Like what?" the booking officer asked.

She waved a hand under her nose. "Overcooked cabbage and wait, is that body odor or," she sniffed delicately, "Stinking Bishop?"

"We don't have any preachers or other religious people in the jail right now, ma'am."

"Stinking Bishop is not a member of the clergy, it's a pungent cheese."

He gazed up at her, his murky green eyes confused. "Prisoners do eat a fair amount of cheese, but usually American or cheddar. Hold out your right hand and relax, please."

Blue sighed and complied. "No wine with dinner, I suppose?"

He narrowed his eyes. "No, ma'am. Forney County is dry and this jail is the tightest ship around."

"What's your name?"

His tongue poked from the side of his mouth as he examined her fingers. "Officer Hugo Petchard. Put the four fingers from your right hand on this pad, please. No, like this. We have to do it right."

"Your father must be Dr. Petchard, right?"

"Right."

"Ah," Blue said before she could stop herself. Dr. Petchard was a frequent patron of the winery, an officious little man who enjoyed slinging his position around. But he was a generous tipper and always bought a few bottles of wine to take home, so Blue couldn't complain. It seemed the son had inherited his father's inclination towards self-importance.

Petchard looked up. "What does that mean?"

She thought quickly. "You favor him."

That seemed to satisfy him and he bent to his work again, rolling her fingers precisely across the ink pad and the fingerprint card, then tossing the card and rolling her fingers again. He hummed quietly and Blue finally recognized the off-key tune as "Jailhouse Rock" by Elvis Presley.

A half smile crossed her lips. "You enjoy your work, don't you, Officer Petchard?"

"There's nothing I'd rather do than police work," he answered.

I'll bet, she thought, and waited patiently as he inked and rolled her fingers again.

BIRD IN THE HAND

CASS RETURNED WITH GROCERY bags overflowing. A new health food store had opened in Arcadia, and she had taken full advantage of their stock. She'd picked up organic chicken, brown rice, and a colorful variety of vegetables. We put the rice on to cook and prepared a marinade for the chicken, then stood in front of the giant sticky notes again.

"We know Blue and Nicole are still alive. What about the rest of these women?" Cass asked.

I shrugged.

"Any children?" she asked.

I shrugged.

"Maxine." She wiggled her fingers at my laptop. "Find out. Each of his wives or ex-wives is a potential suspect, along with any children from those marriages."

By the time the rice was almost done, I'd scoured birth records for children with the last name of Ivy, Ivey, and Ivye with no hits. For a man with such a busy sex life, he could lead seminars on birth control. The only one of his ex-wives to have died was the first, Mary Sterling. Her death certificate was dated early this year.

Cass headed to the kitchen and I followed, then chastised her for stepping onto the balcony without checking for threats. She sighed as she put the chicken on the grill and shut the lid. "I appreciate your safety standards, Maxine, but really, how likely is it that the guy who raped both of us is out there," she poked tongs at the pool area, "waiting for one of us to appear?"

"That's not the point."

"Isn't it? If you want to detect effectively, you'll have to lose some of the paranoia. A little is good. Too much makes you stand out." She left the French doors unlocked as she walked back into the kitchen, and I struggled not to flip the deadbolts home. Thankfully, the doors were in full view of the kitchen island and I took comfort in that thought while she sprinkled olive oil and seasonings on the sliced veggies and wrapped them in foil. "You know, those are only the women Bret made legitimate," she said. "There's no telling who else he was catting around with."

"An illegitimate child?"

Cass stepped into the study and updated the list of potential suspects on the giant pad of stickies, now perched on the easel. I stayed in the kitchen and kept an eye on the French doors. Cass might be right, but paranoia is a hard habit to break. I followed her back to the balcony and watched as she flipped the chicken, which smelled utterly heavenly, and placed the foil package on a shelf inside the grill.

"You really think Blue is innocent?" I asked.

"I think these three cases deserve more examination before we're sure she did it."

"But since Hoffner has an arrest, he won't want to look any more?"

She nodded.

"Why not?"

"Bird in the hand," she said. "Even if I were at work, it would be hard to convince him to look at more suspects. The DA could make a case and probably get Blue convicted of killing all three of them."

I hesitated before asking my next question. "Did you ask her?"

"She says she didn't."

I thought about that. It seemed logical that even the guilty would protest their innocence. I didn't know Blue well, and though she had threatened to kill Bret on an occasion or two, she didn't seem the type to follow through. "What about Poison Ivy and the Dismembered Bunnies?" I asked.

"Why would one of Bret's old band mates kill him and two of the women he'd slept with?"

"I don't know, but shouldn't we add them to the board? The wrecked music rooms are too coincidental to ignore." I filled her in on the band's history as delivered by Stan Overheart that morning, and recent sightings of Sonny Arellano.

"I guess it's a possibility, but we need a motive."

"Do you want to hear the album Stan loaned me?"

"I don't know. Do I?"

She took the food off the grill and I followed her inside, salivating. "Why don't you cook more often?"

"Are you kidding? Bruce would want to share duties once the new wears off the kitchen. The last thing I want to do is sweat over a stove when I get home from work. It's therapeutic for him. We're all better off if Bruce thinks he's the only Elliot with culinary skills."

Cass filled a plate for me and though I protested at the portions, she tutted, telling me again I was too thin. I caved and was glad I did. We ate and I played the album for Cass. Between bites, she made notes on the lyrics, only wincing once or twice.

"What do you think?" I asked.

"I wouldn't buy it, but it must've appealed to quite a few people if they were going gold." She ate another bite of chicken. "Those first two songs are very political. Maybe the lyrics from the second album were even harsher, and somebody wanted to stop the band, so they stole the tapes. I have no clue why those two guys would be coming back for Bret, but there's no evidence they were near the murder scenes."

I wrote the band name on the sticky anyway. "Anything's a possibility until it isn't."

"I can live with that."

I stood and cleared the table. "What now?"

Cass stretched, but gingerly, favoring her shoulder. She pulled her phone out and checked it. "It's only eight. Let's go to the gun range. I've got a surprise."

FIRST NIGHTER

BLUE LAID BACK ON her jailhouse bed and found it bearable. The blanket was rough, but the mattress was thick enough that she couldn't feel the springs beneath it. The toilet was a lidless affair, but at least it had a wide lip as a seat and didn't smell to high heaven.

For the first time in weeks, Blue let herself relax. She absently rubbed ink from her fingers with the alcohol wipe and then deepened her breathing, slipping into a doze. She awoke refreshed. A still mind always improved her perspective and helped her find solutions.

Being arrested for murdering three people wasn't traumatizing for Blue, simply because she knew she was innocent. She also believed that the police, perhaps barring Sheriff Hoffner, wanted to convict the right person, not simply the most convenient person. And that was the nub of the matter, wasn't it? Who was the right person? The guilty party?

If she thought through her almost five years with Bret, she could point to nothing that would lead to a suspect or motive. No negative interactions with suppliers, no disturbances at the winery, no disgruntled neighbors irritated about late night traffic or noise. Her mind flipped through the list of employees they'd had since Blue had joined Bret, and she found none who had left on such a bad note they'd need violent revenge. Instead, there were highlights from their time together. The first set of tables and chairs Bret had built and placed in the winery's wide open dining room. The first set of dishes she had thrown and fired. Opening the first bottle of wine and finding it not just good, but excellent. The full house the first night the restaurant opened and having to find outside seating for overflow guests.

Wonderful memories, now tarnished as she questioned whether Bret had slept with employees, suppliers, customers. She couldn't believe he was dead. His huge personality was a force of nature, and she would miss him. But Blue had been missing him for months now, grieving over the man she'd loved and their disintegrating marriage. His death only added another layer to her grief. In reality, she was already moving forward. She was simply the kind of woman who wouldn't be kept down.

Since she could find no possible suspects or motives in the spaces she and Bret inhabited together, she concentrated on the spaces that existed between them. Those times when she and Bret were apart, which were many given their busy schedules. The winery was such a small business there were rarely opportunities for the two of them to travel together. A Main Street open house in one city usually ran on the same weekend as a food fair in another. A catering event for a business in Shreveport happened on opening night for the Texas Wine and Grape Growers Association's annual conference. Then came the cookbook and her parents.

That last thought sparked two more. The first was that the cookbook might benefit from her time in jail, and she vowed to take notice of everything that happened here. The second was the realization that she had tickets booked to go see her parents in two weeks. Her time in jail would have to be over by then.

The arranger in her nature took over and Blue patted her orange jumpsuit, looking for a pen, then remembered her jailer hadn't allowed her to bring anything to her cell, saying she was a suicide risk. Blue had been too tired to argue, but now she needed that pen. And something other than toilet paper to write on.

There was no 'call' button, so Blue did what she figured every prisoner did when they needed something: she banged on her cell door and hollered.

An older gentleman answered the noise with a wry smile. "Ma'am?"

"I'm sorry for all the racket. May I have a pen and some paper?"

"You won't use them for anything naughty now, will you?"

"Cross my heart."

"In that case, I'll be right back." He was. He passed her a pencil and a pad of paper, and then asked, "You own the winery out in the country, right?"

Blue nodded.

"I've been there. The food and wine are excellent."

"Thank you. I am so blessed to be able to do what I love. It doesn't feel like work that way." She hesitated. "I don't suppose you could use any help in the kitchen, could you?"

"Are you hungry?"

"A little."

"Dinner's over, and it's probably a good thing you missed it. I'll make you a deal." He found a key and unlocked her door. "If you make two of whatever you have, you can spend the rest of the evening in the dining room. Since you're our only female guest at the moment, we thought it wise to keep you separated from the men. But you seem capable of taking care of yourself. I don't think the boys will bother you."

Blue stepped across her cell's threshold and into the hall, and felt a burden lift from her shoulders. "You, kind sir, have got a deal."

THE CASS ELLIOT SCHOOL OF GUN OWNERSHIP

I PESTERED HER ALL the way out to Hamilton's Gun Shop, but Cass wouldn't give me a hint. The sound of guns blasting on the range behind the shop told us plenty of folks were waiting until the worst of the heat disappeared before coming out.

Mitch called as we were pulling into the parking lot and told Cass that Grey had confirmed Bret's time of death as occurring between ten Saturday night and two Sunday morning, and Bret was dead when he went into the tank. Cass said that was good news and bad news. Good news because Blue couldn't have put a dead body in the tank by herself. Bad because she might've had help.

I tried to keep an open mind about Blue's ability to commit murder, but try as I might, I couldn't see her wielding a bat like that.

Stepping into Hamilton's was like stepping back in time. The log building had a slat floor that rang when struck by a cowboy boot and flexed ever so slightly under foot. The scent of gun cleaning solvents and oil hung in the air, and a workbench was covered with metal parts and tools. A potbelly stove sat to one side of the shop, cold now, but the rockers in front of it were inhabited by weathered old coots who eyed us with suspicion. I'd taken Aunt Kay's advice and wore jeans, a t-shirt, and a pair of scuffed up boots I'd had since high school. Once a pair of cowboy boots mold themselves to your feet, there's nothing more comfortable and no getting rid of them.

Hamilton - I was never sure if that was his first name or last - met us at the counter. He was the reason this shop was frequented by gun owners from counties all around. An ex-policeman of few words, he ran the place with military precision and an eye for detail. If Hamilton thought you weren't gun-ownership material, he had no problem sending you down the road to the next gun shop. Which was miles away.

"Hey Ham, can I see it?" Cass asked.

He motioned her behind the counter and they disappeared into his stock room, leaving me alone with the coots. I wandered in their direction but made a sharp left into a row of ammunition when a stream of spit stung a brass spittoon. Although Cass and Ham were only in the back for a few minutes, it felt like I was waiting for Oz the Great and Powerful to peel back his curtain. When they emerged, Cass carried a gun case. She placed it on the counter and I joined them.

"I ordered this for you last week, when you said you were serious about working for the agency."

"You got me a gun?" I asked.

She nodded, face still serious. "Ham has the background paperwork in order. You need to sign it and if everything comes back clean, I'll keep your gun until you have your concealed carry license."

My gun. Suddenly, it was real. Excitement coursed through me. My dream of becoming a private investigator was gaining momentum. My eyes filled with tears when Cass popped open the case. "Your very own revolver, a Ruger .38 Special. It's got a shrouded hammer. With all the junk you carry in your purse, I thought that would be safer."

I hugged her. "I think that's the nicest thing anybody's ever done for me, Cass. And look," I stroked a finger down the gun. "It's got a pink handle thingy."

"Grip, Maxine. And don't thank me yet," she said with a smile. "We've got to spend some serious time shooting. And then you've got to pass the concealed carry class. You're not licensed until Ham says you're licensed. Come on."

SHE LET ME CARRY the gun in its case and our ear and eye protection, while she carried ammunition and the paper targets. Since she was on medical leave and her gun was locked up at the courthouse, she had her personal 9mm with her, hooked on the hip of her jeans. It looked cool and I asked where I could get a holster like that.

"When you're ready to carry, we'll shop for holsters," she told me, and I tried not to pout.

We picked a booth at the far end of the range and started my lesson.

Have you ever fired a gun? No? Let me tell you, it's not as easy as it looks on TV, at least not if Cass Elliot is your instructor. Before she would even let me open a box of bullets, she made me learn the name of every part of the revolver, using words like cylinder, ejector, frame, and barrel. She explained how everything worked, then made me repeat each name until I could do so without hesitation.

Then came instructions on how to handle a gun. She taught me to always hold my gun by the grip, with the barrel pointing down or at least away from any potential living target. Hear the potential part? That means if a person *might* be anywhere near my line of fire, I had to make sure to keep my loaded gun pointing away from them. My gun was unloaded at that time, mind you, but Cass made it clear I was to treat the thing as if it were loaded at all times.

When I dared grumble that it couldn't just load itself, she pierced me with a look and growled, "Maxine, this is no joke. If handling a gun safely is too much to ask, I'll send it back."

I begged and pled for mercy and at last she relented, going back to her instructions. Next we covered stance. There's no such thing as 'point and shoot' in the Elliot school of gun ownership. Those nifty grips where the guy holds the gun on its side and shoots gangsta-style? Forget it. She showed me the Isosceles, the Weaver, and modifications to both.

I assumed the stances as Cass directed, shooting my empty gun at a bull's eye target she ran out on a line. She studied me, pressing gently to lower my shoulders because I kept pulling them up towards my ears, and showing me how to grip my gun with my right hand and support it by cupping my left palm beneath it. She fiddled with my hands, fingers, the stretch of my arms, and the placement of my feet. Then she made me watch and imitate her until she was satisfied I understood what a good stance looked and felt like.

And then we practiced some more.

THE COPS AIN'T YOUR FRIEND

BY THE TIME SHE put three Quiche Lorraines in the oven, a small crowd of prisoners and guards had gathered. Word had spread that a cook, a real cook, was in the cells. Blue ignored the hubbub and did what she always did in the kitchen: issued orders. When a scrawny man rebelled at working for a woman, Blue drew her shoulders back and pointed to the exit. "You work, or you don't eat."

The shirker complained to a burly guard, who shrugged. "You heard the lady. If you want a decent meal, button your lip and fold those napkins."

By the time the quiches were done, they had stacks of buttered toast, a salad of crisp greens and tomatoes, and homemade vinaigrette waiting on one of the long tables, which had been properly set with cutlery, plates, and napkins. A tray of shortbread was in the oven, its buttery scent replacing the savory aroma of the quiche.

She sat next to one of the scruffier prisoners, whose shifty eyes conveyed nervousness rather than aggression, and quietly coached him to place his napkin in his lap and how to correctly use his utensils. He ate in small, quick bites at first, but slowed and seemed to enjoy the food and the experience as Blue worked with him.

They finished the meal and the clean-up crew got to work. When the kitchen was put back in order to her satisfaction, Blue asked the guard what happened at night. "Mostly they watch TV," answered the elderly man. "Or read, or sometimes play games until lights out."

Blue filled glasses with milk and put cookies on plates. Most inmates hurried to the TV room, followed by a guard. A few lingered and settled in with their shortbread and cups of coffee at nearby tables. Blue sat alone and built two lists, groceries for the kitchen, and a list of potential suspects.

A middle aged man with a sad mustache and weepy tattoos sat across from her. "I hear you done your husband," he said conversationally. "Did you poison him?"

"That'd be obvious for a chef, wouldn't it? Someone murdered him," Blue said. "But it wasn't me."

"Nobody in here done what they're accused of," he said with a wink.

"In my case, it's true."

He studied her and seemed to realize she might believe it. He sat forward. "They got any evidence against you?"

"I don't know. They've accused me of two other murders in addition to my husband."

"Lady -," he began.

"Blue, please," she said. "What's your name?"

"Hollis. Miss Blue, you have a right to know what kind of evidence they've got against you. You have a lawyer?"

"No. I don't know any criminal lawyers. Besides I didn't do this."

"You better get one. I'd recommend mine, but he's a public defender. A bad one at that."

"Hollis, you don't think the police are interested in the truth, in finding out who really killed my husband?"

"You ever watch TV?"

Blue shook her head. "I don't have time."

He studied her like she was a species of life he'd never encountered. "The cops ain't your friend, Miss Blue. Inside, in this jailhouse? You're the only friend you got."

He thanked her for the meal, then tipped an imaginary hat and slouched to the TV room. Blue tapped the pencil's eraser against her chin as she thought. Detective Stone had advised her to get a lawyer and told her if she couldn't afford one, a lawyer would be appointed for her. But it hadn't seemed necessary at the time. Since she was innocent, she expected everyone to act accordingly and make sure the real killer was caught. Hollis seemed to have a greater knowledge of the legal system than she did. Blue had never even filed any of the legal paperwork related to her businesses. Her lawyer, a demure woman with a stammer, took care of all that. Blue wouldn't begin to know how to find a criminal lawyer, much less which questions to ask to determine if they were the right person to defend her. But suddenly she knew who could help her.

She mentally ran back through all the movies she'd watched, and waved at the elderly guard. "I get to make one phone call, right?"

"You haven't made it yet?"

"I didn't know who to call. But now I do."

He checked his watch. "It's nearly time for lock down."

"I'll make French toast for breakfast," she said. "With sausage or bacon, depending on what's in the freezer."

"I'm off duty at six. I'll miss breakfast."

"Wake me up and I'll cook yours early," she said. "But get some maple syrup tonight. The real stuff."

THERE ARE WORSE WAYS

BIG BILLY FINALLY SPOKE. "What a way to go."

"There are worse ways than ending up in a tank of wine," Sugar said.

"Remember that," the shorter man said.

"What did your dad say?" Billy asked.

"He was happy to hear BB is dead, unhappy we didn't kill him, and furious we haven't found it."

Sugar pulled at his nose. "So, we're not done?"

"No, you're not." The shorter man was still in his work clothes, pacing the small kitchen in his orange shoes, chain-smoking. "These women you saw in Dallas. You think they are from Arcadia. What did they look like?"

"One was red-headed, the other had black hair," Billy answered. "Mid- to late-twenties. Hot."

"Very hot," Sugar added.

The smaller man nodded. "The black-headed one is called Maxine Leverman. Blue hired her to find BB."

Billy scratched his head. "You think she might know where it is?"

"I think it's time to find out," the small man answered.

THE HOTTEST THING AT THE GUN RANGE

WE WERE BOTH SOAKED with perspiration and although the sun had set and the floodlights were on, the temperature hadn't dropped below ninety-five. Hamilton wandered out to bring us cold bottles of water and watch. After Cass finished with my stance training, he slipped on a pair of shooting glasses and nodded for Cass to load me up.

I'll confess: I was feeling a fair amount of fear as I slipped the shiny bullets - cartridges, Cass insisted I call them - into their chambers. Let's face it, a gun is only as dangerous as the hand that holds it. It's an inanimate object with no more ability to kill a human being than a parked car. But I felt a huge responsibility as I loaded my new revolver, and silently vowed I would learn everything Cass and Hamilton had to teach me, to perfection. Hamilton watched with eagle eyes and grunted occasionally, but since he never expressed dissatisfaction, I took those noises as approval.

"It's not very far away," I said, lifting my chin at the target hanging about ten yards out.

"You won't shoot things that are far away," Cass said. "Not at first."

We donned eye and ear protection. I assumed an Isosceles stance and pulled back steadily on the trigger. Nothing happened. I looked over my shoulder at Cass.

"It's stiff. Pull steady, but harder," she said.

I did. The gun kicked and boomed louder than I expected and I jumped, but felt elated when I saw my target flutter.

I turned around, grinning. "I hit it!"

"You nicked it," Cass clarified. "Be still."

Hamilton disappeared into the shadows near the booth's wall as Cass wrapped her arms around me, placing her hands over mine and adjusting my aim. "Squeeze," she said.

I did. My arms stayed steady despite the gun's kick.

The paper rippled and Cass said, "Fire until your gun is empty."

I squeezed the trigger at a steady pace and concentrated on the smallest circle in the bull's eye. Cass released me and we pulled off our ear protection.

"Now that's about the hottest thing I've ever seen," came a sneering voice. "Two chicks making out at the gun range."

We turned to see Hamilton glaring at a skinny figure standing just outside the floodlights. Hamilton took a step forward and the figure retreated.

"What did you say?" Hamilton demanded.

"Uh, hey Ham. Didn't see you there," said an uncertain voice.

Hamilton stepped out of our booth and into the darkness beyond the floodlights. "What do you want, Petchard?"

Cass rolled her eyes at me as the two men walked to the shop.

"Is that Hugo Petchard?" I asked.

She nodded.

"I figured he'd slunk away in shame after realizing he was dating a cross-dresser. He'll never live that down around here."

Cass ran my target back to the booth. "Hoffner has him working in the jail, out of public view."

"Did his daddy pay Hoffner to keep Hugo on?"

"We call them campaign contributions, apparently. Let's see how you did."

My first shot had nicked the right side of the paper, but the following four had all struck within the bull's eye. On the outer circle, but still, I did hit the bull's eye. With Cass's help, of course. "Not bad, eh?" I asked.

"You'll get better," Cass said.

She clipped a fresh target to the line, ran it way out, and fired sixteen rounds. I ran the target back and smiled. All dead center in a tight cluster.

"Wow," I said.

"In time, you'll be that good." She pointed to the table in the booth. "Now you learn how to clean your gun."

HIS FAVORITE PERSON LIST

I WAS FRESH OUT of the shower and toweling off, still elated from my first gun training session, when Cass came into the bathroom with my phone.

"It's the courthouse," she said with a question in her voice.

"For me?"

She nodded.

I tapped the answer button. "Maxine Leverman."

"This is Blue. I've been arrested."

I sat on the toilet lid and motioned Cass over. "I've got Cass Elliot with me, Blue. Can I put you on speaker?"

She hesitated. "I don't know, Maxine. I've been told not to trust the police."

"Cass is still on medical leave, Blue. She's seen all the evidence and she's not sure you're the right person to arrest for these murders, so we're working through your case together."

She released a long sigh. "Okay, put me on."

I did, and she and Cass exchanged hellos.

Blue sounded tired but determined. "I've realized how serious all this is, that I could be convicted of three murders. That would put me away for a while, and I've got too much to do to spend time in prison. Or jail. Whatever this is. Regardless, this is my one call, Maxine, and I picked you. I want to hire you again. I need a lawyer, but I think I need a private detective, too."

"The agency will help however we can," I said, crossing my fingers and hoping we took on this kind of work.

"Find the names of some decent criminal attorneys and we'll go through them. When can you come?"

Cass said, "Visiting hours start at ten o'clock tomorrow."

"Then I guess that will do. Can I count on seeing both of you then?"

Cass and I exchanged a glance. "It's probably best if I stay on the periphery of your case, Blue," Cass said. "Sheriff Hoffner can't stop me from helping Maxine, but I'm not on his favorite person list right now, so it would help you more if I stay off his radar."

"Wish I'd managed to stay off his radar, too." She sounded amused. "Okay. Maxine in the morning it is."

CASS GAVE ME A quick tutorial on the criminal justice system and provided a list of acceptable criminal attorneys in the area, and some great attorneys outside the immediate area. It's not like Forney County is a hotbed of crime, and most of our criminals are rather stupid, so greatness in defense is rarely required.

She refused, however, to give me a rundown on the evidence the police had collected in the three murder cases. "I can't do it, Maxine," she said. "I'm not on duty, but I can't divulge that information. Blue has a right to it, but to protect her and me, her attorney will have to file a motion for discovery."

"Will Hoffner give her attorney any trouble?"

"It's the judge who rules on the motion." She looked at her watch. "I'll call Mitch in the morning and make sure he briefs the DA, so if she manages to retain an attorney tomorrow and he files his motion, maybe we can get the data tomorrow or Tuesday." She held up a finger. "Hadn't you better text Babby and Kay to let them know you've taken another case?"

She was right. I did and Kay responded that we'd meet at seven in the morning. My job was to bring donuts. Babby texted requesting a cinnamon swirl.

I convinced Cass to spend the night, and for the next two hours we wrote notes on the giant stickies. We brainstormed suspects, listing every employee at the winery, going through the list of wives again, and talking through motive for Bret's former band. It was after midnight when we quit and we were both bleary-eyed.

"It's not coming together, is it?" I asked.

"It's early days, Max. There's always a pattern, or some tiny fact or connection that makes a difference. It's there, but we can't see it yet."

"Always?"

She looked at the stickies clinging to my walls. "Always."

MONDAY

MR. ORANGE SHOES

A MUFFLED SHOUT WOKE me while it was still dark out, sending my heart into overdrive. I sat bolt upright in bed, reached for my shotgun, flicked the safety off, and put the stock to my shoulder, ears straining. It came again and I recognized Cass's voice. I hurried to my guest room.

She was thrashing in her bed and as she cried out, I realized she was having a nightmare. I left the shotgun by the door and sat beside her, gently shaking her good shoulder. "Cass? Cass, wake up. It's only a dream."

Her eyes flew open and the terror I saw in them chilled me. It was the same terror I felt every time I had the rape dream. She was panting and her hands were balled into fists so I talked until the fear faded and relief took its place.

At last she sank back against the pillows and put her hands over her eyes. "Of all the things I hate him for, I hate him for this the most," she whispered.

"Me, too."

She looked at me. "You have nightmares?"

"More nights than not."

She breathed deeply. "What triggers them?"

"I've never found any rhyme or reason to when it comes, but it's always the same. Well, overall."

"Mine, too. Sometimes current stuff gets mixed up in it, but mostly it's just him."

I was chewing my lower lip and forced myself to stop. "Do you think you're more careful now than before?"

"Oh yes. I'm not as paranoid as you, but sometimes I get close."

I glanced at the bedside clock. "It's five. Do you want to go back to sleep?"

"I'd rather run."

———

I'LL TELL YOU NOW that I normally run inside on my treadmill. Yes, for security reasons. When I'm running outside and focused on my pace and breathing, I have trouble paying attention to what's going on around me. Before I agreed to run with Cass, I made her promise to wear her gun. She didn't hesitate to say yes and borrowed running gear and shoes.

We set out on the trail that runs behind my apartment complex. It's a paved path that twists fifteen miles in and around the city, through parks, heavily wooded areas, and around the schools. In daylight it's used by bikers, walkers, joggers, and skaters. At night all bets are off, especially in the area called Deadwood Hollow. Cass humored me as I ran through my security regime of peeking out the windows near the door, stepping out the front door and checking the pool area, club house, and the ground beneath my apartment before turning to lock the deadbolts behind us. The sun was painting luminous peach streaks across the sky when we set out, but I kept an eye peeled for men lurking in the deeper shadows.

Cass was still regaining her stamina after her gunshot wound, so her speed was a little off. We set a comfortable pace and worked our way up to the seven-minute mile mark for the next half hour, then slowed as we worked our way home. Several other runners and two women on bicycles crossed our paths, nodding or giving a slight wave as we passed. I was deep into my zone while we ran and the comfort of knowing Cass was armed let me focus only on my form and breathing. We stopped to stretch and it was as I bent over to work my hamstrings that I saw him.

A man had stopped on the trail behind us, and then stepped into the protective embrace of a thirsty-looking weeping willow. I froze and whispered, "Cass."

"What?"

"Don't look, but there's a man behind us."

She was leaning against a tree, stretching her calf, and I felt her awareness grow. "Acting strange?"

"He hid in that big willow we passed."

"Maxine, I need to look. I'm going to turn to talk to you." She did, and casually looked back up the trail. "I don't see him. Oh wait. He's wearing bright orange shoes. Not a good choice for covert work. Let's go."

"Where?"

"Back up the trail, slowly. We're cooling down. I want to see what he does."

We walked towards the weeping willow at a leisurely pace. As we drew nearer, I heard a one-sided conversation and peeked between the willow's feathery limbs to see a dark-haired man with his back to us. He held a phone to his ear with one hand and ran the other through his black hair, speaking a rapid-fire conversation in Spanish.

Cass relaxed and turned around, taking me with her. "See? Nothing. Take me back to your place and teach me how to use that espresso machine."

PLAYING HARDBALL

KAY'S EYES NARROWED WHEN she pushed open the agency's door. "How did you beat me here, Maxine?"

I glanced at the computer screen. "It's six-thirty."

"That's my point." She put her handbag on her desk, yawned, and stretched. "Do I smell coffee?"

I nodded.

"Keep making the coffee and you can come in early any time, boo bear. You want one?"

"Yes, please. Donuts are on the counter."

She returned with two steaming mugs and perched on the edge of my desk. I flashed the agency's copy of the Forney Cater at her. "No news about Blue's arrest."

"Yet. What are you working on?"

"Blue asked for a list of criminal attorneys. Cass helped me build one last night and I'm adding phone numbers and some of the work their websites say they do."

"Let me see."

I twisted the computer screen and she sipped and scrolled through the names.

"Scratch out numbers two and six. They look good on paper but are jerks who charge far too much for what they deliver." Kay gave me three more names before Babby joined us.

After she had a cup of coffee in one hand and a cinnamon swirl in the other, Babby stood behind me and scanned the list. "Knock off three and five."

"Why Conrad?" Kay protested.

"He's not back from his hernia operation."

"That was at least three months ago."

"He played a round of golf and ripped his sutures. Got infected."

"Men," said Kay.

"Amen." Babby took another bite and chewed. "Where's her name?"

"Babby," Kay warned, and I swear my aunt actually bristled.

"I'm serious. Who's the meanest, dirtiest, sneakiest lawyer around, Kay? If Blue is our client again, she deserves the best we can give her."

"Who?" I asked.

"Yvette Hardcastle," Babby said.

My eyes went wide. "She's the one who got Diann Vega off for killing her husband, right?"

Babby nodded. "But that was justifiable homicide. He dumped her clothes in the pig pen."

"After she set his Mustang on fire," Kay said.

"He deserved it," Babby retorted. "She was bleeding from lacerations all over her body when they found her. How many stitches did it take to sew her up? It was weeks before the bruises disappeared."

"What's wrong with Yvette Hardcastle, Aunt Kay?" I asked.

"She plays hard. Has no qualms about throwing feces wherever she can find it to get her client off."

"That's what Blue needs, isn't it?"

"Maybe," Kay said, looking pointedly at Babby. "But Blue has a reputation to protect, and a business to run after all this murder stuff is done. Diann was a cheap slut who hit the right set of circumstances to justify killing her no-good-dog of a husband."

"You're saying the attorney she chooses could impact how people in the community see her?" I asked.

"I'm saying if she killed three people, she needs somebody who can show how dire her situation was and that she had no choice but to act. And then convince a jury it was self-defense."

"That's Hardcastle," Babby said.

"And if she didn't do it, she'll need somebody who can dig into the evidence to demonstrate without a doubt that she didn't."

"Hardcastle can do that, too, but she loves throwing poop more," Babby said, and popped the last bite of cinnamon swirl into her mouth.

"Blue picked Lost and Found because she liked the idea of an all woman agency," I said. "Ovaries might win the day again."

"If they do, they do. I'm not sure how she'll feel about working with us, though." Babby looked at Kay. "Can you play nice?"

"Don't bring that up, Barbara."

"It's relevant, Kay. Our duty is to provide the best service possible to Blue. If you slip into cat-fight mode with Yvette, Blue's the one who suffers."

Kay lifted her chin. "I can work with anybody."

"The past is the past?"

I tried not to ping pong back and forth between them, but this was interesting.

Kay's look was steely. "Was it a problem on the Smith case?"

"No, but we were working for the prosecution. You'd have to work side-by-side with her on this case."

"Maxine would have to work side-by-side with her."

"You know what I mean, Kay."

I couldn't stand it anymore. "What happened?"

"No," Kay said in a flat tone that brooked no argument.

"She needs to know," Babby replied.

"That's water under the bridge. It has no bearing on my ability to work with Yvette Hardcastle, and you can be sure if hourly billings are involved, it will have no bearing on Yvette's ability to work with me."

"Yvette Hardcastle is meaner than a water moccasin. If she thinks she needs to rattle Maxine, she will. For Blue's sake, Maxine needs to know."

Babby and Kay engaged in a silent stand-off and it was all I could do to keep my mouth shut and wait.

"Fine," Kay snapped, and stalked off. "You tell her."

FAMILY SECRETS

THE BATHROOM DOOR SLAMMED behind Kay and the office settled into an uneasy quiet.

I waited.

At last Babby pulled a chair next to my desk and sat. "Cindy doesn't know this," she began. "And I don't think she'll need to."

"What happened?"

"Your Uncle Charlie had an affair with Yvette."

I swear my eyes nearly popped out of my head, but I had the sense to keep my jaw from dropping. I swallowed. "Aunt Kay's Uncle Charlie?"

"The very same. It was a long time ago. But it nearly destroyed Kay and Charlie's marriage."

"What happened?" I was stuck on that two word question.

"She did some work for his business before she went into criminal defense. Kay walked in on them in his office - on their only time together, according to Charlie - and pulled her gun on Yvette."

"Walked in on them as in *walked in* on them?"

Babby nodded.

A picture of the scene popped into my head and I blinked to eradicate it.

"She threatened to kill Yvette if she ever came near Charlie again, and made her walk out of the office right then, taking only her purse."

"No clothes?"

"Naked as the day she was born." Babby shrugged. "It was late. I doubt if anybody saw her but her ego was bruised."

"Wow. What did Aunt Kay do to Uncle Charlie?"

"Tried to shoot his balls off. Almost did. If you look close you can see the repairs in the wall behind his desk. He broke down and told her how sorry he was. Kay and I had been spending a lot of time at the agency, our husbands were working all hours, and both marriages suffered. Charlie and Yvette had a late dinner and a few drinks, and one thing led to another. Charlie told Kay that Yvette was the aggressor, and I guess Kay believed him. That woman truly is a man-eater."

Babby's use of my self-imposed nickname gave me pause, but I decided to think about it later. "I don't remember anything about this."

"You wouldn't, peanut. Kay and I went to Europe for a month to let Charlie cool his heels and both of them decide whether they wanted to keep their marriage."

"I still have the Paddington Bear you brought me. I had no idea that was why you went. I guess it worked."

"The time apart did them good and they stuck with marriage counseling. It hasn't been smooth sailing, but Kay and Charlie have one of the strongest marriages I've seen."

The bathroom door opened and Kay emerged, steel in her spine and fight in her eyes.

"You so rock," I said.

Kay harrumphed but my words brought a small smile. She sat again on the edge of the desk. "Don't you ever tell your Uncle Charlie that you know, do you understand? It would kill him."

I nodded.

"And Cindy -"

"Will never hear it from me."

"It was done and over years ago and I swear, if we didn't live in a town the size of a snotty handkerchief, we'd never see her or be reminded of it."

"Should I take her off the list?"

"No," Kay said. She looked at Babby. "I can handle working with her. But anyone Blue picks from that list will do a good job."

I hesitated. "If she'll sleep with a married man, will she be antagonistic to Blue, the injured spouse?"

Kay and Babby shared a grim smile. "Things like this always come full circle, baby," Kay said.

Babby piped up. "Yvette caught her husband cheating about the same way Kay caught her and Charlie cheating. Turns out he liked them young and often."

"Underage?" I asked, wondering why I'd never heard any of this.

"He wasn't stupid, just horny. But he had taken photographs and rumor has it Yvette wrecked him financially. Their divorce made the papers. He fled for some industrial town up north."

Maybe Yvette and I would have something in common after all.

"So she'll likely be very happy to defend Blue," I said.

"It's hard to predict Yvette, but probably."

I looked at the computer screen. "I've got six names. What do I do?"

"Go see her," Kay said. "The sooner the better. Have her sign a new contract, explain her choices on an attorney, and we'll figure out where to go from there."

"Visiting hours start at ten."

"Go now, sweetie pie. As soon as word gets out she's been arrested, people will decide whether she's innocent or guilty. Every minute counts."

"But how do I get in?" I asked.

Kay waved a hand as she headed for the kitchen. "If you can't think of something on your own, lovey, figure out what your aunts would do."

BREAKING IN

IT WAS ALMOST SEVEN-thirty when I got to the county jail, now a modern building housed off the square. It used to be part of the historic Forney County courthouse building, but as lockup needs expanded, the locals decided they needed a bigger hoosegow. There are still a few cells at the courthouse, but those are only used by the town drunks who need a night to sleep it off, and those who are waiting to make an appearance in one of our fine courtrooms.

I consider myself a cynic, but I was shaken after the revelation of my sainted uncle's affair and feeling decidedly unkind towards the entire male population. I pushed the ringer next to the double doors, pulled my shoulders back, and waved up at the camera in the corner. Not knowing what the day would bring but certain a girl can never go wrong with chic professional, I'd worn an Elie Tahari sheath dress with a scoop neck. It hugged me in all the right places, but in a subtle gray with black accents down the sides, looked suitably demure. My feet were clad in a pair of black patent Fifis by Christian Louboutin. After our run this morning, my calves and thighs were feeling toned, and the dress and shoes showed them to a perfect advantage. Little did I know how soon I would need that advantage.

A buzzing sounded and the doors unlocked with a metallic click. A shade went up on one of the heavily glassed reception windows. I approached and groaned inwardly; Officer Hugo Petchard sat behind the glass, bleary eyed. It had been some time since I'd seen him up close, but his thinning blond hair was longer and instead of slicked straight back, it covered the tips of his ears. I suppressed a smile. His cross-dressing girlfriend had shot him in the ear on the same afternoon she'd wounded Cass. Petchard's injury was superficial, but I'd heard the bullet left a nick in the cartilage that wouldn't disappear without plastic surgery. The hair hid this physical reminder of his failure to realize his girlfriend had a penis, and that he was dating a multiple murderer.

Every police force in the world must have a Hugo Petchard, whose parents are rich or influential. Because their offspring cannot obtain employment on their own, these parents are forced to purchase positions where their kids can hide their ineptitude and hopefully do no harm. In Petchard's case, it was a bet gone wrong on more than one occasion.

He blinked slowly as I approached and I took the high road: I smiled. His confusion morphed into a scowl when he recognized me.

"What do you want?" he demanded.

I placed my briefcase on the shelf in front of his window. "I need to see Blue Ivey."

"Visiting hours -"

"Start at ten. I need to see her now."

"You're not a lawyer."

"No, but she asked me to come this morning. I'm here. Let me in and go get her, please."

He frowned. "She's in the kitchen."

I raised an eyebrow. "Hard labor?"

"She's just cooking," he sputtered. "Somebody else is doing the dishes."

Humor was lost on the boy. "Go get her, Hugo. I need to speak to her now."

He crossed his arms over his skinny chest. "Come back at ten."

Right then I knew what my aunts would do and for once, was grateful I came from a town as gossipy as Arcadia. I leaned forward and exposed cleavage. He noticed. I motioned him closer. "Hugo, if you don't let me see Blue Ivey right this minute, I'll tell everybody that you -"

I lowered my voice to a whisper and watched as two red spots blossomed high on his cheeks.

"Who told you that?"

I stayed silent.

He sat back. "You wouldn't dare."

"I'd post it on every social media site I can find."

We engaged in a staring contest for several seconds. He must've believed me, because a click sounded and the lock released.

GOOD NEWS AND BAD NEWS

PETCHARD TOOK HIS SWEET time bringing Blue to Interview Room 1, but the wait was worth it. A uniformed officer I didn't recognize opened the door and ushered Blue in. An inmate followed, pushing a stainless steel cart carrying coffee and cinnamon rolls that put off a heavenly smell. Both men thanked Blue for the wonderful breakfast before leaving us.

She was dressed in prison orange and it looked good on her. I told her so.

"You're the one who looks good," she said. There were still shadows beneath her eyes, but she looked more rested than when I'd last seen her on Saturday. "You have the best shoes."

"My mother's convinced it's an untreatable illness. Looks like you're a hit with the inmates and guards."

Blue smiled and put a cinnamon roll on a plate, then handed it and coffee to me. "They're good guys, really. Most of them just need some guidance. Several helped in the kitchen last night and this morning, and they're all trainable. I've told them to come to the winery for jobs if and when we ever get out of here." She sipped her coffee. "I thought visiting hours didn't start until ten."

"Kay and Babby recommended I come early to miss the rush, and so we can get your attorney working as quickly as possible."

"But how did you get in?"

"A little trick Kay taught me."

Blue glanced up at a camera in the corner and lowered her voice. "Can they hear us?"

"Nope. The sound system's broken in this room. Cass clued me in."

"I knew working with Lost and Found would pay off." Blue leaned forward. "For the record, I did not murder Bret, Annie, or Daphne."

I opened my briefcase. "Before you say anything else, read this and sign it. It's our standard contract, like you signed before."

Blue held her hand out for a pen, scanned the contract, signed it, and pushed it back to me. "Does that give us attorney-client privilege?"

I was grateful Cass had run through the basics with me last night. "No. Anything the agency puts in writing is subject to subpoena, although we'd fight it. Most of our communications will be verbal instead of written. Any reports we prepare for you or your attorney will be sufficiently vague they would provide no benefit to the prosecution. Make sense?"

"I think so. We can talk now?"

"Yes."

Blue leaned forward. "I mean it, Maxine. I really did not do this. I'm so naive I thought everybody would realize I couldn't commit a crime like this. I didn't take it seriously when Detective Stone arrested me. But I've had a chance to talk with some of the people in here, and it sounds like I can't trust the police."

"That may be a bit harsh," I said. "We need to focus on what we have to do to get you out of here and prove your innocence."

"You've got a list of attorneys?"

I pulled the page from my briefcase.

She blinked. "It's short."

"This *is* East Texas." Blue grinned and I smiled back. "I had input from Cass, Kay, and Babby."

"Did they have a favorite?"

"No. I've listed strengths and weaknesses and given you an idea of the kinds of cases they've handled in the past."

She studied it. "Only one woman?"

"Yvette Hardcastle is the only female criminal attorney in the area."

"What's she like?"

"Tough as nails, according to Babby and Kay."

"Ruthless?"

I nodded. "And probably sympathetic to your cause."

"She's been cheated on, too?"

"Yes."

"Call her."

"You don't want to talk to any of the others?"

Blue shook her head. "I'm not sure I ever want to do business with a man again."

"If you're comfortable with it, I'll ask you to sign a power of attorney so we can hire her and get started. However, we'd advise you to interview several lawyers before you select one."

"The power of attorney gets things moving?"

I nodded.

"I'll sign it." I gave her the sheet of paper. She read and signed it, then she picked up a crumb. "You'll think I'm crazy for asking this, but has anyone told Nicole Ivy that her husband is dead?"

"I have no idea."

"She deserves to know. If for no other reason than to collect any life insurance." She glanced up at me. "I'm not that heartless, but she does need to know. Presumably she loved the man and had no more idea what he was up to than I did. But if she did know about his extra-marital activities..."

"She's a great suspect," I finished for her. I slipped all the paperwork into my briefcase and put my elbows on the table. "I've got good news and bad news. What do you want first?"

"I'm locked up, Maxine. Your news can't be worse than this."

"Bret has been married before."

"To Nicole."

"And others. Many others. Under various names." Blue stared, so I continued. "That's the bad news. The good news is that each of those women is a potential suspect, which gives us a *lot* of hope for proving your innocence."

THE ICE QUEEN

IT WAS ONLY AN hour later when the agency's door swung open and an absolute sex kitten filled the entryway. I'd seen Yvette Hardcastle's photos online and she was a stunningly beautiful woman, but the force of her personality added a whole new layer to the mix. Yvette had man-eater written from the top of her silky jet black hair to the tips of her Alexander McQueen pumps. Her eyes said there was intelligence behind that predatory façade.

"Didn't think I'd ever cross this threshold," she said in a velvety voice, and stepped forward. She wore a black two-piece Akris suit and the pumps were midnight suede. Her briefcase was by Mulberry and downright delicious. She was dressed to intimidate and I felt a twinge of uncertainty about my role in Blue's defense.

Cindy peeked from behind her Japanese screen and stared. Babby, Kay, and I rose as the temperature in the office dropped to frosty. A steel wall wrapped around my insecurities in the face of this woman who'd hurt my aunt, and I stepped forward, hand out. "Maxine Leverman. You must be Ms. Hardcastle."

Her ice blue eyes narrowed. "You're not licensed, Maxine. What are you doing going to the jailhouse to sign up new clients?"

Kay shifted but I spoke first. "I'm working under Kay and Barbara's direction, which is perfectly legal. You've decided to take Blue's case?"

"No, I haven't, but I am curious." Yvette looked Kay and then Babby up and down, her face neutral. "Of all the calls I thought I'd receive, one from your agency was never on the list."

"Your office received the call from me, Ms. Hardcastle." She turned to face me again. "The agency is working with Blue, but I'm her main contact. Would you like to come to the conference room where we can discuss this more comfortably? If you're a coffee drinker, we'll put a new pot on." I gestured to her right.

Yvette seemed a tad put out that the new girl was stealing the show, but I caught Babby's eyebrow twitching. The lawyer hesitated, but when I stepped away from the group, she followed.

I heard Kay speak as I opened the conference room door. "Always lovely to see you, Yvette. I'll join you in a moment. You take your coffee black?"

"With two creams and a sugar," answered Yvette. She followed me into the conference room and Babby closed the door once she stepped inside. We all remained standing.

"A few ground rules," Babby said. Her voice was granite.

Yvette tilted her head.

"The past is the past. All of it. Agreed?"

Yvette nodded slowly.

"We've never worked on the same side before, but I think you'll find us useful. We will share all information we gather with you, and you will provide us the same courtesy. If you fail to be fully forthcoming, we'll recommend that Blue cut you off. Understood?"

"Yes." Her voice was brittle.

"You will refrain from commenting on your history with *our* family," emphasis on 'our', which was very cool, "and we will refrain from dissecting the factors that led to your ex-husband's unfortunate behavior."

A flush crept up Yvette's neck, but she managed to nod again.

"Good." Babby sat and motioned for us to join her. "How much information did Maxine leave regarding Blue's case?"

I do love my aunts.

HE NEEDED KILLIN'

BY THE TIME KAY joined us fifteen minutes later, Babby and I had filled Yvette in on the high points of the case, done a rough sketch of Bret's marriages and divorces, and rebuilt the suspect and motive lists Cass and I had drawn up last night. She'd filled three pages of a legal pad with notes and had just flipped to a fourth when the door opened and Cindy brought in a tray of coffee and cups. Kay followed with a plate of donuts.

Yvette visibly relaxed when she saw Cindy pouring from a communal pot; perhaps she'd expected a dose of laxative with her cream and sugar.

Kay told Cindy to flip the phones to the answering service and lock the office doors, then join us. I thought Cindy was going to jump out of her heels at the thought of working with Yvette Hardcastle. From fear or joy, I'm not sure. I was grateful for the hour I'd had to brief my aunts between leaving Blue at the jailhouse and Yvette's arrival at the agency.

"Questions?" Kay asked Yvette.

"Do you know what evidence the police have against Blue?"

Kay looked at me.

"No," I answered.

"But Detective Cass Elliot was with you the night Sugar Murphy and William Garcia crashed a stolen pickup while chasing Bret Ivey. And she's been working the murder case off the record with you for the last day or two, correct?"

"We were out together for the evening and just happened upon the wreck," I said. Babby's lips moved almost imperceptibly at that lie. "We brainstormed suspects and motive last night, before Blue hired Lost and Found to help in her defense. Cass was helping me satisfy my curiosity, nothing more."

Yvette regarded me with heavily lidded eyes. "Elliot's off limits, that's what you're telling me?"

"Yes, and she hasn't shared any information the police have gathered about the murder cases."

She jotted a note. "Have you talked to Blue about the murders?"

"She told me she's innocent -"

Yvette waved a hand tipped with blood-red nails. "Everybody's innocent."

"I haven't followed up regarding her whereabouts at the time Annie and Daphne were killed. I'm not even sure when they were killed. She has verbally given me a list of suspects."

Yvette studied the timeline of Bret's marriages and divorces I'd written on the white board, then snapped a photo with her phone. "This is a good start. What a busy, busy boy our Mr. Ivey was." She reached into her Mulberry briefcase and placed a contract on the table, then slid it to me. "I'll take her case. It sounds like her husband needed killing, and given his polygamous lifestyle, we have no shortage of suspects to look into. Sign the contract, give me a notarized copy of the power of attorney, and I'll start on a bail hearing."

"Who's on the bench today?" Babby asked.

Yvette smiled. "Shackleford. My favorite."

SHORT ONE HUSBAND

WITH THAT, THE OMINOUS Yvette Hardcastle was gone. Cindy returned to the conference room after showing her out, and glared daggers at us. "How could you let her," she lifted her chin at me, "interact with someone like Hardcastle? She's not even licensed."

"But she's the one of us that's closest to this case, babycakes," Babby said. "Besides, I thought Maxine did fine."

"She busted Yvette's balls," Kay said. "That was a pleasure to watch. I hope you were taking notes, Cindy."

My cousin fumed but stayed silent.

"Now what?" I asked.

"Now you go to Dallas and tell Nicole Ivy she's short one husband," Babby said. "Blue was right, she needs to know. And I want us there to watch her reaction."

"I don't have time to go with her today," Cindy said.

"None of us do. Maxine could go alone, but it might be better if Cass went as a witness and for backup."

"A witness to what?" I asked.

"Honey bun," Babby said. "You're about to tell a lawyer - an entertainment lawyer, granted - that her husband was married to multiple women at the same time, and he's been murdered. She could be glad, mad, or sad. Or any combination. Having an officer with you can only help keep the woman calm. Who knows? The two of you might pull a confession out of her."

Kay nodded. "Call Cass, kiddo. Tell her lunch is on the agency today."

———————

THE LAW FIRM OF Ivy, McLellan and Brown was posh and I was glad to be in the Tahari suit and Louboutin heels. Cass was in jeans, boots, and a button down shirt and looked completely at ease in the rarefied space we occupied. When I'd asked her to come to Dallas with me this morning, she'd readily agreed, stating that it might help Chad the Psychopathic Physical Therapist move on his decision to let her return to work if she missed a session. On the three hour trip to Dallas, I'd called ahead and bullied my way onto Nicole Ivy's schedule by mentioning the police. We got fifteen minutes at one forty-five.

While I was negotiating our meeting, Cass called one of her old colleagues in the Dallas police force to let them know she was coming to town on semi-official business. When asked if she needed assistance, she replied that she didn't expect so, but she'd let them know if things got dicey. She then went into a delicate dance, gossiping about personnel changes and cases that had occurred since she left the Dallas department, gradually steering the conversation around to sexual assaults. Nothing her contact told her led Cass to believe that our rapist had been active in the Dallas area recently; however, neither of us had reported our attacks to the police, and it was logical to assume he was still threatening his targets if they reported him.

The receptionist unfurled from her desk at precisely one forty-four and beckoned for us to follow her. We traipsed down a hall carpeted in a shimmering golden shag so deep you could lose a shoe in it; I curled my toes into the tips of my pumps and held on for dear life. The conference room's centerpiece was a slab of maple polished to a gleam and surrounded by chairs in shiny chrome with black leather seats. She brought us Perrier, a bucket of perfectly formed ice cubes, and a plate of lime slices, then slipped silently from the room. I'd just cracked the lid on a bottle when a panel in the wall slid open and a white ball of fluff bounded in. Then the big bottomed bimbo from Saturday joined us. I was shocked at her transformation and tried not to goggle.

The big haired overly made up woman I'd followed through the mall had transformed into a slick professional. The hair was pulled back in a bun and her makeup was so flattering it was barely noticeable. I wondered why in the world a woman this naturally attractive would hide her appearance under the heavy makeup she'd worn Saturday. The big bottom, tiny waist, and rack of boobs were encased in a beautiful suit by Dior that molded her figure perfectly. Intelligence sparked behind hazel eyes. She actually looked like a lawyer.

After the briefest of pauses, she stepped forward and offered her hand to both of us. "Nicole Ivy. I understand there's a police matter you want to discuss?" Her voice had a nasal quality that was right on the edge of irritating. She sat and the ball of fluff jumped up in her lap. I recognized him as the dog in Marjorie's purse on Saturday - his name was Ted. While he was cute as a button, I hated to think how much work it would take to get Ted's little hairs off that Dior suit.

On the drive down, Cass and I agreed that I would lead the conversation and Cass would intervene in her official capacity only if needed. "I'm Maxine Leverman, Mrs. Ivy, from Lost and Found Investigations in Arcadia. This is Detective Cass Elliot with the Forney County Sheriff's Department."

A narrow line appeared between her brows. "Forney County? Where is that?"

"East of Dallas, near Louisiana." I shut down the geography lesson. "Are you married to a Bretton Baxter Ivy?"

"What is this about?"

"Answer the question, please," Cass said.

The line grew deeper. "Yes, I am. Now, what is this about?"

"I'm sorry to tell you that Mr. Ivy was found dead Sunday morning."

Nicole's eyes moved back and forth between us, her lips twitched, and at last she burst out laughing. Ted looked up at his mistress. "That's a good one. How much is he paying you?"

Cass and I exchanged a glance.

"Mrs. Ivy, this isn't a joke," I said.

"Come on. Bax is always pulling crap like this. The man loves his practical jokes. Lost and Found. Forney County. Really? Wait. Are you recording this?" She swiveled and plucked a tissue from a box on a side table and dabbed at her eyes, then wiggled her fingers at us as if we were holding a camera. She snorted a laugh. "Ha! Gotcha Baxter. You can't fool me."

Cass slid her detective's shield across the table. "I'm afraid this is a serious matter."

Nicole hesitated, then pulled the gold badge closer. "This is real?"

"Yes, ma'am, it is."

Her hazel eyes slid to me. "Lost and Found is real?"

I laid a business card on the table. This one included the agency's details.

That full lower lip trembled. "Bax is really dead?"

Cass and I nodded. Nicole swiveled in her chair and pushed a button on a phone, then said in a clear voice. "Trace?"

"Yes, ma'am," came a brisk male voice.

"Cancel my appointments for the afternoon."

A brief pause. "Even Mr. King?"

"Yes. And cancel tonight's flight to LA."

"Shall I reschedule?"

"Not yet."

She ended the call, grabbed the box of tissues, and burst into tears.

THERE MUST BE A MISTAKE

IN THESE SITUATIONS, IT'S helpful to have someone as calm as Cass as your partner. I was all teared up and ready to have a good boo-hoo with Nicole when Cass tapped my arm. That simple touch reminded me that I might be face-to-face with Bret Ivey's killer.

We gave Nicole a few minutes to weep and then I asked a question, even though I thought I knew its answer. "When did you last see your husband, Mrs. Ivy?"

"Saturday." She composed herself, running her fingers absently through Ted's lush fur. "How do you know it's him?"

"We have a positive ID."

"From who? Who does Baxter know in this place, this Forney County? He's never mentioned it."

I ignored her questions, as Cass had told me to do. "What kind of work did your husband do?"

She slapped the table and Ted jumped. "No. No more questions until you tell me exactly what is going on. How do you know my husband is dead? What happened?"

It seemed there was a lawyer in that head.

I glanced at Cass and she nodded. I hated to do this, but Nicole was forcing my hand. On our way out of town, Cass and I had met Mitch at The Golden Gate Café where we'd picked up coffee to go. He and Cass had previously discussed asking the Dallas police to do the notification, but he agreed having Cass there to watch Nicole Ivy's reaction to news of her husband's death was useful. He'd given us a headshot of Bret Ivey's face after Grey had cleaned all the goo from the body. He looked perfectly normal except for the waxy complexion. I reached into my briefcase and slid a manila folder across the table.

Nicole opened it and the color drained from her face. She swayed in her chair. Ted jumped to the floor and scurried into a corner.

Cass poured a glass of Perrier and pressed it into Nicole's hand. "Drink," she said, and then looked at me. "Find something stronger."

One of the matching maple cabinets housed an impressive collection of liquor, and I poured three fingers of Jack Daniels' Tennessee Honey. Cass swapped the water for whiskey and helped Nicole raise the drink to her lips. Once Cass was satisfied Nicole could hold the glass on her own, she sat.

Nicole's eyes were glazed when she looked at me. "What happened?"

"He was murdered, Mrs. Ivy."

"Why? Who did it?"

"That's what we're trying to find out."

Her vision slowly cleared. "But you're a private investigator, correct?"

"I am," I lied. But only a little.

"Why are you asking the questions? Why isn't Detective Elliot doing the talking?"

I'd dreaded this question. "I've been hired to look into his death. Detective Elliot came along as a courtesy and to ensure the Dallas police know we're speaking with someone in their jurisdiction."

"Who hired you?" The lawyer was returning.

"Blue Ivey."

"Is that a man or a woman?"

"A woman."

"I've never heard of her. Is she one of Baxter's relatives?"

I answered slowly. "Your husband married her in 2007, using the name Baxter Bretton Ivey." I spelled it for her.

"That's wrong. That's not my husband's name. It is very close, I'll give you that, but that's not his name."

I gestured to the photo, which was still on the table.

She looked down again and touched his face. When she looked up, her eyes sparked with anger. "I'd like for you both to leave. Now."

FREEDOM

BLUE STEPPED THROUGH THE jail door and into the bright afternoon. She smiled with relief at Kay Wooten. "The air really does smell different out here. And not because the jail isn't clean. Thanks for the clothes. My others are ruined."

"My pleasure. Blue Ivey, I'd like to introduce your lawyer, Yvette Hardcastle."

Blue smiled at Yvette. "Thanks for getting that bail hearing taken care of so quickly. But why don't I have to pay anything?"

"Judge Shackleford loves Cedar Bend," Yvette answered. "And he seemed convinced you weren't a flight risk, thanks to the winery and the fact that you're going through harvest."

"What happens now?"

"Now," Yvette said, motioning to the parking lot, "we start on your defense. Kay and her agency have shuffled a few things so they can focus exclusively on you."

The three women got into Yvette's Mercedes, Kay riding in back. She leaned forward to speak to Blue. "We've set up a war room and we'll coordinate your defense from there. Yvette has questions for you. We thought it would be more efficient for you to come to the agency for a few hours before heading back to the winery."

"Of course. Where's Maxine?"

"She's in Dallas, notifying Nicole Ivy that her husband is dead, and is also your husband."

Blue snorted. "That should be interesting. I almost wish I was a fly on the wall for that one."

BOOTED

WE WERE HUSTLED FROM the posh law firm in record time and stood on the building's steps, squinting in the blazing afternoon sun. I looked at Cass. "What do we do?"

"We go home and let Mitch know we've notified Bret Ivey's other wife that he's dead and she refused to talk. He'll go through official channels to check her alibi for Bret's death."

"And maybe for the other two girls?"

"That's a good idea," Cass said.

We started for the car. "Do you mind if we make a detour through the mall?"

"What for?"

"I need to return something."

―――――――

I HAD FINISHED RETURNING the blue pajama set and we were in Nordstrom's when my phone rang. The call was from an unfamiliar number. I jostled the driving moccasins I was holding and answered. "Maxine Leverman."

"This is Nicole Ivy. We need to meet. Are you still in Dallas?"

I beckoned Cass over and tilted the phone between us. "We're at Northpark."

"There's a Chinese restaurant located on the south side of the mall. Do you know it?"

"I do."

"I'll see you there in half an hour."

Nicole hung up and I looked at Cass. "What's that about?" I asked.

"She talked to a criminal lawyer and he told her she's a suspect."

"Ah."

Cass put the pair of sling-back pumps she'd been examining on a shelf.

"You don't like them?" I asked.

"They're gorgeous." She ran a finger over the shoe. "But when would I wear them?"

"On a date, Cass."

"In Arcadia?"

"You could wear them to the winery, or over to that steakhouse in Shreveport. Or to bed with Kado."

"*Maxine*," Cass whispered, checking for eavesdroppers.

"Are these your size?"

She nodded. "But what do I wear them with? I don't own any girl clothes and I don't have time to shop today."

It was terribly true that her wardrobe consisted of Dockers and button downs, and I considered this an opening. I waved for a salesman and checked the time on my phone. "Oh ye of little faith. We've got twenty-eight minutes. Come on."

HEADPHONES REQUIRED

"BRET IVEY'S PHONE IS a treasure chest. It's loaded with women's names," Truman told Mitch and Kado. They were in the forensics room and the young officer's face was flushed. "He must've been terrified one of his wives would find it."

"Password?" Mitch asked, settling into a chair at the evidence table.

"WINE0."

"That's not very smart," Kado said.

Truman shrugged. "Being married to more than one woman at a time isn't very smart, either."

"What's on it?" Mitch asked.

"Phone numbers and addresses. Some for legitimate businesses, some overseas, others for people. First names only. One's an international number with 'Shitbird' as the contact name."

Mitch frowned. "Country?"

"Mexico."

"What about his call history?" Kado asked.

"He's called several women in the past few weeks. He's made some international calls but most are domestic."

"International to where?" Kado asked.

"All over. Europe, Asia, Canada, Mexico, South America."

"Are those numbers regular contacts on his phone?"

"Most of them are business numbers and he stores them under the correct business name. I looked them up and they're either wine, music, or finance businesses."

"Finance? Like who?" Mitch asked.

"Big banks. Maybe he was looking for credit."

"Maybe he owed somebody money. That would be motive."

"It would be," Truman agreed. "But most of these calls are outgoing. If he were in debt trouble, the banks would be calling him."

"Good point. Any files?" Kado asked.

"Loads of .wav and .mp3 files."

"Music?"

"They're all labeled music -," Truman began.

"But you won't know for sure until you listen," Kado finished for him.

Truman's face fell. "I hoped Mitch could do that part since he likes Poison Ivy and the Dismembered Bunnies."

"I'd love to," Mitch said. "But you're the forensic understudy. I've got great headphones you can borrow."

"If that's full of folk punk," Kado said with a glance at Bret's phone, "you're required to borrow them."

THE ALIBI

WE SWEPT INTO THE Chinese restaurant with a gorgeous silk trouser set for Cass and three minutes to spare. We took a remote table in a corner near a window and I ordered egg rolls as an appetizer. "I'm starving. All I had was a donut at the agency this morning."

Cass lifted the garment bag to finger the silk of her new outfit and then peered warily at the food on the other tables. "It looks better than the all-you-can-eat buffet in Arcadia."

"It's a different world."

Cass's phone buzzed and she took a call from Mitch. My listening abilities were impaired by hunger, and I asked her for a summary when she hung up.

"Kado finished with the gun the guys tossed in the river."

It took a moment, but I remembered something shiny arcing towards the river after Sugar Murphy and Big Billy Garcia ran from the stolen truck. "And?"

"It's clean. He found Murphy's prints on the cartridges, but the gun isn't in any databases."

"What does that mean?"

"It hasn't been used in a crime, or at least it hasn't been reported as used in a crime."

"Then why toss a perfectly good gun?"

She shrugged. "Maybe they panicked. Mitch said Truman cracked Bret's phone. There are loads of women's names, some of them the ex-wives we know about. Bret's been in contact with most of them recently."

"Why?"

"No idea. Truman's listening to all the music files on the phone now. Poor guy."

We'd polished off the egg rolls when Nicole arrived twenty minutes later with a paunchy little man in tow. She slid into the booth and waved the waiter away, making me glad we'd scarfed the egg rolls. Her eyes were red-rimmed but she'd touched up her face.

"This is my attorney, Ned Shaver. He's advised me to talk to you." Her expression was sheer outrage, and I couldn't say I blamed her. She'd just found out her husband was not only dead, had not only cheated, but was married to another woman.

Shaver sat higher in the booth and looked at Cass. "I've seen the coverage of your most recent," he paused, "escapades. You're still on medical leave, Detective Elliot. Why are you here?"

"The lead detective on the case, Mitch Stone, is my partner. He knows Lost and Found Investigations has been retained to look into Mr. Ivey's murder. Since Maxine was coming to see Nicole today, he asked if I could join her to limit our impact on Nicole's time."

He seemed satisfied with that. "I spoke to Detective Stone when I called to verify your identity. He's arrested someone for the murder, and claims this woman is married to Mr. Ivy."

"She is," I said. "She had no knowledge her husband was married to another woman."

"Are you calling my husband a polygamist?" Nicole asked. Two bright spots rose on her cheeks. "That's an attack on his character and I will not tolerate it."

I could've played the sympathetic friend, but decided to go on the attack. There was an edge to Nicole I didn't like, an air intimating that she lived on a higher plane than the rest of we mere mortals. "I'm not attacking anyone. I'm telling you that a woman named Blue Ivey is married to a man named Baxter Bretton Ivey who looks remarkably like your husband."

"How do you know what my husband looks like?" she snapped.

"Besides your reaction to his photo earlier, there's this." I pulled out my phone and showed her a photo from the mall on Saturday.

Her jaw dropped. "That's where I've seen you before. You and another girl followed us through the mall. You're a stalker."

It seemed our earlier meeting had been lost to shock. "No, ma'am. I'm a private detective hired by -" I started to say 'Mrs. Ivey' but stopped myself. This conversation was already confusing. "Blue Ivey to find her husband. Who also happens to be your husband. I found him by analyzing the business and personal credit card statements he shared with Blue."

That stumped her, so I kept talking.

"Forney County records support Blue's belief that she is married to a man she calls Bret, who is the same man you call Baxter. Bret was spending quite a bit of time away from home, she thought he might be cheating, and she hired me to find out if he was."

"That husband stealing bitch. Blue. Her name is Blue?" She snatched up her phone and pecked at the keyboard.

Cass reached across the table and took the phone. Nicole's face contracted into a ball of fury.

"That's illegal search and seizure. I'll have your badge for that," Shaver blurted.

"No," Cass said. "It's common courtesy to stay off your phone while you're having a face-to-face conversation. Nicole's phone hasn't been seized, and it certainly hasn't been searched." Cass lifted an eyebrow at Shaver, and when he backed down she looked at Nicole. "Mrs. Ivy, you can consider how to react to your husband's infidelity later. Right now, we need to ask some questions. We have information to share with you as well, but first, we need to know about your husband. You told us earlier you last saw him on Saturday. What time on Saturday?"

Shaver waved a hand. "We're not going there. You have the murderer in custody. You don't need anything from my client."

"You *want* to talk to us, Mr. Shaver," Cass answered coolly. "Nicole and her firm handle people with high public profiles, famous actors and actresses, singers, that type of person?"

He nodded warily.

"Mr. Ivy's history with women is complicated. It's in Nicole's interests that we share what we know so she can decide how best to protect her reputation and that of the law firm."

Shaver considered this. "What do you have?"

"It doesn't work that way, Mr. Shaver. She gives us what we need, and we share what we can."

Shaver had been put in his place several times by Cass and didn't seem to mind. I wondered what his home life was like.

He nodded. "Go ahead."

"When was the last time you saw your husband?" Cass asked. She was in super-detective mode and I was happy to watch and learn. I opened a note pad.

"Saturday afternoon," Nicole answered. Anger, fear, and grief played over her face in turn. "We'd both returned from trips early Saturday morning. We dropped our bags at home and then went to Northpark to have breakfast and shop, like we always do." She glanced at me again, but carried on speaking. "When we got back home we discovered the house had been broken into. My husband's instruments were smashed to bits and our papers had been searched. We called the police, they came out and questioned us and when they were done, my husband left. He had a client appointment he couldn't miss."

"Did he return?"

"No," she answered simply.

"Did he contact you?"

"No."

"Did he normally stay away over night without calling?" Cass asked.

Nicole motioned for the waiter and ordered a bottle of wine. We waited while the waiter poured. I was dying for some broccoli beef with egg fried rice, but stayed quiet.

"Ma'am?" Cass prompted after the waiter left.

"We have very busy schedules," Nicole answered, and then sipped her wine. A crescent of blood red lipstick marred the glass. Her eyes shimmered with tears. "Had. We had busy schedules. His clients were a bit erratic and Baxter never knew how long he'd be. Sometimes it was days. Other times, only a few hours."

"What kind of work does he do?"

"He deals in rare instruments." At our blank look, Nicole carried on. "Buying and selling. He travels constantly, all over the states and sometimes overseas. Mostly guitars and banjos, but occasionally he'll purchase other stringed or brass instruments."

"Does he have a shop?"

"No, he works from home. Does a lot of investigating and buying and selling on the internet. His work is very specialized."

That explained the extensive collection in Forney County. I suspected he had a healthy collection in the Oak Lawn house.

"How did you feel when he left you alone to deal with the break-in and all the mess that goes with it?" Cass asked.

"Irritated, but I understand that clients can be difficult. We certainly deal with our share of drama queens at the firm." Shaver cleared his throat and Nicole looked apologetic. "These are highly strung people, which is often what makes them so good at what they do."

"Where were you from Saturday night around eight o'clock until Sunday morning at eight?"

I wondered why Cass was giving Nicole such a wide amount of time to account for, when Grey had confirmed that Bret died between ten Saturday night and two Sunday morning.

"The firm hosted a party Saturday evening. Eighty attended. It started at eight and the last guest left at about one. Is that right?" She looked at Shaver and he nodded. "Several of us stayed until almost three, Ned included. I went home and slept until nearly eleven."

That was a pretty good alibi for Bret's murder.

"We'll need your guest list."

Nicole motioned for her cell phone, made a call, and asked that the list be sent to Cass's email. I heard a faint chime as the message landed in her inbox. The support staff at Ivy, McLellan and Brown was efficient, I'll give them that.

"You don't have any idea which client your husband went to see on Saturday afternoon?" Cass asked.

Nicole shook her head. "We're apart so much we really don't talk about work." She flinched as she slipped into the present tense again.

"Did he keep a diary, or a calendar?"

"Only on his phone, as far as I know."

Thank goodness for wine-proof phone covers, I thought.

"Had he changed his habits in the last few weeks?"

A small smile crossed Nicole's full lips. "Our schedules were chaotic, Detective Elliot. We had few habits, few routines. We spent the little time we had together focused on each other."

Shaver shifted again. "I think it's time you answer a few questions for us."

Cass looked at me. "It might be easier if we start by telling you what we know. Can we order lunch? I'm starving."

THE SCAM

BETWEEN BITES OF BROCCOLI beef, lemon chicken, and egg fried rice, I told Nicole and Shaver what we'd learned about the man she knew as Bretton Baxter Ivy. Yes, I know it's rude to talk and eat, but while Nicole was barely picking at her lunch, Shaver was packing it away. If Cass and I didn't cram in a few calories now, we'd go hungry.

Nicole looked more and more despondent as I filled her in on his multiple names and wives, and I finally asked if she'd had any inkling about Baxter's prior and alternate lives.

"No, I didn't. Not really," she answered quietly. "I suppose there were signs that something wasn't right, but Bax had an answer for everything. Late night calls, sudden meetings with clients that kept him away, a kid even showed up at our house one morning, looking for him."

I gave Cass a blank look. We still had tons of digging to do, but I hadn't turned up any indication that Bret Ivey had a child.

"What kid?" I asked.

"A Hispanic boy, in his late teens or early twenties. Well dressed, very polite. Had an accent. He knocked on the door and asked to speak to BB Ivy. I didn't know who he meant, but Baxter came flying out of the kitchen when he heard me talking to him. He hustled the kid outside and that was the last I saw of him."

"When did this happen?" Cass asked.

Nicole caught her bottom lip between her teeth and gently tugged. "A few months back. Spring. Before the weather got so freakishly hot."

"Did you get his name?"

"No. But I wondered if this could be a child of Baxter's." Her smile was rueful. "I'm not naive enough to think I was his first sexual partner. I never imagined he'd been involved with so many women, but…" Her voice trailed off and we waited. "Unless a man has lived as a monk his whole life, there's always the possibility a kid is roaming around out there. One they didn't know about. Bax was never totally forthcoming about his history. We'd skirted around both of our pasts, and when he told me he'd done some things he wasn't proud of, treated women worse than they'd deserved, I just thought he was embarrassed."

"Did this kid look anything like your husband?" I asked.

"No, but if he'd been involved with a Hispanic woman, it's possible the child could've inherited more of her features than his. It was a silly thought, but at the time, it felt like Bax knew exactly who this kid was, even though he denied it."

"Baxter didn't tell you what the kid wanted?"

"He said he was looking for someone called BB Ivy. Baxter told the kid he had the wrong house, and sent him on his way."

"Did he tell you who BB Ivy was?" I asked carefully.

"No." Nicole's eyes narrowed. "Do you know him?"

I put my chopsticks down and prayed Shaver would leave some food for me. "There's a little more I need to tell you about your husband."

BY THE TIME I explained about Poison Ivy and the Dismembered Bunnies, Shaver looked befuddled. Nicole had polished off the first bottle of wine and was halfway through a second, and her mood had darkened. She crossed her legs and swung one foot under the table, kicking me twice. I was ready to retaliate.

Nicole shook her head as our waiter cleared the table. "You're telling me that my husband was a famous, you called it folk punk, musician?"

I nodded. "On his way. That's what we believe."

"Why wouldn't he have mentioned it?"

"I don't know."

"And you believe this woman, this Blue, didn't kill him?"

"Yes." Wanting to keep the conversation as straightforward as possible, I hadn't brought up Annie or Daphne's murders.

She snorted. "Who did?"

Shaver laid a calming hand on Nicole's and looked at Cass. "What do you think?"

"I have my doubts about her guilt. The evidence points directly to Blue, but it seems contrived."

"You think someone planted it?"

"Before I decide that Blue's the right person to go to trial, I want more."

Shaver glanced at Nicole, and then back at Cass. "What happened to him? How was Baxter killed?"

"We believe he was hit in the head with a baseball bat, and that blow killed him."

"Who found him?"

"The police did. Or more correctly, the fire department. His body had been placed in a vat full of fermenting wine."

"At this winery that he and Blue own together?" Nicole asked.

We nodded.

"Who put him there?" Shaver asked.

"If Blue killed him, she did," Cass answered. "Or she had help getting him in the tank. It wouldn't be an easy task, even for two people."

"Do you have a viable suspect other than Blue Ivey?"

"No."

"I want her to burn," Nicole said, eyes blazing. "Send her to the electric chair. She stole my husband and killed him. Bash her over the head with a bat and dump her in a tank of her own wine. That's better than she deserves."

"Not if she's innocent, Nicole," Shaver said. "You're hurt and angry, but we want the right person prosecuted for this crime. Baxter scammed this woman, just like he did you."

"Scammed?" Cass and I asked in tandem.

I reached for Nicole's bottle of wine and filled my glass. This was getting interesting.

HE USED YOU

NICOLE GLARED DAGGERS AT Shaver and he raised a hand in a placatory gesture. "We've been over this. You say he made you happy, and I liked him well enough, but I never thought Baxter was good for you financially."

"Why not?" I asked, leaning forward.

"He spent all her money," Shaver answered.

"Ned," Nicole scolded. "That's none of their business."

"It might be," I said "He was spending all of Blue's money, too."

Nicole's eyes widened and I could all but hear the gears sloshing in her brain. "He used us?"

"Given his history," I gestured to the napkin where I'd made notes about Bret / Baxter's marital activities, "he knows how to attract wealthy women and gain access to their resources. So yes, I think he used both of you. I think he used all the women he married, except possibly the first, Mary Sterling. He must've married her back in his Dismembered Bunnies days."

Nicole sat back and uncrossed her legs, which stopped the swinging foot. "I want to meet this woman."

"I don't think that's a good idea," Shaver and Cass said together.

Nicole bumped Shaver to urge him out of the booth. She was a sloppy drunk. "Where is she?"

"What about tomorrow?" I asked. "She should've had a bail hearing today, but I haven't heard anything from the agency, so I don't know if she's out yet."

Shaver jumped in. "That's a better idea, Nicole. It's late," he looked at Cass. "Where is Forney County?"

"About three hours east."

"You'll feel fresher in the morning. Will see things more clearly. It might not be a bad idea to meet this woman who claims to be married to Baxter, but let's give it the night."

Nicole nodded slowly and eased back into the booth.

"I have another question," I said.

"Why not?" Nicole said. "You've already ripped my life to shreds. What's one more question?"

I wanted to tell her it wasn't me who had left her life in shreds, it was Baxter. But I wanted the answer to my question even more. "Was every instrument of Baxter's smashed?"

Nicole nodded.

"None were left intact?"

She cocked her head to the side and looked at me. "We have a gun safe in the house. He stuck three banjos in it a couple of weeks ago."

I put my napkin on the table. "May I have a look at those banjos?"

BUSY BOY INDEED

A BANJO MAY LOOK like a tambourine on a stick, but they're heavy little boogers in case you're wondering. I had a theory about the break-ins at all the houses Bret's women frequented, and I thought it would be easy to prove. Shaver convinced Nicole to let me take the banjos back to Forney County, and I gave him a receipt.

On the drive home, I explained my theory to Cass and she agreed that what I was thinking was plausible, but doubtful. It would require some phone work, but that was doable.

We got to Lost and Found at nine o'clock and I was surprised to see the lights still on. We headed inside, me lugging two banjos and my briefcase, and Cass carrying one plus a Nordstrom's shopping bag. I was even more surprised to find Kay, Babby, Cindy, Blue, and Yvette working in the conference room in relative peace. A beautiful smell was wafting from the kitchen and my stomach growled.

Cass looked at me. "Seriously? We just finished lunch."

"You might've had lunch," I grumbled, kicking off the Louboutin's and flexing my toes. I slipped on a pair of comfy old tennis shoes I keep under my desk and switched items from the briefcase to my purse. "But Ned Shaver took advantage every time I was talking and scarfed the fried rice. No wonder he's so chubby."

Three white boards blocked the room's windows and two of them were full of Cindy's scratchings. She'd rewritten, sloppily, my timeline of Bret's marriages and divorces, and found two more ex-wives. Both living in Texas. He'd married them while he was married to Blue and Nicole and was still married to one, which made three concurrent marriages. Busy boy indeed.

She'd also created a timeline of the break-ins and murders, which was revealing.

"How'd it go?" Kay asked.

"Interesting," I said. "Nicole Ivy wants to meet Blue."

Everyone looked at Blue. "Do I need a bodyguard?"

Cass chuckled. "That might not be a bad idea. Nicole's personality really swings."

"Her lawyer is bringing her down tomorrow to officially identify the body, since she was his spouse first, and Nicole insists on talking to Blue."

Blue shrugged. "Fine by me. I'd like to meet her, too."

Cass and I put the banjos in a corner of the conference room and joined the women at the table. "She's not the empty-headed bimbo I thought she'd be," I said. "Given that she's a lawyer I should've expected some smarts, but her emotions do get the better of her."

"What kind of law does she practice?" Yvette asked.

"Hollywood stuff."

"That explains the mood swings."

I wondered about that but decided to ignore her. "When we told Nicole that Bret - she calls him Baxter - was dead, she thought he was playing a joke on her."

Blue frowned. "Why would her husband do that to her?"

"She seemed to think he liked to play practical jokes."

"And once she realized you were serious?" Babby asked.

"She broke down," I said.

"Then kicked us out," Cass added.

"But she called before we left town and we met her and her lawyer and had a chat."

"What's his name?" Yvette asked.

"Ned Shaver. Do you know him?"

She talked as she tapped on her phone. "No, but I'll have someone put a résumé together so we know who we're dealing with."

"They gave me the impression they worked together, Cass. Did you get that idea, too?"

"Yes. I thought it was weird at first, having a criminal attorney as part of a firm that practices entertainment law, but given what actors and actresses get up to, it makes sense."

"Did she have an alibi for Bret's murder?" Kay asked.

"She was at a party the firm hosted," Cass answered. She pulled out her phone. "Give me your email address and I'll send the guest list to you to verify."

Kay did, and then asked, "If she didn't do it, did she have any idea who had motive?"

"Not that she could think of immediately," Cass said. "But her lawyer said they'd talk about it on the drive down tomorrow. Nicole was a little tipsy when we left her."

"She did mention a kid," I said.

"Bret had a child?" Blue asked.

"She didn't know about one if he did, but a Hispanic kid came to their house this spring looking for BB Ivy."

Collectively, eyebrows went up.

"Bret told her he didn't know who the kid was, but Nicole wondered if this child was a product of a union between Bret and a Hispanic woman. He was in his late teens or early twenties."

"What an amazing liar Bret was." Blue pushed back from the table. "I'm starving. Do you mind if I bring our food in here?"

No one objected, and Cindy rose to help her.

"Where does this leave us?" Babby asked as the two women left the room.

"I don't know where we are on the murder," I said. "But I think I know why the instruments were smashed. If I'm right, maybe we can learn something about Bret's death from the people who trashed them."

THE IDEA

THE SHADOWS ON THE courthouse lawn came to life for the briefest of moments, then settled again into the still evening. A trio of men huddled under the sheltering arms of an ancient live oak and peered around its massive trunk to watch the only office with lights on this late.

"Did you see that?" Big Billy whispered.

"How many were there?" asked the shorter man.

"Two."

"No, three," said Sugar. "The other chick had one, too."

"Guitars?"

"Banjos, I think." Sugar pulled at his nose. "You think they're BBs?"

"Who else?" Billy answered. They watched the glowing windows and saw movement behind the blinds. "What now?"

Sugar released his nose. "I have an idea."

THE THEORY

IT TOOK ABOUT TWENTY minutes to run through my theory. During that time, everyone else was eating these gorgeous little puff pastries filled with cheese and prosciutto. Blue stepped from the conference room once and returned with a selection of grapes, cheese, salami, and crusty loaves. Two bottles of wine were on the table, one white and one a blood red, disappearing quickly. Why is it that I pick my time to talk when there's wonderful food around? Thankfully, there were plenty of questions and I managed to sneak a few bites.

My theory went something like this: I believed the tapes from Poison Ivy and the Dismembered Bunnies' last recording session had surfaced, and Bret had them. Maybe he took them from the studio before it burned, maybe the Bunnies' manager had them. If Bret was angry enough to smash Sonny's guitar, he would've had no qualms about taking the tapes. Why bother? Maybe he was pissed off about Sonny's disappearance. Or, maybe he believed there was something of value on them.

When Kay asked what that might have been, I answered, "Decent recordings that could be turned into an album is the logical answer, but there might've been something else. A recording of their joint song writing, of them working through bad takes, of a fight, or perhaps of something damning to Sonny or his family."

Everyone scoffed at this except Cass, but I held fast.

"I think the Dismembered Bunnies found out Bret has the tapes and believe he hid them in one of his instruments," I said.

"Why would he do that?" Blue asked.

"I don't know. But Kado told us the destruction of the instruments was methodical. Remember? Someone took them apart carefully, except for the banjos. I think they did that to see what was in them, and then smashed everything to make it look like a break-in gone bad or maybe a revenge thing."

"Fine, Maxine," Cindy said. "Open the cases. What are we looking for?"

"Cassette tapes. The studio would transfer the recording session to a cassette, mastered or unmastered, and give it to the band."

"The recording studio would have a copy of those sessions?" Cindy asked.

Clever girl. "Yes, and we could probably get them from the studio if it hadn't burned."

We seven women spent half an hour shaking those three banjos and feeling the cases to see if anything resembling recording tapes was secreted away in them. No dice. However, I wasn't willing to give up until we'd found someone who could take the banjos apart to be sure nothing was inside the tambourine part.

The worst part about the empty banjos was that Cindy scoffed harder. I ignored her and explained my plan of action for Tuesday morning. Since the winery's credit card contained recent UPS and FedEx charges in amounts that were for something bigger than a breadbox, and Bret's call history showed he'd made recent contact with his ex-wives, I thought he might be shipping guitars and banjos to them for safekeeping. Heads nodded, but without enthusiasm. To keep from losing momentum, I carried on with my theory. I also believed Santiago 'Sonny' Arellano was alive and well and living in Mexico, and he'd taken the reigns of his family's drug business. The recent sightings of him made this plausible.

"So what?" Cindy asked, licking garlic oil from her fingers.

"If there's something harmful to his family on those tapes, Sonny might want them back now that he's the big cheese."

"What could be so harmful?"

"What if Sonny really didn't want to be involved in the drug business when he was younger and more idealistic? What if he said something on those tapes that could undermine his leadership now, cause a rift in his family, or allow someone to challenge his authority?"

Cindy digested this. "If he'd been reluctant to be involved in his youth but suddenly saw the light regarding the family business, somebody might think he was a snitch?"

I have to hand it to her, I hadn't made it that far in my thinking. I didn't tell Cindy that, of course. "Exactly. Or maybe he gave up family hideouts, drug processing locations, key members of the cartel, that kind of thing. But there had to be a trigger to cause Sugar Murphy and Big Billy Garcia to chase Bret and break into these houses."

"We have no proof they broke into Annie or Daphne's houses," Cass pointed out. "Or into Nicole Ivy's, for that matter."

"No, we don't," I agreed. "And other things were taken during the break-ins, but that was a diversion. What they were really after were the instruments."

"They weren't really after the instruments either, precious," Babby said. "They smashed them up instead of stealing them."

"From what I can tell from the insurance inventory, about twenty are missing," Blue said. "Murphy and Garcia might've stolen them."

"Maybe," I agreed. "But Bret was cautious. He had to be to pull off all his marriages. I think the trigger was the article about the winery." Nobody replied, so I continued. "Think about it. An article comes out last autumn about the winery, including photos of the owners. Bret Ivey was very good at keeping a low profile. There are almost no photos of him online in any of his incarnations. And his DMV photo," I pointed up at the white board, "is awful, as most of them are. He's done an excellent job of hiding his identity by using multiple names. That article is the first time he's truly surfaced since the early eighties and it contains a decent photo of him. Not brilliant, but you get an idea of his features. I believe Sonny saw or heard about that article and got in contact with Sugar and Big Billy. He's using them to find the tapes."

"Say you're right, Maxine," Yvette said. Her shoes were off, her legs tucked beneath her on the chair, and she held a glass of wine in one hand. No doubt, if Uncle Charlie was going to cheat, he'd picked a looker in Yvette. She was over the top on the attitude scale, but her looks more than made up for that shortcoming. "Sonny Arellano is a big fish. A whale. If there's something controversial on the tapes and he believes Bret has them, why not take Bret out?"

"Because they haven't found the tapes yet." I turned to Blue, who was following the conversation with wide eyes. I pointed up at the DMV photos of Sugar Murphy and Big Billy Garcia. "Have you seen these men before?"

Blue got up and studied them. "Yes, they were at the winery for lunch a few weeks ago. Maybe as long as a month ago."

"How many people come in and out of your restaurant in a month, Blue?" Yvette asked. "How could you remember these two?"

"That one, Murphy, he has a tattoo on his neck. Look." I knew what she was talking about. I'd seen tattoos on various parts of the band members' bodies on the album cover. "I couldn't tell what it was at the time because he was wearing a collared shirt. But it's a bunny head."

"Good enough for me," Yvette said.

Cass assumed that fierce expression indicating thought. "How does the kid come into this?"

I knew I could count on her. "When Nicole told us the kid asked for BB Ivy, we thought he could be Bret's biological child. Given his Hispanic appearance, that's unlikely. Not impossible, but unlikely. Instead, what if he's Sonny's child?"

BAD IDEAS

"THIS IS A BAD idea," Big Billy told the shorter man. "His ideas are always bad."

They were waiting on the courthouse lawn for Sugar's signal.

"They're women," the shorter man answered. "It'll work."

Billy eyed the window. "I don't know."

"You can't hit it?"

"I can hit it, easy. But his ideas, man, they always go wrong."

"You got anything better?"

Billy shrugged.

"I'll see you at the truck. Make sure you get all three of them. I'm getting tired of this."

BLACKMAIL?

CASS ACTUALLY CONSIDERED MY comment. "You think Sonny's been looking for BB Ivy for a long time?"

"Maybe, or maybe this is recent," I answered. "If he's a big drug guy, he can't travel to the US, so he'd send his son. But there's something he wants from Bret."

Cass turned to Blue. "Maxine told me Bret started acting strange about a year ago. He bought the Corvette, stayed away longer, had poor excuses for his absences."

Blue nodded.

"Did anything during this time impact the winery?"

"How do you mean?"

Cass pursed her lips. "New vendors. New contracts. Firing people you've done business with for a long time for trivial reasons. Infusions of cash."

Blue reached for her wine, her expression thoughtful. "An infusion of cash. That's not how he put it, but Bret suddenly wanted to make some changes to the winery. New tanks, new sound system, expand the acreage we use for vines."

"That was unusual?"

Blue nodded. "We'd been debating where to go with the winery for a while. Leave it the same size, which was comfortable, or grow it, which would take some investment and a lot of commitment. The business was cash poor and I didn't want to take out any more debt than we already had." She blushed. "Bret got mad because I wouldn't put more of my money in the business. I thought if we were going to grow, we should do it organically. It would be slower, but we'd do it without heavy loan repayments."

"The tanks in the barrel room look new to me," Cass said.

"He came home one day, this was before he bought the Corvette, and said he'd placed an order for the tanks and was starting work on the land where he wanted to plant new vines. He'd even hired an architect to draw up plans for expanding the dining room."

"Where'd the cash come from?"

"That's what I wanted to know. He was absolutely infuriating," Blue said. Her face was flushed now. "He said he'd cashed in some of his own investments because he believed in the future of the business, even if I didn't." She took a deep breath and seemed to gather herself. "His changes have made a difference, but I don't know how we paid for them, and that makes me nervous."

"No new loans?"

"No, and some of our existing loans were repaid."

Cass looked at me. "Blackmail?"

"Over the tapes," I answered.

That was when the lights went out.

———————

BECAUSE IT'S A PRETTY common occurrence for the power to drop in East Texas, nobody was worried. Cass got up and headed for the kitchen and the agency's fuse box. We'd both spent so much time in these offices when we were kids that moving through them in the dark was easy. She was back in a flash.

"Get away from the windows and somebody dial 911. There's a man in the alley. Who's got a gun?"

Babby hurried to her purse and returned with a 9mm and a spare magazine.

Cass checked the load. "Lock the kitchen door behind me."

"No you don't, Cass," Kay said. We'd all moved into the main office area and were huddled in the center of the room. "Not without one of us."

"This is what I do, Kay. Dial 911 and tell them your power supply has been cut and I'm in pursuit. Send backup. Suspect is a white male, slender, close to six feet tall, in dark clothes. He's wearing a dark cap. I've got my phone. Call now."

And she was gone.

THE SHADOWS

IT'S A HELPLESS FEELING knowing it's nearly midnight and your best friend is roaming the streets in pursuit of someone who might want to hurt you both, and you can do nothing to help her.

Except exactly what she tells you to do.

So I did. As I snatched up the phone on Kay's desk and dialed, the conference room window exploded. A chorus of screams sounded and my heart jumped into overdrive. Despite the fear, I surprised myself by dropping the phone and squatting to duck walk into the conference room.

Kay and Babby hissed behind me like a pair of spitting cobras, but I stayed low and ignored them. If our intruder was throwing things, he might be armed. That was bad for Cass. I crunched across the conference room floor, bits of glass glittering in the sparse light filtering through the blinds. As had been the case for months now, there was absolutely no breeze, but the humid air rushed to invade our cool offices. I shifted one of the white boards. The wooden slat blinds were ajar and through the slit I could see into the street. Lights were on around the square and I realized why Cass had reacted so quickly. From the conference room, she would've seen the glow of street lights even against the closed blinds and around the white boards. There was no logical reason for our power to go out.

Smart cookie.

Arcadia has a beautiful old courthouse in the middle of a grass lawn wrapped by the one way street that goes around the square. Seconds had passed since the window shattered, but nothing moved. I stayed low and waited, watching. Cass rounded the corner of the block at a full sprint. A sliver of shadow separated from the base of a giant oak on the courthouse lawn and scurried east.

I shouted through the empty window frame, "That way, Cass. He's on foot." I pointed and watched as she ran after him. Moments later sirens filled the night air, still heavy with a heat that would keep us in the eighties through the night.

My knees were protesting and I was ready to stand when a second shadow moved. I wasn't sure what I was seeing at first, but a dark mass peeled away from the tall war memorial and morphed into the blackness beneath another live oak. I couldn't decide what to do. Cass was out of earshot and I couldn't see clearly where this figure was headed. I kept my eyes on the lawn and whispered for Cindy to join me.

"There's glass everywhere, Maxine. I'm not coming in there."

I resisted the urge to snap at her. "Call 911 again. There's a second man on the courthouse lawn. He was hiding - wait. There he goes again. South. Call now, Cindy."

She backed away and I heard a phone being uncradled and a voice murmuring. More sirens wailed into the night but they were too late. I'd lose this second man if I didn't hit street level.

I think that's when I realized just how badly I wanted to be a detective. Maybe even needed it. I was utterly helpless while my best friend was out risking her life for a case I'd stumbled into. In those minutes when Cass was out of my sight, before I heard the gunshots, a tiny piece of me grew up.

But the rest of me was still impulsively immature.

Then a gunshot cracked and an image of Cass unconscious in a hospital bed those few weeks ago hit my brain. Icy fear flooded my body.

A second gunshot sounded.

I ran for the agency's front door.

HEAVEN'S INTERVENTION

SOMETIMES HEAVEN INTERVENES IN our favor, and it certainly did for me that night when I'd slipped out of the Louboutins and into a pair of trainers. I couldn't have made it down the stairs and taken off after the second shadow in those heels. No chance.

I hit the grass on the courthouse lawn as the first police car tore around the corner and flew through the square, tires squealing. The flashing lights were disorienting but they caused my man to bolt. I hit my stride as the second car rounded the corner and it followed me onto a side street. The man I chased was nimble, even with a decided hitch to his giddy-up. He darted into a narrow alley, leapt a pile of garbage bags, and hustled between two buildings. I raced after him and had the good sense to stop at the corner for a peek.

He was gone.

I charged into the alley at full speed and went flying as his foot came from a doorway. I went down hard on my hands and knees but had time to flip to my back before he pinned me. Air gushed from my lungs and I sucked a huge gasp when he shifted to grab my wrists. My hair was in my eyes but I recognized him as Big Billy Garcia and although a tiny bit of joy stabbed me because I'd been right, terror overruled it. Being trapped beneath a man and unable to move him is one of the most fear inspiring, rage inducing experiences I've ever had. Perhaps it comes from that deep lizard part of the brain where memories of my rape reside; perhaps every woman feels the same way when she's trapped. Regardless, I reverted to the little girl who'd been pushed down in second grade. Aunt Kay's advice flashed through my head: kick him in the balls.

I swung and screamed for all I was worth. Given his photo on the cover of *Hand to the Throat*, Billy Garcia didn't deserve the nickname of 'big' back then, and he certainly didn't now. He was a scrawny little runt who was no match for a furious woman. I managed to get one knee between his legs and thrust upward. Billy grunted and his hands slipped on my arms. One fist connected with my face and I saw cartoon stars, but I tore four strips down his cheek with the nails from my right hand and landed a solid blow on his nose with my left. He howled and grabbed for his face and I shoved his chest with all my might. He was almost in a standing position and was headed backward when I managed to swing my foot with full force. It connected solidly in his groin and his howl deflated into a breathless groan. Just then, a spotlight illuminated his face in all its agony, and I'll admit I felt a perverse satisfaction in not only being free again, but also the victor in this little skirmish.

Billy Garcia was curled in the fetal position when an officer approached, weapon drawn. From my position on the ground, I raised my hands but kept checking to see that Billy was still down. Footsteps pounded the pavement and I glanced behind me to see Cass round the corner. She stopped and bent over, hands on her knees.

"That's. Maxine Leverman. She's. With me. Arrest him for B&E. And vandalism," she told the officer through jagged breaths. Then she looked more closely at me. "What. Happened to you?"

ASSESSING THE DAMAGE

THE PAIN DIDN'T HIT ME until we were back at the agency. Kay had disregarded Cass's order to stay put and marched down the back steps to flip the building's breaker back on. Yes, that's all they'd done. I'm not sure what Big Billy Garcia and his lame brain partners thought they would achieve by turning off the lights and breaking a window. Maybe they hoped the weensy little women would run from the building in terror, leaving the doors wide open. I'm quite sure they didn't expect a foot race.

The place was in chaos when we stopped at the open door. Two uniformed officers and Detective Carlos Martinez were exchanging confused glances while Babby, Kay, Cindy, and Blue simultaneously explained what had happened. Yvette was in one corner, pecking manically on her phone. I guess the adrenaline rush had hit. Cass and I stood on the threshold listening until Cindy noticed us.

She pointed. "Maxine's bleeding."

I looked down. She was right. My knees and one shin were a bloody wreck, my sexy dress was in ruins, and my palms sizzled where the skin had scraped off. I was amazed to see red marks on my wrists where Billy had held them. Kay and Babby went into repair mode, hustling me to the kitchen. Cass stopped them and improvised the collection of evidence from under my fingernails. Then my aunts dug in and cleaned my wounds. One cut on my knee was deep enough for stitches but Babby tutted at the idea of the emergency room, choosing instead to sterilize the slash with a blazing splash of alcohol and then super glue me up as she'd done when I was a child. Tears stung my eyes but I bit my lip and breathed through the pain.

Kay bathed my face with a warm cloth and it came away streaked with blood. She examined me for cuts but found only a raspberry on my chin and that my left eye was swelling and turning red. "Ouch. Did you make contact, sweetie pie?"

I nodded carefully. My entire body was pulsing with pain. "Once in the nose, once in the balls, and I slashed a good two inches off his cheek."

She pressed iced wrapped in a towel against my eye. "All four fingers?"

"Yes, ma'am."

"Good girl." She and Babby stood back and took in my clothes. "That dress is a goner, honey bunch."

"Does the agency have insurance for this kind of thing?"

"Nope, but maybe we can work a little bonus for you."

Cindy huffed behind me. "I've never gotten a bonus."

"You've never ruined a dress subduing a criminal, darling," Kay said.

"I've never *had* to ruin a dress because I know how to catch them safely. Maybe Maxine needs a course in self-defense instead of a bonus."

"That's not a bad idea," Babby said.

"Maybe Maxine needs both," I said, and staggered to my feet. "What time do we start tomorrow?"

NONE OF THEIR BUSINESS

THE TRUCK SCREECHED TO a stop on the side of the road and the small man glared at Sugar as he climbed out of the truck's bed and into the cab. "You shot at a cop, *idiota*." His accent was thicker now.

"That redhead's a cop?"

"She's a detective. Killed a man a few weeks ago."

Sugar pulled on his nose. "Did I hit her?"

"You better hope not." He put the truck in drive and eased onto the blacktop. "How did she find you?"

"I don't know. I flipped the breaker and ran back down the alley. By the time I came around the building, she was coming after me."

"What happened to Billy?"

"I don't know. Did he get the brick through the window?"

"How would I know? I was waiting in the truck. You were supposed to hook up and meet me."

Sugar shrugged. "Should we go back and look for him?"

The small man considered. "No. Since you shot at a cop, they'll be looking for us." He tapped his fingers on the steering wheel as he drove. "We need to let these women know they're messing in the wrong business."

"How do we do that?"

He accelerated. "Get your picks out."

"Another break-in?"

"Yes."

"What are we looking for?"

The small man shook his head. "What have we been looking for all this time?"

"Instruments?"

"Yes."

"We're going to smash them?"

"You're going to smash them."

"Alone?" Sugar asked.

"Yes. And smash everything else."

"What everything?"

"Everything. Destroy it all."

"How?"

"There's a sledgehammer in the toolbox." The small man gestured over his shoulder to the truck's bed.

"What are you going to do?"

"Be your lookout."

Sugar pulled his nose again. "Sounds like I'm taking all the risk."

"We've discussed this. That's why you're paid so well."

"Oh. Right." He released his nose. "Can you pull the truck over?"

"Why?"

"I've gotta pee."

THE THIRD MAN

GETTING OUT OF THE agency wasn't quite that easy. Detective Martinez finally got us subdued and split the officers up to take our statements. It was a brick that had come through the window, and the boys had tied a note around it. Quaint. The note read: "Back of Biches."

Yes, you read that right. There are no Spelling Bee Awards waiting for these guys.

Kado showed up to collect the note and brick, and dust the fuse board for prints. He fussed at Kay for flipping the breaker back on and disturbing evidence, but only gently. I also noticed he was discreetly checking out Cass, probably to make sure she wasn't hurt.

Detective Martinez sat down with me at the kitchen table. "Tell me what happened, Maxine."

The man is built like a bull with a wide chest and a head that drops into a charging stance when he's irritated. His hair is a steel gray in a buzz cut, which makes him look kind of military. If you didn't know how big his heart is, he might scare you. But I know and had no problem unburdening myself. In truth, I probably over-shared about what I was feeling when Big Billy landed on me and how good it felt to sock him in the nose, but I think Martinez credited my garrulousness to adrenaline.

Cass stood behind me, listening and frowning. She didn't say a word but I knew she was angry that I'd gone after the shadow without having a clue what I was up against, and that I'd done it unarmed. Not that I was anywhere near qualified to carry a gun, which probably made her even madder. In my defense, I told her it was the gunshots that had sent me out the door. I was worried something had happened to her.

Her scowl deepened.

"Do you want to give me your statement now, or come to the station tomorrow?" Martinez asked Cass.

"If Maxine can stay, it'll save me from telling the story twice."

It turned out that Billy Garcia's partner got away. The gunshots came from his gun, firing at Cass as he scrambled into the bed of a pickup. She asked Martinez to have patrol officers look for casings and other evidence in the area where the pickup had been parked.

"License?" Martinez asked.

Cass shook her head. "Lights were out over the rear plate."

"Wait a minute," I said. "Who's the third man? I chased Big Billy, his fingerprints will prove it. He must've been with Sugar Murphy, who either ran from Cass or drove the truck. So who's the third guy?"

"Sonny Arellano's kid?" Cass asked.

"You think he's hooked up with Big Billy and Sugar?"

"It can't be Sonny himself."

"Have you heard of the Arellano family, Detective Martinez?" I asked.

He nodded. "But just because I'm of Mexican descent doesn't mean I have a line into the cartels."

I smiled a little at that, even though it hurt. He smiled back. "I just wondered if you've come across any of them in your capacity as Forney County Detective, or if you've heard the rumors that Sonny is the head of the family."

"I've heard the rumors. You think he's mixed up in this?"

"I have a weird theory that goes back a few decades," I answered, uncertain how much to give away. "But I don't have any proof." I turned back to Cass. "Are you coming here in the morning?"

"After I get done with Chad. I wouldn't miss seeing Nicole's meeting with Blue."

"That could spark some fireworks." I tried to stand but found I couldn't move. I held my hand out.

Babby and Kay were vying for position at the kitchen threshold. "You're not driving home, Maxine," Kay said. "I'll take you."

"No, I will," Babby insisted.

From the looks on their faces I knew I was in serious trouble.

"Tonight, she's mine," Cass said. She pulled me to my feet and steered me through the barricade. "You can have whatever's left of her in the morning."

TUESDAY

VIOLATION

IT WAS NEARLY TWO-thirty when we pulled into the lot at my apartment's complex. All was blessedly still. After Cass had nearly lifted me into her truck, I'd endured a non-stop lecture on the short drive about putting myself in a dangerous situation without proper training or protection. I think she talked about the training schedule for my concealed carry license, but I was crashing from the adrenaline rush and found myself listening not to her words but to her voice, waiting to see if she'd take a breath. She didn't and carried on scolding me as she walked around the hood and opened my door. And then she stopped and stood stock still, looking through the truck and out the driver's side window.

I went from groggy to hyper-alert in a flash. "What?"

"I don't know yet."

She helped me from the truck, slung my lucky purse over her shoulder, and supported me as we walked to my building. I saw a form hovering in the shadows beyond the amber bubble of a safety light as we passed the pool.

"Is it the guy who shot at you? Is it Sugar Murphy?" I asked, voice trembling. "How did he find us?"

She was quiet as she took me the long way around the pool. "It's the guy from Monday morning, when we ran, remember? I see his orange shoes. Does he live here?"

"I didn't get a good look at him, Cass." My heart was thudding now, pain gone. "What's he doing?"

"Nothing, as far as I can tell."

She steered me up the steps to my apartment and we were on the first level when his voice drifted up to us. Again, that rapid-fire Spanish. Cass stayed between me and him, peering into the darkness, muttering under her breath about the lights on the balconies being too bright to see anything.

"Security," I said.

"Not when you can't see what's coming at you." When I stiffened she added, "Or *if* anything is coming."

We'd made it to the third floor without incident when Cass pushed me behind a corner, dropped my purse, and unholstered her gun.

"Stop, police," she yelled, and took off in a sprint, leaving me to peek around the corner. She'd already disappeared and I tried to run after her, but my legs wouldn't work. Instead, I stumbled to my apartment, where my heart sank. The one place where I'd felt a tiny bit of safety had been violated. My door hung like a broken arm from its hinges and the frame was cracked in multiple places, leaving a gaping maw opening onto a black nothingness. The cool breath of fear washed over me, heightening my senses, and I waited at the threshold to see if I could feel a presence.

Nothing stirred.

I drew a shuddering breath and stepped inside.

SHE'S SAFER WITH US

"THIS IS EXACTLY WHAT I was talking about, Babby," Kay said. They were in the kitchen with the door closed to block the noise of men covering the broken conference room window. Kay was pacing the small space, stopping to dig in the cupboards and then slamming the doors shut. "I swear. Right now, I wish I still kept an emergency pack of cigarettes around. Where did I hide that last one?"

"It was taped to the crook of the waste pipe under the bathroom vanity. I threw it out a year ago." Babby took a deep breath and settled into her chair. A cup of herbal tea steamed on the table before her. Despite a very long day and the nighttime heat permeating the office, both women looked composed. "I know."

"She won't work out here."

"Maybe not."

Kay watched her sister through narrowed eyes. "There's a 'but' coming, isn't there?"

Babby blew across the top of the cup and sipped. "She showed a lot of heart."

"She showed a lot of impulsiveness. She could've been killed."

"True. But she wasn't."

"Not this time. And there will be a next."

"Next time she'll have her gun license. And she'll have been through a self-defense course. Cindy's right. That's exactly what Maxine needs."

Kay flipped the switch on the kettle. "It's not enough, Babby. Teaching her how to use a gun safely and how to protect herself won't override Maxine's inability to think through the consequences of her actions. If that man had been any bigger, or if he'd had a gun -"

"He could've hurt her badly."

Two bangs sounded in quick succession and the women jumped.

"Nail gun," Babby said, hand to her heart. "We need to talk about what we want the glazier to put on the window."

Kay blinked. "What's wrong with what we had before?"

"I hated that window. Roscoe's repaired it after Hurricane Rita without consulting us, and it looked too masculine."

"You want pink?"

"No, Kay. I want something that better reflects who we are and what this agency is about."

"It's about all kinds of investigations, Babby." Kay opened a cabinet and got down a mug. "Should we list everything we do?"

"I don't know. I know we're getting more and more business through the internet, and I'm grateful for the web site. I'll draw something up and we can look at it in the morning. Back to Maxine. I'm not ready to give up on her yet."

"Do you want to be the one to tell Vivienne her daughter's been injured, or God forbid, killed while under our care?" Kay poured boiling water over a tea bag. Babby lifted her cup for a refill.

"She's not a child any more, Kay. Her actions aren't our responsibility."

"Even though she's working for us?"

"We can give her all the training available, but it's down to Maxine to use it wisely. I think she's serious about this PI thing. Finding Bret Ivey on Saturday fueled her passion for it. Could you tell? And if she doesn't work for Lost and Found, she'll find a job somewhere else."

"She's safer with us, that's what you're saying?"

"Maybe." Babby sipped, and then nodded slowly. "But beyond that, she's got good instincts. She doesn't quit. She follows her heart."

"But can she follow instructions?" Kay asked, sitting at last.

"Maxine will always have an impulsive streak. It's our job to channel her strengths in the right direction and help minimize her weaknesses." Babby almost smiled. "After watching her for the last few days, after seeing her dedication to finding the truth, are you really willing to give up on her?"

Kay heaved a great sigh and closed her eyes. "I want more than anything to protect Maxine *and* the agency, Babby. But I'm not sure we can do both."

ABSOLUTE DESTRUCTION

I ADVANCED SLOWLY, OPEN-mouthed at all the damage. It was utterly complete. My whole apartment was upside down. My beautiful red sofa was in tatters, its stuffing strewn around the living room like shredded marshmallows. The kitchen was a wreck, cabinet doors open, crockery crunching under foot.

The fear that engulfed me when I saw my damaged front door evaporated and despair expanded in my chest with every step.

I followed the intense smell of a perfume I couldn't identify into the bathroom. My towels were in strips, the contents of the cupboards tossed about. My makeup was in the toilet. Bottles of perfume had disintegrated on impact and amber liquid streaked the walls. Light from the bulbs remaining around the mirror glittered on the glass shards underfoot. The shower was running and I reached in, intending to turn it off, then remembered Kado's distress over Kay's handling of evidence. Water was draining so I left the shower running.

My mattress and box springs had been upended and slashed, the duvet and pillow torn apart. Feathers littered every surface like freshly fallen snow. I couldn't see my shotgun anywhere and panic coated me in a cool slick. Drawers were missing from the chests, my lingerie was strewn about in silken mounds, the drawers themselves reduced to kindling. I advanced on the closet with dread, only to find its contents untouched. My intruders either had a conscience, or were aware of the consequences Diann Vega's spouse encountered when he'd tossed her clothes in the pig pen.

The guest bedroom was in the same shape. The equipment in my exercise room looked as if someone had taken a sledgehammer to it. I crept into the study and my panic bypassed anger and blossomed straight into fury. My computer was a jagged island of broken plastic and glass. The massive stickies Cass and I had filled with notes about Bret Ivey's marriages and divorces, our thoughts about motive related to winery staff and Poison Ivy and the Dismembered Bunnies, were gone. I hurried to the stereo and found the album on the turntable. The original sleeve in its plastic case had fallen behind the unit. I breathed a sigh of relief as I slid the record home. Stan would've seriously hated me if his album had been abused.

A crunching sounded, then stopped. I grabbed a splintered desk leg and ducked behind the study door. A figure entered and whispered, "Maxine?"

My knees went weak. "Jeepers, Cass. Don't sneak up on a girl whose apartment has just been trashed."

"Sorry. I wasn't sure if you were inside." I stepped from behind the door and she raised an eyebrow at the desk leg. "Seriously?"

"They stole my shotgun," I said, and burst into tears.

CASS PACKED A BAG and had me back in her truck in record time, leaving officers in place to guard my apartment until Kado could process it. She'd called Bruce and told him to get one of the spare rooms ready. I'll admit it; this wasn't how I'd imagined my first night sleeping under the same roof as Bruce Elliot since I was a kid, but it would do.

"Poor guy," I said. "Does Kado ever get to sleep?"

"When it rains, it pours," she said. "Crime seems to breed crime. He'll get Truman out of bed to help and they'll do the urgent stuff tonight."

I yawned. My supplies of adrenaline were spent. "You didn't catch the guy again?"

Cass frowned and I realized how rude that sounded. "He disappeared into the woods. Mr. Orange Shoes is gone, too."

"You think they're working together?"

"It's possible. I sent Kado a text, telling him where Orange Shoes was hanging out. Maybe he'll find a cigarette butt or piece of gum and we'll get DNA."

"You don't sound optimistic," I said.

"It rarely ever happens that way, but most criminals are stupid and don't know it. We've got to try."

TELLING PAPA

THE SMALL MAN CLOSED his phone and then his eyes. Sugar waited for the explosion; the shouting coming through the phone had been beyond furious.

The big pages he'd ripped off the chick's wall were crumpled in a corner. Once they'd got back to the hideout, they'd turned up the lantern and read through the notes. Again. And then again. Each time, the smaller man's agitation grew. It took Sugar some time to figure out why, but at last realization dawned: the girls knew about the tapes. Or at least had a theory involving the tapes and BB's former band mates.

That was very bad news for the small man, and even worse news for his father, which was confirmed by the violent reaction Sugar overheard.

So he waited, picking up Maxine's shotgun and sighting down its barrel.

The small man, usually in perpetual motion, was utterly still. Sugar had to pee, but he waited. At last the small man raised his head and Sugar braced for the explosion. But it never came.

"That's it," the small man said.

"What's it?" Sugar ventured.

"Papa's sending the enforcer to take them out."

"Who?"

"Everybody. Everybody who knows about the tapes."

"That's what he should've done when BB made the first call."

The small man glared.

Sugar pulled at his nose. "Um, sorry."

"Good. Because you and Billy are in the same pile of *mierda* that I'm in."

"What does that mean?"

The small man was silent for several moments. "He told me not to come back unless I find the tapes."

"Never?"

"Yes."

"What about me and Billy?"

"You are dead to him."

Sugar blinked. "Like really dead?"

A ghastly smile crossed the small man's face. "Like really."

Sugar rubbed his eyes. "What's on those tapes?"

"I don't know."

"How can you not know?"

"How can *you* not know?" the small man said. "You were there."

"He kicked us out when the chick showed up," Sugar protested.

"What chick?"

"Some scary Mexican chick."

The small man studied him. "Scary how?"

"All scarred up. Her face." He motioned to his cheeks.

The small man nodded. "Ah."

"'Ah' what?"

"That woman is my *abuela*, my grandmother. She was kidnapped by the Sinaloa Cartel when it was falling apart. My family thought she was dead."

"Whoa. That explains why Sonny freaked. He saw a ghost."

"That meeting is legendary, but I didn't know it happened at the studio."

"What did your granny say? We were on the way, man. To stardom. It had to be something heavy to make Sonny walk away."

"I have no idea, but that conversation is the reason Papa wants the tapes." The small man paced. "We must find them. Any bright ideas?"

"The girls know about the tapes, so we follow the girls."

The small man eyed Sugar with something approaching respect. "Clever."

"That's what I keep telling Billy. Let's go find him. Billy's good with girls."

DOMESTICITY

I WOKE TUESDAY MORNING to the smell of frying bacon and had no clue where I was or how I got there. My muscles were so sore they were almost in spasm but I leveraged myself upright and from the odd angle of the room's ceiling, realized I was in the Elliot house. The curtains blocked most of the morning's light, but the clock on my phone read six-thirty, and I relaxed.

Although I remembered getting into Cass's truck, I didn't remember actually arriving at the house or getting inside. I eased out of bed, stretched until I felt somewhat human again, and dug through my bag to find a robe. A mirror that was losing its silver hung over an old dresser, and I gently touched my eye. It was deepening to a lovely shade of black, but the swelling had dropped a bit. The raspberry was scabbing over on my chin, and rather than fret about it, I was grateful I hadn't knocked a tooth loose. There was nothing I could do about my looks, so I ran my hands through my hair and followed the smell of food downstairs.

Bruce glanced over his shoulder as I stepped into the kitchen. "I've got ice ready."

I tried to protest but he pulled a towel wrapped bag of ice cubes from the freezer. I gingerly put it against my face. "What happened? I don't remember getting here."

"You conked out in the pickup and Cass had me carry you inside." He flipped an egg. "She wouldn't let me change you into your PJs, though."

My insides flipped like the egg, and I didn't have any words.

Bruce seemed tickled to strike me mute. "Coffee? Today's Forney Cater is on the table."

"Mmmm," I answered, and sat at the table, enjoying the sense of being served by a man. I wondered if this was what domesticity was supposed to look like. I doctored and sipped the cup he put on the table. "Nice. Blue Mountain?"

"Just for you. I usually make a pot of the grocery store brand because nobody here appreciates good coffee.'

"Untrue," Cass said as she came through the kitchen's swinging door. "We just don't express our gratitude clearly to those who share a branch on our family tree. Are those eggs for me?"

"These are for Maxine. Yours are coming up."

He slid a plate onto the table and I nearly swooned. Fried eggs, bacon, a pretty little heart shaped pancake, and a pile of blueberries topped with whipped cream. "That's romantic," I said.

"That's the only pancake mold he's got," Cass said. "I'm getting him a hammer shaped one for Christmas."

She opened the newspaper between us. "Love Quadrangle Murder Suspect Released" read the headline in huge font. The article provided a recap of the murders and named Blue Ivey as the primary suspect in all three. A separate piece summarized Bret and Blue's marriage and the winery's history. Photos of Blue, Annie, and Daphne were positioned above the fold.

"Guess they couldn't find a photo of Bret, either," I said.

"At least Wally added the caveat that all leads are being followed," Cass said.

"In tiny print at the bottom of the story. It sounds like Blue's a deranged killer who's on the loose again."

"It's not that bad. It'll probably boost business for the winery," Cass said. "How are you feeling?"

"I'm stiff. How are you?"

"Fine. I'm skipping physical therapy again today."

"Chad won't like that," Bruce offered.

"Chad can deal. We've got some bad boys out there with details about Bret Ivey's ex-wives in their hot little hands."

I knew where she was going with this.

"So?" Bruce said as he slid a plate in front of Cass and joined us.

"If they're really after the Dismembered Bunnies' tapes, they might think he hid them with an ex-wife," Cass said.

"My ex-wives wouldn't be my first port of call if I needed help," Bruce said.

"You wouldn't be married to three women at the same time, would you?"

"That's too much work."

Cass nodded at my plate. "Eat up. We need to get on the phones."

ALL HIS EXES

COFFEE WAS ON WHEN we got to the agency. Kay, Babby, and Cindy had come in early to extract contact details from the various databases for the wives so we could test my theory about the instruments. After last night, we needed to warn them about the dangers of the Dismembered Bunnies, too. I was moving slowly and Kay tutted over my injuries while Babby checked to ensure the super glue was holding on my knee. Then they took me into Kay's office, slid the glass partitions closed, and laid into me. First one, then the other, tag-team wrestling-style without the masks and flying chairs. I don't think any of my high school escapades earned me this much grief, but memory fades with time.

They were right, of course, about how foolhardy it was to chase someone in the dark with no backup, no weapon, and no means of communication. Or even to chase someone in daytime under those conditions. I listened and nodded. After they'd fussed themselves out, I promised I would never do anything like that again, and at the time, I meant it. They looked at each other, realized they had nothing left to beat me with, and released me.

I hobbled to the kitchen and caffeine. After I filled a cup, I left a message notifying my insurance agent about the break-in and destruction. Then I found the Nordstrom's bag I'd brought in last night and took it to Cindy.

"Get your trash off my desk," she said. "I'm busy."

"It's not trash, Cindy. Look."

She pulled her gaze from the computer screen and tipped the bag forward. Her eyes narrowed. "What's this?"

"A thank you."

She pushed the bag at me. "I'm not for sale, Maxine."

Why does my cousin make everything so hard? "I'm not trying to buy you, Cindy. I'm thanking you for helping me and training me on Saturday. Is that so bad?"

Cass wandered over and peeked in the bag. "Are those the driving mocs you were looking at yesterday?"

I nodded.

"They're my size. I'll take a thank you if Cindy doesn't want one."

That did it. She snatched the bag and shoved it under her desk, grousing a 'thanks, but you didn't have to.' Cass winked at me as she sauntered away. The girl's got some serious psychological mojo going on.

We split the wife list and waited to dial home numbers until eight o'clock Texas time, but that still put it at six California time. To our knowledge, Bret had had nine wives, including the two we'd met, Blue and Nicole. His first wife, Mary Sterling, was dead. That left six women, three in Texas and three in California, we needed to contact. Kay and Babby took the Texas women, and Cass, Cindy, and I took the California girls, using the speakerphone in the conference room so all three of us could listen in.

Once we assured the women there was no immediate emergency and explained their ex-husband Bret or Baxter Ivy or Ivey or Ivye or Ivie had been murdered, their reactions were either relief ('thank God, he wouldn't stop hitting me up for cash') or anger ('he *can't* be dead, he owes me money'). It seemed that although they divorced in sometimes bitter circumstances, Bret never broke contact with these women. His charm must've been immense. Or maybe some other physical attribute was immense.

His second wife, Susan Spikes, cried, and once we probed a little, discovered that *her* second marriage to the other banker's son had turned out very badly. Bret was wooing her again. I wondered how he thought he could make four simultaneous marriages work, but when you've already got three on the go, what's one more?

Most of the ex-wives knew or suspected Bret / Baxter had been married before, but they all said he was so sensitive about his failed marriages - that's how he described them - they didn't probe.

We briefly explained my theory about Poison Ivy and the Dismembered Bunnies. Susan remembered Bret talking about his time as a musician, but she was the only one he shared that part of his life with. Although he had brought instruments into their marriages and acquired more while married to each, he'd never mentioned it to the other women. Susan had thought it incredibly sexy to be married to a guitar player, but wasn't too keen on his banjo practice. They all thought it unlikely a band mate from thirty years ago would want to hurt Bret now, but we asked them to please take precautions for the next few weeks, going so far as to ask them to request drive-bys from the local police on a regular basis at their homes and work.

As I suspected, each of the women had agreed to hold a package for Bret over the past several weeks, which explained the FedEx and UPS charges on the winery's credit cards. On Bret's instructions, none of the women had opened the packages, but all were about the size and shape of a guitar or banjo. We asked them to open the boxes and check for a cassette tape or tapes. All did, although one Texas ex-wife offered to bash the banjo in her box to bits to find the tape. We told her the Gibson she was threatening might be worth thousands of dollars, depending on its age and condition. That saved the banjo, since she figured she could sell the thing and recoup part of Bret's borrowing. Only two guitars contained anything, both of them notes addressed to 'Shitbird', presumably Sonny, telling him he'd failed to find 'it' yet again.

The third current Texas wife, a jewelry designer named Frannie Whitehouse, offered to drive the package to our office in Arcadia, and we took her up on the offer. I think we were all curious to see what she looked like.

I wasn't sure Nicole Ivy was ready to compare notes with Bret's other wives, but when I talked to Blue at a little after eight-thirty, she was all for it. I guess the grief, what there had been of it, was fading. Blue had started the morning at the winery but was coming into the office at ten o'clock to meet Nicole.

When Kay told us that Texas wife number three lived south of Nacogdoches and would be with us by ten to meet the other wives, we were stunned.

Cindy regained her composure first. "Not only was Bret Ivey a lying, cheating, dog of a man, but he must've had massive balls. Imagine having two wives living roughly an hour apart."

Cass checked her phone. "Mitch texted and said they're interviewing Billy Garcia this morning. I shouldn't be there, but Hoffner's in Austin. You want to come with me, Maxine?"

"You'd better get going." Babby checked her watch. "And it's time to call the glazier, Kay. Let's flip to decide who picks the sign for the window."

WE'RE NOT DONE LOOKING

EVERYBODY KNOWS HOW INTERVIEWS of suspects go on TV. Good cop, bad cop, and the suspect caves and confesses. Seems it's not that easy in real life. Big Billy was mute when we arrived, waiting on a public defender. Mitch paced outside the interview room, shaking his head.

"The idiot won't talk," he said. "We've got him dead to rights on the break-in at Blue's, stealing that truck, and assaulting Maxine. That's some shiner, by the way. I hope you've taken a picture of it."

I scowled, which hurt.

"Seriously. How often is it that a hot chick gets a black eye stopping a criminal? You need to start building your portfolio of experience. Nice work."

That made me smile, which also hurt.

Mitch continued. "Turning off the breaker and tossing a brick through the window is a little uncertain, but it's got to be him that did it."

"How long will it be before the public defender gets here?" Cass asked.

"Who knows? Want coffee?"

We took cups to the forensics room and sat while Kado finished a phone call.

"Nice black eye, Maxine," Kado said.

"Yeah, yeah, it makes me look tough."

"Given that Billy Garcia's still not sitting right, you more than look tough."

"Got anything for us?" Mitch asked.

"Several things. Sugar Murphy trashed Maxine's apartment last night, but he did it alone. Your place is really clean."

"Thanks," I said.

Kado nodded. "Fingerprints confirm Sugar flipped the breaker at the agency and Billy Garcia threw the brick. More good news is that Sugar was in Annie's house. Truman went back and lifted all the partial prints from the pieces of the guitar we found at Annie's. We got enough detail to be sure Sugar was there. We've got partials that could be Billy's, but not enough to be sure. We have Billy's prints on the guitar that was smashed at Daphne's house."

"So they did kill the girls," I said.

"I don't think so," Kado said. "I also talked to the crime scene guys in Dallas. They found prints from Billy Garcia and Sugar Murphy at Nicole Ivey's house. There's plenty of evidence that says they damaged all the instruments, but nothing linking them to any of the murders."

"So Blue's still our best suspect," Mitch said.

"Yes, unless you two have found somebody else." He looked at me and Cass.

I shook my head. "But we're not done looking."

Kado snapped his fingers. "There's something else I need to follow up on. I thought I got fingerprints from all the employees at Cedar Bend Winery, but I missed two. A kitchen worker called Oscar Matalan and the guy who was coordinating it all, Will Sterling."

"Can't you go back to the winery and print them?" I asked.

"I called out there this morning. Oscar hasn't been in since Saturday. Truman's going to get Will's prints this afternoon."

The courthouse receptionist buzzed Kado and said Garcia's public defender had arrived. Mitch looked at us. "You can't be here," he told Cass. "And you definitely shouldn't be here," he said to me.

"Then we're not here," I answered. "But if Cass can't help you interview Big Billy, please remember he doesn't know he's not a suspect for three murders."

"He's not."

"But he doesn't know that."

"How does it help us if Billy thinks we're looking at him for murder?" Mitch asked slowly.

"We need to know why he's smashing guitars. I think Sonny Arellano sent him to find those missing Dismembered Bunnies' tapes."

"Why do you think that?"

I bit my lip. "You'll think I'm crazy."

"That's nothing new."

He was right. I explained my theory about the Bunnies' search for those missing tapes.

"That's far-fetched," he said. "But not impossible. How does accusing Billy of three murders help us?"

"If there's something damaging to Sonny on those tapes and Bret is blackmailing him, and if Sonny sent Billy and Sugar to find the tapes, you can bet Billy's more afraid of Sonny than he is of you."

"But if he thinks he's looking at three murder charges," Cass said, "he might be more afraid of you."

IT'S A GOOD ONE

SUGAR PICKED HIS WAY across the rotting floor, unzipped his jeans, and peed in the kitchen sink.

"That's disgusting," said the small man. He raised the flame on the camp stove and watched the percolator.

Sugar lifted a bucket and poured pond water down the sink. "The toilet's stopped up."

"Be a man. Go outside."

"This place is a dump."

"Doesn't matter. We're leaving."

"To look for Billy again? We just got back. I need coffee first."

"We're leaving because Billy knows where we are." The percolator spat and then settled into a steady burble, and he poured two cups of coffee.

"Billy wouldn't tell, man."

"Even if it could save him jail time?"

"We don't even know he's locked up," Sugar protested.

"We can't find him. He hasn't called."

"Maybe he can't find a phone. Nobody has pay phones anymore."

"Why won't he carry a cell phone?" He ran his hands through his hair. "Everybody has a phone."

"He thinks they'll give him cancer."

The small man grunted. "We're going anyway. Get rid of that shotgun."

Sugar picked it up and caressed the stock. "It's a good one. The barrel's the perfect length."

"I said get rid of it."

"Why?"

"It links us to that chick's apartment." He sipped. "You wore gloves, right?"

Sugar pulled at his nose. "Um, yeah."

"Is that a yes?"

"For most of the time."

The small man glared. "What does that mean?"

"I had to pee. I couldn't touch my todger with the gloves."

He muttered to himself in Spanish, then looked up. "Throw it in the pond. Way out."

"But it's a good -"

"What did I say?"

"Throw it."

The small man drained his coffee. "Go do it, and pack up."

"Where are we going?"

"To look for Billy again and find out exactly what the girls know."

LETHAL INJECTION HIGHWAY

MITCH DID THAT SLOW walk thing men do when they're trying to look tough but not too aggressive. He was an attractive man. Tall with blue eyes and blond hair and in his early forties, he was still trim and had that air about him that told you he knew he was good looking, but didn't really know how good. Detective Martinez joined Mitch and the two made a formidable pair. I guessed Mitch would play the good cop, and Martinez the bad.

Cass and I stood in the observation room and watched through the one-way glass. She'd turned the volume up so we could hear the conversation. Big Billy Garcia's lawyer was a smartly if cheaply dressed defender named Chet Rubins. He was a few years older than us, and I remembered him as a shy kid from school. Billy sat with his skinny shoulders slumped, his gaze fixed on his hands, which were clasped atop the table. He kept shifting in his chair as if he couldn't find a comfortable position. I felt a little tug of pleasure at the bruise blossoming on his nose and the bandage on his left cheek. He looked like a beaten man.

Rubins, on the other hand, had a quiet but confident manner and he listened with interest as Mitch explained why Billy was in custody. Once Mitch finished, Rubins said, "Before we go any further, I want to file a complaint against the department on behalf of my client."

"For?" Mitch asked.

"Mr. Garcia was assaulted by department personnel while being arrested," Rubins said.

"He was fleeing a crime scene and captured by a citizen."

"That's not how my client tells it."

"Maybe your client is embarrassed to admit a woman half his size did that," Mitch lifted his chin at Billy's face. "He got in a few licks and she's filing assault charges."

That was news to me, but if it helped Mitch convince Billy to talk, I'd gladly file assault charges.

Billy's chin dropped to his chest.

"Well?" Rubins asked. "It's best if we don't start this session with a false claim about how you were injured."

"It might've happened like that." Billy's voice was deep but quiet. "It was dark. But I wasn't fleeing a crime scene. I was jogging."

"We've got your prints on a piece of paper that was wrapped around a brick that broke a window in a building downtown. We've also got a witness who saw you flee the scene."

Billy shrugged. "It might've happened like that."

"For a man who's already done time, Mr. Garcia," Detective Martinez said, "you're not a very careful criminal. We have your prints and those of your colleague Mr. Murphy at five other crime scenes."

Rubins sat straighter. "I was told it was only four."

"Mr. Garcia and Mr. Murphy broke into a house in Dallas and trashed some instruments there, too."

"Whose house?" Rubins asked.

"We'll get to that," Mitch said. "The important part about three of the four break-ins here in Forney County is that someone from each of those homes turned up dead."

"You've already arrested Blue Ivey for those murders."

"We're keeping an open mind," Mitch said. "Given the evidence, and we're still processing it all, it's very possible Mr. Garcia could end up doing time for three murders. Once we find Mr. Murphy, any benefit of the doubt we might extend to your client will disappear. Instead, Mr. Murphy will have a shot at our benevolence."

Rubins glanced at his client, who was still examining the table.

"I don't know what it's like out in sunny California," Martinez said, "but we don't like men who murder innocent women and law abiding men here in Texas, Mr. Garcia. Often, they enjoy an extended stay in one of our fine prison establishments or receive a bonus, a trip down lethal injection highway. Maybe you'd like to tell us why you're only a B&E man and not a candidate for a permanent resident visa here in Texas."

THE LONELIEST NUMBER

BIG BILLY MIGHT NOT'VE been too bright, but he was smart enough to recognize wiggle room when he saw it. Given that he'd spent time in prison in California, he probably wasn't too keen on repeating the experience in Texas. Rubins asked for a moment to confer with his client, and Mitch and Martinez joined us in the observation room. Sadly, the microphones were off and all we could see were two men talking.

"What do you think?" I asked. "Will he spill?"

"I think so," Martinez said. "Making him think he might be up for a few murder charges was a good idea."

We watched as Rubins leaned forward and tapped the table in front of Billy.

"What's happening?" I asked, biting my lip, but gently.

"His lawyer is telling him to confess to all the break-ins he and Murphy were part of," Mitch said. "Because we've got solid evidence for those."

Billy shook his head, slowly at first and then with more vigor as Rubins continued to talk.

"He's refusing to give up himself or his partner," Martinez said.

Rubins sat back and threw his hands up, then stood and paced.

"And now Rubins is telling him if he doesn't account for his whereabouts at the times of the murders, chances are we'll pin them on him because we prefer cooks like Blue over crooks like him," Martinez said.

Billy glared up at the lawyer and spoke.

"Ah," Mitch said. "Now we get to the good stuff. Big Billy says there's a bigger fish involved. A fish with humongous teeth who will take his swollen testicles off in a single bite, or worse, if Billy talks about the break-ins or anything else."

Rubins stopped walking.

Martinez chuckled. "His lawyer is asking whether it's worth spending life in prison for this big fish. If the fish paid him enough to do the time for those crimes and murder."

Billy crossed his arms over his chest. His lower lip poked out. Rubins picked up his briefcase and paused with one hand on the doorknob.

"Good," Mitch said. "Rubins is telling him if he's not interested in talking with us, he's got other clients to see. Garcia can sit in his cell all alone and think about what's coming next. Rubins will be back after the murder charges are filed."

Billy scrubbed his face with both hands, leaned forward to put his elbows on the table, and started talking.

"Hey presto," Martinez said. "One really is the loneliest number."

FISH FRY

IT ONLY TOOK BIG Billy ten minutes to tell Rubins his story. His lawyer sat and pondered, and then asked questions and took notes. Cass left to get more coffee. By the time she returned, Rubins was talking non-stop and Billy's head was bobbing in agreement.

Rubins motioned to the mirrored window. Mitch and Martinez met him in the hall and left the door to the observation room open a crack. Cass and I eased forward to hear better and although I couldn't see Rubins, I felt the energy crackling from him.

Rubins: "My client has critical information about a high-profile drug family. He would consider sharing this information in exchange for immunity for any and all crimes he might have committed in Texas."

Mitch: "What drug family?"

Rubins: "A prominent family in Mexico with violent tendencies."

Martinez: "No name? We're not interested."

Rubins: "Before my client divulges any information, he needs your assurance that he will not be called to testify in criminal proceedings regarding this family. He would also like protection."

Mitch: "Why do we care about a drug family in Mexico? This is Forney County. I've got three murders, four break-ins, destruction of property and maybe theft, one act of vandalism, and one assault to solve."

Rubins: "He'll confess to the break-ins, destruction, vandalism, and assault. He says nothing was stolen during the break-ins. The murders aren't his or his partner's."

Martinez: "We've got him on everything but the murders, and we're working on those. Why would we deal?"

Rubins: "This family's violence isn't limited to Mexico. Mr. Garcia has information about specific crimes committed in the US, mass graves in Mexico, along with details of drug trafficking routes and high level players here and across the border."

Martinez: "You think the DEA will want what he has?"

Rubins: "Mr. Garcia will also turn over a key member of the family who is here in Arcadia with him."

Mitch: "Let me call the DA."

THE OATH

FORNEY COUNTY'S DISTRICT ATTORNEY was a quirky man called Sammy Mathison. He was forever in pointy-toed cowboy boots, pearl-button shirts, blue jeans with big belt buckles, and a cowboy hat. The press loved him because he was usually a friend to the Sheriff's department and was forthcoming to reporters. Sammy's office was housed off the square, but in the five minutes it took him to make the short walk, he was drenched in sweat.

"I'm ready for this heat wave to be over," he drawled, drying his face with a paper towel.

We were squeezed into the observation room and I was as quiet as possible, but Sammy saw me. "That's from your tangle with Garcia last night?"

I nodded.

"She's got a few other scrapes," Cass said. "But he got the worst end of the deal."

Sammy looked through the one-way glass. "He's sitting like his balls still hurt. Nice job. You working with your aunts full time?"

"Just started," I said.

"Why is she here?" Sammy asked Mitch.

"She thinks Blue didn't commit the murders."

Sammy scratched his lamb chop sideburns. "She thinks Garcia committed them instead?"

"Could be," Mitch answered.

"He didn't," Rubins said.

"We'll see what the evidence says about that." Sammy turned to Mitch. "Maxine shouldn't be here."

"I don't think it'll matter, Sammy. If Garcia confesses to the murders, all the better for Blue. If he implicates her, we'll have to turn that evidence over to Hardcastle anyway."

I bristled because they were talking about me as if I wasn't there, but Cass nudged me. I stayed still.

"And the rest of it, the potential cartel link?" Sammy asked.

"If it weren't for Maxine, we wouldn't have made the connection. We certainly wouldn't have known to push Garcia on the murders to make him talk."

"It's not a bad thing to get in good with the DEA, if this yahoo has anything worth passing on." Sammy fingered his sideburns again, then told me to raise my right hand and repeat after him. "I solemnly swear I will not repeat anything I hear unless it relates directly to Blue Ivey's murder case."

I raised and repeated.

"And if I repeat anything related to Blue, it will only be to Blue, employees of the agency, and her lawyer."

I repeated again.

"I'll hold you to that, Maxine." He turned back to the detectives. "What have you got?"

Mitch and Martinez let Rubins do the talking and by the time he was finished, Sammy was nodding. "I know who to talk to at DEA, but she won't listen without a name."

"Arellano," Rubins said.

Sammy's bushy brows shot up. "Give me a minute."

He was gone for eight. "The DEA wants Garcia's partners. Witness protection is a possibility, but they'll have to testify if it comes to that."

"Immunity?" Rubins asked.

"Depends on what he gives us, but I can't guarantee it for murder."

"He says somebody else did the murders and he might know who."

"All right," Sammy said. "Let's hear what the man has to say."

They left the room and I looked at Cass. "Was that for real?"

"Your oath?"

I nodded.

"It's not like you were sworn before a judge." She pulled a notebook from her pocket and sat. "But that won't matter to Sammy. In his mind, you made a solemn promise to the DA. If you want to have any success as a PI, I wouldn't test him on how seriously he takes something like that."

LIKE BROTHERS

THE TWO MEN SAT on a bench in the shade of a live oak, watching mid-morning traffic circle the square and glancing occasionally at the boarded window. They'd changed vehicles and cruised the streets surrounding downtown again, looking for Billy. They feared the worst.

"He'll talk," the short one said. His leg was bouncing up and down.

"Never."

"They'll offer protection. They'll find us."

"No, man," Sugar said. "We're tight. Like brothers."

The short man seemed not to hear him. "It doesn't matter if he talks about you. All you've done is break into a few places and smash some stuff."

"Better for you, then. You haven't done any of that."

"Who am I?"

"Oh." Sugar scratched his nose. "He won't give you up, either. We go too far back with your dad. He got us out of prison early. We owe him."

"Yes, you do," he said softly. His leg stopped bouncing. "I hope Billy remembers, too."

A chill ran through Sugar, despite the sweltering temperature. "He won't talk. I know he won't."

"Let's hope he doesn't. Because there's no place any of us can hide if he does."

VINDICATION

WITH THE POSSIBILITY OF protection on the table, Big Billy Garcia spilled his guts. He and Sugar Murphy lost contact with Sonny Arellano when he left the recording studio in 1983 after a late night visit from a woman with a scarred face.

Just like Stan Overheart told me, the band fell apart. BB Ivy disappeared. Billy and Sugar tried to start a new band, but failed. Their arrest records from California showed a string of petty crimes that stopped in 1986. The two fell off the map and resurfaced in 2001 when they were arrested for breaking and entering in California. They were in prison for only eighteen months thanks to a contact with the Arellano crime family they made while locked up. Sonny had risen through the cartel ranks but still remembered his former band mates. Through his legal contacts, he helped them get early parole.

That's when the big trouble started. What the two didn't realize was that Sonny wasn't acting for old time's sake; he expected repayment.

Cass and I were in plastic chairs in the observation room when Kado joined us, bringing more coffee. He stood behind Cass with one hand on her shoulder, running his thumb along her neck and jaw. She blushed to the roots of her red hair, but I'm pretty sure she was purring.

I was worried about what I might miss with the wives at Lost and Found, and checked my watch. We had another half hour before they were due to show up, and I hoped Billy would get to the three murders in Arcadia soon.

At first, repayment involved small favors. Picking up packages and delivering them. Nothing too taxing, and the work paid well. But eventually Sonny expected more from his musical compatriots, including acting as lookouts during hits, collecting money from reluctant buyers, and even dropping a body in the desert on one occasion.

Billy had a squeamish tummy and balked at the body dump but claimed Sugar was a willing participant. Sonny used the carrot method for the most part, but Billy had seen enough of the stick to know the consequences for non-compliance were brutal.

Sonny's sights focused on BB Ivy roughly a year ago when their former band mate made contact about the tapes from that last recording session. Talk about vindication. I nearly laughed aloud from the sheer joy of being right. The tapes ran almost continuously during the sessions, like the band wanted. Therefore, they captured everything that went on in the studios. The music, the in-fighting, the band working out a new song, a snatched half hour of passion between BB and his girlfriend Mary Sterling, and a discussion late one night between Sonny and the scarred woman. Apparently Sonny remembered that conversation and flew into a rage when BB tried to blackmail him. The payments didn't start until BB got a piece of the recording to Sonny. That explained Bret's influx of cash about a year ago. It also explained why he wouldn't tell Blue where the cash came from.

Sammy stopped Billy and asked what the conversation between Sonny and the scarred woman was about.

Billy shrugged. "Sonny never said, and I never asked."

Billy was astounded that BB had the nuts to try blackmailing one of the biggest head honchos in the drug business. Even Big Billy, he of the spelling impediment, knew that wasn't very smart. So when Sonny told them what BB was up to, Billy wasn't surprised he demanded they find BB. The tape's copy was postmarked North Dakota, which is where Billy and Sugar started looking.

Thanks to BB's use of multiple last names, and probably to the limited intelligence possessed between Billy and Sugar, the two had no luck finding BB until that article in *Texas Eats* magazine came out. And it was sheer chance they even saw the article. They were in Texas earlier this year on an errand for Sonny when Sugar developed a toothache. Billy was thumbing through magazines in the dentist's waiting room when he saw Blue and Bret's photo.

"We called Sonny as soon as Sugar was out of the chair," Billy said. "He told us to make sure we were looking at the same guy. We had lunch at his winery and saw him working on some of the vines. It was BB, but with less hair. That's when Sonny told us to get the original tape and any copies, at any cost."

Mitch cocked his head. "And that's when you started murdering people?"

"Hell no," Billy said. "We didn't kill anybody. We followed BB. We figured he'd hidden the tape and copies somewhere. He was taking instruments to his girlfriend's houses, and we thought he was being cute."

"How do you hide an eight-track recording tape in an instrument? Those reels are how big?"

"It was the unmastered recordings, transferred to a cassette tape. Maybe a few of them. They'll fit anywhere."

"Did you find it?" Mitch asked.

Billy shook his head.

"Why destroy the instruments?" Mitch asked. "Why not steal them and sell them?"

"Sonny's still pissed that BB smashed his National Triolian. That thing was beautiful. This was payback."

"And the murders?" Martinez asked. "You said you know who committed them."

Garcia shifted. "Some guy was at BB's house Saturday night."

"What were you doing there?"

He shrugged. "Planning to go back in. We hit the music room before, but that tape could be anywhere."

"And?"

"He was in the garden, behind the house."

"Who? BB?"

"No, definitely not. This dude and some chick were arguing. Not BB's new wife. This girl was younger."

"What were they arguing about?" Martinez asked.

"She was jabbing him in the chest, saying something about Annie. You know how a gal will go at you over nothing. We figured it was a lover's tiff." He swallowed hard. "But she had a bat and took a swing at him. He grabbed it and cracked her one."

"What happened next?" Martinez asked.

"He picked her up and disappeared around the house."

Martinez and Mitch exchanged a glanced. "Did you see him stab her?"

"Like with a knife?"

"Like with anything."

"Nope. He just smacked her with the bat."

"What time was this?"

Billy pursed his lips and the wheels cranked. "Late, but the winery was still open. That's why we picked that time. We figured the wife and BB, if he was around, wouldn't be home."

"Describe him."

"Come on, man, it was dark."

"You were close enough to hear them arguing."

He sighed. "Tall. Lots of hair. Not bushy, but thick and kind of dark, I think. White kid."

My skin tingled and a thought skittered around my brain, refusing to be caught.

The DA shifted and leaned forward. "Is there anything else you can tell us about that murder, or Bret Ivey's murder?"

Garcia shook his head. "I didn't even know BB was dead until Sunday afternoon. I thought the wife did it."

"Where were you between ten and two Saturday night and into Sunday morning?" Sammy asked.

"Are you serious?"

Sammy nodded.

"Out behind that house until the chick died. I know we were there before midnight. Then we split and went to the boats in Shreveport. Gambled until about three. I've got receipts for gas and food."

Sammy looked at Mitch, who nodded. "This was helpful, Mr. Garcia," the DA said. "But let's move on. You promised a name. An Arellano family member. Who's that?"

HONOR AMONG THIEVES

"WHAT KIND OF ASSURANCE does my client have that you'll honor this agreement for immunity?" Rubins asked.

"I can't guarantee anything until I hear who he's got and find out how valuable this guy is to the family," Sammy answered. "But I've got an agreement." He opened a folder and passed a piece of paper across the table. "My contact at the DEA has signed it, but it's not final without my signature. So, Mr. Garcia, your future is in your hands."

In the observation room, we leaned closer to the glass. The doorknob twisted and Kado stepped away from Cass. Truman joined us. His eyes were bloodshot and oval indentions marked the skin around his ears.

"I found it," he whispered.

"What?" asked Cass.

"The reason Sonny Arellano's so worked up. I'll fill you in later." He leaned into the wall and looked into the interview room.

Billy drew a deep breath and let it out slowly. "It's Sonny Arellano's second son, Oscar. He uses the last name Matalan when he's in the US."

"That's one of the guys at the winery whose fingerprints we didn't get." Kado looked at Truman. "Did you find out where he is?"

Truman shook his head. "He washed dishes. He's gone."

Back in the interview room Sammy opened his folder again. "Which one is he?"

Billy studied the photos and put his finger on a face.

The DA nodded. "What's he doing in the states?"

"When I called Sonny to tell him we'd found BB, he sent Oscar to help."

"Where is he?"

Billy hesitated again. His hands were moving now, trembling as they twisted over each other. "Man, I don't know. Do you know what these guys do to people who talk?"

Nobody answered, because everybody had seen news of the torture and killing in that violent culture.

"If Sonny gets wind of this, he'll send his enforcer after me. I'll be flayed alive. He'll cut me open and let the buzzards eat me. They'll put my head on a stick as a warning. Man. I don't know."

His lawyer tapped the immunity agreement. "This is the best protection you'll find. If you want this deal, Mr. Garcia, keep talking."

Billy knuckled his eyes. "We have a place in the country. If they haven't split, you'll find him and Sugar there."

———————

SAMMY LEFT TO CALL his DEA contact and Mitch and Martinez joined us in the observation room. "Hear that?" Martinez asked.

We nodded.

"We're going to the house now. Truman, I need you to come with us."

"Yes, sir. But let me tell you about the tapes."

"You found the conversation?" Mitch asked.

"I found a piece of a conversation," Truman said. "It's in Spanish and the recording is poor, but it sounds important."

"And?"

"A man and a woman are talking. At first, there's screaming and somebody slapped somebody. The woman calms the man down and talks about 'the family' and their plans for him. She commits to killing somebody named Rafael if he comes home. It lasts about four minutes, but there's got to be more on the full tape."

"Good work, Truman," Mitch said. "And Maxine, that's a damn fine nose for mystery you've got."

CHOICES, CHOICES

I REALLY REALLY WANTED to go along on the raid to capture Oscar Matalan and Sugar Murphy, or even go with Truman and Kado to Blue's house to look for signs of a struggle in the garden, but I had to get back to the agency. Hearing Billy Garcia's confession had been fascinating and vindicating, but the wives were coming and I didn't want to miss that.

Cass and I had walked from the agency to the jailhouse, and while the earlier walk over had been hot, we sweltered on the way back. She had her phone out and was texting. I kept an eye out for traffic as we crossed the various streets.

"Who's that?" I asked.

"I'm canceling with Chad. I forgot to text him earlier."

"Cass, this is totally unlike you." She looked at me, and I thought about it. Actually, it was exactly like her. She'd decided she was healthy enough to be back on the job, and that was that. But she wasn't. I knew it and I knew Kado knew it, too. Chad certainly knew. "Make an appointment for this afternoon."

"If we've got time."

"We'll make time. I need you back inside the courthouse, finding out what's going on with Blue's case."

She harrumphed. "What are you thinking about?"

"What do you mean?"

"You've been far too quiet since we left the jail. What's on your mind?"

"Nothing, really," I said. "Something Billy said about Daphne's murderer bothered me, but I don't know exactly what."

"Given Bret and Daphne's times of death, Billy and Sugar could've committed both."

"Do you think they did?" I asked.

"No, depending on whether Sugar corroborates Billy's alibi and his receipts check out."

"Do you think Mitch and Martinez will find Oscar and Sugar?"

"I don't know. And I hate not knowing." Cass looked down at her phone. "But I'll give them an hour before I check in."

ONE RING TO BIND THEM

MANY MEN WOULD HAVE been in their element when realizing they were the only male in a room full of powerful women, but Ned Shaver looked like he'd swallowed a toad. He was sweating profusely as he trailed behind a very pale Nicole Ivy when she entered Lost and Found Investigations and appraised the space with a cool glance. Granted, the front window had been replaced by massive sheets of plywood and the carpet didn't threaten to devour your shoes, but the decor was upscale, professional, and undeserving of her sneer.

Grey called Babby after Nicole left the ME's office to say she'd confirmed the dead man was her husband. He sounded bemused when he told Babby she'd demanded her husband's body be shipped to Dallas so she could arrange a funeral, and then changed her mind and demanded he be burned in the pet crematorium and his ashes dumped in the city sewage plant.

We didn't have time to interpret Nicole's degree of inebriation or her mood because a very attractive brunette with an Anita Ekberg-esque figure and the sharp eyes of a New York loan shark came across the threshold, dragging a big cardboard box behind her. Her face was puffy and her eyes watery, but she was a knockout. "Who's the lying bitch who says she's married to Bret Ivye?"

"I am," answered Nicole and Blue in unison.

That stopped Texas wife number three in her tracks.

Cass touched her belt, checking for her detective's shield and gun. Frankly, I was glad she wore both.

Blue motioned towards the conference room with her head. "Anybody who's been married to a Bret or Baxter Ivey, follow me."

Amazingly, they did, the newcomer after leaning the box against Babby's desk. The rest of us, Shaver included, followed. I was last in line and when I managed to get inside the room, the three wives were standing at the far end of the table, eyeballing one another. Each was different, but extremely attractive in her own right.

Cass leaned close. "Bret had great taste in women, I'll give him that."

Wife three walked to the white board and stared at the medical examiner's photo of Bret. Her shoulders shook as she drew a long breath, but she stood erect. "What happened?"

"He was hit in the head with a bat and his body tossed in a tank of wine," Blue said in a flat voice.

Wife three glared at Blue. "A *tank* of wine?"

"Mine. Bret and I own a winery. Owned a winery."

The room grew still as the women took each other in, perhaps unwilling to accept that their husband would marry someone so different from themselves. The icy appraisal didn't end until Nicole caught sight of me and gasped. "Maxine? What happened to your face?"

"It's nothing," I said. "A little run-in with one of Bret's former band mates."

The newcomer wiped her nose and studied me. "The Bunny guys who killed Bret did that to you?"

"We're not sure they killed him," Kay clarified. "But they have been breaking and entering, destroying property, and now they're committing assault."

Texas wife number three turned back to the other wives. "I suppose it's only polite that we introduce ourselves. I'm Frannie."

"Nicole," the lawyer from Dallas whined in that nasally voice.

"I'm Blue." She indicated the coffee Cindy had brought in. "We might as well sit."

Nicole snatched Blue's left hand and turned it so her palm was facing down. I felt Cass tense, but Nicole dropped the hand as if it had stung her. "He lied. Everything was a lie," she whispered as she sank down into a chair.

Shaver slouched beside her and closed his eyes. I felt an 'I told you so' threatening to cross his lips, and willed him to stay silent.

Blue's hand remained suspended in mid-air and Frannie studied it. I knew they were looking at Blue's hammered platinum band with the square cut sapphire.

"What?" Blue asked. "What did he lie to you about?"

"That's my wedding ring," Nicole said to the table. "He took it to have it cleaned and said it must've been taken from his jacket. We reported it stolen and filed an insurance claim." She cut her eyes at Shaver. "You were right."

Blue slipped it off and put it on the table. "If that timetable of Bret's marriages is right, you're the lawful owner. You can have it back."

"I can do you one better, Nicole." Frannie picked the ring up and studied it. A slow smile crept across her face. "I made this. He bought it from me in 2001. Even better... he told me it was a gift for his mother."

HELL HATH NO FURY LIKE THREE WIVES SCORNED

WOE TO THE MAN who lies to his wife. Or wives. The truth always comes out and I counted Bret Ivey a lucky man to be in the morgue. The ring was the ice breaker. Once the women reached consensus on Bretton Baxter Ivey Ivy Ivye's status as a low life, an odd bond formed. The wives studied the timeline of Bret's marriages and the more they talked, the more the pieces fell together.

Nicole summed their opinions up: "What a bastard."

As the only bearer of testicles in the agency, Ned Shaver realized the precariousness of his position and slipped from the building. I peeked around the plywood to see him scanning the square, cigarette in hand, seeking refuge from all the estrogen. He was smarter than I thought.

Kay and Babby turned the Bret bashing back to the reason we were all here: finding Bret's killer and clearing Blue's name.

"Who wanted him dead?" Kay asked.

"If I'd known about all of this," Frannie said with a glance at the white board, "I would've."

"Me, too," said Nicole.

"Not me," Blue said. "I've got too much to do to get into murder." She looked at Yvette Hardcastle. After surveying and dismissing Ned Shaver, the defense lawyer had been busy tapping away on her phone. "Should we tell them about the other murders?"

"You killed somebody else?" Frannie asked. Her eyes were watery but I admired her plucky front.

"The police think I did."

Yvette pursed her lips. "I'm waiting on the DA to send the discovery documents Judge Shackleford granted me. Since Nicole and Frannie round out Bret's current suite of wives, it makes sense for them to hear the whole story. The murders might be unrelated to the winery or his life with Blue." Yvette raised an eyebrow at Cass. "Which side are you playing for?"

"Pardon?"

"I'll start planning my defense today. If you're working for the Sheriff's office, you have to leave. I can't have my strategy getting back to them."

"It's not a contest," Cass protested.

"Don't kid yourself," Yvette stated. "The moment Mitch Stone arrested Blue for three murders, this became a contest to determine not Blue's innocence or guilt, but who's the better lawyer."

I saw Cass's jaw work and knew she was grinding her teeth. But her voice was neutral when she spoke. "I don't think the DA sees it that way."

"I can't afford to believe he doesn't. Blue certainly can't. Now, are you working for us, or for them?"

"I'm interested in the truth. I haven't revealed the evidence the department collected, have I?" Cass looked at me and I shook my head. "I'll protect whatever defense you come up with, Yvette. Unless we find definitive evidence Blue committed these murders."

Blue held her hands up. "I didn't. Really."

Cass nodded. "There you go. Your secrets are safe with me."

Blue's lawyer looked undecided, and Kay spoke up.

"You want Cass on your side, Yvette. She's smart, she knows how the department thinks, and I trust her completely."

"Me, too," said Babby.

"Me, too," said Cindy, and I didn't know if she meant it or was sucking up, but either way, I was glad to hear her voice. I also noticed she was wearing the driving mocs. They looked good on her.

Yvette had the decency to ask her client what she thought, and Blue said she'd value Cass's input.

"For what it's worth," Nicole said. "I like Cass and Maxine. They pissed me off yesterday, but that's Baxter's fault."

Frannie was studying Cass. "You're the cult detective right? And the one who shot that multiple murderer earlier this summer?"

Cass's creamy skin flushed to the roots of her red hair. "You heard about that?"

"A woman detective? Killing the bad guys? It was all over the feminist blogs."

"Great." I knew Cass meant it in the most sarcastic way possible. She hated that kind of attention.

"She'll be fine," Frannie said. "Let's go."

Issue decided.

"I'll make more coffee and call out for donuts," Babby said.

"Make it two dozen," Kay replied. "Cindy, I want you at the DA's office waiting to pick up whatever he releases."

Yvette's phone dinged. "Better get a move on, Cindy. That's Sammy's office. If you see Nicole's lawyer tell him it's safe to come back. If he practices criminal law, he might be useful."

LOOKING GRIM

CINDY WAS GONE LESS than fifteen minutes. Sometimes it's a blessing to work in a small town.

Yvette dug into the files and started reading, tucking one report behind another as she finished them, refusing to share.

Cass looked down at her phone and started tapping. The response was swift and she touched her shoulder as she summarized the texts for us. "The bad news is Oscar Matalan and Sugar Murphy are gone. The good news is Kado and Truman found Daphne's murder scene behind Blue's house."

"What now?" I asked.

"We wait." She settled back in her chair, face inscrutable.

I couldn't sit still, so I followed Kay from the conference room. When we were clear, I whispered, "How are you holding up?"

"Fine," she said, but her face said she was struggling.

"I'm sorry," I said.

"For what, sugar britches?"

"For getting us involved in all this. If I hadn't answered the phone while you were in the powder room, or if I'd told you about Blue's call when it first came in, we wouldn't be here and you wouldn't have Yvette rubbing it in your face."

She smiled that beautiful smile. "She's nothing, baby. And regardless of how the agency came to be involved, three people would still be dead. We'd still have put Yvette's name on the list of lawyers. We'd still be sitting around this table, gagging on obscene amounts of White Diamonds."

I giggled. Kay was dead on; Yvette might be a smart cookie and a sharp dresser, but she needed to learn when to stop with the old lady perfume. Babby was working on donuts in the kitchen and we took plates, napkins, and fresh coffee into the conference room. Yvette was writing on the white boards, making notes about the evidence collected at all three murder scenes. This was the first time I'd seen any of the details.

I was shocked.

Fingerprint evidence. Lots of it. Wine doped with tetrahydrozoline and the eye drops it could've come from collected from Blue's house. A bloody bat found at the winery with microscopic bits of headlight and tail light stuck in the blood. The rope Annie was hung with was an ordinary nylon, but one of the cut ends of Annie's rope matched a cut on a spool located at the winery. The pottery tool stuck in Daphne's neck was made by the same manufacturer of the other tools that belonged to Blue, and could've come from her set. There were no fingerprints on the wine tank Bret had been found in, and Blue was observed wiping down the tank's lid and mopping spilled wine from the floor.

Holy cow. This looked grim.

Blue paled and one hand covered her mouth. Babby noticed and motioned for Cindy to pass the donuts and pour coffee. Babby put a cinnamon roll in Blue's hand. "You need the sugar, Blue. Eat it."

She did, and color slowly returned to her face. "When you see it all laid out like this," she said, "I look guilty."

"You do," Frannie agreed.

"Who are Annie and Daphne?" Nicole asked. She was sitting next to Shaver who was munching on a chocolate glazed.

"Two of our staff," Blue answered. "I didn't know it until last week, but Bret was sleeping with them. Seems he's slept with a few others, too."

"Let's hope Baxter hasn't left us the gift that keeps on giving." Nicole gave in and took a donut covered in sprinkles. "Guess it's time to get tested for sexually transmitted diseases, girls." She dunked the donut in her coffee. "Here's to blood and urine samples."

REFUTING THE EVIDENCE

"THERE'S NOT MUCH HERE." Yvette stood back and examined her handiwork. "The fingerprint evidence? You work in a winery. Anyone could pick up a wine bottle and glass you've touched. When was the last time you were at Annie's house?"

"About three weeks ago," Blue said. "She had a party and most of the winery staff went."

"Were you only a guest?"

Blue frowned. "What do you mean?"

"Did you simply eat and drink?"

"No. It's hard for me to keep my hands off a stove. I helped her make a few appetizers. Ah," she said, her eyes brightening. "You want to know what I touched, right?"

Yvette's lips curved up at the corners. I chose to believe that was a smile. "Do you remember?"

"I was in the kitchen and living room, and I probably went to the bathroom." She cocked her head to the side. "I opened some doors.

Definitely touched the fridge, stove, faucet, countertops, and sink. Probably the computer desk. Maybe the stereo and remote. Did they find my fingerprints in any of those places?"

Yvette looked down at her paperwork and nodded.

"In the kitchen?" Blue asked, voice incredulous.

"Afraid so."

"After three weeks? Annie knew better than that."

I was a little tickled at Blue's indignation, and much relieved Yvette thought some of the evidence could be explained away. In what seemed a perfectly logical manner. Frannie and Nicole were listening intently, as was Shaver.

Kay had slipped the stack of papers from in front of Yvette and was passing them around the table. Yvette scowled and opened her mouth, but Babby glared her down.

Yvette's chin shot out but she shut her mouth.

Kay studied one page for a long moment. "What about the bottle from Daphne's that has Blue's bloody fingerprint on it? Can you do something with that?"

Her question held a tiny note of challenge but Yvette seemed not to notice. Or if she did, acted as if she didn't care. "Blue? Any thoughts?"

"I cut my thumb Saturday afternoon, but didn't realize it until blood ran down my palm." She held up her hand to show us the thumb, which was still wrapped in a bandage. "I was clearing a table and could've touched something before I realized what I'd done."

"Makes sense."

Cindy spoke up. "The eye drops in the wine?"

Yvette shooed the question away. "They might be able to match the residue in the bottle or glass to the brand Blue uses, but so what? How many people use the same brand?"

"How about the bat?" Cass asked.

"The bat that killed Baxter?" Nicole asked.

"Yes, and possibly Daphne."

"That's a little more problematic." Yvette tapped her chin. "It was found in the garage, correct?"

Blue nodded.

"Who has access to the garage?"

Blue dropped her head into her hands. "Who doesn't? We don't lock it because we store stuff for the winery in there. People are in and out all the time. The garage doors are on clickers," she made the universal motion for pushing a garage door opener, "but the regular doors are never locked."

"Perfect," Yvette said. "Who's got the bat report?"

Babby raised her hand.

"Did they find fingerprints on it?"

"Nope. But they found two types of blood." She looked at Blue. "Whoever did this used the same bat on Bret and Daphne."

"Oh no," Blue said. "If we'd kept the garage locked -"

Kay jabbed a half-eaten glazed donut at her. "They would've found something else from the winery to use. So stop that, right now. This isn't your fault. Nothing you did or didn't do caused these murders. Do you understand?"

A murmur of agreement swirled around the table.

Blue bucked up. A little.

"Does anyone know what the words on the car mean?" Cindy asked.

"What are they?" I asked.

"'Now it's over, bitch'," she said.

My jaw dropped and I turned to Blue. "Isn't that what Daphne yelled as she was storming out Friday night?"

"Right after I fired her."

"That might be problematic," Yvette said.

"Actually, it narrows the field," Cass said. "Everyone who was in the winery when Daphne shouted at Blue is a suspect for Daphne's murder."

"Good point, Detective Elliot. Thank you for confirming that you're not batting for the other side." Yvette grimaced a smile at Cass. "Blue, we'll need a list of employees who were at the winery that night, preferably with their photos."

"I think most of the staff have a photo up on the website. If not a head shot, then they're probably in the photos we take during harvest. Would someone print them and I'll check?"

"I will when we break," Cindy said.

"Is there any way to get a list of customers from Friday night?" Yvette asked.

"Credit card receipts will give us most," Blue said. "But some people use cash."

"We can start with those and see who else you remember." Yvette turned again to the white board. "Given all that, we're left with the tank. Blue was cleaning the lid and the floor around it before Bret's body was found. Blue, what was going on?"

"I'd found a sticky spot on the floor. I was a little surprised, but during harvest, all bets are off on our regular routines." She thought for a moment. "I thought I'd better check the top of the tank to make sure the wine hadn't sloshed out while we were filling it. Sure enough, there was a sticky trail down the side, but also on the lid. I wiped the tank down and mopped up the mess."

Yvette tapped her lip. "That could go either way. We can believe you were innocently cleaning the tank and floor, or you were sanitizing a crime scene."

"What motive did I have for all these murders?" Blue asked.

"For the two girls, jealousy and revenge for sleeping with your husband. For Bret? Revenge for cheating on you. Do you have a life insurance policy on him?"

"Several."

Eyebrows went up.

"We have life insurance policies on both of us to cover our business borrowing. The policies were required by our lenders, so there's nothing questionable in them. We also have policies on each other individually."

"What values?"

"A million each."

Cindy whistled, and a furious blush swept up her neck and over her cheeks as we turned to look at her. Personally, I thought a million dollars was a little light.

Blue had the grace to smile. "We were both so involved in running the winery, we thought it wise to make sure the surviving spouse had some financial breathing room."

Nicole's smile was jaded. "That's the first positive thought I've had in two days. I had a policy on him, too."

"Me, too," Frannie said with a laugh. "Better put us on your list of suspects, Yvette."

"We've got Nicole's alibi," Yvette said with a steely face. "Where were you Saturday night between ten and two?"

"Seriously?"

Yvette nodded.

Frannie sobered. "Hosting a show of my new jewelry line until about eleven. I had dinner after that with two friends and got home after one. I set the alarm and it has a log, so you can see I didn't leave the house again until Saturday morning. I went out to get the paper."

"When was the last time you saw your husband?"

"Wednesday. He came home and we took his instruments to my studio and locked them up with my stock. Said there'd been a rash of break-ins in the area and some of his instruments were valuable."

"How many are there?" I asked.

"Four guitars, three banjos, and two very heavy amps. Why?"

"The Poison Ivy and the Dismembered Bunnies tapes might be in them."

"And the men who did this to you," she motioned to my face, "might come looking for them?"

"One is in jail. But until they're found, the other two might."

Frannie pulled a cell phone from her purse and dialed. She told her assistant to put all the stock back in the vault and close the studio for the day, adding that she'd explain everything later. "Yes, Bret is dead... Thanks for that. I think I'm still in shock... I want you to put his instruments in the van and bring them to Arcadia... Yes, you'll still get paid for a full day."

"You brought a package with you, Frannie," Cass said. "What's in it?"

"It arrived Friday and Bret had told me not to open it, so I didn't. Let's find out."

It was a battered old guitar and when I held it up and peeked inside, I saw wadding. "Hand me the tongs from the kitchen, Babby."

She did, and I pulled cotton packing from the guitar's interior. It took ages, but at last I saw the edge of a paper package. Cindy's hands are smaller than mine and she took over, eventually teasing it free with a pair of tweezers Kay found in the bathroom.

Cass took the padded envelope with gloved hands. She slit the top and pulled out a single sheet of notepaper. "'Try again, Shitbird'," Cass read. "I presume that's meant for Sonny. Does this look like Bret's handwriting?"

The wives nodded.

"Okay," I said. "One down, quite a few more to go."

"We should tell you there's a witness to Daphne's murder," Cass said. At Yvette's startled expression, Cass added, "Billy Garcia said he and Sugar Murphy saw someone hit Daphne with a bat in Blue's garden."

"Well?" Shaver said. This was the first time Nicole's lawyer had spoken since he'd slithered back into the room. "Who killed the girl?"

"We don't know," Cass told him. "Big Billy saw the murder but didn't recognize the suspect."

"That's not much help."

She checked her little notebook. "White kid - that's what Billy called him. Tall. Lots of hair. Not bushy, but thick and kind of dark."

"It's not much to go on," Shaver said.

"It's more than we had last night," Yvette retorted. She looked at the photos of Garcia and Murphy on the white board. "Garcia's hair is dark, but neither his nor Murphy's is bushy."

Cindy's stomach growled and she blushed. "Can we have lunch now?"

"Only if the winery can supply the food," Blue said. "Any objections?"

"I'm in if the winery supplies wine," Frannie said. "I could use a drink."

A DRUG LORD'S KID DOES MY DISHES?

ORGANIZING A MEAL FOR nine women with varying dietary needs and one tubby man should've been a nightmare, but Blue handled it with ease. Or maybe I should say that her staff handled it with ease, because although it was after noon and the winery's lunch service was in full swing, we had a beautiful spread on the table by one o'clock.

Everyone took a chance to stretch and take a potty break, and Yvette went back to her office to check on things. Frannie's assistant turned up and there was much confusion as people walked up and down the building's staircase, carrying food and instrument cases and trying not to knock each other over. Arty and Steve from the law office on the other side of the building helped us bring everything in, then stayed for lunch.

Cindy was attaching photographs of the winery's employees to one of the white boards when Arty first entered the room. She actually blushed when he kissed her on the cheek and again when Steve did the same. Both men were in their element with so many beautiful women around. Yvette made it back just as we opened the wine, and greeted the two men warmly. She'd taken the time to touch up her makeup and spray on a little more old lady perfume. Images of Pepé Le Pew's fuming tail swirled through my head. I saw Babby waving a funeral home fan under her face and I lowered the temp on the thermostat to get some air circulating.

Babby showed Steve and Arty her ideas on the new sign for the agency's window, which was an elegant Arts and Crafts design, and both approved. Kay shrugged. "The next time somebody tosses a brick through our window, I get to do the drawing."

We were helping ourselves to sandwiches on freshly baked bread, hand thrown pizzas still warm from the oven, salads, and platters of cheese, meat, and grapes, when Nicole wandered over to the white board. She studied the photos of the winery's employees and pointed at a group shot taken outside.

"I'm pretty sure that's the kid who came looking for BB Ivy," she said.

Arty was standing beside her and studied the image. "Steve? Isn't this the guy we saw this morning?"

Steve looked over his shoulder and nodded.

"When was this?" Yvette asked.

"I talked to him this morning at The Coffee Shop. And I think he was sitting on a bench on the courthouse lawn when I did my mid-morning coffee run. He wears these loud orange shoes." A shiver ran up my spine and Cass and I exchanged a glance. Steve thought for a moment. "He was with another man, a blond guy."

We crowded around. Nicole pointed to a handsome young Hispanic man with strong features. He had a hand lifted to shade his face from the sun, but he was looking directly into the camera. His smile was wide and toothy.

"That's Oscar," Blue said. "He's one of our dish washers."

"What's his last name?" Cass asked.

Blue thought for a moment. "Matalan, I think."

"He's Sonny Arellano's son," Cass said.

"I had a Mexican drug lord's kid washing my dishes?" Blue asked.

"Looks like it."

"Jeez."

"When did you hire him?" Yvette asked.

Blue shrugged. "A few weeks ago? Maybe longer. People in these positions come and go."

"Baxter saw this kid when he came to the house. Talked to him. Why would he give this kid a job at the winery?" Nicole asked.

"Chef or our scheduler probably hired him," Blue said. "Dishwashers work in the back. Bret was only back there when he was romancing a waitress. That man could pull them."

"He was a looker his whole life," Frannie said. "Even when he was a kid he was super cute."

"You've seen photos of him when he was young?" Blue asked.

"How young?" Nicole asked.

"Early twenties and older, probably." Frannie looked at the other two wives. "You've never seen photos of his early life?"

"I begged him to show me family photos," Blue said.

"Me, too. But he said everything burned in a house fire," Nicole added. "Frannie, where did these come from?"

"The boxes he keeps in the attic," Frannie said.

"What else is in those boxes?" Yvette asked just as I started to ask the same question.

Frannie shrugged. "More photos. Some paperwork. Old music stuff."

"Does your assistant have keys to your house?"

Frannie nodded.

"Tell her to go get those boxes and bring them here."

Yvette looked at Nicole. "Anything of Bret's at your house?"

"Some paperwork, but only current stuff. Like I said, he told me everything burned in a house fire."

"Blue?"

"He's got boxes everywhere. The house, the attic, the garage, the garage attic, the shop."

Yvette checked her watch. "Let's take a break. Anybody object?" No one did. "Give us a couple of hours to go through Bret's stuff. Let's reconvene at four. Does that work for everyone?"

We agreed and I noticed Cass tapping on her phone. "Who's that?"

"The Psychopath. I'm checking to see if he's got time for me." She looked me over. "It wouldn't hurt you to get in a workout. That might loosen you up a bit. Come to therapy with me."

I bit my lower lip. "Let me see if Harvey's available."

"I didn't mean *that* kind of workout, Maxine."

I laughed. "Even I'm not up to a tussling match with Harvey. But a little stretching and some light weights might do me good."

A TRAP

HARVEY'S GYM IS BLESSEDLY quiet in the early afternoon, after the soccer moms have come for their yoga and spin classes and before the hard core heavies turn up to rock the free weights.

He took me in with a single gaze and pointed at the locker room. When I joined him on a yoga mat he placed a palm against my head and stroked his thumb down my uninjured cheek. "What does the other guy look like?"

"He's battered, but not broken."

Harvey lifted my hands to look at the bruises on my wrists. "He pinned you?" I nodded and his face tightened. "Not today, but soon, we start self-defense lessons. Today, we'll work some of that soreness out."

And we did. Over the next half hour, Harvey helped me through stretches that I held progressively deeper and longer, working the kinks out of my neck, shoulders, arms, torso, legs and even my ankles. I knew I hurt, but I didn't realize how much I hurt until we'd finished and I was feeling better. Throughout the exercises, Harvey kept his touch light, as if he were afraid he'd hurt me more.

I followed him to the juice bar and eased onto a stool, accepting a carrot, ginger, and apple juice concoction that soothed as it went down.

"I saw the broken window. It was you who chased that guy down?"

I nodded.

"Was he important to your case?"

"As it turns out, yes. He's the one who's been smashing all the instruments. The guy who hired him really wants those tapes"

"But he didn't murder the winery guy, right? His wife killed him and two other women. I saw it in the Forney Cater. Crazy gal."

"I don't think she did it."

"Why? The cops think she did."

"Killing three people doesn't fit with her personality. And if you look at the evidence, Harvey, she's being set up."

"By who? The guy you caught last night?"

"I don't think so. But he says he saw the man who killed one of the women."

"So who did it?"

"He didn't know. He gave us a general description, but his partner might've seen more."

Harvey took a pull on his protein shake. "Then go get his partner."

"He's gone. Vanished."

Harvey smiled. "Set a trap."

"What do you mean?"

"He's after those tapes, right? The Bunnymen tapes?"

"Poison Ivy and The Dismembered Bunnies, but yes."

"Have you found them?"

"No."

"He doesn't know that, right?"

"Right."

"If he's hot to get them, convince him you have them. He'll come and you can grab him."

We clinked glasses. "Smart boy."

"I'm more than just a fabulous body."

GROUND ZERO

BLUE SAT ON THE garage floor and let the tears come. She'd given Yvette a pair of shorts and a t-shirt and the women had methodically pawed through all of the boxes and files Bret had stashed at the winery over the years.

"You've never seen this stuff?" Yvette asked.

Blue shook her head. "The winery was Bret's. I joined him to start the restaurant. All this," she flapped a hand at the paperwork, "was here. It never occurred to me to snoop."

Yvette found a box of shop towels and joined Blue on the floor. She handed the other woman a rough blue cloth and awkwardly patted her shoulder. "It's the best I can do. Are you okay?"

"I haven't cried this much in years." Blue blew her nose. "I can't believe he's maintained three separate lives for so long. Seeing it up on the white boards at Lost and Found was one thing, but this," she lifted a piece of paper from a box, "makes it real." She looked closer. "Make that four lives. This one is a divorce decree for a Charlotte Ivie." Blue spelled the last name. "Four wives at one time? How is that even possible?"

"You really had no clue?"

"I really didn't. I can't believe I was so stupid."

"It wasn't just you, Blue. He must've been a master manipulator. Nicole and Frannie are pretty smart cookies."

"But still. To believe him so completely? To never wonder why he was gone so much? I can't believe I didn't question him at all."

Yvette waited for Blue's sniffling to stop and motioned to a partially filled box. "That looks like ground zero. Is there anything in it that helps us clear your name?"

Blue pushed the box to Yvette. "I can't take any more."

Yvette dug. To her relief, Bret Ivey had kept meticulous records of the significant events in his life. Everything was in date order, and the divorce decree Blue had found was his most recent: he'd divorced Charlotte Ivie earlier this year. Bret had kept some photos, perhaps to ensure he kept all his wives straight. She came to a batch of paperwork tied in a bundle and used a pair of wire snips to cut the faded red ribbon. A clutter of yellowed newsclippings, letters, and photos fell loose. She read.

"You can rest easy knowing Bret didn't suddenly suffer a mid-life crisis and start philandering." She held up a letter. "His first wife, Mary Sterling, dumped him because he was catting around."

"She's the one that's dead, isn't she?" Blue asked. "Maxine's notes said she died this year."

Yvette moved the paperwork around. "Here's her death notice."

Blue took the page. It was a printout from a newspaper's website from the previous year. "She's a pretty woman."

"She looks like you."

"She does, a little. How did he find this?"

"He must've had a search set up on the internet to notify him when her name is mentioned. He probably has that stuff set up for all of you."

"That's creepy."

"But fitting for a man who'll use four names to marry four women at a time. Look at this." Yvette gave Blue a photo. "Do you recognize him?"

Blue laughed, a genuinely happy sound. "Bret must've been in his late teens. Look at all that hair. Lord, he was skinny." The smile faded. "He was good at it. At making us believe we were the only ones." She dropped the photo. "Is there anything here that proves I didn't kill him?"

Yvette shrugged. She scraped the pictures and documents back together and tossed them in the box. "Not that I can see, but let's pack it all up and take it to town. Bret's other wives might see something we don't. And I hate to say this, but the women at Lost and Found are pretty smart."

"Why do you hate to say that?"

Yvette patted the skin under her eyes. "A long story that's long over. Let's get this crap in the car."

A CUNNING PLAN

I WAS WORKING ON a plan to lure Oscar Matalan and Sugar Murphy to us when everyone returned to the agency. Blue and Yvette brought boxes of paperwork from Bret's former life, and his other two wives fell on them like starving wolves. Blue and Yvette started on the boxes and instruments Frannie's assistant had delivered.

Cass was flushed from her therapy with Chad and I pulled her to one side, explaining what Harvey had recommended.

"Good idea," she said. "But the police have to be involved."

"No, Cass. It has to be simple and believable, and we need to get it done tonight."

"Why tonight?"

"I have a bad feeling about these guys. Like they're getting desperate. They've been on the edge of violence all along and I'm afraid arresting Big Billy might push them over the edge."

"That's why the police should be involved."

"I think it'll scare them away," I told Cass in a low voice, and then I flashed a grin. "What if you and I came up with a cunning plan?"

"Like?"

"Pretend we know where Bret's hiding place is and make sure they know it."

"How do we do that?"

"Steve saw the guy in the orange shoes, Oscar, on the square twice today. What if he ran a quick reconnaissance?"

STEVE AND ARTY THOUGHT the idea of identifying a major drug criminal was a hoot, but were also indignant at the thought that their neighbors might be under surveillance. We explained the issue of the missing session tapes and how we needed to capture Oscar Matalan and Sugar Murphy to find out more about Daphne's murderer. We warned them of the dangers but Steve put his shades on and was out the door almost before we finished telling him what we wanted.

"And," Cass told him as he grabbed the door knob, "I want to know if he's still in the orange shoes."

"No problem."

"Limited contact, Steve. Right?"

"Right." He flashed an adorable grin and was gone.

"He's got a big heart, that guy," Arty said with a soft smile. "If Matalan is out there watching, Steve will find him."

TO CATCH A CRIMINAL

TO CATCH A CRIMINAL, you have to think like one, Steve thought as he made his way down the building's stairs. *And then you have to out think him.*

He stepped onto street level and stopped to stretch, as he always did, taking a long look around the square, as he always did. There was no sign of Oscar, but given that it was late afternoon and the unbearable heat was at its worst, that was no surprise. If he was watching the agency, he'd do it from an inside vantage point. That meant he'd be in The Coffee Shop because besides the courthouse lawn, there was no better view of the building housing Lost and Found.

Steve set off on the walk he took around the square two to three times a day. In part for exercise, in part to get coffee or lunch, and in part to pick up the latest gossip. He waved to the gals in the flower shop beneath the offices (it reeked of cigarettes, so he never went in); stopped to finger a pair of biking shorts at the new store selling upscale sporting goods (it would never survive in a town the size of Arcadia); stepped into the jewelry store to see if his watch repair was done (it wasn't) and talk about Blue's arrest; bought a pack of gum at the drugstore and confirmed Blue was being represented by that ball-buster Yvette Hardcastle; narrowly missed flattening Mrs. Springer as she left the men's haberdashery with a new suit for her husband; said hello to the receptionist at the investment firm who wanted to know if it was true Maxine had caught a murderer; said good-afternoon to the snooty woman who ran the pawn shop (who'd never so much as nodded in reply, but one has to try); helped the waiter at the Italian restaurant adjust a sun umbrella; and finally stepped into The Coffee Shop and breathed a sigh of relief.

The air was crisp and smelled of coffee and the roast beef that was always on Tuesday's dinner menu. Early diners were at a few of the tables, but only one booth near the windows was occupied, by the man in the orange shoes Steve now knew was Oscar Matalan. A skinny blond man sat at a nearby table, pulling on his nose. Steve nodded at Oscar and walked to the counter like he always did, and ordered two skinny lattes to go, like he always did.

As the espresso machine hissed to life, he caught Oscar watching him. Steve offered a half smile and Oscar smiled back. The owner wanted the poop on last night's festivities and Steve filled him in while he paid, confirming that while Maxine was a mess, he'd heard the fellow who attacked her still wasn't sitting right. He doctored their lattes like he always did - one sugar for Steve, two of the pink packets for Arty - and finally turned to leave.

Oscar motioned to Steve. "I saw you come out of that building," he said. "Is that your office with the broken window?"

"No, it's our neighbors, a detective agency."

"What happened?"

You crafty bugger, Steve thought. "Someone threw a brick through it last night. One of the girls caught the guy who did it."

"A girl?"

Steve nodded and sipped his latte. The blond man opened a copy of the Forney Cater and pretended he wasn't listening.

"Why did he do it?"

"Something about stealing old tapes." Steve leaned close. "Turns out the girls found them and are picking them up today." He checked his watch. "They might already have them. It's all very cloak and dagger."

"Mmmm," Oscar said.

Steve put the coffees down and pulled out his phone. "What are you up to?"

"Looking for a job." Oscar tapped the Help Wanted section of the Forney Cater.

"What kind of work do you do?"

"A little of this, a little of that. I've worked in a kitchen and did maintenance at a hospital."

"Maintenance? Really?"

Oscar nodded.

"Any plumbing?"

"Of course."

"This is kind of sudden, but we've got a leaky sink in our office and I think the ladies at the agency have the same problem. Would you take a look at it?" Steve typed in his phone's password and his thumbs flew over the screen as he texted Arty: *Remember the game we played last week? I'm bringing a new friend. Get the toys ready.*

Oscar eyed him. "When?"

"Sorry, it's rude to text and talk, but that one had to go. Would now work for you? We can pay cash."

"Absolutely." Oscar's gaze darted to the blond so fast Steve almost didn't catch it.

Oscar scooted out of the booth as Steve picked up his coffees and smiled. "You have no idea how much help you'll be."

BONDAGE

WE WERE WORKING OUR way through Bret's paperwork when Cindy's phone buzzed. A wide smile crossed her face but quickly faded. She leveled a laser beam gaze at me. "Arty wants you and Cass to come to his office. Now."

We left quizzical glances in our wake but I wasn't inclined to explain unless Steve had news. We hurried down the hall and pushed open the door to see the man we knew as Oscar Matalan bound to a chair and struggling furiously. Steve sat behind his desk looking like the cat who'd found the source of the cream. Arty had a hip up on the desk and was swinging a leg, looking amused.

Cass and I circled their prisoner, who was red-faced and sweating. His legs were bound with black silk scarves, his hands were locked behind him with a pair of fur-lined wrist-cuffs, and he was biting on a ball gag strapped to his head. His nostrils flared as he sucked in air, but the glint in his eyes told me he was more angry than distressed. The orange shoes were still on his feet.

"I feel like I've walked into a bondage flick," Cass said. "Do I want to know about the handcuffs?"

"Nope," Arty answered. "But if you want to keep him, you'll have to trade mine for yours."

"How did you manage this?" I asked Steve.

"I asked him if he wanted a job fixing our plumbing."

"I didn't know you had a problem with it."

"We don't." He looked at his hostage. "But he didn't know that. I told him your office had a drip, too, and that's probably why he came so willingly. I think he wanted a peek at all the investigating you've been doing."

I couldn't help it, I giggled. The thought that a major crime lord's son got caught over a leaky faucet was too funny. He stilled then and stared at my face, and his eyes crinkled. Just a bit. I knew he was working through the realization that I was the one who had captured Garcia and was enjoying my black eye. And then it hit me: we had the second oldest son of one of Mexico's nastiest drug czars in our offices. If Sugar Murphy had been on the square and watching us too, he'd wonder where his buddy Oscar had gone. That could be bad.

I chewed my lip. "What now?"

Cass looked thoughtful. "I should probably read him his rights and take him to jail. But I'd rather talk to him first." She studied Oscar. "We know you're Santiago Arellano's son."

His eyes widened.

"Where's Sugar Murphy?"

It was just a flash, but his gaze flicked to the windows overlooking the square and returned to her face, trying for defiant but revealing only fear. He jiggled in the chair and it thumped against the floor. Tears shone in his eyes and I realized he'd probably never been in custody before. That might work to our benefit.

"I can't guarantee anything with regards to your status, Mr. Arellano," Cass said. "Or do you prefer Matalan?"

He scowled and a strangled reply squeezed around the ball gag.

"How rude of me." She looked at Arty. "Do you want to take it off, or should I?"

Arty unbuckled the gag and Oscar worked his jaw. "*Puta*," he spat at Cass.

"There's no need to be ugly," Steve scolded.

"*Cabrón*," Oscar replied with a reproachful glare, then wiped his nose against his shoulder.

"I need information, Mr. Arellano. If you cooperate, I'll let the District Attorney and the DEA know. They may view you more favorably."

"No English," Oscar said, his jaw jutting forward.

"Liar liar," Steve sang.

"Seriously?" Cass asked. "You're playing the language card?"

"No English," he repeated, and his lower lip quivered.

"It's your funeral." Cass pulled out her cell phone and dialed. "Martinez? Can you come to Arty Henderson's office? He and Steve have a surprise for you... Yes, a good surprise... Come now. You'll be glad you did."

NO ENGLISH

WHILE WE WAITED, CASS continued to chastise Oscar for not talking to her. He kept protesting that he didn't understand English. While Steve held his hands, Arty uncuffed Oscar and Cass replaced hers for his. Since we weren't sure how desperate he was, the scarves stayed on his legs.

The door opened. Cindy poked her head in and gasped at the prisoner. "Is that...?"

"It is," I confirmed. "And Steve and Arty caught him."

"Holy cow," Cindy gushed. She's quite pretty when she glows. "A major player in the drug business. You two are something else." She landed big kisses on each of their cheeks, Arty's perilously close to his mouth.

Both men beamed.

"What are you waiting for?" Cindy asked.

"Mr. Arellano claims he can't speak English, so I've asked Detective Martinez to join us," Cass said.

"Oooh, bad choice," she said to Oscar. "Cass is much nicer."

She was leaving as Martinez opened the door. He took in the situation and rubbed both hands over his face. "You're kidding."

"Nope," Cass answered. "Steve lured him in and he and Arty tied him up."

Martinez high-fived the men. "Nice work. So?"

"No English," Cass said.

"A common problem with our visitors from the south when they encounter representatives of the establishment." Martinez launched into bad cop mode, got in Oscar's face, and drilled him in rapid-fire Spanish.

"What's he saying?" I whispered to Cass.

"He told Oscar he's a suspect in three murders. That's as far as my Spanish gets me."

Oscar stayed silent, so Martinez kept talking. I heard the word *padre* and *familia*. Martinez was going down the shame route. Oscar kept his gaze down but couldn't stop the tears. Martinez squatted and looked up at him and talked more. And some more. At last, Oscar shifted and spoke.

Martinez pulled out his radio and asked for a patrol car to pick them up behind the building. No lights, no siren. He looked at Steve and Arty. "Did you frisk him?"

"Tempting," said Steve.

"But no," Arty said. "We decided to leave that to the professionals."

Martinez surveyed the silk scarves. "Nice knots."

"Lots of practice," said Steve as he knelt to untie them.

"Do I want to know?" Martinez asked.

"No," answered Steve and Arty together.

Martinez hauled Oscar to his feet and emptied his pockets. Fifteen hundred dollars and change in cash, a set of keys, a switchblade, a pack of Juicy Fruit, and a Mexican passport. "Fake, no doubt," said Martinez as he tossed it all on Steve's desk.

Cass opened the passport as Martinez sat Oscar down again. "Oscar Matalan from Chihuahua."

"Let's take Mr. Matalan downstairs. His chariot awaits."

"What about the murders?" I asked.

"He says he's got something to trade, but he wants to talk to someone with bigger *cojones* than me."

"Good idea, sending the car around back. Murphy's still out there," Cass said. "But I know how to catch him."

Oscar's head jerked up and Cass smiled. "No English, huh?"

MAYBE WE COULD DO SOMETHING S&M

CINDY WAS ALMOST DANCING with excitement when we got back to the agency. She'd filled the wives in and they were congratulating each other on having identified and stopped a high-ranking member of a Mexican cartel. I was a little put-out that nobody remembered it was me who made the initial connection, but I decided to be gracious and joined in the general hoopla.

Cass studied the photos of Bret's wives for a moment, and then raised her voice over the din. "Does anybody smoke?"

Shaver and Nicole raised their hands.

"I need you to go downstairs and light up."

"I just had one," Nicole protested. "And I'm trying to quit."

"One more won't kill you. Probably. We need a diversion. Martinez is taking Matalan down the back stairs. We need people on the street to keep Sugar Murphy focused on the front of the building."

"He's here?" Blue asked.

"I think so."

Nicole picked up her bag and she and Shaver hustled out of the agency.

"Now," Cass said. "I think I know how we can catch Murphy and find the Dismembered Bunnies' tapes. But I need some inside information from Babby."

TWENTY MINUTES LATER, Cass and I hurried down to street level talking while trying to look excited. In truth, it wasn't hard. I was hopping into Cass's old truck when I caught a flash as sunlight bounced off The Coffee Shop's door, and I hoped Arty had been right. As we were leaving his office, he'd whispered to Cass that he thought Sugar Murphy was waiting on Oscar there. He also told her Sugar had heard him mention that we knew where the tapes were.

Rush hour in Arcadia lasts from about four fifty-five to ten past five. Five-fifteen if the chickens who live on the square toddle into the street. We eased into traffic. We'd both slipped on our shades and were busy checking the people rushing around the square, trying to get out of the heat. Cass lifted her chin at a dark pickup. "I think that's him."

"Should we wait?"

"No. If he's out here, he'll follow us."

We made our way slowly around the square, watching. At last we hit Highway 79 headed east to Shreveport. Cass drove the speed limit and we kept a close eye on the mirrors. The dark truck followed and I felt really good about her plan. It was simple: Blue suspected Bret liked big bottoms and given the average cheek size of his various wives, she was correct. We'd originally spotted Bret leaving The Bicycle Club, and Babby confirmed that if you were into big rumps, that was the place to be. Cass thought it possible Bret had a girlfriend at the club, and if so, he might've left the tapes with her. It was a long shot, but we suspected Sugar Murphy would follow us, especially if we looked excited to be going somewhere. Even if we didn't find the tapes, we had a good shot at catching Sugar.

Traffic thinned the further east we drove, but the dark truck stayed with us, between a quarter of a mile to half a mile back. A comfortable distance to ensure he didn't lose us.

The Bicycle Club's parking lot was almost empty when we arrived, but the neon wheel was still spinning and the words "Crystal Tonight!" were on the marquee below it. We went ahead and entered the building, trusting Sugar to follow us in or wait for us to come back out. I supposed his choice would tell us how big his balls were.

A middle-aged man was wiping down the bar, his shirt sleeves rolled back to reveal surprisingly delicate wrists. His eyes were bright as he took us in. "We're not taking applications. But I'll put you on the list if you want a call when a spot opens up. That black eye's a good twist," he said. "Maybe we could do something S&M."

"We're not applying," Cass said, and showed him her badge.

"Easy mistake, as hot as you two look." He studied her credentials. "This is Louisiana, sweetheart. That badge is no good over here."

"Consider this part of your greater civic duty," Cass said. She slid a photo of Bret onto the bar. "Do you know this man?"

"Sure. He's here all the time." He kept polishing and we followed him down the bar as he worked. "What do you want him for?"

"Do you know his name?"

"Goes by Baxter."

"Does he come in here regularly?"

He nodded. "Few times a week. He's dating one of the dancers."

Score one for Cass. "Is she in?"

"What's this about?" he asked. We reached the end of the bar and he faced us fully.

"He's dead."

The bartender's eyebrows shot up. "A natural death?"

"Nope."

He looked at a set of beads hanging over an exit from the stage. "You think Crystal did it?"

"She the type?"

He dried his hands. "She's one of the more balanced dancers we've had, but with chicks, you never know."

"Is she in?"

He sighed and ran both hands over his slicked-back hair. "Any chance you're going to arrest her?"

"If she needs arresting," Cass said.

"Let me know as soon as you know, all right? She's the best dancer we've got. If she's not here tonight, I need to change the marquee and call the twins. Which isn't a bad thing. Those girls pack 'em in, too."

A SANDPILE OF A GRAVE

SUGAR MURPHY PULLED INTO the strip club's lot, parked between two cars under a shade tree, and checked his phone. No calls, no texts. He wasn't sure what happened to Oscar after he disappeared inside the building, but he'd been gone long enough that whatever had happened, it couldn't be good.

Heat inside the truck quickly grew unbearable and he cranked down the window, wondering what to do. There was no doubt the girls were on to the tapes. The guy at The Coffee Shop said so. If Sonny was so desperate to get those tapes back that he'd disown his son, it was a matter of time before Billy and Sugar ended up in a sandpile in some desert.

So here Sugar sat in an oven of a beat-up pickup truck, the last hope to keep himself, Billy, and Oscar alive. He wasn't optimistic about his chances.

Sugar pulled at his nose and took a look around the parking lot, wondering how long the girls would be inside and why he and Billy hadn't figured out BB would hide the tapes with some skanky stripper. Given BB's love of the fairer sex, they should've known. The only positive thing to come out of today, from Sugar's point of view, was seeing the shiner on that black-headed girl, Maxine. She might've caught Billy, but he'd whopped her a good one in return.

He was twisting in the seat, looking for a comfortable position, when his bladder spoke up. Sugar crossed his legs and willed the women to hurry.

SQUEEZE THEM DRY

WALKING THROUGH THE CURTAIN of beads was like stepping into another world. Not that the strip club we left behind was lush, but after my eyes adjusted to the near blackness, I realized that back stage was harsh. The walls were unfinished drywall. The floor was rough concrete. A faded white line led us to a set of rooms built from plywood. Music played softly and white light seeped beneath a closed door. Cass knocked and when a voice told us to enter, we did.

A woman sat before a battered vanity whose top was packed with colorful tubes and jars, and cups bristling with brushes. A three-way mirror shone, its bulbs casting a bright light. She was drawing a mole above her lip and held up a finger as we entered. "There," she said, leaning back and examining her face. "When I use the mole, I always want to add in a curly black hair, just to see if the drunks notice when I swoop down to take their tips."

She smiled at us in the mirror and then turned around and stood, straightening her short robe. Crystal was young. Not jail bait young, but barely. She had the hour glass figure Bret prized, and a sincerity that upped the wattage on her smile. "I'm Crystal. Bud must've sent you back. You looking for work?"

"No," Cass said, and again offered her detective's shield for inspection.

She glanced at it and then back at us. "Police?"

"Yes, ma'am. This is Maxine Leverman. She's a private investigator." I will admit I felt a thrill at hearing those words spoken aloud, even if they weren't true. Cass held out the head shot of Bret on the autopsy table. "Do you know this man?"

Crystal took it and sank onto her chair. "It's Baxter. Is this? I mean…" she turned the photo back to us. "Is he dead?"

We nodded.

"How did you know him?" I asked.

"He's a regular and we started dating." She was staring at the photo again. "Nothing serious, but we had a good time."

"He didn't want to marry you?" I couldn't help it. It seemed like he married most of the women he came across.

"Nope." Crystal handed the photo back to Cass. "What happened to him?"

"Where were you this past Saturday evening from around nine o'clock until three Sunday morning?"

"Here."

That should be easy to verify.

"What happened to him?" she asked again.

"He was murdered and we're trying to figure out who killed him."

Her eyes grew wide. "How terrible."

"Forgive me," I said, "but you don't seem too upset about his death."

"I am sad," she said, and then shrugged. "I'm from Idaho. I have a real boyfriend there, and he's who I'll marry. I'm studying accounting and finance at LSU and the money I earn here pays the bills and my tuition. Baxter was for fun." She half smiled. "He really was a nice guy and a good tipper. I'll miss him, and his tips. Oh no." Crystal's hand went to her mouth. She stood and dug through a rack of costumes. After a moment she turned and held out a small box. "Baxter gave this to me last week. He said if something happened to him, I should give it to the police."

Cass pulled on a pair of latex gloves and took it, easing the top off. Inside lay a black cassette snugged in bubble wrap. I was incredibly proud. I was right, and we'd found the tape. Cass asked if she could have a plastic baggie from the box on the vanity. Crystal opened it for her, and Cass slipped the box and the tape inside and positioned them so both were visible.

"There are people who want this and are willing to use force to get it," Cass said. "So be very careful for the next week or so."

"Honey, I take my clothes off in front of drunk men and squeeze their wallets dry with lap dances. I'm always careful." She cocked her head to one side. "What's on that cassette?"

"Something that will make the DEA very happy."

IT ALL GOES HORRIBLY WRONG

THE CLUB DOORS OPENED and the girls emerged, blinking against the stinging sunlight. Sugar tried to crouch and willed his bladder to hurry. The redheaded cop held something up for the black-haired chick to see. Sugar squinted and spotted a small box and a black cassette tape inside a clear baggie. His heart fluttered.

The girls high-fived and hurried to the old pickup, barely sparing him a glance. Sugar zipped up and cranked his truck, blasting onto the road. He blinked. It was empty. Mashing the gas pedal, he groaned along with the old truck. He had to catch them, because a plan had come to him right before he got out of the truck to pee. He'd driven this stretch of highway many times. One of the blind curves up ahead had a verge that fell away at a gentle angle to a secluded spot by the Sabine River. It was perfect for bumping someone off the road and ensuring the car wouldn't be spotted from above.

He hadn't wanted this to get violent, certainly not with a police officer. But he had to have that tape. Keeping his eyes on the road, Sugar reached beneath the seat and pulled out the short-barrel shotgun he'd taken from the chick's apartment.

Oscar didn't have to know everything.

"WHAT WAS HE DOING?" I asked.

"Peeing."

"Slow down so he can catch up."

"I've got a better idea."

She punched the accelerator and I snugged my seatbelt around my waist and across my chest. We rounded the first curve and Cass slowed enough to make a tight right-hand turn. She spun a u-turn in the middle of the small county road, and stopped beneath a copse of sagging oaks. We waited.

Sugar blew past and Cass grinned. "Let's get him."

SUGAR ROUNDED THE CURVE and stared down the length of highway. It was still empty. He stomped the accelerator and wondered what kind of engine she had that would let her disappear so fast. He hit a straightaway and pushed the truck harder. It slowly gained speed. A car appeared in his rearview mirror, coming up fast, and suddenly he had to pee again. The only thing that moved that fast was a state trooper. Sugar fingered the shotgun resting on the seat beside him and took his foot off the gas. The blind curve was just ahead and he slowed to the speed limit, thinking through plausible reasons for speeding.

As he entered the curve, the vehicle behind him materialized into the girls' truck, and Sugar had only a moment to think, "Wha-?" before the redheaded cop tapped his bumper and sent him careening off the road.

CASS TURNED HER TRUCK off the highway and drove down the verge at a sedate pace. The pickup was an old Ford handed down from her father through her six brothers and Cass until at last it became a spare vehicle at the Elliot house. But through those years of passing from one child to the next, its engine had gone through several modifications. It was now a souped-up monster that was the envy of high school boys for miles around.

The body was still in excellent shape despite the abuse it had taken, and boasted a homemade cow-catcher over its bumper and grill, which made it ideal for nudging vehicles off the road. Cass suspected Sugar might be desperate enough to attack us, and she'd insisted we take the old truck.

She pulled to a stop next to Sugar's pickup and I cranked my window down to see better. The truck was upright and he was still strapped in, but he gazed at us with dazed eyes. The bridge of his nose had a nasty gash and blood was smeared over the steering wheel.

"Think he's got a concussion?" I asked.

She opened her door and unholstered her gun. "Doubtful. Stay put until I say you can get out."

Her gun was up and ready when she rounded the truck's hood. Sugar lifted a shotgun and waved it in Cass's general direction. I looked closer. Fury flew all over me and I wrenched open the pickup's door.

"Stay in the truck, Maxine," Cass called.

"That's my shotgun," I shouted.

"You can have it later. Get back in the truck."

I did, but my blood was boiling.

Cass eased forward. "Police, Murphy. Put the gun down."

His eyes rolled from Cass to the shotgun and he cocked his head, as if he were surprised to see it in his hands.

"Put it down," she said, and took a step. "We've got Oscar Matalan and William Garcia. We know Oscar is Sonny Arellano's son. We've got the tape. Garcia's working a deal with the witness protection people. Shooting a cop only makes things worse for you."

The shotgun wavered and Cass stiffened, but his hands dropped into his lap. Sugar's eyes rolled up and he slumped forward, banging his nose into the steering wheel again. I bolted from the pickup but Cass got to him first. She gave me my shotgun and lifted one of Sugar's eyelids.

"Maybe he does have a concussion," she said. "Better call 911."

INVISIBLE PEOPLE

BY THE TIME THE ambulance carted Sugar Murphy off, handcuffed to the gurney with an officer by his side, and a tow truck arrived to take his pickup back to town, I was beat. My muscles were stiffening up again and general fatigue from all the excitement of the last few days was setting in. Cass took shells out of my shotgun, and I cradled it in my lap.

She poked me in the ribs as we drove back to Arcadia. "You've got about fifteen minutes to snooze, then we're back in work mode."

"Why?"

"We've got to give statements and see what's going on with Oscar."

"But Cass," I whined. "None of that matters. Yes, they're bad drug people, but that's for the DEA to work out. Arresting them solves the break-ins and instrument bashing, but it doesn't get us any closer to finding out who killed Bret and the girls."

"Maybe, maybe not."

"What are you thinking?"

"Whoever killed Bret had good knowledge of the winery and Blue's house. They had access to the bottles and glasses with fingerprints, to the wine bottle with Blue's bloody fingerprint, the bat, and that pottery tool."

I thought as she drove. "That makes sense, but other than getting a general description of the man who murdered Daphne from Sugar, what good will the tattered remnants of the Dismembered Bunnies do us?"

She smiled at that. "Oscar worked at the winery, for at least a few weeks."

Suddenly I was wide awake. "You think he saw something?"

"Or heard something. Blue said he washed the dishes. Nobody would've noticed him."

The invisibles, I thought. This is exactly what Aunt Kay had tried to teach me. The people nobody notices are sometimes in the perfect place to gather information.

"But how do we get him to talk, Cass? We've got nothing to trade."

"Oh, I think we do. I'm not sure Oscar is cut out for the drug business. He was bawling like a little girl while Martinez drilled him."

"You think we can offer him something better?"

"If it solves three murders, I think it's worth a try."

THE BRET'S WIVES CLUB

BY THE TIME I got to the agency, the wives were packing up and heading to Blue's for a sleepover. Nicole's lawyer Ned Shaver was off to a hotel on the Loop.

I filled them in on how we captured the third member of the marauding Bunnies.

"Sugar is at the hospital, getting thumped over," I said. "Detective Martinez and the DEA are working on Oscar Matalan, trying to determine if he knows anything related to the murders."

"Anything that would clear me, you mean," Blue said.

"Yes."

She looked at her lawyer, who was stacking paperwork. "It's not looking good, is it?"

"It's not looking bad, Blue, and we're just getting started," Yvette said. "Maxine, what was on those tapes that was so important to Sonny Arellano?"

I shrugged. "Kado was looking for a cassette player when I left the courthouse. He called Stan at The Golden Gate, but his is out for repairs."

"There's a stereo with a cassette player in the music room and it didn't get smashed," Blue said. "I guess that's why Bret bought it, to play those tapes. Kado can borrow it, if he needs it."

"I'll come get it," I said. "Later tonight?"

"Fine by me. I plan to sell all his unbroken music crap as soon as I can."

Frannie perked up. "Are those instruments I brought today evidence, Yvette?"

"Nope, why?"

"I'll take them to Blue's and have them appraised with his other stuff."

"There's a thought," Nicole said. "I'll take those banjos to Blue's, too."

Shaver spoke up. "We've got contacts in Los Angeles or Nashville who will give you a fair appraisal. They'll also let you know if anything is worth repairing."

The women gathered their things and we helped them carry instruments down to the various cars.

"Seriously?" I whispered to Kay as the wives discussed plans and exchanged phone numbers. "Would you want to hang with the women your husband was cheating with?"

"No," Kay said. "But they've formed a weird bond. It makes sense in a way. Instead of an ex-wives club, it's the Bret's Wives Club." She studied the women as they left the conference room. "They're all his victims, and they're just figuring that out. They might be a support system for one another."

Yvette was pecking away on her cell phone at the head of the table and Babby was putting empty coffee cups and wine glasses on a tray. I joined her. "We didn't learn anything new today, did we?" I asked.

"We certainly did," Yvette said. "We know beyond a reasonable doubt Blue didn't kill Bret or those two girls."

"We do?"

"We do. But until we figure out who really murdered them, it's my job to convince Sammy Mathison that she's the wrong woman, and Bill Hoffner to put three murders back on his open case list."

THE ERRAND

THE KILLER WATCHED THE cars drive past the winery and down the drive to Blue's house. The women's silhouettes were just visible through the darkened windows. Rumors swirling through the winery had Blue meeting the two women Bret was currently married to today, and had his marriage count up to over twenty women.

Tuesdays were usually slow and the killer called to another staff member: "Watch my station. I need to run an errand."

She nodded absently and carried on rolling silverware in napkins. The killer stepped out into the early evening and eased behind the shop building. The sun was slowly sinking and the pines surrounding the winery threw long shadows that devoured the tall, slender form slipping between them.

FACING REALITY

"TURN THAT CRAP OFF," Frannie said. "I can't believe anyone would buy that stuff."

Babby had driven out to Maxine's destroyed apartment and collected the Poison Ivy and the Dismembered Bunnies album so the wives could hear it. None were impressed.

"That sounds kind of like the stuff he practiced at our house," Nicole said. "But it was hard to find anything musical in it."

"Put on some Joan Jett. I could do with some hot chick rock after that noise."

A chime sounded and Blue looked down at her phone. The women had migrated to the music room and were surrounded by the ravaged remains of their husband's instruments. "Thank goodness. The photos from the white grape harvest are finally in."

"What are they for?" Nicole asked.

"I'm writing a cookbook and the publisher has sent a photographer out several times. She's coming back this week for the red grape harvest."

Blue opened the file and started flipping through the photos, and then stopped. "I don't know whether to laugh or cry."

"Why?" asked Frannie.

Blue turned her phone around. "If this wasn't the last time I saw Bret, it was close." She looked at the other two women. "Do you want to see these, or had you rather not?"

"Might as well face reality," Nicole said. "Where's your computer?"

"I DON'T BELIEVE IT." Frannie's wine glass tipped at a precarious angle as she pointed over Blue's shoulder. "When was that picture taken?"

Blue looked at the date and told her.

"Bret drove in that morning, didn't he?"

Blue thought for a moment. "I think he did."

"He came from my house. He was wearing that hat when he left. The man always had a hat on his head, but I hadn't seen that one before."

"I've never seen it, either," Nicole said.

"That's his lucky harvest hat," Blue said. "He wore it constantly during harvest, worried something would go wrong if he took it off. I had to make him take it off when he came to bed."

They grew silent.

"Well this is awkward," Frannie said. "I can't believe he could leave my bed one morning and be in yours," she looked at Blue, "or yours," she looked at Nicole, "that night. No offense, but that's icky."

"Too right," said Nicole.

"And it's worse than that, because he was sleeping with women other than us," Blue said quietly.

"It's been about twelve hours since I learned my husband was a polygamist," Frannie said. "I've adapted pretty quickly. Why is that?"

"Maybe we knew," Nicole said. "Knew deep down but didn't want to believe."

"He was good," Blue said.

"At making you feel you were the only one," Frannie said.

"Bastard," said Nicole.

"I'll drink to that," Frannie said, and tossed back her wine. She dragged up a conga whose top was slit but body was intact, and perched next to the desk. "Let's see the rest of those photos. I don't think I've got anything more current of him. He was easy on the eyes and easy to insure. At least I'll enjoy his life insurance money."

Blue looked up and cocked her head.

"What?" asked Frannie.

"I thought I heard something." She walked to the music room door and stuck her head into the hall. It was empty. She slowly returned to the other wives, who were flipping through the photos. Blue was explaining how the harvest and wine-making process worked, when Nicole stopped her. "Go back one."

Blue did.

"Who's that?"

"The winery's host, Will."

"He's the spitting image of Baxter."

"No," said Blue. She leaned closer. "You think?"

"Wow," said Frannie. "He's a looker. Where are those photos of Bret when he was younger?" She tottered to the boxes they'd brought with them and grabbed a stack of photos. "Here," she said. "In this one. And this one."

They were casual photos of BB Ivy and the Dismembered Bunnies in the studio, at gigs, rehearsing, and preparing for a photo shoot. The women looked back and forth between the old photos and the new.

"I can't believe I didn't see it," Blue said.

"Pull up the current photo of Baxter," Nicole said. "He's got about twenty years on that kid. His hair is short now and Will's hair is darker. There are similarities, but if you didn't see them together, you wouldn't notice."

"He can't be Bret's child," Blue said. "He never had any kids."

"That we know of," Nicole clarified. "How old is Will?"

Blue frowned. "Mid to late twenties?"

"That would put Baxter in his early twenties when Will was born. Who was he married to then?" Nicole opened her phone and studied the photos she'd taken of the white boards. "Here we go. He married Mary Sterling in 1983, divorced her in 1987."

"Nobody else?" Frannie asked.

"Only Mary as far as we know."

"Do we have a picture of her?"

Blue motioned to the boxes. "Somewhere in there."

Nicole found the death notice and accompanying photo. "Could be her kid. Hey Blue," she held up the photo. "She looks like you."

"Yvette said the same thing," Blue said. "Do you think Will is their kid?"

Frannie was still digging and came up with the photo of a younger Bret that Blue had seen earlier. "Yeah, Will's definitely his kid. Look at this." She turned it to face them, then examined the back of the photo, squinting to see better. "Unbelievable. He knew."

"What do you mean?" Nicole asked.

"He knew he had a kid. This is Will, not Bret. Look." She shoved the photo at Blue and dug deeper in the box, pulling out more photos and looking at their backs. "He's got pictures of Will when he's an infant through to his high school photos. That one," she pointed to the photo Blue still held, "must've been taken when he was about college age."

Blue studied the pictures of Will. "How did he get these? Mary divorced him because he was cheating. There's a Dear Bret letter somewhere in that box."

"She must've sent them to him."

"I wonder if Will knew his father?" Nicole asked.

"How could he?" Blue asked. "None of us knew he had a kid. Bret traveled a lot, but he didn't spend that much time in California."

"How could a man have a son this cute," Frannie said, holding up a studio photo of Will as a toddler in a jon-jon romper with a rubber ball in one hand, "and not adore him?"

THE FALL

I WAS WALKING DOWN the stairs to ground level, my head bent over my handbag digging for my keys, when I fell into the door and stumbled out onto the street. A pair of strong arms caught me and the next thing I knew, I was looking up into a pair of warm brown eyes flecked with gold. Butterflies came to life in my stomach. Bruce looked as surprised as I did, and was slow to put me back on my feet.

"Easy there," he said. "You in a hurry?"

"I can't find my keys. Would you hold this?" I held out my bag.

He took it warily and balanced it on two hands. "What do you have in this thing? It must weigh twenty pounds."

"The essentials. Stop looking. There's girl stuff in here." I found my keys right where they were supposed to be: on that cute little strap inside the bag. I raised them in triumph. "Thanks."

"No problem." Bruce shifted the purse back to me and I slung it over my shoulder. "Are you headed somewhere?"

"I was going to call Cass and see if she wanted to come to my place and order dinner in. A cleaning crew was supposed to clear out stuff that can't be repaired, and I need to make a list of what has to be replaced."

"Kado's taken her out." He glanced across the square at Arcadia's only Italian restaurant. The decor was cheesy, but the food was carb rich and very good. "I could cook while you inventory."

That was a bolt out of the blue and although it was a welcome one, I wasn't sure how I felt about having a man in this apartment. It was sacred ground, my bolt hole, the place I had felt safest in the world. Now, I wasn't sure how safe it was and in truth, I was reluctant to go back alone. Logically, I knew my interlopers were safely tucked away in Forney County's fine jail, but the fear lingered. I wanted to explore a relationship with this man, but I was struggling with the thought of letting Bruce into my abode when it struck me that he wasn't the first man to have been there. Yes, the complex's manager and the maintenance guys had been in and out, but they didn't count. But Sugar Murphy had been there. He was a man. And he'd certainly made himself at home, evidenced by the fingerprints Truman found on the toilet handle. So why not let Bruce in? If things didn't work out, I could always move.

"Sounds great. I need to run out to the winery later, and I don't know what I've got in the fridge."

A smile split his face and he ran a hand over his hair. "I'll stop by the grocery store on the way. Are you allergic to anything?"

I assured him I wasn't and gave him my apartment number. The butterflies soared into full flight and it was all I could do not to burst into song as I climbed into the Lexus.

SECRETS

HOW INDEED? WILL THOUGHT from his position outside the music room. He'd crept through the house and to the second floor, cringing when he stepped on the squeaky stair by mistake. He'd ducked into a room just before Blue stuck her head into the hall, then moved slowly to stand by the door. He listened to their conversation with morbid fascination, growing more disgusted by the minute with his father and the women he'd bedded.

Will had never known hate until right before his mother died, when she told him the truth about his father. He'd found the box his mother had secreted on a high shelf in her closet and finally understood why her mouth had always been a little pinched. Why she'd been so watchful whenever they were out of the house. Why she'd always been so protective.

His mother's life had been wrecked by a blackmailer whose lies and half-truths had sent her to an early grave. Bret had only gotten what he deserved when he ended up in that tank of wine. Now the women who'd helped him would get what they deserved.

Will tightened the grip on his bat and waited.

A KISS ISN'T JUST A KISS

BRUCE BAKED AN AMAZING white fish and used a dented pot to steam vegetables while I wandered around the apartment, despairing at the damage. The cleaning crew had done an amazing job of scrubbing away the fingerprint powder and salvaging what they could. But most of the apartment was a loss. Thankfully, I am meticulous about taking pictures of my belongings for insurance purposes - I don't know where I get that obsessiveness, but I'm glad I've got it - and keeping them in a safe deposit box. I knew my insurance agent would thank me when I delivered my list and photos tomorrow morning. Or maybe not, given how much they'd have to pay out.

The crew managed to salvage four plates, a cereal bowl with three chips on its lip, and two salad plates. Bruce surveyed the contents of my cabinets and said, "Minimalist is in."

By the time I finished my inventory, dinner was ready. The crew had glued two of the barstools back together, and although they listed severely to starboard, we balanced and ate a fabulous dinner at the bar. Bruce had brought a bottle of the pink stuff from Cedar Bend Winery, and I asked how he knew that was my favorite.

"I have my ways," he said with a sly smile. "Hey, how come nobody heard the guy trashing your place?"

"There are only two apartments on this floor. The other one is empty, so are the two directly below me."

He looked around the nearly empty space. "Are you okay to stay here tonight?"

I hadn't thought about that. The mattress and box springs in my bedroom and the guest room had been slashed and were gone, whisked away by the cleaning crew. My beautiful red sofa was also gone. "I think I have a sleeping bag in one of the closets," I said.

"That's not what I meant," Bruce said. "Are you okay to stay here alone?"

I hadn't thought about that, either. Not directly. It was one of those things I could avoid until I had to face it head on, and now was the moment of truth. Tears stung the back of my eyes and my lower lip quivered. I bit it to keep it still.

Bruce watched, and then took me in his arms, pulling me close. I don't think I've ever felt so safe in my life. I rested my head against his chest and let the rhythm of his breathing and his thumb tracing circles on the back of my neck relax me. He leaned into the kitchen bar and we stood like that for a long time.

At last I lifted my head, intending to thank him, but he brought his lips to mine and kissed me. Softly at first, and then with more heat. I lifted my arms to his broad shoulders and stood on my toes to reach him, and he circled my waist with his arms. His hands, rough with calluses, slipped under my blouse and electricity crackled through me. He pulled my hips to his and desire coupled with a pulsing panic exploded through me.

The old images arced through my mind. Flashing lights, thumping bass, Richard Nixon's crumpled face. I'd never had sex since the rape without the images intruding. Usually I was drunk enough to push them away, but tonight I was almost sober. Fear overwhelmed desire, and I pushed away from Bruce.

His soft brown eyes shone with lust and concern in equal measure. "Are you okay?" he asked. "We can stop whenever you say so."

There's nothing sexier than a man who puts control of his lovemaking in a woman's hands. I trembled with desire and gratitude, then cleared my throat. "I promised to go to the winery to pick something up for Kado."

He tucked a strand of hair behind my ear. "Why don't you pack some clothes and stay with us for a few days? At least until your new furniture arrives."

"I could stay with Babby or Kay."

"Or Vivienne?" he asked with a sardonic grin. The angst between my mother and me was legendary.

I snorted. "Never with Mother."

"Stay with us. Please. I promise I'll stay out of your room. Unless you tell me to come in."

His face was so open and full of hope I couldn't help but say yes.

"Good," Bruce said. "I'll do the dishes while you pack."

A man who cooks *and* does the dishes? That's the second most sexy thing out there. My knees trembled as he picked up a sponge.

REVENGE

"I'M WORN OUT," FRANNIE said, and gestured to the neat stacks of paper on the floor. "This is too much to take in. Can you believe one man can keep communications going with all these women?"

The wives had gone through most of the paperwork and arranged it by wife and in date order. Mary's letters to Bret were stacked chronologically, as were the photos of Will. They'd found no information about any other members of Bret's family. Not parents, siblings, aunts or uncles, grandparents, or cousins.

Nicole walked to the CD player and slipped *The Best of The Guess Who* into the tray, then began slow dancing to "These Eyes."

One box remained and Frannie eyed it with suspicion. "I wonder what we'll find in there."

"I'm not sure I want to know," Blue said. "Poor Mary. She had the worst of it for all these years."

"He got a lot more money out of the other wives," Nicole countered in her nasally voice, her eyes closed as she swayed to the music. "Us included. I wonder if the kid inherited any of his father's philandering ways? He certainly got Baxter's looks and wouldn't have any trouble with the girls." She opened her eyes and surveyed the wrecked music room. "I'll go get some water and we can finish that last box, then get some sleep. Wine, anyone?"

"I'll go," Frannie said. "I've got to pee anyway. And yes, I could use another glass. Anybody else?" The Guess Who swung into "Laughing" and she'd nearly crossed the threshold into the hall when she snapped her fingers and turned back. "I'll take the dirty dish -"

Her words died in a shriek of pain. Blue and Nicole stood transfixed as a baseball bat whipped out of the dark hall and connected with Frannie's left arm, just at the elbow. The shriek faded to a whimper as she looked at the broken arm and slipped to the floor.

"Frannie!" Blue yelled, racing to the other woman and crouching beside her.

Nicole was right behind her but pulled up short as Will materialized in the doorway, bat raised for another swing. Nicole grabbed the collar of Blue's shirt and yanked her off balance. Blue fell on her butt and did a fast crab-walk backwards. His bat missed her head by inches.

He was hissing as he stalked into the room, bat raised again. "Bitches. Every one of you, bitches in heat."

"Will," Blue said, her voice quiet but shaking. "Calm down. We're no threat to you."

"No threat?" He coughed a laugh. "Do you have any idea what my mother suffered because of women like you?"

"No, but we know a little. We've got her letters." Blue pointed at the neat stack on the floor and watched as Will grew still. She and Nicole inched away, stepping carefully to avoid the musical clutter. "She did suffer, Will. She loved you very much and wouldn't want you to do this."

Will turned his gaze on them, his beautiful gray eyes now the color of a troubled ocean, blazing with hate. "Oh yes. She would."

He raised the bat and took a step forward.

FROM A HORROR MOVIE

THE DRIVE FROM MY apartment to the winery was shorter than usual because I was in a lust-fueled trance and missed most of the trip. How I managed to arrive without doing a mischief to myself or anyone else is a mystery.

I waved at the officer stationed on the county road just before the winery's entrance and he waved back. The parking lot was positively packed, and I left the Lexus along the drive to the house. I excused my way through the crowd on the patio and stepped inside to the sound of the three piece jazz band from Friday night. The guitar player was crooning Chet Baker's version of "Funny Valentine", yet he managed to wince at the sight of my face and blow me a sympathetic kiss.

I glanced around, looking for Will, but didn't see him. One of the waitresses fussed over my black eye and said he'd left to run an errand and she wished he'd hurry back.

"Business is booming since word of the murders and Blue's alleged role in them got out. People adore Blue," she said. "They were a little leery of Bret, maybe because he was such a flirt, but nobody can imagine Blue killing anyone. People are coming from all over to show their support. Even the publishers want to include something about the murders in the cookbook. Long may it continue."

I saw Wally Pugh, reporter for the Forney Cater and KOIL, the local radio station, sitting with an attractive woman near the stage. His eyebrows twitched at the sight of my battered face, and I remembered I had a bone to pick with him over how he portrayed Blue in today's newspaper. But that would have to wait.

When I asked if Blue was in the kitchen, the waitress directed me to the house. The wives' cars were parked in the drive and lights glowed in some of the upstairs windows. I was reaching for the doorbell when I realized the door was ajar.

If I'd been smart, I would've hightailed it back to the winery and called the police, letting them investigate. But you've probably figured out that I've never been one to follow my head. As it turns out, it was a good thing logic didn't prevail.

I slung my lucky purse higher on my shoulder and pushed the door open enough to slip inside. Music drifted down the stairs and I recognized "Laughing" by The Guess Who. I grabbed the banister and headed up, apologizing to my healing knees as I went.

I'd made it only a few steps when the first shriek sounded. My blood ran cold and my pain disappeared. I bounded up the rest of the stairs and stopped in the hallway. More screaming and the sounds of scuffling were coming from Bret's music room and I ran to it.

The scene I found was from a horror movie. Frannie lay unmoving on the floor near the door, her left arm splayed at an unnatural angle. Nicole was yelling at a man stalking towards them, baseball bat held high. She stumbled over a piece of drum kit and sprawled on her butt, then grabbed a cowbell and heaved it. The man ducked but kept moving.

Blue's face was ashen as she helped Nicole up, but I realized she was speaking softly to their attacker. Given the amount of clutter on the floor, there was little space for the women to retreat. A shot of adrenaline flushed through me. I dropped my lucky purse, stepped over Frannie's body, and grabbed a mostly intact banjo.

I hefted it and swung with all my might, smacking the attacker in the back. He went down with a 'whoof' and Blue and Nicole jumped him while he was stunned, but he pushed his upper body from the floor. I grabbed an orange extension cord and dropped to my knees, scrambling to wrap it around his legs. I got it around once, pulled it tight, and felt a surge of glee as he fell face forward again.

He was still struggling but Nicole engaged in a tug-of-war over his bat and won, then raised it over her head in a double-handed grip, letting loose with an unholy scream. The CD changed tracks to "Undun" and despite the fight swirling around me, I couldn't help but think how appropriate the opening lyrics, "She's come undone," were to the scene.

Nicole started a vicious downward swing but Blue stopped her. "No," she said, shoving the bat away. "We can't do this."

"Yes we can," Nicole screamed. "He killed Baxter."

The man flipped to his back and kicked the extension cord away. I was shocked to see Will the host staring up at me. His gray eyes were wild and his face so twisted in frustration and fury that he looked like a different man. I was still on my knees and lunged for his legs.

"We can't kill him," Blue said. She grabbed a guitar neck and shoved part of a microphone stand at Nicole. "But we can defend ourselves. Hit him with this."

The women set to whacking and Will curled into the fetal position. I squirmed forward and tried to get the extension cord around his legs again, but he kept kicking at me. Blue whacked his calf and Nicole got after his thigh and I managed to wrap the cord around his legs three times and tie a knot. Will grabbed one of Blue's ankles and yanked, but she maintained her balance and kicked him in the face. When he covered his bleeding chin with both hands, Blue and Nicole fell on him and rolled him onto his chest, then fought to pull his arms behind him. I grabbed thick metal strings snaking from a pile of broken equipment and tied his hands. Then the three of us stood, sweating and panting, and studied our handiwork.

"Frannie," Blue gasped, and staggered to the third wife. "Call an ambulance, Maxine."

"Not yet," Nicole said, all the nasally whine gone from her icy voice. "Let's get him in a chair."

THE CONFESSION

IT ONLY TOOK NICOLE and Blue ten minutes to have Will blubbering and spilling his guts. I couldn't hear him because The Guess Who had shouted their way through "No Time", and now "American Woman" was blaring from the stereo. I thought about turning the music off, but it was a fitting soundtrack to Bret Ivy and the incredible mess he'd made of these people's lives.

As soon as I saw Will's lips move, I dialed 911. The room was a disaster of broken equipment, scattered paperwork, and spilled wine. I moved some of the clutter out of the way and sat beside Frannie. The knees of my linen trousers were a bloody mess and I knew Babby would want to super glue me up again. I wondered if a split knee could garner me a trip to the emergency room.

Frannie was regaining consciousness and I helped her find a more comfortable position. Her left arm was in bad shape and I hoped the break wasn't so bad she couldn't make jewelry anymore. She'd promised to create a set of turquoise earrings with matching ring, bracelet, and necklace for me. Shallow, I know, but there you have it.

A siren's wail cut through the music and Nicole and Blue stepped away from Will, leaving him sagging as far as he could in the straight-backed chair. It had taken all three of us to lift him into it and we'd wrapped duct tape around his chest to ensure he stayed put. The wives filled me in on Will's status as Bret's child as we worked, and suddenly the itch in my brain was scratched. That was the connection I'd been trying to make for days now and I was dismayed I'd missed it.

"What'd he say?" I asked.

"He killed both women and Bret," Blue said, her eyes glazing over. "He was planning to kill us all."

"Who all?" I asked.

"All of Baxter's wives," Nicole said. "Past and present. Except for Blue."

"What was he going to do with Blue?"

"Frame her for the murders so she went to prison. She looks enough like his mother that Will has a soft spot for her."

"It's not your fault Bret was obsessed with -" I almost said 'big bottoms', but managed to stop myself. "Women."

"That's not the way Will sees it," Blue said. She sat heavily on the conga, sticking her arms out as it wobbled. "I need a drink."

A LITTLE LIE

DETECTIVE MITCH STONE FOLLOWED the paramedics into the music room. "I need to carry duct tape and scarves instead of a gun. Seems to work better."

The Guess Who had made their way to "Do You Miss Me Darlin'?" when Nicole walked over and snapped the stereo off. "No," she said. "I do not."

I scooted out of the way so the paramedics could tend to Frannie. My movements were stiff and I was struggling to stand when Mitch held out a hand. "Knee pads would be a good investment, Maxine. Maybe Santa should bring you some." He eyed my face. "That's a nasty cut over your eye. Might need stitches."

A cut? I patted the area above my brow and felt something sticky. One of the paramedics checked me over and agreed I needed stitches in my forehead and knee. I knew I would miss all the fun if I went to the ER and asked if super glue would do the trick.

"Might leave a scar, but yeah, it'll work," he answered as he cleaned my wounds and applied bandages. There was a touch of respect in his voice, and I treasured that.

Mitch led the three of us downstairs and I introduced him to Nicole and Frannie. He waited while Blue poured three good measures of scotch and even let us down the first glass and start on refills. Nobody talked over anybody else this time, and Nicole and Blue shared what Will told them.

He'd never known the truth about who his father was until just before Mary died. She was on intense pain medication and didn't paint a very clear picture, but after her death Will found the box of letters that told the whole story. Bret had met and married Mary in his Poison Ivy and the Dismembered Bunnies days and loved her madly. She'd booted him when she discovered he was cheating, and he'd sent heartfelt letters of apology and promises to remain faithful. As many youngsters do, Mary relished her power and made him suffer. Then she found out she was pregnant and expected him to come running when she called. But Bret's proclamations of undying loved died and he vamoosed, leaving Mary and their son to fend for themselves.

She was a wreck during her pregnancy, and in the first few months after she gave birth her agony turned to bitterness. But she eventually met a man who swept her Cinderella-style out of her penny-pinching existence and into a lush world of money and privilege. During their courting, he naturally asked about Will's father and Mary told a lie. A tiny one, but in the way lies often do, it had massive ramifications.

She told her beau that Will's father was dead, killed in a military operation so secret that his death wasn't announced to the public. Something to do with intelligence gathering in Libya. Bear in mind that Mary was an exceptionally beautiful woman and smart enough to keep her suitor out of her panties until she had a ring on her finger. He bought into that little lie to the tune of five sparkling carats set in gold.

Perhaps all predators have a sixth sense for weakness in their prey. Although not interested in assuming his parental responsibilities while Mary was single, Bret became fascinated with his child once she was married to a wealthy stockbroker. So fascinated that he demanded photos of Will and cash, lots of it, to ensure Mary's dead hero stayed in the grave. Bret continued to write, Mary continued to wait anxiously for the mail each day, and she continued to supply Bret with a stream of cash and photos of young Will.

Over time, Mary's marriage to the stockbroker grew chilly while Bret's letters grew wistful. He reminisced about their years together during the Dismembered Bunnies days and proclaimed his regret at not knowing his son. When Mary offered to leave her stockbroker husband and join Bret, he refused, claiming simultaneously that he couldn't provide for her in the way she'd become accustomed and asking for more money.

About this time, Mary learned how to Google. She found references to Bret's marriages to Susan Spikes Ivy and Nicole Hartford Ivy, all during the time Bret was allegedly pining away for Mary. She challenged him on his nuptials, but he assured her he was the victim of their feminine wiles and his love for her remained pure. He was unable to leave Nicole because she had taken control of his assets and he would lose everything in a divorce.

Mary's bitterness over Nicole, and perhaps her early years of drug fueled living, turned into liver cancer. She was dead within months. But not without first leaving her son the gift of knowing who his real father was and how the bitch Nicole had ruined Mary's chance at happiness.

After Mary's death, Will found the box of letters and discovered his father was nothing more than a con man whose promises and lies helped send Mary to an early grave. He set out to find his father. Will first saw Bret at Nicole's house in Dallas and followed him to Cedar Bend Winery, then to Frannie's studio south of Nacogdoches. All in a single day. In every location, Bret acted as if he belonged and felt free to fondle various females. Needless to say, Will was confused.

It took a little time, but he realized Cedar Bend was the hub of Bret's hanky-panky and he asked for a job. When he confronted Bret several weeks ago, Bret steadfastly denied having any offspring and then promptly fled. That was when his disappearing act began.

Bret wasn't avoiding Blue by limiting his time at the winery, he was avoiding his son.

THE DEAL

MITCH SAT BACK AND stroked his chin, his blue eyes distant. While we waited, Blue poured another round of scotch. The third glass of amber liquid seemed to bring us all back to life. At last he stood and opened his cell phone.

Cass ran into the kitchen, breathless, and nearly knocked him over. "You got him?"

We repeated an abbreviated version of events while Mitch sat and listened again. His eyes still had that faraway look when he stood and opened his cell phone. He headed for the front door.

"Where're you going?" I asked as Cass checked out the new cut on my forehead.

"Hmm?"

"What do you think about Will's confession?"

"Oh, that," he said. "As long as he repeats it, we're good. Kado'll find evidence and it'll be a slam dunk."

"Are you calling Sheriff Hoffner to tell him I'm innocent?" Blue asked.

"Nope. I'm an unnamed source calling Wally Pugh at the Forney Cater. It's best if he hears the unvarnished truth before Hoffner has a chance to twist it to make himself look good."

"And then you'll call Hoffner?"

"Then I'll call Hoffner." He hesitated. "You're not the suing type, are you? For false arrest?"

"What are you talking about?" Blue asked.

"The department's kind of low on funds right now, and a lawsuit could push our liability insurance through the roof."

"From what we heard today, you've got a solid case," Nicole said. "I'll represent you."

"I hadn't considered it, but now that you mention it…" Blue tapped the island with a finger as she thought. "Tell you what. Keep those police cars away from the winery's drive, and I won't sue."

"It's a good deal, Mitch," Cass said. "We've never made an arrest out here. It's a waste of money."

Mitch nodded, a slow smile spreading across his face. "My wife loves the winery. Throw in dinner for two and a bottle of that pink stuff, and I'll let Hoffner know you were frothing at the bit but I managed to talk you down."

Blue held out a hand. "Deal."

NO CREDIT

LIGHTS WERE BLAZING AT the Elliot house, though it was almost midnight when we got there. After she realized I'd had three glasses of scotch, Cass had all but breath-o-lyzed me before letting me follow her home in my Lexus. I'll admit my reserves of adrenaline were shot, but I managed to keep her tail lights in sight and pull safely into the drive behind her.

Abe, Harry, Bruce, and Goober were waiting up for us and the rich smell of chocolate cake filled the kitchen. I've got to figure out how the Elliots eat like this all the time and stay so thin.

"Gosh, Maxine," was all Goober could say when he saw my bloodied clothes and battered face. He shifted from foot to foot, fingering the hook on his overalls, and I thought he was going to faint. But to his credit, he pulled clean kitchen towels from a drawer, filled a bowl with hot water, and left both on the kitchen table.

This time it was Bruce and Harry who fussed over my wounds. As we told them about the arrests and confessions, they peeled the bandages off my knee and eyebrow, disinfected me, and applied super glue. Harry cleaned the raspberry on my chin, which was scabbing over nicely. "No offense, but I'm not sure you're cut out for this private eyeing thing, Maxine," he said.

"None taken," I told him. "But it's too late to back out now."

"Then you'd better get some self-defense training."

"It's top of my list as soon as I can move again."

Bruce poured hot icing over the cake and Abe filled glasses with milk. His gentle brown eyes reflected concern, but he only squeezed my shoulder as he put my glass on the table.

"You caught a murderer?" Goober asked.

"He killed three people and would've killed more if Maxine hadn't stopped him," Cass answered. "What do you think about that?"

Goober swallowed a bite of cake. "That's brave."

"Your case is over, Maxine?" Abe asked.

I felt that free-fall sensation of loss again. "Looks like it."

"What do you have lined up next?"

"Working cases will probably take a back seat to studying and getting my concealed carry license."

"Well, you're off to a good start," Abe said, and drained his milk. "But I doubt Bill Hoffner will give you any credit for helping identify and arrest a triple murderer, or those three men tied up in drug trafficking."

I laughed aloud, and it felt good. "I wouldn't want his credit if he gave it, Abe. The people who matter know how I've bumbled through this case, and that's good enough for me." Truth be told, it was.

"I'm going to bed," Harry said. "If you want hot water, Maxine, you'd better get in the shower first. Bruce hogs it all."

"He does," Goober added.

Bruce shrugged. "Some of us like to be clean. But you're welcome to the shower, Maxine. Let me know if you need me to scrub your back." Except for Goober, eyebrows shot up around the table. Bruce shrugged. "She's injured."

"Well, well," said Abe.

"Just remember the walls are thin in this house," Harry said as he took his plate to the sink.

"What does that mean?" Goober asked.

"Never mind," Cass told him. "I don't think we'll have to worry about it tonight."

WEDNESDAY

A SMALL TOWN

I SLEPT SOUNDLY TUESDAY night, probably thanks to feeling so secure in the Elliot house. The hot shower wiped me out and loosened my tired muscles enough that I found a comfortable spot as soon as I slipped into bed. The nightmare stayed away and instead I dreamed of bad music, angry rockers, and a vengeful child. I woke to the smell of frying sausage and baking biscuits and knew any diet plans were worthless. Instead, I swore I'd make it to the gym and do what I could to work off a few calories.

All six of us crowded around the Elliot's breakfast table and came to life over a huge breakfast and wonderful coffee. Harry was the first to leave, to pick his girls up and drop them at a day-camp. Abe followed not long after to start on a long-haul run, picking up and delivering cars for a local dealership. Cass was next, hurrying to the courthouse to get the poop on our prisoners. She took Goober to drop him at his trailer so he could pick up fresh clothes. That left me and Bruce to do the dishes, and we listened to the news on KOIL while we loaded the dishwasher.

There was very little related to our capture of a triple murderer, and nothing relating to the two incarcerated members of Poison Ivy and the Dismembered Bunnies or the drug lord's kid. We did get an update on the dismal state of cattle prices, the Junior League bake sale scheduled for Saturday, and a notice that the animal shelter was offering free vaccinations until four o'clock today. Some things do make living in a small town worthwhile.

Bruce didn't bring up the fact that he'd stayed out of my room last night, and I didn't mention it either. For some reason, I was content to let this relationship develop organically.

I dressed for work and sent a text to Simon, confirming a date for Friday night. Yes, I am very interested in Bruce, but we had a long road to travel before I was willing to commit to exclusivity.

A girl can't be too rash about her dating options, can she?

NO JUSTICE FOR THE LOCALS

THE FLOWER SHOP'S DELIVERY van pulled away as I rounded the corner to the square, and I eased the Lexus into the empty spot. My knees protested loudly as I wobbled up the flight of steps, and I stopped on the landing to take a breather. After the last six days, it felt a little surreal to be standing outside the door with "Lost and Found Investigations - No Job Too Big or Small" written on the frosted glass. I'd loved every minute of it, even the time spent battling Big Billy and Will, and I wasn't sure I'd ever find a case that could keep me so interested. Yes, a short attention span is one of my weaknesses. I still looked forward to finding mine and Cass's rapist, but I was having trouble seeing how the day-to-dayness of the business would challenge me.

Too late to back out now, I told myself, and twisted the doorknob before my Tory Burch sling-back flats walked me right back down the stairs.

Cousin Cindy looked dismayed when I stepped into the agency at eight forty-five. "No fair. You're not supposed to be here for another hour."

Babby held out her hand. "Pay up, Cindy. Nice work, Maxine. I had the eight-thirty to nine o'clock slot. Oh, and you brought donuts. I hope there's a cinnamon swirl for me. Ten bucks, everybody. Cindy, go get my winnings from Arty, please."

I pulled off my over-sized shades and placed the bag from The Palace on Babby's desk. "Yes, there's a cinnamon swirl for you, Aunt Babs. There's a glazed for Aunt Kay. Cindy gets a cake donut."

"I hate those," she said, slapping a ten spot on Babby's desk and stalking to the door.

"I know," I replied with a sweet smile.

Kay and Babby examined my super glued injuries and murmured approval. I sipped my extra large coffee from The Golden Gate and watched Babby slip the cinnamon swirl from the bag.

She took a bite and her eyes rolled. "Beautiful."

"We might have to call off the pool on Maxine's arrival time," Kay said, peeking in the bag and taking the glazed. "If she can get here only forty-five minutes late after the trauma of the last few days, she'll soon be coming in at eight like the rest of us."

Babby licked her fingers. "I don't think Maxine's ready for that kind of consistency."

"Hey," I protested. "I'm right here."

"Sorry, sugar pie. But timekeeping has never been one of your strengths."

I thought about promising to do better, but Babby was right. I found a thick new binder on my desk. "What's this?"

"Your study materials," Kay said.

I groaned. "I have to learn all this to be a private investigator?"

"There's more online, pookie."

I lifted the binder's cover and flipped through the pages, feeling mollified. The margins were wide and the type large. There were pictures. I could manage it.

The agency's door opened and Cass came in, followed by Cindy, who put two ten dollar bills on Babby's desk. "Arty says he's out, but Steve still wants to play," she said.

Cass chuckled. "Maxine's arrival time?"

"Yes," Kay said. "Want a half hour slot?"

"I'm a terrible gambler," she said. "I just stopped by to fill y'all in. Yvette's talking to Blue now."

"Are you back on duty?" Babby asked.

"Not yet, but I think Chad'll sign me off this week. Mitch is tied up with paperwork and asked me to come see you."

"Have a donut," I said, and held out the bag.

Cass took a plain glazed and passed the bag to Cindy, who pulled out a chocolate glazed in triumph. "You said you got me a cake donut," she said.

An apple fritter and the cake donut were all that remained. I took the apple fritter, pretty sure the cake donut would end up in the trash. "So?" I asked Cass.

"Big Billy Garcia is gone."

"What?" four voices chorused.

"Two US Marshals plucked him right out of the county jail last night and whisked him into witness protection."

"I guess that's what he bargained for," I said. "But it's annoying that I don't get to press assault charges."

"What about Oscar?" Kay asked.

"There's some dispute going on between Homeland Security, the DEA, and the FBI over who gets first crack at him, but he'll be gone, too. Probably this morning."

"And Sugar Murphy?" Babby asked.

"He's still in the hospital with a mild concussion, and he hasn't said a word. Martinez tried to convince him to talk last night, told him Big Billy was singing the "Hallelujah Chorus", but he's staying mum. The DEA's taking a shot at him this morning."

"Silly thing," Cindy said. "Will they put him in witness protection, or let him go to prison based on Big Billy's testimony on whatever charges the FBI or DEA presses?"

"I have no idea, but he won't be a guest in the Forney County jail for long."

"Is there no justice for the locals?" Kay asked. "Don't we get to prosecute them for breaking and entering, property destruction, and assault?"

"The DA might try to roll our charges up with the DEA's, but in the great scheme of international drug trafficking and murder, will they care about the petty stuff that happened here? Probably not."

"It's not petty to me," I grumbled.

"That's the way the cookie crumbles, darling," Babby said, peeking at the cake donut.

"What about Will?" I asked.

"We keep him," Cass said. "Sammy's filing murder charges this morning. He's dropping all charges against Blue."

"Thank goodness for that," Kay said. She lifted her coffee cup in a salute. "We did what Blue asked us to do, which was help her find the real killer. But special kudos to Maxine and Cass."

I really, really wanted all that praise for myself and Cass, but if this Lost and Found thing was going to work, I'd have to learn to be a team player. Starting now. "Truth is," I said, "if it weren't for Cindy and her database digging, it would've taken us a lot longer to figure out that Bret was leading multiple lives."

She preened, as I knew she would, and it felt right.

"And," I continued. I'd thought about this overnight and while it hurt, knew humble pie was on today's menu. "I need to apologize for taking a case when I'm not licensed. I thought it would be a simple matter of finding a spouse who didn't want to be found, but it turned out to be a lot more."

"It did indeed," Kay said. She looked at her nails, her face tense. "I have to say that I'm proud of you, punkin. If you'd let things go after you found Bret, we'd have the wrong woman in jail and worse, Will might be out there killing Bret's other ex-wives."

"Hear hear," said Babby. "But don't do it again, okay, sweetheart?"

I nodded and Cass stood to go.

"Lunch?" I asked.

She lifted the cover of my binder. "On your first day of studying? I wouldn't miss it."

Aunt Babby took the cake donut from the bag, studied it, and then took a bite. She chewed and nodded. "I'm off to the post office and the bank. Given that it's hot enough to fry chicken outside, I'll be driving."

THE TEST

I SPENT THREE HOURS alternating between studying, posting invoices and client payments, and working through the backlog of paperwork. The whole time, I eavesdropped on Kay's phone calls. There was a little variety. More missing people. Some who had been found. A few days of mystery shopping, which might be fun, depending on the shop. Some forensic accounting. And the ever-present insurance work. My black eye was throbbing and my spirits sinking by the time lunch rolled around.

"Does it ever change?" I asked. "Or is it always this boring?"

"Most of it's repetitive, peanut." Kay smiled sympathetically. "But we do get the occasional request for protection services or investigating corporate espionage. Depending on the client, that can be very exciting."

"Espionage? Like bugging? Spy stuff?" This sounded promising.

"Sometimes. How's the studying coming?"

"I'm making progress." I stood and stretched, relishing the pops my spine made. "But I could use a break."

"Call Cass and grab some lunch. Go to Chubby's, get a chocolate shake, and try to pick up some gossip. You're too thin and you need more contacts in town." She looked me up and down and I nodded but didn't commit. Kay was still right.

"The invisible people?" I asked.

"You're learning, angel. I'll be back. No phones, right?"

"Right."

Kay headed for the powder room and I checked the clock. Almost noon. Cass would be done with physical therapy and because I hadn't heard from her all morning, extremely unhappy because Chad still hadn't released her to go back to work. Not that I blamed him. She needed a little more time to heal. But only a little.

I pulled up her number and just as I was about to dial, the phone rang. Not my phone, the office phone. I looked towards the powder room. No Kay.

Please believe me when I tell you that I hesitated.

I debated.

I considered the pros and cons.

But in the end I snatched up the handset and in my most professional voice said, "Lost and Found Investigations. How can I help you?"

I couldn't help it.

THE END

ACKNOWLEDGMENTS

Writing this book was a blast, but it wouldn't have happened without prompting from the real life Babby, Cindy, and Kay. They're not detectives (although they could be), but they helped spark the idea of Lost and Found Investigations when Maxine Leverman walked out of her debut role in *Avengers of Blood* and decided she wanted a book of her own (characters do that sometimes). To Kay, Babby, and Cindy, many thanks for letting me totally rewrite your lives. I hope I've done you justice as the awesome women of Lost and Found, and that Forney County will offer up many mysteries for your alter egos to pursue.

Thanks again Kathy Shelton for your sharp eye and attention to detail, and for the bump on the title. And even more thanks for letting me know you laughed in all the right places - that, as much as anything, keeps me going.

Jeff and Dan, thanks for your comments on Maxine's visit to the gun range and keeping me in line on terminology. All errors are mine alone, and if you find any, please don't give up on me. I'm trainable. Really.

To those readers who picked up this book by an unfamiliar author, you have my sincere gratitude. Reading time is precious and for most of us, far too limited. It's tough to take a risk with your time and hard-earned cash on an unknown author and set of characters, but I hope you've enjoyed reading *A Case of Sour Grapes* as much as I enjoyed writing it. For more on the good (and bad) characters in Forney County, check out the rest of the Cass Elliot Crime Series.

As was the case with my earlier novels, the idea behind *A Case of Sour Grapes* was sparked by events from real life. If you want to know more about the origins of this story, visit GaeLynnWoods.Blogspot.com and check out the following post, Genesis of a Novel: That Dirty Rotten Lousy Stinking No-Good Dog of a Man. (Yeah, the title kind of gives the post away, but it's a good read, nonetheless.)

To the women in my life who've suffered at the hands of a cheating spouse: rock on. Your grace, courage, and resiliency are amazing and an inspiration. I know with absolute certainty that there's more joy to come in your future stories than you can imagine. Keep hanging in there.

Gae-Lynn Woods
May 2015

p.s. The folk punk band name Poison Ivy and the Dismembered Bunnies arose because (1) poison ivy jumps on me from great distances and I was itching as I was writing, and (2) our rescue kitty, The Dude, was wreaking havoc on the bunny population in East Texas as I was writing. Enough said. I'll leave the rest to your imagination. On a positive note, bunnies are again hopping through the yard and eating my garden. Perhaps The Dude and the bunnies have reached a truce. Only time will tell.

ALSO BY GAE-LYNN WOODS

THE DEVIL OF LIGHT

A Cass Elliot Crime Novel

AVENGERS OF BLOOD

A Cass Elliot Crime Novel

www.ingramcontent.com/pod-product-compliance
Lightning Source LLC
Chambersburg PA
CBHW020357260626
47156CB00007B/2147